ANGLO-SAXON ATTITUDES

ANGLO-SAXON ATTITUDES

a novel by

ANGUS WILSON

"What curious attitudes he goes into!"
"Not at all," said the King. "He's an Anglo-
Saxon Messenger—and those are Anglo-Saxon
attitudes. He only does them when he's happy."

Through the Looking-Glass.

New York
THE VIKING PRESS

FOR CHRIS AND PAT

CHARACTERS IN ORDER OF APPEARANCE

GERALD MIDDLETON: Professor Emeritus of early medieval history.

ROSE LORIMER: Senior lecturer in medieval history.

CLARISSA CRANE: A novelist.

PROFESSOR CLUN: Professor of medieval history.

MRS CLUN: His wife.

THEO ROBERTS: Assistant lecturer in history.

JASPER STRINGWELL-ANDERSON: Lecturer in history.

SIR EDGAR IFFLEY: President of the Historical Association of Medievalists.

PROFESSOR PFORZHEIM: Professor of medieval history in the University of Halle.

MRS SALAD: Former ladies' cloakroom attendant and ex-charlady of Gerald Middleton.

FRANK RAMMAGE: Property owner in Earl's Court.

VIN SALAD: A waiter, grandson of Mrs Salad.

LARRIE ROURKE: An Irish boy.

ELVIRA PORTWAY: Secretary to John Middleton and mistress of Robin Middleton. Granddaughter of Lilian Portway.

JOHN MIDDLETON: A radio celebrity and journalist, younger son of Gerald Middleton.

ROBIN MIDDLETON: A company director, elder son of Gerald Middleton.

MARIE HÉLÈNE: His wife.

TIMOTHY: Their son.

LILIAN PORTWAY: An ex-actress and suffragette, grandmother to Elvira.

STÉPHANIE HOUDET: Companion to Lilian Portway and aunt of Marie Hélène Middleton.

YVES HOUDET: Her son.

MR BARKER: Once coachman and chauffeur to Lilian Portway and her brother-in-law, Canon Portway.

ALICE CRESSETT: His daughter.

HAROLD CRESSETT: Her husband. A market-gardener.

MAUREEN KERSHAW: His daughter by his first marriage.

DEREK KERSHAW: Her husband. A former naval petty officer, now a garage proprietor.

INGEBORG MIDDLETON: Wife of Gerald Middleton.

KAY CONSETT: Their daughter.

DONALD CONSETT: Her husband. A sociologist.

LARWOOD: Gerald Middleton's chauffeur.

MRS LARWOOD: His wife. Housekeeper to Gerald Middleton.

DOLLIE STOKESAY: Widow of Gilbert Stokesay, formerly mistress of Gerald Middleton.

CUSPATT: A museum expert.

M. SARTHE: A biographer.

MRS JEVINGTON: A sculptress.

CAROLINE JEVINGTON: Her daughter, in love with Timothy Middleton.

OLD EMMIE: A friend of Mrs Salad.

CHARACTERS ALREADY DEAD BEFORE THE ACTION OF THE BOOK

EORPWALD: Seventh-century Christian missionary at the court of King Aldbert of the East Folk.

ALDWINE: Eighth-century Christian missionary to Heligoland.

PROFESSOR STOKESAY: Regius Professor of English history.

GILBERT: His son. Essayist and poet.

CANON PORTWAY: A noted Churchman and antiquarian.

DR WINSKILL: A young general practitioner.

CHARACTERS OFF STAGE

MR PELICAN: A civil servant.

MR GRIMSTON: A small manufacturer.

PART ONE

COLUMN IN *THE TIMES*, NOVEMBER 1912

It is now possible to make a tentative statement about the extensive archaeological excavations undertaken this summer in the former kingdom of the East Folk. The work was originally carried out by the East Coast Antiquarian Association under the direction of the well-known antiquary the Rev. Reginald Portway, who is Secretary of the Association. The later stages of the excavation were supervised by Professor Stokesay. Excavations were carried out at many sites on the marshy tracts of land near the coast between Bedbury and Melpham. Apart from traces of a pagan Anglo-Saxon cemetery near Bedbury, the outstanding discovery was the tomb of Bishop Eorpwald in the grounds of Melpham House, five miles outside the village of Melpham. The whereabouts of this tomb have long been an historical mystery. Eorpwald, who died in 695, was buried at Sedwich. In 867, when the Norsemen were approaching, the monks of Sedwich carried away his coffin and buried it elsewhere. Tradition spoke of Melpham or Bedbury. The excavation, of course, reveals this long-hidden secret. The stone coffin has inscriptions and ornaments of great interest to historians of the seventh century. The most remarkable discovery, however, is undoubtedly that of a wooden fertility figure. Similar Saxon figures have been found twice before, preserved in the marshy bogs of Jutland and Friesland. But this discovery is unique in English archaeology. Its presence in the coffin of Bishop Eorpwald has given rise to a number of theories among historians of the period. A satisfactory solution must wait upon the publication of the reports of Professor Stokesay and the Rev. Portway. At a coroner's inquest the tomb and its contents were found to be the property of the owners of Melpham Hall—the Rev. Portway and his sister-in-law, Mrs T. Portway, well known to the public as Miss Lilian Portway, the actress. It is understood that negotiations are in progress for the sale of the objects between the owners and the Trustees of the British Museum.

For further documents relating to the Melpham burial see the Appendix at the end of the book.

CHAPTER ONE

G ERALD MIDDLETON was a man of mildly but per-
sistently depressive temperament. Such men are not at
their best at breakfast, nor is the week before Christmas their
happiest time. Both Larwood and Mrs Larwood had learned
over the years to respect their employer's melancholy moods
by remaining silent. They did so on this morning. The house in
Montpelier Square was as noiseless as a tomb. Mrs Middleton
had rung up from her house in Marlow as early as eight o'clock
to enquire what arrangements her husband had made for his
annual Christmas visit to her. Would he, she asked, arrange
to bring down their son John? Mrs Larwood had tactfully
refused to wake Professor Middleton; she would see that he
phoned Mrs Middleton during the morning, she said. The
message was placed with the letters and newspapers beside
Gerald's plate.

The prospect of speaking to his wife on the telephone and,
even more, of the family Christmas party greatly heightened
his depression. He decided not to open his letters until he had
read the news or to open *The Times* until he had softened his
spirits with the more popular daily newspaper which always
accompanied it. It was an unwise decision: the optimistic
presentation of decidedly bad news on the front page turned
his passive gloom into active irritation. On the middle page
was a lengthy article by his son John. He always swore that he
would not read John's articles, yet he always did so. Their
cocksure and sentimental tone at least lent justification to his
hearty dislike of his younger son, particularly if he accompanied
his reading by a mental image of his wife's cooing admiration
of their son's talent.

"Once more," he read, "John Middleton investigates fearlessly a case of tyranny and injustice in this overgoverned England of ours. In each investigation that he undertakes, John Middleton goes directly to the centre of the ill, exposes the canker, and proposes its remedy. He is at once physician, surgeon and healer of the serious illnesses which threaten the freedom and decent living of everyone of us in England today, of you and me and of every ordinary citizen. The *Daily Blank* does not share John Middleton's political views. He describes himself as an independent radical. The *Daily Blank* is not a radical newspaper, but because it believes that any man who is prepared to fight these deadly evils without fear of person, office, or party is a friend of England, it is proud to publish these courageous articles. John Middleton showed himself a friend of freedom as a Labour Member of Parliament: he showed himself even more so when he resigned from the Labour Party and the House of Commons to fight your battle without the restraints of red tape. If you have grievances, if you know of neighbours suffering under the injustice of government tyranny, big or small, send your problems to John Middleton. He will investigate your case without fear or favour."

Gerald tried to tell himself that he should be fair to John. The purpose surely was a good one, if the manner was necessarily nauseating. He had no right to judge his son's career by his knowledge of his popularity-seeking character, his histrionic, self-deceiving temperament. Never, after all, had he himself been prepared to face the truth in life, either in his family or in his profession; he had less than no right to judge the manner in which his son did what he had not the courage to do. He settled himself to read this particular case. A Mr Harold Cressett, a market-gardener of outer London, had suffered expropriation of his land by a Ministry which wished to build a government factory on the site. After months of delay, in which Mr Cressett had dismantled his greenhouses, ceased trading and so on, a curt letter informed him that the

land was not needed and that the compensation money must
be repaid. The simplicity, the decency, the bewilderment of
Mr Cressett and his wife were painted in glowing colours; the
tragedy of old Mr Barker, Mrs Cressett's paralysed father, was
dwelt upon. He had, it seemed, been a coachman of the old
school—a school long vanished. Only at the end of the article
were the villains named. Bureaucratic clerks in all their hideous,
inhuman behaviour were charged with the deed; but they were
only the instruments of tyranny. The real villain was the head
of the department—a highly esteemed administrative civil
servant named Pelican. Did Mr Pelican, John asked, know the
minutiæ of his department as his reputation for thoroughness
demanded? If so, he had erred by commission. Was he ignorant
of his clerks' and executives' incompetence? Then he had erred
by omission. Much play was made with Mr Pelican's name.
While we all loved the pelicans in St James's Park, it was said :
let them suffice. We needed no more pelicans in Whitehall. It
was not, it seemed, upon the blood of his own breast that Mr
Pelican fed his bureaucratic young, but upon the life-blood of
hard-working citizens like Harold Cressett, etc.

Gerald's first reaction was to decide that Mr Pelican must
be a charming man and Mr Cressett a rogue. Then angrily he
told himself that he knew nothing of the world around him;
he had no right to judge. Who was he to dismiss John's stories
of bureaucratic tyranny? A man with large enough private
means to scorn complaints against taxation as vulgar and irresponsible; a family man who had had neither the courage to
walk out of the marriage he hated, nor the resolution to sustain
the rôle of father decently. An ex-professor of medieval history
who had not even fulfilled the scholarly promise of studies
whose general value he now doubted. A sensualist who had
never had the courage of his desires; an aesthete who could not
even add to his collection of drawings without pangs of conscience about his money or his neglected historical studies. A
sixty-year-old failure, in fact, and of that most boring kind, a
failure with a conscience.

His heavy, handsome dark face flushed with disgust at the tediously repetitive chain of self-recrimination at which he had once more arrived. Before he opened his letters, he set himself resolutely to refresh his depressed spirits. For all the boredom of this evening's meeting of the Historical Association, for all the wretched prospect of Christmas at Inge's, today promised to be really a very pleasing one. The new catalogue of the Gruntvig collection had arrived. There was nothing to prevent him spending all day on it—to vary the pleasure of his own Johns and Daumiers and Cotmans with memories of Leonardos and Raphaels that would never be his. There was the pleasant prospect of trying to persuade old Grantham to part with that Fuseli this evening. But he felt no more cheered. He thought of that girl in Asprey's who had sold him Inge's Christmas present yesterday—he dwelt slowly upon the pleasures of her bust, her hips, the easy movement of her thighs. He could remember only that he was sixty-four, could wonder only whether his growing lust was a simple case of enlarged prostate that would "have to be dealt with." His spirits remained depressed.

He turned to the two letters that lay beside his plate. The handwriting of the one he recognized as Sir Edgar's; the other was unknown. He preferred the unknown. "Dear Sir," he read, "I am preparing a Ph.D. thesis for the London University School of English Literature. My subject is 'The Intellectual Climate of England at the Outbreak of the First World War.' As you may imagine, I am anxious to concentrate on what posterity has shown to be really vital in that age rather than on the conventional aspect—Shaw, Wells, Galsworthy, etc. Whilst, therefore, paying some attention to the foundations of the Bloomsbury school in the Cambridge thought of the early years of the century, I am devoting the major part of my thesis to D. H. Lawrence and Wyndham Lewis. In relation to the latter, I am investigating the careers of such less-known figures as T. E. Hulme and Gilbert Stokesay. I believe that you were a close friend of Stokesay's, and I should be glad of any personal information you may care to provide me with upon this neglected and important young poet and essayist, whose work in retrospect appears, to my generation at any rate, to reflect a seriousness and a final significance which criticism today teaches us is the only true criterion of literary merit. In particular I would be glad of any light you can throw upon his relations with his father, the historian Lionel Stokesay, and, in particular, upon the part Gilbert Stokesay played in the Anglo-Saxon excavations made at Melpham, East Folk, in 1912. I believe that his practical association with art historians may throw valuable light on his aesthetic themes.

"I have already corresponded with his widow, but she is not able to provide me with any information of importance. You may wish to know my qualifications for carrying out this task. I am a graduate of Minnesota University and North-Western University. I have majored in aesthetics, music and literature, paying special attention to the metaphysical poets. I have attended courses in creative writing given by such eminent poets as . . ."

Gerald laid aside the letter without reading the signature. He had long ago decided that he had nothing to say about Gilbert Stokesay which could interest these many young people who so admired his work. He had never been able to get through any single thing that Gilbert had written.

So Dollie, he reflected with amusement, had been able to provide no information. She was probably drunk when she got the letter. He pushed her image out of his mind. He had long vowed that he would not think of her, and yet every day he did so. She had after all been the one really happy passion of his life, and, through his ineptitude and cowardice, he had ruined that happiness.

This brash young American little knew what sore places he was invading with his clumsy fingers. Dollie and Melpham! The two forbidden subjects of his thoughts, the constant underlying preoccupations of his depression. If he were to tell what he sometimes believed to be Gilbert's real part in the

Melpham excavations, he would indeed throw light on his dead friend's aesthetic theories.

He turned to Sir Edgar's letter in desperation. "Dear Middleton, I should be glad of a word with you before Pforzheim's lecture tonight. You will find me in the ante-room. It is possible that Association business may come up at the end of the lecture, if Pforzheim doesn't go on for too long. If it does, we may be sure that the question of the editorship of the *History* will be raised. While I do not in any way want to force you into a premature decision, I should be glad to have some idea of what you intend. I have already told you how deeply I, and not only I, but the great majority of your colleagues, hope that you will accept the editorial duties, but we cannot for too long postpone our decision. In any case, some intimation of your feelings before the lecture would be a helpful guide to me in my direction of any discussion that may arise.

Yours sincerely, Edgar Iffley."

They already knew his decision, Gerald thought angrily; he had made it as plain as he could that he did not intend to become editor. It was sheer sentimentality their asking him, a refusal to give up the belief of "promise" in a man over sixty. If they did not want Arthur Clun, and he could well understand that they might not, then let them have the courage to say so and appoint some younger man. The trouble was that, through fear of Clun's appointment, all the younger people— Roberts, Stringwell-Anderson and the rest—had made him their candidate.

Well, he would not be bullied into it by the affection of old-stagers like Sir Edgar or the fears of his ex-pupils like Roberts. As to "intimations of his feelings"—his feelings were his own affair. If he were to tell them, it would be that he had long felt that detailed scholarship such as Clun favoured was insufficient, disreputable, crossword-puzzle work, and historical generalizations were an equally disreputable pseudo-philosophic moralizing of the kind that old Stokesay had indulged in at the end of his life. All this seeking for the truth of the past should be in abeyance until we had reached some conclusions about the truth of the present. In any case, who was he to dabble in truth-telling when he had evaded the truth, past and present, for most of his life? If they chivvied him, he would raise the red herring of his projected work on England under Edward the Confessor. The long-promised work to succeed his book on Cnut was by now an old enough chestnut to embarrass any of them if he brought it up.

He rose from the table in bitter mood. Weighed down with doubts, struggling with his depression, he made his way to his study to telephone his wife. As he walked through the hall, he caught sight of his handsome, flushed features, his tall erect figure in the long gilt mirror and was disgusted. "Good God!" he thought, "what a bloody, shameful waste!"

Rose Lorimer, struggling with weighed-down shopping baskets, made her immense way among the marble and mosaic of the Corner House, caught a passing view of herself in a mirror and was pleased. She had always affirmed that women scholars were primarily women and should not disregard the demands of feminine fashion. To advertise learning by disregard of dress was to be odd, and Dr Lorimer disliked oddity more than anything. The vast intellectual excitement of her researches since the war had not left her a lot of time for thinking about clothes, but her mother had always said that with a good fur coat, however old, one could not go wrong; and for her own part, she had added a bold dash of colour to cheer our drab English winter—woman's contribution to banish gloom. Twenty years ago, of course, she reflected, straw hats with flowers would have been out of place in December, but the dictates of fashion were so much less strict nowadays, it seemed. And then Dr Lorimer had always loved artificial flowers, especially roses.

There was no want of artificial flowers in the Corner House entrance hall. An enormous cardboard turkey and an enormous cardboard goose, owing their inspiration to somewhat vulgarized memories of Walt Disney, held between them the message MERRY XMAS made entirely of white and pink satin roses. As the tableau revolved, the turkey changed to a Christmas pudding and the goose to a mince-pie, each suitably adorned with a wide grin and two little legs; AND A PROSPEROUS NEW YEAR they announced, this time in real chrysanthemums. Dr Lorimer thought amusedly of Christmas, so rich in pagan symbols; the Real Masters of the Church had taken small pains to disguise their victory there. Muffled voices at the back of her mind pressed her to change her tense—*take* small pains, it said. In two days' time, she thought, Initiates everywhere—in Northern Europe, and further even than that—will be working their old magical spells of health and renewal over their unsuspecting Christian flocks. In England here, their archbishop —King Fisher—she smiled to think of the significance of the name, would be at the head of them. So old a mystery concealed for so long from so many, but not from her. She shook herself and drove off the voices. Knowledge led one into such strange dreams. It was all over along ago, of course. Nevertheless, the early Christian missionaries bought their pagan converts at high price with the ceremonial adulteration of their Saviour's birthday.

She tucked her giant legs with difficulty beneath one of the small tables and looked at the menu with a certain puritan alarm at its luxurious array of dishes. Choice was made simpler for one, she reflected, at her usual "ordinary" Lyons or A.B.C. She sighed at the uneasy prospect of sensual choice. Clarissa Crane, however, appeared to be such a distinguished novelist, and novelists, no doubt, were used to living luxuriously. A few years ago, she would not have imagined herself introducing a novelist as a guest at the Annual Lecture, but Miss Crane's letter had sounded so very interested; and if the academical world insisted on its narrow limits, then other means of disseminating the truth must be found.

Clarissa Crane, searching the vast marble tea-room with a certain distaste, suddenly recognized her learned hostess and felt deeply embarrassed. In all this drab collection of matinée-goers and pantomime parties, that only could be her. She had expected somebody dowdy, indeed had worn her old green tweed suit in deference to the academic occasion, but she had not been prepared for someone quite so outrageously odd, so completely a "fright". Dr Lorimer was mountainous, not only up and down, but round and round as well, and then her clothes were so strange—that old, old fur coat, making almost no pretence of the large safety-pins that held it together, and, above the huge, aimlessly smiling grey face, a small toque composed entirely of artificial pink roses and set askew on a bundle of tumbling black coils and escaping hairpins. Clarissa, with a sensitive novelist's eye, dreaded to think into what strange realm the poor creature's mind had strayed; with a woman of the world's tact, however, she cried, "Dr Lorimer, this is so awfully kind of you!"

"Not at all, dear, I was only too glad to be of help. It's so seldom that Clio can aid the other muses, isn't it?" Dr Lorimer's voice was strangely small coming out of her massive form, like a little girl's reciting a party piece. Its childish effect was the greater after Clarissa Crane's sophisticated, strangled contralto: "I do hope I can help you," Rose said, "because your novel sounds so very, very interesting." Her mind strayed away over the novels *she* had read—*The Forsyte Saga*, *The Last Days of Pompeii*, a book called *Beau Sabreur*, and, of course, a number more when she was a girl. *They* hadn't been interesting at all, she remembered.

"Thank you," said Clarissa, "I'm sure you can. Taking me to this frightfully important lecture in itself, and then, I wanted to know . . ."

Rose Lorimer interrupted her question, "We'd better choose something to eat, dear, first," she said, and looked at Clarissa over the top of the menu with a sort of shy leer. She was not normally given to calling people "dear" or to leering at them, but she had somehow arrived at this approach as suitable for so unusual a companion as a smart lady novelist. It was a manner that recalled a poor stage performance of a bawd and suggested a subconscious appraisal of her guest that was hardly complimentary. "Will you have an ice, dear?" she asked, and then, remembering the seasonable cold weather, she added, "or there seems to be sundries," and she lingered over the wondrous range of dishes in print before her.

"Oh, no, just some tea," Clarissa said, and then, fearing to hurt the poor creature's feelings, added, "and some toast would be nice."

"Toast," repeated Rose. "What with, dear?"

"Oh just butter." Clarissa feared being involved with sardines.

"I don't see toast and *butter*," said Rose, who *had* in fact got involved with the sardine section, "Oh, yes, I do. It's further down. *Buttered* toast," she explained.

"Of course, I've no right at all to consider doing a *historical* novel," said Clarissa, her eye trying to avoid the glistening circle of butter grease that grew ever larger around Dr Lorimer's lips. "But somehow I feel the past speaks for us so much at this moment." It was the critics, in fact, who had spoken so determinedly against her knowledge of modern life in her last novel. "And then those extraordinary dark centuries, the faint twilight that flickers around the departing Romans and the real Arthur, the strange shapes thrown up by the moment-ary gleams of our knowledge, and, above all, the enormous sense of its relation to ourselves, its nowness, if I can call it that. The brilliant Romano-British world, the gathering shadows, and then the awful darkness pouring in."

Rose, who, when the muffled voices of her *idées fixes* were not working in her, was a very down-to-earth scholar, could make nothing of all this darkness and light business. She con-tented herself with eating as much of the buttered toast as possible; then, taking out a packet of Woodbines, she lit one and blew a cloud of smoke in Clarissa's direction, as though she was smoking out a nest of wasps. "I'm afraid you won't find much of all that in Pforzheim's lecture, dear," she said kindly, "it's about trade."

"Oh, but *that's* so fascinating," Clarissa felt shy and was unable to stop talking. "The furs and amber from the Baltic, the great Volga route. Yes, even in the darkest times, the persistence of trade. Think of Sutton Hoo! the homage of the barbarians to civilization, that great Byzantine dish!"

"Inferior factory workmanship," said Rose, and she did not this time add "dear".

Clarissa collected her poise around her embarrassed shoulders. "But what I want from you," she said, a simple, intelligent seeker once more, "is the whole story of the clash of the pagan and Christian worlds in England."

"Oh! that's a very large request, I'm afraid," said Rose. She had suffered too much for her theories not to be suspicious of such a frontal attack. "Did you read the articles I sent you?"

"Oh, yes," said Clarissa, "and found them fascinating, absolutely fascinating. But it was the background that I wanted: you see, I'm no scholar. I know nothing really, for example, of comparative religion. Of course, I've read Frazer and Dr Margaret Murray about the witches . . ."

She stopped, alarmed at the sudden change in her hostess's expression. A deep pink had spread over Rose's rather grubby cheeks, giving them a curious likeness to the soiled flowers in her hat.

"I'm afraid, dear," she said, "if you want to talk about witches, you've come to the wrong person. I'm a very plain scholar. An historian, you know, is not the same thing as an anthropologist." Her little girl-voice took on quite a hard timbre. Frazer, Margaret Murray indeed! She was always being confronted with this awful confusion. Her theory, her *knowledge* of the nature of the early medieval Church, was not based on folk-lore and fancy and that sort of thing. She was a factual historian, trained by Tout and Stokesay. And then—what she saw so clearly sometimes nowadays—the conspiracy, the strange age-old conspiracy which she alone had guessed at, was something beside which Dr Murray's Dianic cult and Divine Victims paled into childish insignificance. Clarissa, realizing the magnitude of her blunder, began to extricate herself, but Dr Lorimer was listening now to voices quite other than Clarissa's cultured tones.

Really! thought Clarissa, if collecting historical material is going to be as tiresome as this, I wish I had accepted the offer of writing a travel book on Angola. Seeing Dr Lorimer's blank expression, she raised her voice. Heaven knew how deaf the old thing was!

"Of course, the Melpham excavation seems to me so fascinating," she shouted, averting her eyes from a nearby party of goggling schoolchildren.

"Yes," said Dr Lorimer distantly, "it is very fascinating." She decided not to tell this stupid woman just how fascinating. She would return the conventional judgment, "But you must remember that Bishop Eorpwald was a very unusual person. So much we know from Bede alone. We can't judge everything by Melpham."

"Did you take part in the 'dig'?" asked Clarissa in a sporty voice that she somehow felt necessary for the colloquialism.

"Bishop Eorpwald's tomb was excavated in 1912, dear," said Dr Lorimer sharply. "I was only a girl."

Clarissa poured herself out a cup of cold tea and drank it in her confusion. "I've always been awful about dates," she explained.

"Well, you must try to get them right in your book, mustn't you?" said Dr Lorimer; then noticing her guest's embarrassment, she relented, and said, "There was no reason why you shouldn't think I helped at Melpham. Fifty-five must seem as old as the hills to a girl like you."

Clarissa reflected that the simple, too, had their charms. She almost regretted her Woman's Hour talks in the "Middle Age Looks Back" series.

"And anyway," Rose added, "I *look* as old as the hills. As a matter of fact, it was a great compliment to pay to a pupil of Professor Stokesay's. Melpham was the crown of his work, in my opinion. No. Everything he did was wonderful. He taught me all I know. And so vigorous right up to the end, though he rather left his old colleagues behind then. He became a man of affairs, dear," she ended, as though this was some sort of physical metamorphosis.

"Yes, I remember," said Clarissa. "He was one of the men of Munich, wasn't he?" and instantly regretted the contribution. But she need not have been anxious, for Rose smiled vaguely, "Yes, bless his heart," she said, "he'd gone quite beyond my little world."

"And you really think that the wooden figure . . .?" Clarissa tailed away in query.

"Oh, a fertility god, dear," said Rose. "No doubt of it at all. Of course, the carving's very crude. Much cruder than the few finds they've made on the Baltic Coast. Due to native workmanship, no doubt with the Continental tradition almost lost. That accounts for the large size of the member, you know." Clarissa felt that she need not have feared to finish her sentence. "But it's an Anglo-Saxon deity all right. A true *wig*. One of the *idola* Bede was so shocked about. Or pretended to be, shall we say?" she added mysteriously.

The significance of the mystery, however, was lost on Clarissa. "And is there nobody alive now who was with Stokesay at Melpham?"

"No," said Rose ruminatively. "Or wait a bit. I believe Gerald Middleton was there. But he was only a young student, of course, and it's quite outside his period."

"Oh," said Clarissa, "Middleton's *World of Canute*. Of course, I've read that, or looked at it, perhaps I should say. It's rather heavy, isn't it?"

"Well, we think Gerald Middleton's a great stylist," said Rose, and added archly, "but then we're not novelists."

"Fancy Middleton being alive," said Clarissa. "Shades of the schoolroom!"

Rose was nettled. "Gerald Middleton can't be more than ten years older than me. He only left off lecturing two years ago. He's not much over sixty." she decided.

"He hasn't written for a long time, I think," Clarissa sought forgiveness.

"No, I'm afraid not. He doesn't thrive any more than I do in this world of increasing specialization. He'll be there this evening though, I'm sure. All the serious early medievalists will be, you know. You're quite privileged. I'll introduce you to him and then you can ask him about Melpham. Not that he can tell you anything that isn't in Professor Stokesay's articles."

Clarissa saw a chance for independence. "As a matter of fact I know someone who was a friend of Professor Middleton, a very *great* friend at one time," she added with a coy laugh. "Dollie Stokesay. But you probably know her too."

Dr Lorimer, who was not willing to accept from Clarissa the suggestion of old scandal about a colleague, said, "I saw her, of course, once or twice when she kept house for her father-in-law. But she never helped Professor Stokesay with his work, whatever she may have done in the home." And then she added, "I'd no idea *she* was still alive."

"Oh, indeed, yes. We're near neighbours," Clarissa cried, as though this gave Mrs Stokesay a peculiar claim to life. "Darling Dollie! I simply can't imagine her in the academic world. She's such a marvellous Philistine." She paused, and added reverently, "But a wonderfully integral person."

This was not a concept that claimed Dr Lorimer's attention. "We must be going, dear," she said, and she beckoned to the waitress. "Pforzheim's a brilliant lecturer—the greatest medievalist in Germany today. You're quite privileged, you know. I'm sure you'll find a lot of inspiration in his talk." She picked up her two shopping-bags. "But there won't be any witches, I'm afraid," she added with a chuckle.

Clarissa insisted on taking one of the bags from her and instantly regretted her politeness. It seemed incredible that any shopping-bag could be so heavy. She did not know, and Dr Lorimer did not remember, that at the bottom of this bag were many milk-bottles that should have been returned to the dairy, as well as many empty tins intended for the dustbin. A most

peculiar smell disturbed Clarissa as they walked out of Lyons'.
Dr Lorimer had also forgotten a tin of dog's meat she had
bought for her fox-terrier a month ago.

"Let's go by underground, shall we, dear?" said Dr
Lorimer. "I love the rush-hour tubes; so full of interesting
types. *Your* raw material, I suppose."

Clarissa's heart sank.

Mrs Clun's heart sank, as she recognized her husband's
mood. Her thin frame shivered as much with alarm as with the
intense cold. She had followed him out on to the porch to ask
him about the sherry, and now she had been there over ten
minutes listening to his strictures while the east wind whistled
into every open crevice of her afternoon frock. Mrs Clun was
extremely thin and not very young; also she had never worn
enough underclothes since a time many years ago at the college
garden party when her husband had reproved her publicly for
looking "lumpy". She tried always to tell herself how proud
she should be that after so many years he noticed her figure
at all.

Professor Clun's dapper, soldierly little body was well
padded. "If, of course, you're going to regard every suggestion
I make as a criticism," he said, and his hard green eyes glared
above his toothbrush moustache, "then I must wash my hands
of the whole matter."

Mrs Clun knew that she must listen carefully so that she
might interpose a softening word at the right moment, but her
mind kept travelling to her blue woolly upstairs in the bedroom. She smiled, a vague watery smile. Professor Clun
noticed her red, frostbitten nose and resented it.

"I'm sure," he continued, "that I've no wish to give my
time to these household matters. I have, as you very well know,
a great deal of work on my hands. It's bad enough that I have
to go to this lecture. I don't relish the idea of spending an hour
listening to Pforzheim, able though he is, let alone the prospect
of hearing Rose Lorimer air her crazy theories afterwards. If

Sir Edgar were a better chairman, or even if Middleton had some modicum of the sense of responsibility which his position ought to give him, we should not waste hours of precious time on these pointless generalities. The whole concept of these Stokesay Annual Lectures is entirely out of date. If we want to know what Pforzheim or any other Continental authority has to say, we can perfectly well read it in the journals. Any sensible executors with a little more *savoir-faire* than Sir Edgar or Middleton would have had the terms of Stokesay's will annulled long ago. The money could be most conveniently used for research projects or publications. When I think that I shall have to pay my own fare to the Verona conference next summer . . ."

"Yes, Arthur," said Mrs Clun.

"What do you mean 'yes'?" said her husband sharply. "You know nothing at all about it. This affirmation of statements of which you are entirely ignorant is among your most irritating habits, Ada. But, for heaven's sake, let us stick to the point we're discussing. If we are to entertain the Graysons this evening, and I've already said that it was necessary, we can at least do it competently. Why you should choose this moment to suggest South African Chablis, I cannot conceive. The Graysons will hardly wish to come out to Wimbledon to drink an Empire wine. What sort of story do you want them to carry back to Manchester?"

"I was only thinking of what you said about economy. . . ."

"That was on the occasion of the research students' party. Do have *some* sense of what is fitting. We're not rich people, but there is no need for contrivance. We haven't got large private means like Middleton, but we're not paupers." Indeed, with his own salary and his wife's private income, they were really very comfortably provided for.

"I shouldn't think that Muriel Grayson would know one wine from another," said Mrs Clun, stung by the cold into contention. "She's a very nice, homely Lancashire body, but not stylish at all."

"That's hardly a matter for you to judge, Ada," said Professor Clun, beginning at last to feel the cold himself. "You don't pretend to style, and I shouldn't wish you to do so." Although, after long years of bullying, his wife had acquired a certain suburban gentility, she had brought him her private income from a distinctly plebeian source. Arthur Clun fully recognized the limits of her achievement and required no more of her. "Well," he added, "I hope that the rest of this evening's entertainment can be left to your own judgment, unless you wish me to contract pneumonia. You may well feel pleased that you have not to travel in a draughty underground train as I have."

"Do you really need to go, Arthur?" Mrs Clun asked, hoping that a little cosseting would thaw his mood.

"Has anything I have said suggested that I am making this journey on a frivolous impulse?" he snapped. "Of course I must be there. You seem to have no sense of my position, Ada. Besides, all sorts of things come up after the lecture. The editorship of the new *Medieval History* series is on the agenda. Heaven knows what silly suggestions may be made about that. Middleton's well aware that he's past that sort of thing, but if some of those disciples of his, some of his bobby-sox fans,"— and he laughed at his little modernism—"get going, they may over-persuade him. Roberts and Stringwell-Anderson will try hard for it. They know very well that their contributions will have to be confined to scholarship, not to philosophical generalities, if I'm the editor."

"I'm sure you *ought* to be," said his wife with sincere reverence.

"Yes, yes, dear. The occasion is really too obvious to make the observation gratifying. We don't wish to indulge in the sort of domestic billing and cooing that fellows like Roberts go in for, with their wives playing university politics. Besides, you're not a member of the University Press Syndic, so it's irrelevant. Stick to your last, my dear." He turned to go and then stepped back to give her the customary sharp peck on her cheek. Looking at her scarlet nose, he relented for a moment.

"I dare say you'll be glad when spring comes," he said, as
though paying tribute to the peculiarities of the feeble-minded;
but he was immediately embarrassed by the implication of
sentiment in his remark. "Goodbye," he said, "and whatever
you do, don't fuss this evening." He set off to walk briskly
across the common.

"Whatever you do this evening, Theo, please don't get into
a fuss," said Jasper Stringwell-Anderson. He stretched his long
tweed-clad legs across the sofa, reclining on his hip. Then he
flicked a piece of fluff from his orange suede strap shoes, as
though suggesting the sort of nonchalance he would prescribe.

"My dear chap, what is the good of telling me not to fuss?
I'm always in a fuss." Theo jangled the coins in his flannel-
trouser pocket, screwed up his face, and ran his other hand
through his wiry black hair, as though he, too, would illustrate
the sort of acrobatic muddle he claimed to have been born
into. "Of course, I *can* be kept under. By a strong hand. Now
if only Betty had been able to come this evening, she'd have
done it. But, of course, she had to choose this evening to go
and see her ruddy mother. The old woman's got a pain. It's
her habit at such times." In his excitement he stuttered
more than usual and his Yorkshire accent was almost that
which he used when he told funny stories of his home town.
"Betty's fonder of her mother than of me, you know," he
added, by way of explanation.

Jasper never knew what to do with these sudden confidences
of Theo's. He would not have thought of revealing any personal details of his own life—indeed, he had no personal life to
reveal. Like Betty Roberts, he was devoted to his mother, but,
since he had no feelings deeper than social or intellectual
approval for anyone else, he took such filial devotion for
granted in anyone he esteemed worthy of his acquaintance.

"Fussing will only drive Middleton back into his shell. It
will annoy Sir Edgar and give Clun every opportunity to shine
as the cool-headed administrator."

Jasper was in something of a "state" himself and he fancied that lecturing Theo would steady his own nerves. He reached a long arm for a cigarette from a small satinwood box inlaid with mother-of-pearl. It was just out of his reach, and Theo, coming to his assistance, knocked over a lamp and a small saucer. The saucer smashed into irreparable fragments.

"Oh!" cried Theo, "There you are, you see."

"Or rather, there *was* a rather nice piece of Lowestoft," said Jasper sharply.

"I can't think what you want all this junk for," Theo stuttered, his eyes blinking through his thick glasses. "You'll go the same way as Middleton. It's all this picture-collecting that's kept him from doing the work he should. Good taste and all that doesn't marry with serious thinking. I've always said it . . . "

"You're working on a false premise if you think that re-iteration will persuade me of its truth," said Jasper testily. He got up and, in going out of the room, pointed to the sofa with its starched white chintz cover and its gold fringing. "Sit down," he said. In a moment he had returned with a small jade-green dustpan and brush, and hitching up his trouser creases he knelt and carefully brushed up the minutest pieces of china. Then getting tissue paper and a brown cardboard box from a drawer in the desk, he began to sort the fragments into the paper. He gave the occupation a full, careful and spinsterish consideration.

"The truth is," said Theo, "that it's bad to have money in our job. Surplus wealth may make culture, but it turns scholars into antiquarians. Learning needs decent poverty. They recognized that in the Middle Ages. All this," and he waved his hand round the elegant room, "is so much paltry distraction."

"And wives and children?" asked Jasper, whose nervous tension had found a new, more satisfactory outlet. "Where do they fit into your romantic, Helen Waddell, view of scholarship?"

"Betty's a great help," Theo protested, "when her mother hasn't got a pain."

Jasper closed the cardboard box and tied it with string, cutting the ends with a small ivory sheathed penknife from his waistcoat pocket. He took out a fountain pen and wrote across the lid "Fragments of a Lowestoft saucer, broken by Theo Roberts xxii–xii–liv."

"Now, Theo," he said, "we have other things to discuss than your mother-in-law. How are we going to jockey Middleton into accepting the editorship that will undoubtedly be offered to him?"

"I imagine I shall tell him bluntly that he owes it to us all to accept it."

"And I imagine that his laziness will be proof against the appeal of such sentiment."

"Then I shall tell him straight out that if he doesn't take this on, he may as well pack up. It'll be Middleton's 'Canute', it'll be Middleton the man whose lecture notes and tutorials have inspired two generations; but it won't be Middleton who saved English medieval studies from the dead hand of Clun. He'll die a second-rater who left a tidy little fortune and a bloody gallery of drawings that any other fool with money could have collected. And if he thinks his lecture notes will make him another Acton, good though they are, I shall tell him where he can put that idea."

"Yes," said Jasper, "that's probably the right tone. I think perhaps you *had* better stick to your Northern bluntness. It has its specious charm for the older generation. I shall use *my* talents in prolonging the discussion. It's difficult to think what Pforzheim can possibly say that will allow us to discuss for an hour. With God's help, however, and the assistance of dear Rose's *idées fixes*, we may succeed. Sir Edgar can hardly 'pass to other matters' if a good discussion gets going. It would be most impolite to our distinguished visitor, and Sir Edgar's old-world courtesy never deserts him. Luckily there will be a number of talkers there—with half a word about coin hoards we shall have Praed on his feet, and, if Pforzheim idly mentions Roman town survivals, we shall have Grayson giving us what Manchester thinks for at least half an hour."

"Grayson's a sound man," Theo said, in tones of heavy reverence.

"We are considering tactics, my dear Theo, not estimating abilities. The time for that will come if and when Middleton becomes editor. Your estimate of relative 'soundnessess'," he spoke the word in inverted commas, "will be most valuable when we advise him on contributors. Meanwhile, if we can postpone the discussion on editorship, we shall have almost a month in which to work on Middleton, with Christmas and New Year intervening." Jasper went to the corner cupboard with its painting of ample eighteenth-century goddesses undergoing the polite scrutiny of Paris.

"I wish," he said, pouring out two white Cinzanos—he allowed no questioning of the Continental form of apéritifs he offered—"I wish that Middleton had some slight share of his ghastly son's ambition."

"Well, now, I don't know about John Middleton," said Theo. "I think he's a smart chap, you know. Betty and I see him pretty often on television, and he certainly has personality."

Jasper thought it underbred to be snobbish about television, so he forbore to mention that he had no set. "An odious, smug personality," he said.

"Oh, come now," Theo was exaggeratedly Yorkshire. "Just because the problems he deals with don't touch your pampered life. He's done a great deal to fight the bureaucrats in this country. I like him, he's against the Cluns."

Theo was pleased with this application of their professional life to national affairs. He leaned back for Jasper's comment but none came. Annoyed, he looked sharply at his host and went on: "I thought it was great of him, resigning from the House of Commons like that. Being an M.P.'s no job for an individualist like him, especially a Labour M.P. He's no planner, he's a good old Tory Radical like Cobbett."

Once again he waited for a comment, but that too did not come. Jasper, in fact, rather delighted in the fact that Theo, with his working-class background, should be so staunch a Tory, while he had always voted Labour. He felt it brought him into personal contact with the modern topsy-turvy social order. He often quoted it at dinner parties as an instance of modern English life.

"Middleton never speaks of his family," he said, forgetting that he never spoke of his.

"No," said Theo, "Betty met Mrs Middleton once. She and Middleton live apart, you know. She's a Dane or Norwegian or something, anyway Scandinavian."

"Scandinavian anyway," said Professor Pforzheim, taking the small carved ivory box to the light of the window, "Walrus ivory, I suppose. Perhaps Norwegian, no? Of the late ninth century, I may suggest. Perhaps from the Hebrides Islands?" He turned his tall, distinguished figure towards Sir Edgar, and his clear blue eyes smiled in anticipation of applause.

Sir Edgar's heavy grey eyebrows drew together in distaste. The fellow's a mountebank, he thought. We're not playing parlour games. Nobody asked his opinion. All the Germans are the same, histrionic nonsense! Had Pforzheim been other than a distinguished visitor, he would have answered sharply. As it was, he slumped his already hunched shoulders forward and moved to the door of the lecture-room. "Will an hour be enough for you?" he asked, turning his bald head and looking back over his hump.

With his dwarfish height and his little bent legs he might have been an insect, and Professor Pforzheim, towering above, might have been about to crush him. But the professor, if not sensitive to the emotions of others, was quickly aware of the response he evoked. Running his long hand through his prematurely grey hair, he laughed, all pearly teeth, a high-spirited, boyish laugh. "Oh, my God!" he cried, "I am showing off. That will never do in England." It was a spontaneous exhibition that had served its purpose on many different occasions. Sir Edgar, however, disliked it even more than his earlier performance. He fell back on the old English courtesy that he had consciously perfected to combat the increasing irritability that came with old age and arthritis.

"My dear fellow, you must excuse the abstraction of a very old man. I oughtn't to be here, you know, no one of eighty should hold any sort of office." He gave the small twinkling glance that always charmed, coming out of a face so severe in repose. "You're perfectly right. It was dug up in Iona in '24. It's one of the few objects I haven't given to the museums. I think the president's room has the right to a little beauty. I've left it to the Association. They'll probably put it in a case, and quite right too. I've always been far too inclined to treat important objects as part of my own petty existence. It's a nice piece though, isn't it?"

"Quite marvellous. And to proclaim its history so easily," Professor Pforzheim belittled his own performance, "that for me is a most excellent quality. I have no love of historical puzzles, pieces that do not fit. Things like this Heligoland burial, for example."

"Ah, I've been wondering about that. You fellows have kept pretty dark about what you've found." Sir Edgar glanced with amusement at Pforzheim.

"I do not care for premature publication, you know, Sir Edgar," the visitor said, and his manner, for so charming a man, was quite stiff.

"Oh, quite right, my dear chap," said Sir Edgar. "Well, we'll know when we're intended to, no doubt. I liked your article on the functions of the Carolingian Chancellery. We've got a young chap from Leeds working on the same thing at the moment. He'll be here this evening. I think he's got a bone to pick with you. Something to do with your interpretation of the seals. So we'll give you a bit of a run for your money. By the way, don't hesitate to carry on beyond the usual hour if you want to. We normally have a short Association business meeting after the discussion, but I wouldn't be sorry to post-pone it. I get very easily tired these days, you know. So use all the time you want."

Once again Professor Pforzheim ignored his chairman's references to procedure. "Sir Edgar," he said, in that abrupt, overloud tone that people so often use when they have made up their mind to speak, "Will there be Press here this evening?"

"Oh! I expect so. *The Times* and the *Guardian* usually send chaps along. Stokesay was a bit of a national figure, you know. Are you going to say anything about him this evening? It's usual, of course. But you don't have to."

"But of course," said Professor Pforzheim, "I shall pay tribute to his great historical work. I do not think it will be exact if I make mention of his political work—as a foreigner."

"Oh, no, my dear fellow. Certainly not. Not 'exact' at all." Sir Edgar was delighted that his question had so quickly elicited what he wished to know. He always faced the Stokesay Lecture more easily if he knew that no reference would be made to the founder's unfortunate last years. "Quite candidly, the old chap made an infernal nuisance of himself with all that . . ." His voice tailed away as he realized that "pro-German nonsense" would not be exactly polite to his guest.

"By the way," said Professor Pforzheim, "are the Melpham objects on exhibition still?"

"I don't know," said Sir Edgar, "I haven't looked at 'em for years. I don't care for these nonesuches, and Eorpwald's tomb is one of them. Anyway, I never look at anything that isn't beautiful these days unless duty compels me, and I haven't touched the seventh century for years. I expect you'll find them in the gallery, though you never know now, they change things about so much in all these museums. All this display fiddle-faddle. Educating the public and so on. We're back to the Prince Consort. Anyway, Cuspatt'll produce the things for you, if you want to see them. What's the interest in Melpham, any-how? Stokesay said all there was to say about it. How does it go? 'We may search all the annals of the English conversion until the end of time before we find a spirit so strange, a character so enigmatic as Eorpwald, the Janus-headed missionary of East Folk. This man, so learned, so credulous . . .' I forget how it goes on. I had a wonderful memory once. Could recite you hundreds of the old man's purple passages. But you'll find it all in his *Conversion of England*; the serious stuff's in the *E.H.J.* for '13, and he wrote it up again in '22."

"Yes," said Professor Pforzheim, as though in answer to a too often repeated story.

"Ah! Middleton!" said Sir Edgar with pleasure. He liked Gerald Middleton at all times and especially when he promised relief from a Hun visitor. "You know Middleton, Pforzheim, don't you?"

"We have not met since before the war," said Professor Pforzheim. He was careful not to bow but to shake hands.

"You were not at Florence in 1950, Professor Middleton, nor again at Vienna last year?"

"No," said Gerald Middleton. "I'm too old really for international congresses, and certainly too lazy." His voice, though drawling, was warm and deep.

"Oh, you are quite right, I am sure," said Professor Pforzheim, and he smiled sophisticatedly to show his superiority to congresses. "One hears only platitudes. Nevertheless," he added, "there is always a certain stimulus about the interchange of ideas."

"Ah, yes, the interchange of ideas." Gerald Middleton reiterated the phrase, and his handsome, sensual face with its contour-map of lines and furrows assumed a perfunctory gravity in courtesy to foreign pomposity. "The trouble is, of course, when, like me, you haven't any to interchange. However, there's always the scandal, isn't there?"

"Ah!" said Professor Pforzheim. "Alas, we historians have so little scandal. We are not palaeontologists to display our Piltdowns." He gave a sly look: "*Albion perfide*" he said in a guttural French accent. There was nothing, he always believed, Englishmen liked so much as a joke against themselves.

Neither Sir Edgar nor Gerald seemed to realize the joke. Gerald said, "One should always mistrust amateurs," and his heavy eyelids seemed almost to close. Sir Edgar said, "Ah, my dear fellow, we pursue humane studies, we're not technicians. All this spectographic analysis and fluorine tests and what-not. There's no place for 'sweetness and light' in all that."

"No, no," said Professor Pforzheim, shaking his head, "The Tyranny of the Tool."

Gerald Middleton seemed to take this more jocularly. He glanced at Sir Edgar, but the old man would not share the joke.

"I was told you wanted to see me," Gerald said.

"Ah, yes, my dear boy," said Sir Edgar, for so he regarded Gerald's sixty-two years. "This infernal business of the editorship may well come up this afternoon. I do hope you won't make a fuss about accepting it."

"I see no likelihood of fuss," said Gerald. "But don't count on my taking it. I can't say."

"You're very wrong, you know," Sir Edgar said gravely. "We need a certain breadth of interest, we need imagination, and we need someone who can write at least tolerable English, if the series is to be of any use."

"There's plenty of young fellows with all that," Gerald said.

"The next candidate is Clun," Sir Edgar said grimly.

Gerald's tone became sulky. "I can't say at all," he said.

"Well, be prepared to discuss it," Sir Edgar insisted, then taking out a gold hunter watch, he said, "Two minutes."

Professor Pforzheim bowed this time, then he said, "Professor Clun, always so exact and methodical. How is he?"

"Always so exact and methodical," said Gerald.

Pforzheim raised his eyebrows, "And Dr Lorimer?" he asked.

"Always so inexact and unmethodical," Gerald replied.

"No, that's not fair, Middleton," said Sir Edgar. "She has a fine brain, Pforzheim, but she's not been well lately."

Gerald turned almost angrily on Sir Edgar. "You don't understand my praises," he said irritably.

Professor Pforzheim intervened tactfully. "But, Middleton, I was forgetting. You are exactly the man I wish to talk to. The last survivor of Melpham," and he laughed. "You were *there*, were you not?"

"I was there, but I know nothing about it," Gerald said, dismissing the subject.

"But you can tell me something about the circumstances? We must talk afterwards."

"I was simply an undergraduate staying with the family, a friend of Stokesay's son Gilbert, you know. I didn't arrive until the excavation was practically over. . . ." He seemed about to say more, then he checked himself.

Sir Edgar led the way through the door on to the platform. Gerald's dark, flushed face had grown more and more irritable. "There's not a chance in a hundred that I'll take the editorship," he whispered to Sir Edgar, "you'd better know that."

CHAPTER TWO

"I DO not think," said Sir Edgar, and his cracked old voice was additionally broken with emotion, "that the Association has been privileged for a very long time to hear a speech at once so learned and so humane as the one we have heard this evening. Professor Pforzheim, in his survey of Dark Age and Early Medieval trade, has taken us on a vast geographical journey from Canton to the shores of the Iberian Peninsula, and from the Baltic to the Upper Nile; but he has taken me, and, I dare say, many of you on an even wider spiritual journey, for he has recalled, to me at any rate, a time when historical studies demanded, as their simple prerequisites, learning worn lightly, high courage of imagination and strong intellectual discipline."

Sir Edgar glowered at a number of scholars whom he felt to be pre-eminently lacking in these qualities. Gerald Middleton moved uneasily in his chair. He had strongly approved the speech himself, but he disliked a show of emotion in those whom, like Sir Edgar, he regarded as champions of reserve and decorum. How very unpleasant the effects of old age are, he reflected.

Jasper Stringwell-Anderson crossed his legs elegantly and observed Gerald closely through narrowed eyelids. He guessed that Sir Edgar's unwonted emotionalism would affect Gerald adversely and feared that it would stiffen his reluctance to become editor. "Yes, yes," he muttered, "we're delighted to know there is still some heat in the dying embers, but don't go on for too long." Sir Edgar, however, had more to say.

"The study of history is not a simple amassing of knowledge," his voice seemed to gain strength, "less still a technique;

it is not even an exercise of wise judgment or clever analysis. It is, it must be, a discipline of the spirit, an act of faith in civilization."

Clarissa Crane, conspicuously chic among the audience, felt that this was all she had hoped for: Professor Pforzheim's distinguished air and the "magical" names he had mentioned—Damascus, Aleppo, Baghdad, Canton—had quite enchanted her. She was well on the golden road to Samarkand; indeed, had quite forgotten once or twice the annoying prohibition against smoking. And now this famous old man burning with dry fervour. "A pocket prophet in short black coat and striped trousers, burning with dry fervour." She was delighted with the phrase—it would serve so well to interpret the academic world to her literary friends.

"It is peculiarly fitting," Sir Edgar was saying, "that we should have heard this note again at the annual Stokesay Lecture. In his latter days, Stokesay spoke too often in those tones of generality, of popular rhetoric which is not the voice of history but of journalism. I can say this now, because I often said it to him," he chuckled grimly.

Theo Roberts whispered to Jasper, "I'd like to have heard that."

"But," Sir Edgar continued, "Stokesay was one of the last great historians. At his best, he was very great, at his least, he never fell into that paltry, document-grubbing pedantry that now so often serves us up petty detail, preliminary field work, and supposes that it is giving us history."

Rose Lorimer's eyes were shining and the artificial roses bobbed up and down in her excitement; she turned and smiled at random to the company behind her. A young woman lecturer from Sheffield catching one of these smiles was quite disconcerted; but Jasper, practised in the art, received two or three and dexterously returned soothing glances.

"Above all," Sir Edgar ended, "it would peculiarly have pleased Lionel Stokesay to know that the best of his memorial lectures—and having heard them all, I can confidently say it was the best—was given to us by a visitor from Germany, for Stokesay loved that country and delighted in its great tradition of scholarship and the breadth of its view of history's claims and functions."

Sir Edgar sat down, feeling that perhaps he had gone a little too far, but after all, the fellow had given a fine speech, even if he *was* a Hun. He shook Professor Pforzheim's hand. "Thank you, my dear fellow," he said, "a memorable and splendid occasion."

The audience broke up into little groups. Gerald Middleton started to edge his way out before the discussion began. Professor Clun, however, had other ideas.

"Well," he said, "I don't think we learned anything new from that." His protuberant green eyes stared up at Gerald's great height in intelligent terrier challenge. Gerald looked down at the little withered rosy apple face. He noticed flecks of spittle on the little, ridiculous moustache. His sensual lips broadened into a contemptuous grin.

"I'm sure you didn't, Clun," he drawled, "You read all the *Jahrbücher* and *Forschungen*. But it was all new to me. I'm damnably lazy about reading German. I must say I thought the fellow's English very good."

"I fancy he knows very little Arabic," said Professor Clun. "He made a curious jumble of that tenth-century North African trade manual. Of course, I don't profess to know Arabic myself, but then I don't set up as an authority on Mediterranean trade."

"No," said Gerald with a smile, "I suppose not. I fancy though he was translating from the Latin version current in Western Europe. After all, he was using it to illustrate French and Italian trading customs, and if the only version they had was a jumble of the Arabic, perhaps that was the point. But I dare say I got it wrong."

Professor Clun saw no possible response but an ambiguous smile. A uniformed attendant brought them sherry and biscuits.

"Thank you, Norton," said Gerald, "Merry Christmas to you."

"Yes, yes," said Professor Clun, taking his sherry, "Of course."

"Thank you, gentlemen, and the same to you," said Norton. "Thank you for the doll for Jessie, sir. We're not letting her see it till Christmas, of course."

"Oh they sent it, did they?" said Gerald, "you never know with these shops nowadays."

As Norton moved away, Professor Clun said, "They're all the same, these old soldiers. On the scrounge. They know very well which side *their* bread's buttered."

"Norton was my batman on the Marne," said Gerald, and flushed red at what he felt to be his own priggishness.

"I hear your son-in-law didn't get the Sociology lectureship at Exeter," Clun said after a pause.

"No," said Gerald.

"I noticed he didn't get Oriel or Bristol either," Clun added.

"Thank you for showing such interest," Gerald laughed. "Donald hasn't a very good manner at interviews."

"All this good manner business," Clun said. "They take far too much notice of it now in my opinion."

"I suppose," Gerald laughed again, "that interviewers have always preferred a good manner to a bad one."

"Charm," snapped Professor Clun.

"Ability to get on with people, I should think," Gerald suggested.

"Get on with people," Clun held the concept up in the air for inspection, then dropped it heavily. "Get on with the work is more important."

"I must get on with *my* own business," said Gerald, glancing at the clock. "There's just a chance I may buy a Fuseli drawing this evening, but I'm afraid the dealer's too knowing. He'll ask more than I am prepared to give."

"I'm surprised," said Clun, "that you should consider *that* in pursuit of your hobby."

Gerald was suddenly very annoyed, "Oh my dear fellow, don't you know," he said, "cheese-paring's always the mark of the rich."

As Gerald began to move away, Professor Clun hesitated, he did not wish to remind Gerald of the coming discussion of the editorship, but his anxiety was too great to allow him to remain silent.

"The proceedings of the Association," he said, "the question of the editorship's sure to come up."

"Oh, I don't suppose there'll be time for anything after the discussion," Gerald said carelessly, "and in any case, there are two or three excellent young chaps they ought to consider before they get down to you and me." And he moved off.

He was not to be allowed to escape so easily, however, for Theo and Jasper were in wait.

"Well, didn't that make you feel grand?" asked Theo. Even his somewhat obtuse sense of situation had seen in Professor Pforzheim's lecture an opportunity to rouse Gerald to the need for action. "*Absit* Clun, eh?" he laughed.

"Oh, Clun feels doubts about Pforzheim's proficiency in Arabic," Gerald said.

"I hope he raises that in the discussion," said Theo, "Pforzheim looks to me a heavyweight. He'll make rings round our Arthur."

"Well you must let me know if he draws blood." Gerald made to move on.

"You're not getting out of this so easily," said Jasper, smiling, and fitting a cigarette into a Dunhill holder. "Your place is here and you know it."

"My dear chap, I know nothing whatsoever about Dark Age trade, or at any rate no more than befits a gentleman."

"Then you must sit patiently like a gentleman," said Jasper, "until the association's business comes up, Gerald." Both he and Theo were perhaps a trifle over-jocular in their anxiety. Then he added in mock American, "Who do we need for editor? One, two, three—M...I...D... Middleton."

"Rah, Rah," added Theo.

"Thank you very much," said Gerald, "but I'm not staging a come-back. You should get yourselves a job as agents for Mistinguette."

"There won't be another Medieval series for twenty years," said Theo, "this is a serious matter."

"The more reason," said Gerald, "for not appointing a played-out man. Look, if it's Clun you're worrying about, I've already told Sir Edgar to appoint one of you younger chaps. If they don't like either of your two faces, there's Prescott or Drake, or Hilda Ferguson, not to forget Edinburgh and the fair sex."

"You know perfectly well," said Jasper, "that if it isn't you, it'll be Clun. And if by some odd freak, one of our generation did get the job, you know very well we wouldn't have either the prestige or the connections to make a success of it. Your ex-pupils make you a present of the compliment—you're the only man who has all that."

"In the first place, I haven't," said Gerald, "and in the second place, if I were to be active again I should give my energies to *England under the Confessor*." He spoke the title of his work, so long mooted and never realized, in ironic inverted commas.

"Ah," said Theo, knocking his pipe out on the heel of his shoe, "if I really thought that, you know . . ."

But Jasper interrupted, "If you don't take the editorship, Gerald, you'll never write another thing: if you do, you'll write *The Confessor* and much more."

Gerald was about to be angry, then he checked himself and said drawlingly, "Well, at the moment anyway, you must excuse me. I have a chance of buying a Fuseli drawing and I don't intend to miss it."

Jasper showed *his* annoyance. "Overrated modern *chichi*," he said.

Gerald smiled and began to walk away, when Theo, red in the face, produced his prepared piece. "Look here," he said, "we all know your *Cnut* was damned good *and* your lecture notes. But you're not Acton. It's not enough. If you don't help history now, she won't help you. You'll be classed as a second-rater."

Gerald flushed and his heavy jowl trembled slightly. "I don't think you mean to be impertinent, Theo," he said, "but you are. And what's worse, you're being melodramatic," and he walked away.

As he got to the doorway, Rose Lorimer bore down upon him, with Clarissa Crane in tow.

"Hello, Rose," he said with an affectionate smile, "Good, wasn't it? I've got to run now, my dear, but a Happy Christmas to you."

"Oh, Gerald, you're not going before the discussion, that's too bad of you."

"You do my discussing for me, my dear."

"Oh, I'm afraid I shan't be able to say anything for you," Rose took such conventional facetiousness quite seriously, "I've a most important thing to ask Pforzheim myself about trade and the Christian mission, and about St Boniface. . . ."

Rose's breathless excitement was interrupted by Clarissa's strangulated sophistication. "Since Dr Lorimer's so excited, I'll have to introduce myself. I'm Clarissa Crane," she announced in the simple, direct voice she used to take the celebrity off her name.

Gerald did not recognize the note or the name, but his sensual eye took in her slim feminine figure. He smiled.

"I know a novelist has no place here," said Clarissa to repair the ignorance that her practised eye had recognized, "but I'm foolhardy enough to be writing about the seventh century, and Dr Lorimer kindly brought me along. I wanted particularly to meet you, because you can tell me something about Melpham."

This second mention that evening of Melpham finally removed any glamour that Clarissa might have had for Gerald. His professional eye had already detected a shop-soiled frigidity beneath her chic. "I know nothing whatsoever about Melpham," he said curtly. "If I remember rightly, Bishop Eorpwald died in 698; my interests begin roughly at 950."

"Oh, but you knew the Stokesays frightfully well. Dollie's told me a lot about you. She's a great friend of mine."

At the mention of Dollie Stokesay's name, Gerald's face softened again. "How is she?" he asked eagerly.

"Oh! wonderful, as usual," said Clarissa.

It seemed a curious description to Gerald of chronic dipsomania, but he let it pass. "I haven't seen her since before the war," he said. "I wish I could help you about Melpham, but there's nothing to tell. I was simply a friend of Gilbert's and I knew even less then than I do now of the seventh century."

"Gilbert Stokesay? Oh, that's terribly interesting. Everyone talks about his work now, except, of course, Dollie. It seems so incredible to think of her in connection with Futurist manifestos and so on. I don't suppose she's ever read a line. Gilbert Stokesay! Oh, I shall certainly ring you up," Clarissa said. Melpham might just help with the novel, Gerald Middleton was rich and distinguished, but Gilbert Stokesay was a smart name; there was no doubt of Clarissa's determination to keep in touch. Gerald had refused to see innumerable Americans who were writing theses on his dead friend's work, but *they* could not bring him news of Gilbert's widow. It would tax his ingenuity to avoid saying anything about Gilbert or Melpham for half an hour, but it was an ordeal he was prepared to undergo if he could hear from Clarissa a first-hand account of Dollie. Anything to get news of her, without actually seeing her. "That will be delightful," he said, and disappeared through the doorway.

Clarissa said loudly to Rose, "I'd no idea he was such a charmer."

Sir Edgar was piloting Professor Pforzheim round the room. He advanced towards a tall military-looking man wearing orange suede shoes. "Professor Pforzheim, you must meet

Colonel Brankscombe," he said, "he's the fellow who's going to bear witness against you in *The Times* tomorrow."

"Fascinating lecture," said Colonel Brankscombe. "Afraid I can't hope to do you justice, but I've got the salient points, I think."

"Are none of your colleagues here?" asked Sir Edgar.

"No, Ottery doesn't seem to have made it." The colonel turned to Professor Pforzheim as if in apology. "If you'll let me know where you're stopping, I'll let you see what I've written tonight if you like."

"Oh," said Professor Pforzheim in chuckling delight, "this is quite wonderful. *The Times* is willing to be checked. I don't think any foreigner would believe it. Thank you very much, but I am sure that it is quite unnecessary," he added, with a little bow, "the accuracy of *The Times* is proverbial, you know."

Once again Sir Edgar was forced to avoid catching a compatriot's eye. That was the trouble with foreigners, the unnecessary embarrassing things they said.

"But where is Middleton?" cried Pforzheim, as they watched Colonel Brankscombe leaving. "I wished so much to speak to him."

"I'm afraid he's left," said Professor Clun, seizing an excellent opportunity.

"What?" said Sir Edgar with annoyance, "Middleton gone?"

"He had some rare drawing to see," said Professor Clun, suggesting almost that it might be pornographic. "The rich can never resist a bargain." And he laughed, not so much at the observation, as at the pleasure in turning Gerald's words against him. Sir Edgar, however, was not favourable to malice.

"I suppose we can none of us do that, Clun," he said shortly.

Professor Clun's dislike of Sir Edgar was very great, but he was anxious to avoid any overt disagreement. He turned to Pforzheim, "Well," he said, "you gave us just the thing for the occasion. I only wish there was an opportunity to talk a bit on the more scholarly level."

Sir Edgar frowned, but Professor Pforzheim only smiled. He estimated Professor Clun's abilities more highly perhaps than his English colleagues, and suffered less than they did from his deficiencies.

"Oh, but you are quite right, my dear man," he said. "My lecture was a *Denkschrift*. You, of course, want something more solid. Well, the discussion is yours."

Poor Professor Clun was perplexed. It was gratifying to have his point of view taken seriously, but then, of course, it was only to be expected; Pforzheim was a good Continental scholar, and it was only in England that serious scholarship was underrated. On the other hand, the last thing he wanted was to prolong the "discussion". "I hardly think Sir Edgar would care for a discussion of technicalities this evening," he said with a confiding smile.

Sir Edgar's reply was lost, however, in another of Clarissa's gestures. "I'm Clarissa Crane, Sir Edgar," she said, "I've really no right here. . . ."

Sir Edgar did not exactly recognize the character of her intervention, but he could see at once from her appearance that it was a time-wasting one. "Not at all," he said. "Delighted. Well, I'm afraid we must cut our conversation short. The discussion's four minutes overdue. Fire any questions you like at Pforzheim. He's told me to give you all *carte blanche*," and he led the way back to the dais.

The discussion, to Professor Clun's discomfort and to Jasper's delight, went with a bang. Praed was deeply interested in Professor Pforzheim's view about the Kharkov hoard, didn't he perhaps lay a little too much emphasis on the presence of Bactrian coins? Naturally the greatest interest attached to anything from that area, but, after all. . . . Grayson was interested in the Carolingian decrees to Marseilles merchants, but surely this was only another instance of brilliant imperial propaganda, to talk of Roman survival seemed to ignore. . . . Prescott gave other instances of the restrictive decrees of the Cordova Caliphate . . . Drake questioned the relevance of St Gregory's attitude to the slave trade.

Jasper's purring was almost audible, Clun's terrier-barking could even be *heard* once or twice—"Perhaps I may say Mr. Chairman . . ." But Sir Edgar seemed deaf to such interruptions. Professor Pforzheim's survey had been broad, his replies were as rich in depth. It was not Sir Edgar's intention that such a remarkable performance should be curtailed for a lot of tiresome association business. He equally ignored all Rose Lorimer's flustered bobs, becks and smiles. He was convinced that the growing oddness of Rose's views was only a temporary aberration in a fine scholar due to overwork. His whole aim was to protect her from herself until he could persuade her to have a long holiday. As to Clarissa's occasional attempts to rise from her chair, he had already marked her down as a time-waster and he was not quick to change such judgments.

Now little Hilda Ferguson, fiercely Scots with her flaming red hair and shrill soap-box voice, rose to express her agreement with the lecturer's very clear exposition of the Ethiopic position, but at the risk of being theological she would like to stress the very deep mark on the whole social order of that area left by the Monophysites. . . .

Professor Pforzheim dealt with this point also very aptly, but the introduction of religion into the discussion was too much for Rose Lorimer. She was on her feet. Clutching her old fur coat around her and smiling benignly from beneath her roses, she spoke, her childish voice almost cooing the carefully enunciated syllables.

"Those of us who worked most closely with Professor Stokesay and to whom his memory is not only most dear but always alive, have experienced this evening a quite remarkable pleasure in listening to Professor Pforzheim's wonderful lecture."

She paused and, throwing back her fur coat from her shoulders to reveal a purple crochet jumper, she smiled vaguely round the room as a signal that she had much to say. Professor Pforzheim bowed from his chair at the compliment and smiled as to an old friend, but Rose seemed oblivious to individuals.

"I am among those who owe all that they know to Lionel Stokesay, and not only all that I know, but all that I have dreamed of what the past can yield up to us if we approach it with reverence and dedication. And not only the past but the past that lies in the present." Here she smiled mysteriously. Sir Edgar began to look uneasy, but Jasper sat back with a smile of delight. "I was one of those, common in my girlhood, for whom the study of history was a very dry discipline, and I well remember, how, in that old hall at Manchester, now I understand pulled down, I went, with a certain reluctant scepticism, to hear the famous Lionel Stokesay lecture. That scepticism was soon washed away through the floodgates which his discourse opened for me."

Jasper could not forbear giving a special smile at Professor Clun, as though including him in a bond of peculiar pleasure at Rose's reminiscences. It was more than the little man could bear, and he muttered audibly, "It's a pity a lot of other things weren't washed away." Theo, who was as disgusted at Clun's lack of chivalry as he was delighted at the likely length of Rose's contribution said, "Shame!" in his broadest Yorkshire. Rose noticed no interruptions.

"Sir Edgar has criticized Professor Stokesay's last years, he has called the writings of those last years journalism. Well, I have crossed friendly swords with our President before now and I do not hesitate to do so again." She smiled archly at Sir Edgar, who slumped into his chair until he seemed to be no more than a black hump. "I saw a lot of Lionel Stokesay at the end of his life, and I know how deeply, how seriously, he felt that it was his duty to bring his great historical knowledge to bear upon the troubled events of those years. Nobody, of course, likes the Nazis." She said this as though referring to the usual antipathies to spiders or muddy boots in the house. On political matters, her mind was as naïve as her voice. The embarrassment of the audience was perhaps greater than that of Professor Pforzheim, who had blushed scarlet. "But Lionel Stokesay felt above everything that he must do all in his power to preserve peace. In his efforts to do so, I believe, he showed himself a great statesman as well as a great historian, and his sadness when all his efforts proved unavailing was tragic to see. It killed him."

Rose was unable to continue for a moment, and then, pulling her fur coat around her, she leaned forward and, smiling through her tears, she said: "But these are now only memories. What is important is that we have heard this evening a lecture which can, if we follow its lead, take us out of the petty lanes and alleys, along which students of medieval history tend nowadays too easily to stray, to that broad road with its glorious ideal prospect upon which Lionel Stokesay trod all his life. So commanding is the scene which our lecturer laid before us this evening that it may seem churlish to ask that it should have been even wider. All the same, there is one aspect of that strange, important watershed period of the past, which has been given the foolish label of the Dark Ages, that I would like to mention. Professor Pforzheim has told us something of the continuous trade of the Northern pagan world and something of the spread of trade which went with the preaching of the Gospel, but does he not think that the division between these two worlds—the pagan and the Christian—is really rather artificial? Was there so much that finally separated them? Once there had been compromise, that is. It has always seemed to me, and I fear I have laboured the point more than once in print,"— she smiled in childish glee round the room—"that in their eagerness to keep the saving of souls for themselves, to destroy the Church of Iona, the Roman missionaries made so many compromises." She seemed now to be listening to two voices and her utterance became increasingly confused. "Is there not, or perhaps I should say, was there not, a filling of the holy vessels with blood that came from more ancient sacrifices than that which we remember on Good Friday? And I would ask perhaps, if the older force which conquered then in the realm of spirit may not also have overflowed and transformed even the material life of the time, even the trade?"

She paused, looking strangely at Professor Pforzheim. The Professor stood up deeply embarrassed.

"I'm not sure I have truly understood the meaning of Dr Lorimer's question. The interchange between the pagan and the Christian world, of course . . ."

"I'm afraid, I don't speak at all well," said Rose simply. "I'm so familiar perhaps with these ideas, live with them so much, that . . ." her voice tailed away. "Well," she said more brightly, "I could give so you many examples. But to take our east coast of England, surely from the fifth century onwards an essential part of the trading world. What do you make of King Redwald's idols? What do you make of the implications of Bishop Eorpwald's tomb? These, I would remind you all, were the results of Rome's mission. . . ."

Before Professor Pforzheim could answer, Arthur Clun was on his feet. "Mr Chairman, I really must protest. The association has business to do. I cannot conceive how the circumstances of Eorpwald's burial can possibly . . ."

Rose Lorimer turned a bewildered, worried stare upon him. "Perhaps Professor Clun thinks that we should not allow ourselves an imaginative leap beyond the strict barriers of fact?"

"I think," said Professor Clun, "that some people have made one imaginative leap too many and show little sign of being able to return to the realm of reason."

Sir Edgar was about to protest, when Professor Pforzheim, whom years of courageous opposition to Nazi rule had made peculiarly susceptible to any sign of bullying, rose to his feet.

"I should like to speak something about this." He looked down at the lectern and his long body pivoted uneasily from foot to foot. "What I am going to say is an indiscretion. I had not intended to speak anything about it this evening. Indeed, I should perhaps correct that—I had intended most definitely *not* to speak anything about it. But Professor Clun's belittling of the importance of the Melpham tomb makes me feel that I *should* speak and, as the gentleman from the Press is no longer here, I hope that I can trust this great body of historians to allow my confidences to go no further. As you know, we have been making excavations along the North Sea shores of Heligoland, an important centre of Saxon life and the scene of the conversion of King Eltheof by St Boniface's disciple Aldwin. Well, we have discovered Aldwin's tomb. The material is in very bad condition and anything I say must be regarded as very tentative. Nevertheless, there seems reason for us to think that the conditions of Aldwin's burial were the same as those of Eorpwald nearly one century earlier. There are fragments that suggest the same wooden pagan deity. I fear that most of what Dr Lorimer is saying goes beyond what I would call historical fact, but I think we should be careful before we dismiss the Melpham discovery so easily as an exceptional event."

He sat down, with folded arms, his head buried in his waistcoat.

If for some of the audience it was Pforzheim's manner rather than what he said that was rousing, the many specialists were clearly in a state of great excitement. There was silence for some seconds, then a small clerical figure at the back of the hall rose to speak. Father Lavenham, the great Benedictine scholar, had a distinguished ascetic face which was yet strangely goat-like, his bleating voice equally had an unexpectedly diplomatic, soothing note.

"Mr Chairman," he said, "since Professor Pforzheim has been so good as to honour us with this remarkable confidence, I think we should repay him by refraining from discussion of it until greater certainty allows him and his distinguished colleagues to make public their more definite conclusions."

He sat down with the air of having nipped some potentially insidious nonsense in the bud.

Once again there was silence. Rose Lorimer had the air of a martyr vindicated by a sign from Heaven which she did not quite understand; it was Professor Clun who now smiled vaguely as though there were no end to the childish folly of his colleagues. Clarissa alone had failed to realize the importance of Professor Pforzheim's statement. Holding her bag, her gloves, and her small felt cap in one hand, she rose to her feet.

"Mr Chairman," she said, "I don't know whether a mere visitor has any right . . ."

But her question remained unspoken. Sir Edgar had decided that the moment had come to put an end to the proceedings.

"I fear we have no more time for questions, and," he added with a chuckle, for he had conceived a great dislike for Clarissa, "little inclination to hear them with all we have to think about."

He turned to Professor Pforzheim. "Once again, thank you," he said, and led the way through the door at the back of the dais to the accompaniment of the association's applause.

CHAPTER THREE

MRS SALAD came each year to get her present from
Gerald before luncheon on Christmas Eve. It was always
the same present—a five-pound note and a large pink cyclamen
in a gilded basket tied with pink ribbon. This year, Gerald had
attempted a variation by presenting her with a scarlet poinsettia, but he knew at once that he was wrong.

"Oh, it's a lovely foreign thing. Bright as blood," Mrs Salad
said in her old, croaking tremolo, and she peered at it through
the haze of mascara'd moisture that always clung to her eye-
lashes and stuck in little beads on her black net eye-veil. "I
dare say it'll draw the flies. But lovely for them that likes bright
colours. Just like the stuff the girls put on their finger-nails
now. Like a lot of old birds giving the glad in the Circus, or the
York Road, Waterloo, more likely. Trollopy lot."

And Mrs Salad's black-dyed curls and fur toque with eye-veil
shook in disgust, though whether against the painted nails of
the modern girl or the behaviour of prostitutes was not clear.
In either case, it was righteous disgust, for, despite her scab-
rous imagination, Mrs Salad always boasted that she had kept
her body clean "as Our Lord had given it to her," and for
make up, although her face was liberally covered with rouge
and mascara and enamel, she had never used nail-varnish.

"Now the cycerlermums," she continued, "is as delicate as
my sister-in-law's skin. Her husband wouldn't have her wear
a soiled garment not a day longer than was needed. Spurgin's
Tabernacle they was," she added. Many of Mrs Salad's images
were drawn from the anatomy of her family. "Well, there it is,"
she said, giving the poinsettia a final survey, "More of a leaf,
really." For all their cloudiness, Mrs Salad's eyes were very sharp.

It was not an auspicious beginning for the visit, and this year Mrs Salad seemed more frail than ever, her agile mind more random. Her shrunken little body in its black cloth coat with a bunch of artificial Parma violets was bent with arthritis and her match-stick legs trembled on her high-heeled patent leather boots with grey kid uppers.

"I came from 'Endon by Underground," she said, "and a musty, high-smelling lot they are that go by it now. My son-in-law offered to bring me in his car. But Gladys wouldn't have it. Wanted it herself for a bit of la-di-da, I dare say. Lovely chap, he is. Used to be in the Navy. Often I've seen him of a morning when he's taking his tub, stripped to the waist. Better than any boxer. But it's all for Gladys. He's not the one to give it away to any little cheap bit that comes along."

Gerald, who was well used to Mrs Salad's reminiscences, handed her the customary glass of sweet sherry and asked her how she liked living at her daughter's.

"Oh! it's a loverly residence," Mrs Salad said, carrying her glass with shaky hand to her smudged scarlet lips. "Gladys isn't equal to it," she added with dignity, "though she's my daughter. My son-in-law saw it at once, 'Mother,' he said to me, 'you make the place like a palace and it fits you like a glove'." Mrs Salad here moulded one of her black kid gloves to her small, knotted hand to illustrate the point. Then she continued, "And a beautiful class of neighbours too. Though it's a trashy lot next door. Makin' h'objections without call. My grandson Vin come at weekends and he likes to sun himself in the garden. He strips thin but very delicate, and a lovely choice of the trunks. Gold and white satin. They starts makin' hobjections. I didn't lose my dignity. I just said, 'You filthy trollopy lot,' I said. Well, you know me, dear. How's Mr. John?" she asked, giving Gerald a sharp glance. "I seen him on the Tele. Very quick he was helping the lot that won't help themselves. Poor chap. Answering a lot of silly questions from the poorest of the poor. They won't thank him for it. Vin's met him often. A la-di-da lot they move with. It doesn't do any good to ask about it. We shouldn't understand it if we did. But there you are, it doesn't do to criticize, just because their larks aren't ours, does it?" Gerald had no idea what Mrs Salad was driving at, but he agreed. "I had a lovely powder-puff from Miss Dollie. She always remembers me. You goin' to her for Xmas?"

It was Gerald's turn to look sharply at the old woman, "Now Mrs Salad, you know very well that I haven't seen Mrs Stokesay for years."

"No," said Mrs Salad, "more's the pity. You took what you wanted and passed on, as men will. Oh well, who can blame you?" She shrugged it off with an *ancien régime* worldli-ness. "Nobody wants to wear an old pair of shoes. But you had lovely larks while it lasted. And very nice to work for, you both were, sin or no sin."

Mrs Salad looked round the walls and fixed her eyes on a John drawing of a woman putting on her stockings. She gave it an approving smile as though to illustrate her broadmindedness.

"That's the trouble with Gladys, doesn't know life," she said. "I was talkin' about the old days at His Majesty's the other night when we had company. After they'd gone she says to me, 'Can't you find nothing to talk about but lavatories?' 'I've met better class in the Cloakroom than you'll ever know,' I said. 'Programme girl seems more refined to me,' she answered. Silly cow! I could have been programme girl over and over. But, no thank you! Save your feet's my motto."

Mrs Salad's dim old eyes took on a distant look and she brought out a small lace-edged handkerchief from her old black velvet vanity bag, filling the room with the scent of violets.

"Many's the time Sir Beerbohm Tree's stood outside the theatre, *and* Mr Lewis Waller too, lovely little body *he* had. 'I'd strictly advise you,' they'd say to their lady friends, 'to use Mrs Salad's lavatory, it's on the left of the stalls going in.' And they'd come, all the upper tens! I wouldn't have the trash —the demimondes and débutantes—I didn't want that filth.

'There's a cloakroom on the other side,' I'd say, and send them to old Mother Rogers. And now you want *your* present," she said abruptly, as reminiscence and invention both gave out, and opening a brown paper bag, she produced a huge white silk handkerchief on which were embroidered a number of large orange flowers.

"Thank you," said Gerald, "I like that very much. I'm glad you're able to keep up your embroidery."

"Art's in the bones or it isn't," said Mrs Salad sententiously. "I'm sorry it's marigolds, dear. I know you like the birds better, but I can't see to do their beaks now. The Mayor of Southtown," she added rather vaguely, "was looking into my eyes only the other day, 'It seems against nature, Mrs Salad,' he said, 'to see those lovely little horbs dimmed.' But there! Time takes and it gives, for all its called the Great Healer. And so I tell Vin. 'Your time's now,' I tell him. Slim as a girl he is. But he don't seem to settle down now 'es out. I don't see what good it's done him. Delicate made 'e is and only a boy. Stands to reason 'e couldn't rough it with the others."

"I shouldn't worry too much, Mrs Salad," Gerald said. "Of course, I loved soldiering. But National Service doesn't do any harm, even to those who don't."

"National Service!" Mrs Salad repeated. She smiled to herself and then she looked sharply at Gerald, but she only said, "H'm."

Gerald laughed. "You and John should get together," he said. "National Servicemen's problems. That's one of John's great specialities. He's been urging a reduction in the Services all this autumn in his articles."

Once again Mrs Salad looked strangely at Gerald. "Say toodle-oo to Mr John for me," she said. "You tell him from me there's some company that's not to be helped and it's better not to try. But there you are, life's no easy lottery they say. As we've seen who've lived it."

Her feelings about the poinsettia she made very clear, for she ostentatiously left it behind when she said goodbye.

Since Frank Rammage had grown fat, he liked to spend his time doing odd jobs indoors. With his short legs and his pot belly, he couldn't do much that required the use of a ladder, but he laboured hours painting shelves or fixing electric wires. It was easy to spend so much time on these small tasks with four houses to keep in repair, and in Frank two instincts were very strong—orderliness and economy. His innate inclination to keep things tidy had been developed into a mania by his years of service in the Navy; his passion for saving reinforced since he had become a property owner. These two obsessions were always at war with a third—his philanthropy; he did not mind that a large number of his lodgers were petty crooks, drunkards, tricksters and middle-class down-and-outs, indeed it was what he chiefly esteemed in them, but he hardly knew how to support their untidiness, their dirtiness, and their extravagance with light and gas. As he busied around putting up a new shelf in his large bed-sitting room, which was all the space he reserved for himself, he prepared to do battle with a lodger over the question of old pilchard tins.

"It's no good. I've told you twice about it and you've done nothing," he said, gobbling like a Norfolk turkey and thrusting his fat, smooth pink face at the girl before she had fully entered the room. "You'll have to go, duckie." He called everyone duckie or dear.

"I'm sorry, Frank. I've been so tired coming back in the mornings," she said plaintively. Her thin, white face, greasy with vanishing-cream above her dirty roll-topped sweater and jeans, looked hungry rather than anxious.

"We all get tired," said Frank, and his little rosebud mouth closed tightly with the moral air of a reproving hospital matron.

"Oh, God!" said the girl, swinging her emaciated boy's body on to the divan bed with its crimson coarse weave cover.

Frank had ideas about interior decoration and the room was filled with modern Scandinavian furniture and little lamps with coloured paper lampshades. Upon the walls, each painted a different colour—crimson, grey, apple green and lilac pink—

hung ferns in wicker cases. A naval motif was given by cross-ings of arty ropes and crimson anchors.

"You're too bloody fat, Frank, that's your trouble," she said.

"I've reduced considerably of late," Frank snapped, "and that doesn't answer all those fishy tins. That'll smell the place out." It was only in his use of "that" for "it" and in an occasional glottal stop that Frank's East Anglian origin could be detected.

"Well, it wouldn't do much harm if it did smell a few of the stinkers you've got here out of the place," the girl said, and she took off one of her sandals and shook it over the floor.

Frank's bald head with its ring of carroty fuzz shot forward at her.

"Stop that at once," he said. "No wonder you don't get any work at the studios. You'll spend the rest of your life in the ice-cream factory if you don't smarten yourself up a bit. Look at those jeans."

"Well, what are *you* wearing?" said the girl.

It was true that Frank also habitually wore jeans and a woollen T-shirt, but they were scrupulously clean, if, perhaps, a little unsuitable for a man of fifty-nine. It was this aspect that the girl seized on. "I've never seen anything so silly at your age," she said.

Frank was now really angry. "You'd better go," he said, "and if you land back in the approved school don't come to me for a good character. Pilchard tins and rudeness, I've had enough of it."

"You know what," said the girl, "you're a bloody hypocrite. You don't care about the pilchard tins. Not a damn. You're just frightened about your rent. Only you won't say so. Not Mr Frank Rammage, the friend of the down-and-outs, the man the police come in to tea with, the pal of all the social workers and snoopers in South-west London. Oh no! It's just that he wants to help, that's all."

The mention of rent put Frank on his mettle. "That's all right, dear," he said, "you pay when you can."

Each time that he spoke this familiar phrase, and sometimes it was as often as twenty times in a week, he felt overcome by the sadness of the situation. It was seldom, he knew, that any good would come of his sympathy, but it was the hopelessness, the endless hopelessness of the lives with which he had surrounded himself, that awoke his compassion. Frank Rammage's attitude could hardly be called sentimental, for it went further than mere feeling—he regarded the dishonest and depraved as almost sacred. As usual, however, the little scene had satisfied the mixture of bullying and masochism that lay on the surface of his strange, Dostoevskian philanthropy. He felt quite jolly. He seemed more like matron in an expansive mood as he picked up a piece of yellow material from the table and showed it to the girl.

"Buttercup yellow," he said. "It's very difficult to get that exact shade."

"Lovely, Frank," said the girl abstractedly. She, too, had got what she had intended—a further extension of credit. "Well, so long, Frank," she said, "I've got a date."

The chance to moralize was too great to resist. "You ought to leave 'dates' alone," Frank called after her reprovingly, "and rest yourself. To keep them healthy and good to look upon, that's what God gave us bodies for."

"Like Mr Rammage, I suppose," called the girl from the landing.

"You do talk cock, Frank, don't you?" said Vin Salad in his refined drawl, which sounded as though he had got rid of a Cockney accent by swallowing it. He called back upstairs to the girl. "Put something on your face, Myra, before you go out to meet him." Then seating himself demurely on the divan, he said, "That girl's face looks terrible naked. That's nice," he added, pointing to the yellow material. "Six and eleven?"

"No," said Frank sharply, "seven and five."

"You've been taken for a ride," Vin replied, "as usual."

He sat for a while very still and tall and languid on the divan. There was something almost Egyptian or Persian about Vin

Salad's stillness and languor, with his long, docile, almond-skinned face and his huge liquid black eyes. His clothes were far from Eastern, however, for Vin was very careful to avoid anything that suggested the ornate or even the flashy black of the Teddy boy. He wore a very plain dark grey worsted flannel suit, with a cream silk shirt, dark red tie and light suede strap shoes. It was rather a fragile covering for the winter season, but it was all he had at the moment, and in any case, Vin was always shivering slightly with cold even on a hot summer day. Suddenly his eyes flickered in his stillness and the tip of his tongue appeared between his even teeth. It was a saurian movement, but too quick to be sinister.

"She's a lying little bitch," he said. "Have you got rid of her?"

"I had it out with her about the pilchard tins," Frank said petulantly.

"Oh! Christ!" Vin exclaimed. "You get on my tits."

He reached over for a box of chocolates from a small crescent-shaped table and, placing it in his lap, ate the chocolates slowly but greedily one by one as he talked.

"You knew she was a filthy slut when you took her in. But you haven't got the guts to kick her out. All you can do is to nag and natter at the silly bitch."

He seized the apple-green silk cushions and punched them feebly, then placing them behind him, he lay back languidly and half closed his eyes, looking at Frank through his long lashes.

"Why don't you twist her arm or punch her face, if that's what you want?" he drawled.

Frank got up from a kneeling position and stood arms akimbo, a hammer held at his hip. He wore the broadminded smile with which he accompanied certain of his lectures.

"Sex and violence—that's why you're only a waiter, Vin," he said. "Your dirty little imagination can't carry you any further. You think you're so bloody smart, but your mind doesn't take in more than a quarter of what it could. Get what you can how you can. It's so bloody easy, and look where it gets you."

Vin stared at Frank like a young ruminating cow, then he held out the box of chocolates. "Have one." he said, "They're marvellous."

His pronunciation of the word was like a mixture of a small boy's and a Kensington hostess's. He had as many variations of speech as had his grandmother. "Crime doesn't pay," he said, closing his eyes. "I wonder you don't get tired of all that crap. You know why I'm just a waiter as well as I do. Because I don't want to get mixed up with the police again. If I liked to troll the 'Dilly like Larrie, I could live as grand as Madame de Pompadour, or pretty near." He got up lazily and stretched his arms. "I don't know what's the good of being good," he said in a Shirley Temple simper. "By the way," he added, "you'd better tell Larrie to lay off it. The silly . . ."

A large black face appeared round the door.

"Ah, Mr Rummage," said a deep West Indian voice, "I want you to give me evidence. Gloria says she didn't have a man up there last night and I know she did. Did you see anyone go up?"

"Now, Artie, landlords don't tell stories," Frank said. "You ought to know that."

"If I find her with some man, I'll spatter them both," said the head and vanished.

Frank called after him, "And my name's not Rummage either, as you perfectly well know. . . . Oh dear," he said, "I expect he will. They're as excitable as children, those West Indians," and he clucked his tongue in disapproval.

"I can't think why girls frequent them," said Vin in refined tones. "I shouldn't think of it," he added. "You won't see me for two days now, Frank. But don't let any of the dear lodgers use my room, see? We work late tonight and I'm going straight down to Gran's for Christmas."

"That's good," said Frank. "There's nothing like a family Christmas."

Without any relatives himself, he believed that family life infallibly spelt decent living. Vin said nothing this time, he just looked.

"I've got a little present for you," said Frank and, going to his desk, he produced a bright yellow tie.

"Thank you," said Vin. "Funny how some boys like those bright ties. I haven't got a present for you," he added. "I don't see any sense in giving things to rich people; well, you tell Larrie . . ."

But once again there was interruption. "Can I come in?" said a very deep voice.

"Of course, Major," said Frank.

A tired-faced military-looking man with grey wavy hair and a much cleaned, much pressed check suit opened the door. "Can you change this for me, Rammage? Left myself without anything over Christmas and it's too late to go up to the ruddy bank!"

"I can do you ten," said Frank, counting the money from a very full wallet.

"Perfectly silly of me to have my bank up in Piccadilly," said the major, a little over-eager in pocketing the notes. "I must get my account moved down to Earl's Court. Well, a Happy Christmas to you," and the major left them.

Vin looked at Frank, "Well, I don't know," he said. "Him you give ten pounds. Me you give this," and he picked up the yellow tie.

"It may bounce and it may not," said Frank. "Trust is the only thing to give him back his self-respect. Besides, it's hard for him to get work and he pretty nearly conked out in November with that pleurisy. They only saved him with penicillin."

"Silly, isn't it, what they do?" said Vin. "Any fool could see he'd be better dead. They've got it in for your blue-eyed Larrie. You tell him from me. And if he thinks because he's such a dear friend of Mr John Middleton's, they won't book him, he's a sillier cow than I thought. There's a war on in our world."

"Now, Vin," said Frank, "I know you don't like Larrie, but he's a good boy at heart. He's Irish and wild and he doesn't tell the truth, but he's not really bad. All this going about with John Middleton's gone to his head, that's all. I'd like to put a stop to it."

"Yes," said Vin, "I'm sure you would." Then, looking at Frank's round apple face, he added, "And I believe you honestly don't know why. Or ever will, for that matter: no wonder you've got that old clergyman's photograph stuck up on the desk. Who is he anyhow?"

Frank looked at the conventionally handsome, clean-cut features in the picture—it was the face of an old-fashioned matinée idol playing a clergyman.

"He was a very good man," he said, "Canon Portway. He was rector of Melpham, where I was born."

"And you were in the choir. Christ! isn't life boring?" drawled Vin. He looked at Frank for a second. "You've gained weight since then," he added, then taking a piece of holly from the profuse Christmas decorations of the room, he placed it neatly on Frank's bald head. "It's you and the plum pudding," he said, and sauntered out of the room.

Like his grandmother, he left his Christmas present behind.

"No, I don't think it's at all funny, Larrie," said Elvira Portway, John Middleton's secretary, and taking the sheet of paper on which he had typed "A Happy Xmas to all our bleeders," she crumpled it up and threw it into the waste-paper basket. "John," she said, "stop him touching the typewriter, or, much better still, get him out of the office altogether."

"The darlin' girl doesn't like me, Johno," said Larrie, all Irish eyes and smiling.

"You'd better beat it, Larrie," said John Middleton, his earnest, boyish tones a little more edgy than his great wireless public would have recognized. "Cut along and have a lovely Christmas. I'll see you Tuesday."

"Look after yourself, Johno, and don't eat too much," Larrie began a playful sparring at John, hitting him lightly on the belt. "You don't want to add to that, now do you?" he asked.

It was perfectly true. At thirty-three, John Middleton had the air of a boy who was getting gross.

"Give my love to your Mum, Johno. Tell her it was the grandest day of my life that I spent at her lovely house. Did you know I'd been to Johnnie's mother's for the day?" Larrie asked Elvira, and, noted that, although she made no reply, she also looked down at her desk. "The top of the morning to you, Johnnie. And to you, my lovely," he said to Elvira, who again did not answer. "Isn't she gorgeous?" he called to John, and left the office.

It was perfectly true. Elvira Portway was exactly gorgeous —tall, dark, voluptuous in the Roman style. Perhaps she inclined a trifle to the heavy in that same style, but it was as yet but the briefest inclination. She was a Roman matron before her time, and yet there was about her a quality of naïveté that suggested the English rose. A nice English girl's upbringing, of course, is guaranteed to withstand the impact of many years' persistent Bohemianism, or rather, it controls and makes its own Bohemianism. It was not so much that Elvira's devotion to the arts was insincere, but rather that it brought with it something of the fresh keenness of the hockey field.

"Well, that's all taped then," said John, sprawling in the scarlet leather armchair.

The office had been furnished two years before under South Bank influence in scarlet and white. He ran his hands through his thick black curly hair and pulled his small leathery face into a monkey-like grimace which, largely owing to his white even teeth, came out as his famous impudent grin.

"Correspondence complete. Parker's doing that now, isn't she?" At Elvira's affirmative nod, he went on. "Wednesday's *Globe* article, script for next Friday's broadcast, speech for Co-op luncheon."

He smiled a more natural smile to himself. There was only one thing he liked more than "clearing off arrears," and that was "getting down to a new batch."

"You've forgotten the Macclesfield Chamber of Commerce," said Elvira, yawning and stubbing a lipsticked end of cigarette into an already overful square glass ashtray. "Will you address their dinner on February 3rd?"

"Yes," said John. "I'll give them the works about London the Octopus and the need for provincial culture."

"Why?" said Elvira.

"Why on earth not?" said John, kicking a ball of screwed-up paper from the floor and catching it. "It's a very good speech *and* a very important problem. It's all very well for cosmopolitan Bohemians like you, but it's serious for the country's vitality." He looked stern through his horn-rimmed spectacles, like a prefect "jawing" the House on slackness. "Oh, I know what you're going to say—it's inevitable—up to a point it is, but there's nothing like fighting inevitability." Then to soften the priggishness, he said, "That's why I fight the approach of age. Larrie's quite right, I must get this down," he patted his stomach. "Get on to Jock Henning after Christmas and see if he'll play squash again with me regularly."

Elvira made a note of this, then she said, "I wasn't going to mention inevitability. I don't care about London the Octopus and the provinces. I just meant why are you going to Macclesfield?"

"But, good heavens! Why not? I've nothing against Macclesfield, it's a most important place."

"Yes, I suppose so," said Elvira. "I think I meant just why? Why any of it?"

John frowned, took out his pipe and sucked as he lit it. "That's the sort of pointless question the people you go about with ask," he said, then waiving her possible objection, he added, "Oh! I know very well what the point's meant to be, but I *still* don't think there's any point."

"No," said Elvira, "I know you don't. Well, don't let's discuss it now. God! how I hate after lunch."

"You sit up too late," said John laughing.

"We were discussing Malraux," Elvira said, as though that explained anything necessary. "There was an American there who knew him in his Commie days. And Hardy was back from New York with some frightfully funny stories about the New Criticism boys."

"I haven't seen Hardy for over a year. I suppose he's just the same as ever."

"Yes," said Elvira, "I don't know why, but he hasn't got less interesting since you stopped seeing him."

"You *are* in a bitchy mood," John still laughed.

Elvira got up and put some papers away in a filing cabinet. She moved with the heavy gait of one about to make a difficult pronouncement. "I'm sorry," she said, "I expect it's Christmas." Then going to the window, she looked out on the wet waste of Sloane Square. Late Christmas shoppers were pushing their way into the doors of Peter Jones; its wide expanse of glass gleamed sadly with the watery sun's reflection. At the other end of the Square, someone dashed from a taxi into the theatre. Water poured from the taxi roof as it lurched off. It spelt death to Elvira.

"They're very late," she said, coming back into the room.

"Who?" asked John.

"Johnnie," she said, "I've made a Christmas resolution. You're always saying I'm so drearily unconventional, so I shan't keep it till New Year. I'm going to give you a month's notice."

"Good heavens!" John sat up in his chair. "Why?"

"Oh God!" said Elvira, "It's so awful. You really are surprised. You see you just don't notice people any more, you're so busy being Miss Lonelyhearts to your public."

John thought desperately for the best approach, "I did notice you were depressed," he said laughing, "but I put it down to drink, my dear."

"No, Johnnie," said Elvira, "It's no good. It doesn't work any more. I still like being with you, but I know everything you're going to say. I can't bear it."

"Don't you think," asked John, "that we might approach the matter from a less personal angle. You're the ideal secretary for me. You've been with me for four years and I've absolutely no complaints. . . ."

"You've got Miss Harrington and Joan," Elvira interrupted, and when John was about to deny their value, she went on, "In any case, I *must* approach it from my personal point of view and not yours. I took the job because *you* interested me. Oh! I don't mean your being an M.P. Though that was interesting too, because it was a new world to me. But when you resigned in November, I'd about had politics, as much as the Labour Party'd about had you."

John was going to protest at this version of his dramatic and courageous resignation, but he thought better of it.

"Well then?" he asked.

"Well," said Elvira, "it isn't interesting any more."

"Is it Larrie?" asked John abruptly.

"Oh! God, of course not," said Elvira. "He's a crashing bore and I wish he wouldn't come to the office. But he'll get tired of that soon." She took out her lipstick and did her mouth.

John got up and straddled before the electric fire. "Is it Robin?" he asked in a rather self-conscious voice.

"Oh! Johnnie!" said Elvira, throwing the lipstick on the desk angrily. "Don't put on that knowing air and don't be so dramatic. I've known for a long time that you knew I was having an *affaire* with Robin. I thought you didn't say anything because it wasn't your business, and all the time you've been thinking how clever you were and waiting to produce your knowledge at the dramatic moment. No, it isn't Robin. I do my work or don't do it because it interests me or bores me, not because of my private life."

"I know my dear brother doesn't think so highly of me. I thought perhaps he'd infected you with his opinion," said John stuffily.

"You're wrong, as a matter of fact," said Elvira, "Robin's immensely impressed by your act. But I'm not going to discuss

Robin. Look," she said, trying to explain, "you came out of the war with ideas, with some capacity for thinking. You'd even written one or two good short stories, and then the Labour landslide of the election made you an M.P. when you'd never thought you'd be elected."

John laughed. "You can hardly blame me for trying to cope with the situation."

"No, you started off as an excellent M.P.," said Elvira. "As you know, I'm old-fashioned enough to be on your side there against Hardy and all the anti-political crowd. But in a way, you were glad. You'd had a couple of stories turned down by the highbrow magazines and politics was a good way out. Then, bit by bit, you found you weren't holding your own in the political world, so you went in for this individual business. Helping individuals against State tyranny, the unit against the monopoly, talent against money power, the old radicalism and all that. It was all right up to a point, when it was simply attacking abuses in the House, but then you found radio and the newspapers. And then it wasn't all right, at least not for me. I'd started in with something interesting and ended with *Peg's Paper*. You made a lovely public figure and you made lovely money. And then to cap it you made your dramatic resignation."

"Elvira, you can't have been with me through all that ghastly time and think it was sheer publicity."

John was not angry at Elvira's charges. Most of his thoughts were the result of sympathetic association, and as soon as he heard any statement, even one hostile to himself, he began to see its truth, even to elaborate it.

"I didn't say publicity," said Elvira. "There you are, you see, you'll drift into any view put forward. If I told you that you were a public fraud, you'd take on *that* rôle and exaggerate it. But you're not, you just move along into any standpoint that's going and play the part to perfection—budding intellectual, good Labour Party man with ideas, public figure fighting the little man's cause. But it only needs someone who really thinks about the subject, someone who's not just interested in the rôle, to come along and oppose you and you drift into something else." She waved her cigarette in the air, as though to dispel his fears with a magic circle. "Don't worry, Johnnie," she said, "I'm not prophesying ruin. You'll get by—indeed, you'll probably drift from strength to strength, but *I* don't want to go with you."

"The trouble is," said John, "that the simple issues of people's lives I'm concerned with now aren't smart enough for you, Elvira. You want 'good talk' with Hardy and his friends, and little clique jokes about Camus and Heidegger, or whatever they're talking about now," he added, as he saw Elvira smile. "You're an intellectual snob."

Elvira got up and moved towards the door.

"Saved by the bell," she said. It was a phrase of her father's which came strangely from her lips. "Thank God! You see, Johnnie, where you've got to. Even a year ago you wouldn't have used a dreary, middle-class expression like that. You're full of comforting, protective catchwords. You've become a bore, Johnnie. For me, that is. For your great public, you're absolute heaven."

John picked up a letter from a lady in Lincolnshire whose watercress farm was threatened by a new drainage scheme. Another Cromwell defying centralized tyranny, he thought, then reflected that Cromwell had been foremost in fen drainage. But the letter had served its purpose; the terms of its references to him had dispelled the insidious effect of Elvira's picture. He looked up, surprised, as Gerald followed Elvira into the office.

"I was ready to leave rather early," said Gerald, "and I thought perhaps I could pick you up here. Inge will be pleased if we get down there early. Family Christmas, you know," he added in explanation to Elvira, from whom he found it difficult to keep his eyes.

"You don't know my father, of course," said John, "I always forget how repugnant the activities of public life are to you, Father. It was brave of you to venture into this office. This is Miss Portway."

Elvira looked at Gerald with pleasure; it was enough that he reminded her of Robin. Gerald was only concerned that his face did not reveal his interest in her. That sort of thing was all too liable to happen when one got old. His sensual desire, however, was mixed with a certain irritation as he heard her name. The past seemed insatiable in its encroachments upon his life today. However . . . "Are you related to Canon Portway?" he asked.

"Remotely," said Elvira. "He was a sort of great-uncle or something. My grandmother was the 'great' Lilian," she added sharply.

Gerald was surprised at her tone. "One of the few great actresses of my lifetime. You inherit her beauty," he said.

"I hope that's all," Elvira replied.

"Oh, in quite a different style," Gerald hastened to say. "Lilian Portway was never . . ." he was about to add "my sort of choice," but ended "quite human to my idea."

"Unfortunately," Elvira answered, "my experience of her was quite otherwise. I'm sorry. As you see, I don't care for her. Ethereal-looking grandmothers aren't in my line. She's so noble, she's even sent me a Christmas present, although we don't speak. I hate that sort of thing from people who behave like goddesses."

The malaise that the revival of Melpham as a topic had aroused in Gerald compelled him to go on, "I stayed with her in my undergraduate days at that lovely house at Melpham," he said.

"Oh, yes," Elvira replied shortly.

John came to their rescue. "Well, she's safely settled in the Tyrol now," he said, "with an aunt of Marie Hélène's for a sort of companion. That's how I came to meet my perfect secretary." He smiled at Elvira.

Gerald saw that this topic, too, did not appeal to Elvira. He disliked "choosey" women as a rule, but the promise of Elvira's figure seemed superior to any defects of temperament.

"My daughter-in-law Marie Hélène knows everyone. She's the perfect cosmopolitan," he said sharply. "Look here," he went on, "you must have invented that fellow Pelican. There can't really be a civil servant with that name."

John laughed. "He's all too real I'm afraid," he said. "You should ask Cressett."

"You've certainly got a wonderful case," said Gerald. "Of course, the Minister'll have to take responsibility, but Mr Pelican won't easily wriggle out. What sort of chap is the wretched Cressett? My heart bleeds for him like that of all your readers," he said, with a touch of irony in his voice.

John noticed this, but before he could answer, Elvira said excitedly, "Oh, we don't *meet* our correspondents. That might destroy the illusion. We're concerned with injustice to individuals. Nice abstract individuals—Pelican the wicked bureaucrat and Cressett the exploited little man. We don't want to get mixed up with personalities."

Gerald frowned. He disliked pretty girls who showed hysteria, particularly in the form of strong opinions. Irritation with John, however, seemed to him so reasonable an emotion that he quickly returned to the more pleasant spectacle of her physical form.

"Well, I know nothing about it," he said. "I wouldn't read the newspapers if it wasn't for this ridiculous idea that's been implanted in all of us about being well informed. Conscience stirs me every now and again, and then I come into the middle of something like this Pelican business and believe everything I'm told. People like me should be governed by our betters." He looked at John sharply, hoping that he had aroused annoyance. It infuriated him to think of this attractive girl in his son's office.

John was, in fact, roused to the intense dislike of his father that always lay below the surface, but its effect was to push him into a decision. If Elvira was going to leave him, he would get rid of her first. His work came before such personal considerations.

"Elvira's on the side of the big stick in these things," he said.

Having made the decision to part with her, his voice took on a sneering note that surprised himself, but he felt that it was in keeping with his new line. "She moves in *very* highbrow circles, Father, where dear old Nietzsche's all the thing these days."

Elvira felt an abysmal sense of defeat. After four years, to have made so little impression that he could dramatize her out of his life. If John was convinced by every individual he came in touch with, Elvira always felt emotionally guilty for every emotion she aroused in others.

"Actually, Johnnie's doing a very useful job," she said to Gerald, then felt ashamed of her betrayal of her views. Gerald's smile, however, seemed to reassure her. She found herself liking him immensely and wondered that Robin as much as Johnnie seemed only to care for that tiresome mother of theirs.

"Mrs Salad sent you her love," said Gerald to his son.

"God! how the wicked prosper," said John. "You ought to meet her, Elvira, she's the living example of that Marxist myth, the lumpen proletariat."

"She sent you a message," said Gerald. "She thinks you do too much for people who can't be helped. She's never liked the poor, you know." He laughed. "Her grandson's one of your fans. Met you somewhere or something. I can't remember what it was all about. Vin his name is."

John recalled all too clearly his meeting with Larrie's friend Vin. If he had only known that he was also called Salad! However, he giggled nervously and said, "I meet so many undesirable people."

Elvira, hearing the giggle, thought immediately of Larrie and wondered whether she ought not to put aside her views and stay with John in case he ran into trouble. These things could be so tricky and John was so stupidly cocksure.

There was nothing she could do though, she decided.

"I mustn't keep Larwood waiting too long," said Gerald. "He's taking us down, but I've told him he can come back tonight for his family Christmas. Robin'll have his car if we need one. Anything that'll save us from your mother's driving."

"I could have run you down," said John, "if I'd known it was inconvenient for Larwood."

"You drive too fast," said Gerald, "anyway, Larwood's paid for some inconvenience. Goodbye, Miss Portway, I shall be sad if we don't meet again."

"I'm sure we *shall*," said Elvira, taking his hand.

When the two men were safely out of the office, she picked up the telephone and dialled.

"Mr Middleton, please," she said. And a minute later, "Robin, darling? I've told Johnnie. Yes, he will, I'm sure. Well—I only managed it by being bloody nasty really. He'll be all right when he's thought up reasons to give his friends, only he's done such an act about my being with him for ever that it's a bit difficult. No, not really, A bit sharp, but that was all. He couldn't say much because your father was there. No, I thought he was enchanting. Just like you. Well, not really like you, because he has a moustache and is older, but awfully sweet. I told you. I'm going to a sort of party. No, of course not, it'll be hell without you. Oh! I know you have to go there. Anyway, it's part of the way we have to go on. No, no, darling, I just *said* 'have to', I didn't mean it. Well, as long as you don't enjoy yourself too much or forget me for a minute. And don't be nasty to your father. Well, as a matter of fact I have taken a fancy to him. He's much nicer than any of the rest of your family. Well, not perhaps than Johnnie, but less embarrassing, anyway. No, darling, I'm not really depressed. I'm like that at Christmas anyway, even without all this business of your having to go down to Marlow. I should think your mother must be awful at Christmas. Oh! not especially. I don't like *any* old women much, as you know. No, darling, I will. Anyway it's only until Tuesday. I only hope I shan't have that pain I had the last time you went away. Well, you ought to be flattered really, but I do see that you wouldn't be. Goodbye, darling, I'd like to say dream of me like that girl in the dairy, only it sounds rather dirty."

Elvira put down the telephone and stared into the ashtray. Her feelings for Robin were not at all intellectual.

Robin Middleton ran up the stairs of his large Hampstead home like a schoolboy after talking to Elvira. Then, outside the bedroom, the depression of reality slowed his step. His wife Marie Hélène was packing his dressing-case as he came into the room.

She was in an ostentatiously calm and efficient mood that allowed her to exercise all the tyranny of fussing without being accused of it.

"That was Elvira," said Robin, who used sincerity to his wife as his only protest against her existence.

"Yes?" said Marie Hélène, and going to the door of the bedroom she called across the corridor, "Timothy, stop reading and get on with your packing." As a good Catholic, she remained an excellent wife to Robin without condoning a moment of his adultery.

Timothy appeared at the door, already at sixteen nearly six foot, trying by excessive neatness to disguise his gangling figure. He blinked through his steel-rimmed glasses and said, "The packing's done," and went back to his book. Robin laughed affectionately. He was sure of his son's love, but suspected that his respect went with community of religion to his mother.

Marie Hélène said, "His manners want so much improvement." She spoke the word "manners" with the reverence she felt for it. "I've bought your mother's *present*," she went on. Her English was nearly faultless, but she pronounced certain words like "present" in italics as though she thought they were slang words. In fact, she had a belief that such words were "popular speech" and that it was distinguished to use them. The dictionary word was "gift", but its use would have been bourgeois. She was herself of rich *petit-bourgeois* Lyonnais origin and much possessed by it. "Do you want to see it?" she added. But when Robin said "Yes", she merely sat down on one of the upturned suitcases. "Do you think that this year your mother will make a scene when Timothy and I go into Henley for Midnight Mass?"

"No," said Robin, "I think you put an end to Mother's protests against Mass last year."

He noticed his wife's full olive-green wool skirt billowing around her feet and shivered. She always seemed to wear dead greens or purples that, with her sallow, distinguished camel's face, filled the room with cold. It was true that even in this centrally heated room, offering such warmth against the bitter air outside, Marie Hélène's tall unbending figure suggested the funereal, shuttered cool of a meridional house in the glare of summer's heat.

"I have put in a pair of your stout walking shoes," she said, "your father likes to take a walk on Boxing Day."

"Oh! Don't let us encourage him," said Robin, "that walk always upsets Mother's Christmas arrangements and she hates it."

"Yes," said Marie Hélène, agreeing, and then added, "but the arrangements, after all, are for her husband. If he doesn't like them . . ."

Robin laughed, "You know very well Mother never arranges anything for Father, only for her children."

Marie Hélène did not accept a humorous approach to such matters. "Then the arrangements are not serious," she said.

She had no compassion for her mother-in-law's rôle as a wronged wife, when it sprang from such derelictions of wifely duty. Her own similar position had no element of justice in its cause, only Robin's indulgence of lust.

"Tante Stéphanie has sent Timothy a leather wallet for Christmas," she told Robin. "It is quite hideous Tyrolese peasant work, but he seems to like it."

"I can't think why she's so generous," said Robin, "after that lawsuit. If I were Madame Houdet I'd never speak to us again."

"She's my aunt," said Marie Hélène. "Because she took a stupid law case against me for money to which she had no right and lost it, does not make her lose her sense of what is correct."

Robin smiled. "I wish she'd won it. I can't think why she *didn't* in a French court."

Marie Hélène laughed. It was a loud satisfying sound when it came, which was rarely. "My dear Robin, you are not quite so English as that. Fortunately French courts are not like the English picture. They are just."

"All the same," said Robin, his handsome, dark face frowning at the prospect of an unpalatable truth. "After she'd been in Auschwitz and had come back to find the lawyer had tricked her of all her money . . ."

"He committed suicide," said Marie Hélène with a grimace of horror and disgust. Then, with a look of reverence, she went on: "Tante Stéphanie is a very courageous woman. She refused the money we offered."

"Well, I can't say I blame her *after* we'd defeated her in the law-suit."

"I said she is courageous. Of course, she could not accept, but we were right to offer."

"I see," said Robin.

"In any case," Marie Hélène remarked, "she will be well paid by that old Mrs Portway. Tante Stéphanie is not a fool about such things. No doubt she will get the old lady's money when she dies."

Robin winced. "I hope Elvira doesn't mind too much," he said.

"Why should she mind?" his wife asked. "She recognizes no duty to Mrs Portway, she should expect no reward. Of course, the old lady will leave her a legacy, since she is her granddaughter."

"French law would demand a little more than that," Robin laughed.

"French logic sometimes falls into English sentimentality," observed Marie Hélène, with the smile she kept for wit,

"Tante Stéphanie writes to me that Yves will come to London this summer. I have written that he will be our guest."

"Good heavens!" said her husband, "he's a monster, or, at least, you've painted him as such."

"*I* don't like him," said Marie Hélène, "but he's my cousin."

Once again Robin could only say, "I see." He added, "I hope I shall be able to entertain him."

"You are a wonderful host, darling," said his wife with absolute sincerity. Save for his sentimentality, of which she regarded his infidelity as a by-product, Marie Hélène thought her husband perfection.

Robin began to change into a heavy tweed suit. "I hope I shan't have a row with John about this business of poor old Pelican," he said, folding his discarded trousers with obsessive precision. "It's quite intolerable that he should write all that nonsense in the paper about one of the few thoroughly competent civil servants the country's got. The firm's dealt with Pelican ever since '41 and I've never known a more sensible and useful person. Just because this Cressett—probably some small dealer's who's incompetent to run a whelk stall—complains of an injustice, John starts a public pillorying of a man whose position forbids him to answer back. If Pelican has made a mistake, it's not surprising, with all the work his Ministry carries. It's typical of politicians and journalists, they want a state-run country and they're ready to employ thousands of bureaucrats at our expense to do it, but when one of their employees really *can* administer, they turn on him. All this self-publicizing sentimentality about individual cases when the country's fighting for its life makes me absolutely sick. Especially that it should be my brother. No business man would dare to be so irresponsible." Robin as a businessman was neither old-fashioned, individualistic nor sentimental.

"John is a fool," said Marie Hélène. "But I don't think you should take up a stranger's cause against your family."

"I take up the cause of the logic that stares anyone in the face who knows what the economic needs of this country are,"

Robin said defiantly. He heard the note of pomposity in his own voice that always accompanied anger and calmed himself by brushing his tweed suit very meticulously. "Well, there's one piece of family piety that I'm thinking of letting the firm in for which should please you," he said.

He looked expectantly at Marie Hélène, but she dilated her camel's nostrils slightly and said, "I do not give blank cheques." It was one of her favourite English phrases, the very enormity of so prodigal a behaviour fascinated her.

"It's Donald," he said. "He's failed for these University posts again."

Marie Hélène smiled—a look that matched her somewhat frostbitten mouth. "I am sorry," she said, "but perhaps he is not so brilliant as Kay thinks him. Not everyone can be a university lecturer." For Marie Hélène, to be *agrégé* was quite something.

"Oh, he's brilliant all right," said Robin. His brother-in-law was a luxury that the family paid for. He never cared for his purchases to be depreciated. "But he obviously gets off on the wrong foot with his colleagues. Kay, bless her heart, is worried about their taking so much family money and her husband earning nothing. Mother wrote to me all about it and asked if I could find him something to do. Of course, he's a bit up in the clouds. All this Anglo-Catholicism makes him think we can put the clock back, but there's a tough core of common sense there all the same. A lot of it is bitterness over not getting the posts. That's why I want to do what I can. As I told Mother, there's no need for Kay to get a conscience, she's entitled to the interest on her dividends as much as anyone else." He looked to his wife for confirmation of his beloved sister's rights but none was forthcoming. "Anyhow, I've agreed to give him something to do while he's waiting about. As a matter of fact, these evening lectures at the works have been a great success, despite all the jeremiads I was treated to when I started them. Even some of my dear brother directors have changed their tune, and the union bosses are quite enthusiastic now. Up to now, of course, they've been largely technical, but I don't see why we shouldn't include a bit of training for citizenship, so I'm going to get Donald to do a series on current affairs. A few of his utterances are liable to make our union chaps cry blue murder, but as long as he's kept in check, it won't do any harm for them to be made to think a little beyond their mental horizon of the Depression and watered-down Fabianism."

Marie Hélène began to put on her hat before the dressing-table mirror. As she talked, she did not turn, but watched her husband. "One must never be foolish about business," she said.

Robin looked annoyed. "After all, he is my brother-in-law," he threw back at her.

She saw the force of this. "You are probably right," she said. "In any case, these lectures are nice, but hardly impor-tant." Commerce was commerce to her, not a matter for "frills".

As she moved to get her gloves, Timothy appeared in the doorway "If we don't hurry up we shall be late. It's after half past six," he said in a self-satisfied voice. He had finished his book.

It was Robin's turn now to be annoyed with what he felt to be the boy's priggishness. Marie Hélène, however, was always just in her dealings with her son. "You are right," she said with a smile. "I am glad that you are learning to be prompt. That is very important."

Lilian Portway, Elvira's grandmother, walked with a stick; for all else, with her graceful, willowy figure, she might have been forty rather than seventy. She moved with firm strides through the crisp snow, throwing back observations in her commanding, low-timbred voice to little Stéphanie Houdet who came panting behind with the laden shopping-baskets.

"They've done nothing, literally nothing, about my band-stand," she said in the voice of tragedy. "I shall see the mayor, Stéphanie, and tell him that they won't get a penny more of my money until they've painted my bandstand. Gold," she said dramatically, "a deep red gold and black. I shall give them a lake with black swans and twenty tubs of agapanthus lilies."

"But my dear Lilian,"—Stéphanie Houdet, unlike her niece Marie Hélène, spoke English with the most uncompromising French accent—"No one will come any more to this part of the town. It is quite finished."

Indeed, the broken-down baroque bandstand, which stood —a relic of Hapsburg glory—in the neglected little garden, seemed almost to have ceased to pretend to be more than a ruin.

"People will come where one draws them," Mrs Portway said.

She had brought crowds to see her play Shaw's heroines in Sloane Square, she had brought crowds to hear her speak of women's rights in Norwich, she had brought crowds, more select, to hear her praise Mussolini's Italy in Knightsbridge and Mayfair drawing-rooms, she could bring crowds to listen to music from "her" bandstand in a forgotten quarter of Merano any day she willed.

"Can't," she said, "is a word people use too easily today. It's the current cant," and she laughed her wonderful high-comedy ripple. "I don't think I ever heard my brother-in-law Reggie say 'can't'," she said, and turned back upon her little companion as though daring her to deny this.

As Madame Houdet had only heard of Canon Portway through a very great deal too much hearsay, she could not deny it.

"My brother-in-law knew," Mrs Portway continued, drawing her long, old-fashioned chinchilla coat around her, "what had to be done, and it *was* done. He knew that the people must be given back their old services, the age-old services of beauty and dignity. There were protests, but the Sarum rite was sung in his church. He knew that Eorpwald's tomb would be found on our estate. He told them: 'Dig!' They dug and they found nothing. Even the great Professor Stokesay lost heart. But my brother didn't. He said: 'Dig again', and they found the famous Melpham tomb. And when I came to him and asked him to appear on *our* platforms, he knew at once where the Church's place was. Up there alongside Mary and Martha, yes, and Mary Magdalene. He stood with me beside Emmeline Pankhurst and he spoke for Women. The little hearts, the 'can'ts', said his career in the Church was finished. I wonder how many of them remembered *that* when they read what *The Times* had to say of Canon Portway when he died—moral leader, outstanding antiquarian, lover of beauty, fearless fighter, great Churchman."

Mrs Portway paused to wind the pale mauve tulle that hung from her chinchilla cap around her willowy neck. It was poor protection against the bitter wind, but, as she grew older, Lilian Portway dressed more eccentrically. Particularly she demanded "a piece of lovely colour" about her, whatever the weather or place.

"Very few, I imagine," she said with a bitter laugh. "The 'can'ts' of this world have small memories as well as small souls.—But I'll have no 'can't' from the mayor about my bandstand."

She strode forward impatiently, like some erect, silky-haired bear in the landscape of snow and dark evergreens.

Madame Houdet teetered precariously behind. She would have been more comfortable in her high-heeled patent leather shoes than in the fur-topped boots that Lilian had bought for her. For all Lilian's striking appearance, it was Stéphanie Houdet who was the better-known figure in the Tyrolese Kurort. To the inhabitants, Austrian and Italian alike, Mrs Portway was just another rich English eccentric: but *la vedova francese* was something really extraordinary. With her chic black dresses, her flowing crêpe veil, her rouge and lipstick, she moved not a step from the garb of the old-fashioned Provincial French bourgeoise widow. In Poitiers or in Châlons-sur-Marne or in her own Lyons she would have passed un-noticed, but in the little medieval colonnaded town or on the

picturesque hillside walks designed in such careful miniature
Alpine style for the Austrian invalids of 1911, she was as odd as
some macaw got loose among the autumn crocuses. Stéphanie
Houdet knew that she was a local figure, but she did not guess
the reason. She thought that she was feared because she saw
through everyone, "*sales boches*" and "*fous italiens*" alike. She
thought she was respected because of her munificence to the
poor, and here she was right, for she held Mrs Portway's
purse-strings.

At her friend's return to the subject of the bandstand, she
drew tight her scarlet lips and pulled down her plump little
cheeks until the beads of rouge and powder showed in the
creases. She had already vetoed this scheme in her own mind
as *une grande folie*, but she never spoke precipitately. Madame
Houdet had her own ideas of philanthropy, more nineteenth
century in form than Lilian's theatrical gestures. Crippled
children and bent old women brought tears to her eyes and she
liked to administer very small sums of her friend's money with
lots of gossip and, at the end, a little talk about *le petit Jésus* and
Notre Dame de la Charité. In a foreign but Catholic community
it was considered behaviour suitable to her age, but impertinent because of her alien origin. She always, however, got her
own way in her schemes. Lilian's extravagant wishes, of which
"her" bandstand was typical, were considered quite absurd for
her age but entirely suitable in a rich foreigner. They hardly
ever came to anything. As to the origins of their surprising
friendship, the common experience of concentration camp
horror that had brought them together in the hotel in Geneva
after the war, these had been buried in oblivion in the Kurort,
as they would have been elsewhere, with all the other boring
details of recent history, never so boring as when they are
connected with a war which people wish to forget.

Madame Houdet, then, avoided any comment on her
friend's scheme. They had left the little gardens now and were
ascending the hill. On each side loomed vast villas, once
splendidly vulgar in their sentimental chalet style, now

decayed and squalid beneath their covering of snow. Human habitation, however, set Madame Houdet's tongue on its natural, rapid course of scandal. The Weissblum's eldest son was bankrupt, the Schneiders could get no more credit, as for old Signorina Paccelli, former mistress of a silk magnate, it seemed that she was now completely paralysed down the right side. "The good God," said Madame Houdet, "does not pay on Saturdays, he pays in his own time."

It often irked Lilian Portway to be confined to such petty talk and she wondered that Stéphanie could be so triumphant about the sins of others when her son behaved as he did, but a friendship that had begun in gratitude for kindness when she was fighting her war nightmares was now her only barrier against loneliness, and, in any case, Stéphanie was such a wonderful manager. It was not only that she managed all the money, but she also managed the present, and Lilian found increasingly irksome anything that cut her off from the past. As usual, she shut her mind to her friend's talk and wandered back in memories—to the Vanbrughs, like herself some of the first real ladies to win success on the stage; to the praises and rebukes of George Bernard Shaw; to Emmeline and Christabel Pankhurst—dear Christabel, so sensible, had resisted all her enthusiasm for Fascist Italy; and, as so often nowadays, to Melpham. She remembered the shrubbery with its tangle of St John's wort and, cutting into her friend's gossip, she said, "The Victorians did awful things to gardens. Melpham must have been so charming when it was simple parkland, and then my mother-in-law made formal beds and shrubberies, and such hideous ones—St John's wort and double begonias and horrors like that! You know, in a way, Stéphanie, I'm glad that I sold the place when Hugh was killed, it was only association that made it beautiful—being there with Reggie and when Hugh was a little boy. It was an ugly place in itself, and for an old woman on her own it would have been cruel as well as ugly."

Madame Houdet gave Mrs Portway a sharp glance, she regarded any reminiscences that went back earlier than their own

association as a sign of growing mental enfeeblement in her
friend and her attitude to such decline was equivocal.

"Perhaps if you had lived at Melpham, Elvira would have
come to live with you," she said, looking inquisitive. With
Madame Houdet curiosity was always malicious. "It is sad to
think of a young girl without a real home."

Lilian Portway gave a throaty chuckle, "Oh, my dear, how
we differ," she said. "My advice to any girl would be: 'Leave
home! Break away! Take all the wonderful things that life has
to offer while you can! The gods grow tired of showering
their gifts on those who don't make use of them.' You don't
know the battle *I* fought, Stéphanie, to get away. I was like a
canary released from a cage in those first days in London; I
just sang and sang." Mrs Portway's enthusiasm often carried
her into such doubtful metaphors. "And then came love and
marriage. I hesitated, Stéphanie, I hated bondage. But the urge
to motherhood, to creation was too great for me. Liberty and
creation. Those are the things I have cherished. Little Hugh
was born. I was a mother! I'm afraid, Stéphanie, that when soon
after I became a widow, I was glad to get back my old freedom.
You would think that was wicked, but *I* know that it was life
speaking in me. The greatest was still to come—*Major Barbara*,
Candida, *Mrs Hushabye*, and the little I could do for Women!"

Madame Houdet had heard it all so often before. In some,
of course, it would have been wicked, but in Lilian Portway
she preferred to think it was merely senile folly. She noted how
her friend's head shook when she was excited. Soon all this
senseless talk and pride would be broken, she would be like a
little child and then she would need her friend as never before.
Our Saviour had said Blessed are the meek, and, again, Blessed
are the Peacemakers, so she only said, "You were a good
mother, Lilian."

"Perhaps," said Mrs Portway, stopping as they reached the
gate of their villa to pluck some evergreen for the house, "perhaps. Yes, I was! I gave Hugh life! When he was only six, he
knew the world. He was happy and at home in dressing-rooms

and on public platforms as much as in his nursery at Melpham. That's why I shouldn't wish to have held Elvira, had
she been ever so different to what she is. But, in any case,
it wouldn't have done, Stéphanie. The girl has a common
streak. Oh! I don't mean common as it's usually spoken. I
have known fine people of simple origin—Old Barker, for
instance, our coachman, you've heard me speak of him."

As he was one of the few people to whom Mrs Portway referred that fitted into Madame Houdet's category of 'good'
people, she said with relish, "Ah! the poor, brave, paralysed
man!"

Lilian Portway flashed her eyes in scorn. "What does it
matter if his body is paralysed?" she said. "You can't paralyse
the souls of straight, honest, noble folk like that. Elvira has
none of it. She's her mother's daughter. There's a core of
cheapness there for all her clever Bohemian talk. People would
say that I shouldn't speak of my daughter-in-law so because
she is dead, perhaps particularly because she died in an air-
raid." She paused dramatically before the door. "When that
bomb fell on the Café de Paris," she said, "what mattered was
not on whom it fell, this person or that. On my son who was
somebody, or my daughter-in-law who could never be anybody. What mattered was that it destroyed vitality, happiness
and life." She flung the door open as though showing the way
to a world of such riches.

Had she believed this, she would have been incurably insane,
for the drawing-room which they entered was a centrally
heated mausoleum. Signed photographs were everywhere—of
Shaw, of Wells, of Irene Vanbrugh and Mrs Pat, of Gordon
Craig and Granville Barker, of darling Christabel and dear old
Flora Drummond; the famous photograph of the Duce had
been consigned to the dust-heap, but D'Annunzio still threatened Corfu with his poet's head to remind Mrs Portway of
Italy's glorious past. The signed copies of Shaw's plays stood
on a table separate from the bookcase, and with them a photograph of Canon Portway with his parishioners, all dressed in

their costumes for the Coventry Mystery Play. It was the wonderful past so eagerly sought by Mrs Portway in her memory, but standing there to greet her in photographic form it petrified her world of living ghosts into the mummified dead of the tomb. The photographs of Madame Houdet's past were there, too—Yves, luscious-eyed with the white communion band on his arm, Yves ostentatiously virile in his conscript's uniform, Yves with the smallest of bathing trunks showing off with a medicine-ball on the beach at Cannes, Yves superb in the uniform of Free France. Stéphanie Houdet, however, had no eyes for these cherished images, for she had caught a glimpse of the boot of a Lagonda in the garage and she knew that the reality was asleep upstairs. Lilian Portway's much vaunted 'life' filled the house for *her* at least.

The post lay scattered on the table where Yves had searched it eagerly for possible evidence of cheques. There were three letters with English postmarks. Madame Houdet opened the one that was hers. "Oh, such an elegant card from Marie Hélène," she cried, "she has such good taste."

Everything Marie Hélène did seemed to her unusually smart since she had shown such smartness of another sort in winning the law-suit.

"It seems to me in very poor taste to write at all," said Lilian, "after the way she has behaved."

But Madame Houdet did not hear this. She was overjoyed that Marie Hélène had invited Yves. She had feared lest her obvious desire for this invitation should be ignored. "It is a very elegant house, I believe. Yves will be happy there," she said.

"I have no doubt," said Mrs Portway drily. "All the same, I'm surprised you should want him to stay in *that* house."

"They are cousins," said Madame Houdet simply. Then she asked, "Where do your cards come from?" She longed to know whether there was one from Elvira.

Mrs Portway, realizing this, was mortified, but at least had the comfort of knowing that Stéphanie knew nothing of her own peace-offering, which had received no return.

"A wonderful rich, old-fashioned Christmas card from Barker," she cried, "All robins and holly! Exactly what one would wish him to send." She hoped to imply a certain pretentiousness in such elegant cards as Marie Hélène sent. "His daughter Alice Cressett must have chosen it. That splendid countrywoman! It seems strange to think of her living in London and married to a man whose name is in the papers." The noble simplicity of Barker, of all the world of peasantry who were not "common", seemed somehow out of joint when one of them should be mentioned in the news.

"And the other card?" said Madame Houdet. Much of the pleasure of their isolated life together lay for her in the invasion of privacy.

"That," said Lilian in a voice of high scorn. "An impudence from that scoundrel Frank Rammage. Some pretentious picture of *blue* horses." She had so far forgotten this unpleasant bit of her past that she could only produce her anger by acting it, and her voice rang out as it had done when as Portia she withered Shylock. It was a poor performance: she had never played well in Shakespeare.

"Ssh," said Stéphanie, horrified at the raised voice, "Yves is sleeping."

Lilian Portway sat down on a high-backed chair and leaned her elbows on the table, she cupped her chin in her hands and raised her long swan neck towards her friend.

"Stéphanie," she said, "Yves has got to behave himself this time he is here. No! don't interrupt me. I don't mind his being drunk with that ghastly old Italian woman if she's fool enough to spend her money on him. But if he wants to carry on in that way he should stay with her in Milan or Genoa or wherever it is."

She knew perfectly well, but she could not bring herself to say "Florence". That *she* should have to stay up here in this remote place, while some vulgar industrialist's widow should live in her beloved city. When the doctors told her she could not return to Fiesole, she had cried as she had never done off the stage. Merano was only Italian in name to her. "My heart simply *will* not stand these scenes," she said dramatically.

Madame Houdet looked at her with the hatred she reserved for those who knew the true state of her relations with her son. She was about to burst forth in anger, when she was interrupted by a familiar voice.

"Oh my God!" shouted Yves in an American accent even more extravagantly French than his mother's English one. "What the hell are you making all that noise for? Cheep-a-cheep, Cheep-a-cheep. That's my mother all right. Why don't you put a pillow-case over her head, Mrs Portway? She'd be a hell of a sight more lovely as a corpse."

Madame Houdet laughed, as always, at her son's Quilpish humour.

"It's not like the country is it, Father?" asked Alice Cressett, as she wheeled the heavy grunting man to the window of the front room, "nor like the Cathedral Close neither."

If Mr Barker could have done more than grunt, he might well have answered that it was not much like the town. It was indeed like nothing on earth except a stretch of arterial road on the very confines of London. In one direction could be seen the banks of gorse bushes which made lovely the dual carriage-way that led motorists on through the countryside without their having to realize it. Their loveliness seemed, however, a little spare and grim in midwinter. In the other direction, towards London, light industry was embodied in a splendid compromise between functional and more conventional English taste, in which a considerable expenditure of glass was surrounded by ornamental designs in green tiles. Loveliness, in this case, perhaps, was marred by a certain tendency to prettiness and fuzzing of outline. It was here that Mr Cressett's market-garden flourished or would have flourished under any management but that of Mr Cressett. At the moment, however, Mr Cressett's ineptitude was happily disguised by the dismantling due to Mr Pelican's bureaucratic muddle.

"He's thinking of the horses, aren't you, father?" said Mrs Cressett.

In the days when old Mr Barker could still speak, he had been known to think of many things other than his profession of coachman; indeed that profession had long been behind him when paralysis struck him down. He had been valet and chauffeur and handyman to Canon Portway for many years after horse-transport had ceased to be the current mode of travel. In all that time he had thought and spoken a lot of drink and women and the degeneration of the times, and of money, especially of money. But, since he ceased to utter his thoughts, his daughter had decided that he thought only of horses. It seemed a pleasant subject for an old man to ponder on and had the additional merit of calling for no attention from anyone. As to money, Mrs Cressett herself was prepared to give *her* undivided thought to that subject.

"Now you can put the paper down, Harold," she said to her husband, "we've all seen what John Middleton has to say about you." As Mr Barker was no longer able to read, she presumably meant that *she* had seen it. "Very nice. But that won't bring the compensation money back."

Her slow country voice was matched by her slow, dignified movements. Alice Cressett was a big, regal, Junoesque woman. She was not wholly unaware of her queenly manner and dressed usually in purple. "I told you not to be so quick in returning it," she said, moving backwards and forwards through the room as she talked, laying the table for supper. "But there you are, those that don't listen get no reward. It just means that encyclopedia'll have to go back where it came from. You can't expect to use Father's money for foolishness." Mrs Cressett always referred to the money which she administered as "Father's money". It made the old man happier, she said. It also made easier her refusal to assist her husband. "I dare say he won't grudge you your half pint, will you, Father?" she added, "though there's those that might. But don't think having your name in the paper's going to mend matters."

Harold Cressett looked pitiable enough at any time, but, at the mention of returning his encyclopedia to the booksellers, his dismal, little rabbit face might have moved any heart less hard than his wife's. It could not be said that she had a heart of stone, for this usually implies some conscious rejection of pity. Mrs Cressett's heart was more likely made of wood, as people are said to be wooden-headed; she just did not notice other people's emotions. With her maternal figure and her slow comfortable movements, this complete absence of feeling made people think that she was dependable. Canon Portway had thought it, Lilian Portway had thought it, Harold Cressett, a lonely middle-aged widower with savings, had thought it when he married her. And, indeed, she could be depended upon to go her own way, gathering any money that came within her path. Perhaps if a stone rolls slowly enough, it *will* gather moss, and what Alice Cressett gathered, she didn't waste on foolishness.

Even at the risk of his wife's annoyance, Mr Cressett could not leave the article in which his name appeared. He had always been very fond of reading. During his first marriage, he had read most of the time. His first wife had run the confectioner's very competently and Mr Cressett had sat behind the counter and read.

He liked facts: articles that gave the length and breadth of rivers and the rainfall in the world's capitals, reports of the largest goose egg ever laid or the number of peasants drowned yearly by the flooding of the Yellow River. In encyclopedias he found his greatest pleasure. Old editions of *Pears'* or *Chambers'* pleased him best, he didn't care for the distracting photographs of the modern editions. And now his own name appeared in print, and with it some facts—the acreage of his market-garden, the amount of compensation he had had to return to the Ministry, even his own age. It was like an encyclopedia article headed CRESSETT (HAROLD).

He hitched his fluffy grey flannel trousers even further above his ankles than their normal short length and said, "I wouldn't be surprised if there was a subscription got up for me after this article. Help towards restocking the place."

"I don't see who'd spend their money like that," said Mrs Cressett, placing a dish of very round home-made cakes on the table. Everything on the table was a bit like that—round, plain, solid, comfortable-looking and hard. Mrs Cressett tended to make things in her own likeness.

"It says so here," said her husband, and read from John's article. " 'And now, as the Ministry informs us, everything is back to normal. Mr Cressett (at what cost of worry and anxiety officialdom does not state) has returned his compensation money, the Ministry has returned the market-garden. What or who these gentlemen are who have so kindly returned to Mr Cressett his own property is not made clear. That is a point that will be pursued further in these columns. But one thing the Ministry report does not mention—nothing is said of Mr Cressett's stock that he disposed of when he was so peremptorily told that he must leave his own land. Nothing is said of the tomatoes, the dahlias and the cucumbers. Perhaps this is another oversight of Mr Pelican's department. It is an oversight that will be noted by other smallholders, to say nothing of the harassed housewife. They will wonder that the law which gave Mr Cressett compensation, however inadequate, for his land when some official decided to take it from him, does not allow him some compensation for a business that has been ruined by vacillation and muddle when some other official has decided to give it back.' There! " said Mr Cressett triumphantly.

Mrs Cressett paused; she was uncertain but interested. She took a napkin and tied it round old Mr Barker's huge, scarlet neck. "If there's money coming," she said, "it won't go into *this* place, that's certain. I'm done with vegetables and flowers. We'll sell up here and go in for lodgers. That'll pay its way and more. We might go to Cromer. You'd like to go back to Norfolk, wouldn't you, Father?"

Mr Barker's staring eyes swivelled round in his great crimson moon face.

"I knew you would," Alice said. "But no more plants."

She had wrongly supposed that Harold would know how to make a market-garden pay, and, when he failed, she had even tried a hand at it herself; but, countrywoman though she was, her talent lay in getting money out of people rather than vegetables; they were more susceptible to pressure.

She went to the sideboard and, taking a lace tablecloth from one of the drawers, she held it before her father. "Mrs Portway sent me this," she said. "Real lace from Italy."

"Ah," said Mr Cressett, "Mantua's the great lace-making town in Italy. It gave the name to . . ."

But Mrs Cressett was not interested in Mantua. "Seventy-five, Mrs Portway must be," she said. "Their thoughts go back kindly to the past at that age. She won't go for leaving that Elvira anything by all accounts."

Mr Barker's eyes swivelled round the other way this time.

"Father's right," Mrs Cressett said, as she poured his tea into a saucer. "It's no good to have false hopes. There's no justice in law, as we soon found when the Canon died. All that money to Rammage! Sinful it was, and shameful sin, if the truth's to be told." She dried Mr Barker's walrus moustache with the napkin. "Not that there was so much he left," she said. "Living at the end of the old man's life had been shamefully high," and she gave a deep, throaty chuckle.

"Nothing from your blessed Maureen," she said to her husband. "What a way to treat her father. Well, if it's too far to send a present from Slough, it's too far to come over in fancy motor-cars, that's one comfort. There'll be no iced cake for that Derek of her's another time."

Mr Cressett sighed; his daughter's quarrel with her stepmother seemed to have cut him off from his last link with the outside world.

"Well, come along to table," said Mrs Cressett.

Gerald's Daimler sped along the Great West Road. "I'm surprised that Portway girl was so restless," he said to John,

"I thought all that sort of thing had gone out now. Female neurosis was the curse of my time. It's particularly infuriating when they're attractive like that."

John said, "She aims above her intellectual station."

"Probably gets it from her grandmother," Gerald said. "A great actress, but like most of them had no real idea of what she was playing. Actually she'd have been a better actress if she'd been a bit more of a fool. She'd have just acted instead of trying to make sense of her parts. I'm not surprised the girl doesn't get on with her. I remember well when I stayed there what an egoist she was. Stokesay had just opened Eorpwald's tomb and she went round as though she owned the thing—'My tomb this and my tomb that'. Actually, to do her justice, she *did* own it, or rather her brother-in-law Canon Portway did. They sold the stuff to the Museum for a very nice sum for those days. Most of her share went into the pockets of Mrs Pankhurst and her wild women. Lilian Portway had plenty of money of her own anyway. She was always a crank. Got a bee in her bonnet about Mussolini later on—the Shavian great man, you know. What's happened to the girl's father?" he asked.

"Her parents were killed in the Café de Paris raid," said John. "She's very unhappy really."

It occurred to him to tell his father about Elvira's relations with Robin. He had decided now that this was the cause of her resigning, and so foolish an action could only spring from an *undesirable* relationship. Looking at his father's face, however, he decided against telling him anything—a confidence to Gerald appeared to him as something very strange, almost incestuous, certainly the sort of thing that would upset his mother.

"A pity," said Gerald. "Tragic beauty tends to be a bore."

Silence settled upon them. As they approached Slough, John said, "Do you think we would have time for me to see someone here?"

Gerald, surprised, looked at his watch, "Well, you'll have to make our peace with your mother."

"Oh, Thingy'll forgive me," said John and he gave the address to the chauffeur. They drew up at a small semi-detached house in a nineteen-thirties street. "I shan't be long," said John, getting out, then he added, "Would you care to come in?"

Gerald was about to refuse. He could think of no reason why he should go into a house in Slough with his son, then he felt annoyed at his acquiescence in his family's habit of isolating him. He was not going to let himself be held to blame for it. Besides, he thought, who knows there might be another Elvira here, and one less likely to be a neurotic pseudo-intellectual. "I think I will," he said, getting out of the car.

John reflected doubtfully on presenting his father to Maureen and Derek Kershaw, but he saw no way out of his offer.

Derek Kershaw opened the door to them. His advertisement good-looking face creased into a smile on seeing John. The even white teeth gleamed as though from a hoarding, but the smile had more reality in it.

"My father," said John. "This is Derek Kershaw, Father. We're on our way to family Christmas at Thingy's, Derek. I couldn't pass so near without wishing you both a Happy Christmas."

Gerald was annoyed to hear his wife's nickname mentioned to a stranger, but Derek said, "Give all our wishes to your mother, won't you, John? Come in," he said, "Maureen's cooking and I was just going to play this." He laid a long-playing gramophone record on a little plain wood table, then, again to Gerald's surprise, shook hands with them both. "Maureen," he called, "here's John."

A young woman with black garçon-cut hair, wearing a lime green woollen dress with a smocked neck and frill skirt, came in, wiping her hands on her apron. She also shook hands with them. "My present to Derek," she said, pointing at the record. "*Salome* with Welitsch. It'll keep him quiet over the holiday."

"Aren't you working?" John asked, surprised.

"Oh no," said Maureen, "he's a bloated capitalist now," she laughed. "We've got an assistant and they work alternate Bank Holidays."

"How is business?" John asked.

Derek shook his hands in the air, boxer fashion, "First rate," he said, "I've got a wonderful 1935 Bentley for you if you'll take it off me."

"Oh, do, John," said Maureen, "otherwise we're going to die a gory death in it."

Derek grimaced behind her back cheerfully and, going to a corner cupboard, brought out a gin and Noilly Prat. "Will this do you?" he asked Gerald. "Aren't you a professor?" he asked, and, when Gerald assented, both he and his wife put on a pious church-going face in reverence for higher education.

"Well, what do you think of the room, John?" said Maureen, "you haven't seen it since Derek did his worst on it."

Gerald, looking around at the pink walls, low glass book-cases and complicated gramophone and radio installations, was depressingly reminded of his wife's Scandinavian furnishing, but he said, "*I* think it's delightful."

"Thank you," said Derek, with a coyness that Gerald did not expect from him.

"I'm sorry you couldn't find a job for Larrie," said John.

"Nothing here that was any good to him, I'm afraid," said Derek. He turned to Gerald, "I wish *I* knew some history," he said. But before Gerald could answer, Maureen said, "Where on earth did you find *that* specimen, John? Derek couldn't have employed *him*. Crooked stands out a mile in those Irish eyes . . ." She stopped as she saw her husband frowning at her and contented herself by saying, "You need Derek to look after you, you know."

"Well, whose fault's that?" John asked, and they all laughed.

Gerald, looking at the books, vaguely wondered why science-fiction should seem to him discreditable.

The subject of Larrie seemed to have made them all silent. Then Maureen said, "Well, you're doing Father proud all

right!" John looked puzzled. Derek roared with laughter. "I
told you he didn't know," he said to his wife. "Your protégé
Cressett, John, is none other than my esteemed father-in-law."

"Good God!" said John.

"Only we don't esteem him very much," said Maureen.

"You're sure you've got the right end of the stick, John?"
asked Derek. "I know these civil servants can be bloody fools,
but I can't see anyone being a bloodier fool about business than
my father-in-law. That market garden of his . . ."

It was Maureen's turn to interrupt. "Father's business is
his own," she said shortly. "But whatever you do, John,
don't get mixed up with my stepmother. She'll take the skin
off your back."

John seemed as unhappy with the subject of the Cressetts as
with that of Larrie. He swallowed his drink. "If you're ready,
Father, I think we'll have to go," he said. He fished in his
overcoat pocket and brought out two tissue-paper-wrapped
parcels. "Just to show I don't forget old friends," he said.

"Thank you," said Maureen, and she smiled. "In any case,
we see you on television or, if we don't, the neighbours
remind us of it."

"There's a smashing blonde two doors away who's scats
about you, John," Derek said.

"Thank you, I'm sure," said John. Once again they all
laughed.

"Oh my God," said Maureen, "that's my *risotto* burning."
She rushed into the kitchen.

Gerald got up to follow John to the door. "Thank you for
the drink, Mrs Kershaw," he called.

"Thank you for coming," she called back, "we don't have
a live professor at Caldecott Avenue every day, you know."

Gerald did not know whether the remark was friendly or not.

John had walked ahead with Derek to the car. "Sorry about
what Maureen said," Derek mumbled. "All the same, you
want to watch your step with young Larrie, John." John gave
no answer.

"Come again, won't you?" Derek said to Gerald, once more shaking his hand. "Perhaps you can tell me what happened in history after the Tudors. We never got any further than Sir Francis Drake and his bloody bowls at school. The glorious Armada, and back we went each year to the Ancient Britons in their woad. Not a word about why things were like they are now. . . ."

John, seeing that Derek was launched on the imperfections of the English educational system, said, "Father only knows about Canute. The chap who didn't want to get his feet wet."

As they drove past the factories of Wembley Exhibition design, Gerald said, "Nice people."

"Yes," said John. "Derek's a good man. He was a C.P.O. Tel. with me in the *Rodney* in the Med. Maureen's all right, or would be, if she didn't always know best. She's a Bevanite," he added with a grunt of disapproval. His own position as M.P. had been Right-Wing Radical.

Gerald looked at his watch. "We're going to be very late at Inge's," he said.

Ingeborg Middleton, coming downstairs to greet the village children, said to herself, "Oh God, let the carol-singing be a success and let the family arrive in time to hear it and I shan't mind if on Christmas Day there are rows and difficulties. I honestly shan't expect *everything* to go right on Christmas Day, if I have what I want now," she added, as though God might not believe her willingness to have only part of her own way. She feared, perhaps, that God would know her own temperament as well as she did. A more inner voice added, "Let Robin and Johnnie, but especially Johnnie, think that only I could have made such a little Christmas occasion." She was careful, however, not to listen too carefully to this second prayer lest its demand for filial adoration might be too outrageous and so annoy God that He would refuse her all her wishes.

If, at fifty-nine, she had no strong personal experience of God, she still believed that if she accepted any disappointment she should be recompensed for her self-denial. She had brought every power of her personality to convince other people of this in childhood; and she still did so. On occasion, of course, she overreached herself, but on the whole it had worked very well, except perhaps with her husband. In return, as she often reflected, she gave people everything she possessed—warmth, liveliness, love, natural gaiety.

The village girls were removing their overcoats, but, despite the central heating of the hall, they were shivering, for the long white muslin dresses Mrs Middleton had had made for them were very thin.

"No! No!" cried Ingeborg, towering above them, a Norse goddess from the stairway. She used her Danish accent with exaggerated emphasis, lengthening all the vowels in a marked singing tone. "Don't shiver so. Give yourselves up to the happy time."

She felt radiant with happiness. Her tall, ample figure, carefully corseted, moved everywhere in stately command. Her corn-coloured hair was greying now, but it was still thick and soft; her complexion was like a fairy-tale country girl's, her long pastel-blue silk dress showed her still lovely arms and shoulders. She used her arms a great deal—in stroking the children's heads and in gestures of kind command to the servants.

"Amalie! Monica! Irmgard," she called to the servants who were still arranging chairs and refreshments in the long morning-room, "please, where are the flowers? Take these cyclamens and this lovely cineraria into the room. You can't sing without flowers can you, Norma?" she cried to one of the older girls, but she did not wait for an answer. "No, one moment, please, Irmgard, we must have some of these beautiful crimson cinerarias to put in little Mollie's black hair, mustn't we, Mollie?" and she arranged the little flower heads around the child's ears. "Little red stars in the black, black night," she said. Some of the girls still giggled when Mrs Middleton talked, but most of them took it for granted by now.

The maids ran about chattering like starlings, for Mrs Middleton loved them to be happy; she would not put up with

glum faces. Her servants were always of three nationalities—
English, Danish and German—to mark her own triune nature
—English by marriage, Danish by birth, and with her own
darling mother, "*min kjaere lille mor*," a Bavarian. For long years
she had said, "See! the two great giants can lie down together
like little lambs when little Denmark tells them it must be so."
During the war she had not said it, indeed had not wanted to,
for the occupation of Denmark had deeply upset her. Nevertheless, it was the kind of thing she liked saying, and now she
was glad to be able to repeat it once more. She said it in a
playful, deprecating little voice, but, whatever she may have
thought of its application to the nations, she had no doubts of
its truth in her personal life.

Now she began to fit the crowns of candles to the girls'
heads. "Of course, Saint Lucy is not Danish you know," she
said. Since the rehearsals of the preceding week it was, by force
of repetition, one of the few facts about Scandinavia that they
did know. "She is Swedish. But *we* follow the custom too,
and now little English girls are going to do so. And why
not? It is a beautiful custom. Christmas is not national. Oh
dear no!"

Soon the parents began to arrive, and for every one of them
Mrs Middleton had a word about their children. "Little Harry
would like to have a crown too, wouldn't he? But I'm afraid
the crowns are only for little girls. Later the little boys will
sing too. Everyone will sing in the *Heilige Nacht*, Mrs Adams,"
and when she noted that lady's discomfiture, she cried, "Oh
yes! everyone. And they will love it." Once again there were
to be carols in English and Danish and German, and she had
even taught two little girls to sing "*Dans cet étable que Jésus
est charmant*," in compliment to Marie Hélène.

When everyone was seated, Mrs Middleton clapped her
hands high in the air and all the lights went out, leaving only
the holly wreaths, the mistletoe and the thirty little spruce trees
illuminated with red and white candles in the Danish fashion.
Then coming down between the two ranks of chairs, she

walked on tiptoe with candle in hand. "Hush!" she whispered, her finger to her lips.

There was no need for admonition, for her giant shadow had cast a silence upon the audience that just hovered on the edge of nervous giggles. Miss Butterfield, the infant-school teacher, had rescued Ingeborg from more than one such situation before now and she instantly struck up the first carol on the grand piano. And now all tendency to laughter was submerged in parental admiration as the little girls advanced singing "*Es ist ein' Ros' entsprungen.*" They held their white gowns bunched in one hand and in the other a candle. There was a certain amount of squealing as drops of hot grease fell on hands and heads, but Mrs Middleton had found no way but spartan courage to meet the situation.

She had told them the story of the boy and the fox at rehearsals, making it sound strangely pretty. "And though the little fox bit and bit the little boy's tummy," she had said, "did the little boy make a sound? No! He was a very brave little boy, and little girls can be brave too," and her singing, rising accent put all the sweetness she could command into the word "brave".

Now that she saw some of the girls faltering in their steps, she bent down from her great height and said, "Poppy, Eileen, remember the little fox." She was determined to have no tears to mar the day.

Carol after carol they sang and, before each of them, Mrs Middleton said a few words: "This is a *most* pretty story. Mary and her little infant Jesus are riding on a reindeer. Imagine! a reindeer! Of course, those little people that sang the song could not imagine anything else, for they lived right up," and her voice rose as she said it, "in the north of Norway. I have been there!" she said as simply as a little girl to the village audience.

The Vicar, despite years of practice, still got hot under the collar when she addressed him like this, but he turned and smiled at a small boy in the audience as though Mrs Middleton intended her words for the children only.

And now it was a little Jutland peasant song that the children were to sing, and Ingeborg led them with a deep contralto, her well-supported pastel-blue bosom heaving, her grey eyes round with surprise. "*Ole Dole, din din,*" she sang, or that, at any rate, was what it sounded like to the smaller children, who, thus reminded that they were hungry, began to cry.

At the end of the song, Mrs Middleton called up a very angel-pretty little boy of six from the audience—there was nothing she liked more than angelic faces in children—"And now little Maurice Gardner will sing a verse of 'Holy Night' and we shall sing the choruses. Little Maurice is a very shy, special little boy," she said to the audience, "so we must all help him."

When no sound came from his terror-struck mouth, she bent down from the heavens above and placing her huge doll's face close to his, she asked, "What is the matter, Maurice? Have the trolls bewitched your tongue?" so creating a deep psychic trauma that was to cause him to be court-martialled for cowardice many years later in World War III. Miss Butter-field coaxed Maurice out of his fright, and *Heilige Nacht* filled the room.

Ingeborg was by now so delighted with her little party that she had quite forgotten the absence of her family. When her daughter Kay and her son-in-law Donald were ushered into the room, she took them for late arrivals from the village, and said "Hush" very loudly and pointed to Maurice, whose special character had to be considered.

Maurice's needs, however, were quickly forgotten when she recognized her own kin. "Kay," she called, and ran to the end of the room. "My darling little Kay. And how is big Donald?" and then, with a special cry, she flung herself upon the baby, "*Min lille barnebarn,*" she cried. " 'No,' he says, 'I don't want a grandmother to swallow me up.' "

"We're all right here, Mother," said Kay, "Don't, for good-ness' sake, let us interrupt the singing."

By now, however, Maurice had burst into tears and a right-eously indignant Mrs Gardner had taken him back to his seat. Mrs Middleton was unable to persuade him to resume his solo, and Mrs Gardner was almost at the point of losing her temper when Ingeborg made what she believed to be a conciliatory remark. "Never mind, Maurice," she said, "you are not the only little baby in the room now. See!" she added, pointing towards her grandchild, "there is another one. But I think per-haps he is a braver little baby than you."

Kay blushed scarlet; Donald took his usual defensive action on such occasions by carefully analysing the social elements involved; Mrs Gardner got up and took Maurice from the room.

Mrs Middleton, however, was too occupied in announcing the next carol to notice what had happened. The arrival of her daughter had reminded her that her two sons were not yet part of the audience and she determined to prolong the proceedings so that her prayer should be answered. "And now a little English carol," she said. "'Lully, lulley, lully, lulley; the falcon hath borne my mate away.'"

The obscurity of the words baffled the audience; and they were not much helped by Mrs Middleton's demonstration of a bird in flight. The Vicar felt uncertain whether there was not an impropriety in the whole proceedings: he had not remem-bered that carols embodied so much of what, if not secular, seemed like an unhealthy mysticism. He feared there might even be some unsuitable element of pagan survival mixed up in the whole proceedings. Indeed, there was something about Ingeborg's Brunhild figure and her general passion for the charms of folklore, Christian or otherwise, that would have delighted Rose Lorimer herself.

When this carol drew to its strange end, the Vicar got up and announced that his Christmas duties forced him to leave. It had been a most delightful occasion, a real unity in rejoicing all too rare in these days when communal life was at a discount. How Mrs Middleton had managed to produce anything so really unusual in so short a time, he did not know. It seemed only yesterday that these charming dresses had just been strips of material, but then he did not profess to understand the powers of feminine magic. The realization that he had said "magic" embarrassed the Vicar, and he could only murmur, "A rare and unusual occasion."

Any further remarks he might have made were cut short by Mrs Middleton, who turned to the children with a knowing look. "Now just imagine! Mr Bilston thinks he has heard all our carols. He does not know how much little children like to sing, does he?"

But, alas, when she turned again to the audience, many other people had risen to support the Vicar in his signal for departure.

Mrs Middleton played her last card, "I know, children," she said, "the Vicar is hungry, that is what it is. I expect he has his eye on those meringues. Now, all of you, off! and see who can get there before him. Please," she said to the audience, "to eat," and she pointed to the huge array of food and drink. "Then," she added, "we will all be ready to sing again."

Kay, watching the gigantic form of her mother bearing down upon her, was filled with affection. Surely, she thought, no one could be irritated with the absurdities of someone so ingenuously kind and in love with life. Donald, seeing his wife's energy fading in the presence of her mother, felt all his hostility coming to the surface. He had resolved to be patient in face of the many difficult situations that he knew must arise during the Christmas visit, but, remembering previous years, he noted that he was unlikely to be able to keep his resolution.

Happily, perhaps, the worst of all such moments came immediately. Mrs Middleton took the baby from Kay and, looking at her daughter's withered hand, she said, "No, *liebchen*, you will have to be content with your grandmother, poor little Mummy cannot manage the big elephant baby."

Kay, catching a sidelong glance of her husband's face, said, "Darling, it's wonderful. I'm just like the Vicar. I can't imagine how you've done it all."

What Donald did not guess was that as soon as Mrs Middleton had alluded in this way to her daughter's deformity, she was overcome with shame. She could not love her daughter as she did her sons, but it was only when she felt cornered by life that she ever wished to be cruel to anyone. Today, despite Maurice Gardner, everything seemed to be giving way to her, and she felt very loving. "Darling Kay, you look so pretty," she said. It was something, at least, to have her daughter's praise.

But wishes gratified never occupied Mrs Middleton so completely as those as yet unfulfilled. "Where can Johnnie be?" she asked. "I knew it was a mistake for him to come with your father. Christmas is not a time for Daimlers and chauffeurs. It is a simple time."

"Christmas the season of the small owner-driver," said Donald. But Mrs Middleton did not regard the things her son-in-law said. She knew that they tended to be "bitter", but then she also knew that he was an orphan, and therefore she felt able to love him just the same.

Contrary to Ingeborg's expectations, refreshment only seemed to strengthen the determination of the audience to leave. She cajoled and cooed, but all to no avail; and, when she found even Miss Butterfield unwilling to return to the piano, she stood on the stairs, looming above the departing guests with a face so dead and empty that she might have been Brunhild in her long sleep. God had not answered her prayer, despite all her assurances, and, as always happened on such occasions, Mrs Middleton remembered that she was getting old and soon must die. "Not even Robin, usually so faithful, can do this small thing for me. To be here on time."

As it became increasingly clear that the performance she had been prepared to give would not be asked for, all her histrionic reserve drained away, and even her smooth, doll-like face seemed to crumple and grow grey. "Good-bye, good-bye," she called from the stairs in a monotonous, falling tone, "No more singing—Merry Christmas."

Donald even passed her on the stairs without receiving any comment. Coming back to the morning-room, where the maids were clearing away the dirty plates, he said to Kay, "It looks like being a quieter Christmas than last year. Your mother seems less edgy." Kay, however, when she went out into the hall, was immediately anxious. If she did not fan her mother's energy until John's coming revived the fire, they would be in for a Christmas Day far worse than she had feared.

"Darling," she called, "Donald's spoken to Robin about doing something with the firm and it seems there's a most interesting job going for him giving lectures. He's already full of ideas." She put her arm round her mother's corseted waist. "It was a wonderful idea of yours as usual. I really think he may be able to help Robin and it'll take his mind off things until the next lot of vacancies comes up. He just *couldn't* go on with his book and I was really frightened for him. And now, thanks to you," she leaned across and kissed her mother very gently on the cheek, "thanks to you, everybody's happy again." Why do I have to do it? she wondered. What am I so frightened of?

Mrs Middleton stirred very slightly, as though from a very far distance a faint sound had broken her immortal sleep. "That is good," she said, but she could indeed only see her daughter through a deep fog of all the injustices life had brought to her. She was old and tired and Gerald would arrive full of the energy of his selfish life; it was too hard to bear.

"Don't mind me, darling! if you want a good cry," said Kay, practised as an augur reading the entrails of chickens. "You do too much for everybody."

But at that moment the purr of the Daimler could be heard from the drive outside. Mrs Middleton, started into life, pounced on a small girl who was still struggling with her goloshes. "Winnie," she cried, "all the others have gone, but you will stay and sing one little song for my son. We will sing together the *Tannenbaum*."

Winnie, however, took one look at her hostess's face and was out of the front door before another word was spoken. Mrs Middleton, running after her, fell into John's arms.

"Thingy," he cried, "you *mustn't* come out into the bitter cold in that thin dress."

"Johnnie," she murmured, "Oh! Johnnie, you have missed all the little children and their singing."

Larwood came in with the luggage and Gerald followed him with many parcels. "You're here early," he said to Kay.

"No, Daddy, *you're* late." She was quite snappish.

Gerald did not notice her tone, he only saw her appearance in an old skirt and jumper and her hair scruffy and dead. More even than her marriage to Donald, it annoyed him that his daughter should let her looks run to seed in that sort of academic dowdiness. "You've got powder on your skirt," he said, and went into the morning-room. Seeing only Donald and the baby, he came out again. "You didn't say you were going to have some short of show or we'd have come earlier," he remarked to his wife.

John looked up quite angrily. "It was the carol-singing," he said, "we oughtn't to have been late."

Gerald thought it useless to remind his son of the reasons. "I'll get you a drink, Inge," he said. It was the only contribution he could find to make to his wife after all these years of the children's management of her.

Only once did Mrs Middleton come to life again that evening. Christmas Eve supper was one of her special offerings to the family, the real Danish Christmas Eve dinner, but, unlike that held in Denmark, this was only a prelude to an English dinner on Christmas Day. This evening as usual they sat down to the Danish rice pudding followed by roast goose. Gerald dreaded the effects it would have on his digestion. "I shan't eat much tonight, old dear," he said, patting his wife's shoulder. "I'm frightfully tired."

Ingeborg put down her knife and fork and smiled at John and Kay. "Papa doesn't change," she said, winking at them in special intimacy. "Even now he believes that he is tired when he is just hungry. Give your father a large piece of goose," she said to Donald. "There, Gerald, no one can have indigestion from *my* roast goose."

But if Gerald was to be forcibly fed, what would be the re-action of Marie Hélène, about to receive the Sacrament? In her present mood, Ingeborg would have no mercy towards hunger-strikers. Donald was the first to think of this and was delighted, when his mother-in-law ordered food to be kept back for the late-comers, to be able to say, "Not for Marie Hélène surely. I imagine she'll be going to Midnight Mass."

It was soon apparent that Mrs Middleton was going to insist on the same scene that she played each Christmas. "But, my dear Donald, why should you think she wishes to go to church with an empty tummy?" she laughed.

Donald was left by the others to argue the dogma of the Real Presence with her this year. After all, he had raised the subject.

"Very well," Ingeborg said at last. "If my daughter-in-law is this kind of cannibal. . . . But Timothy will be very hungry, he grows so fast."

"I expect, Thingy," said John, coming to Donald's rescue, "that Marie Hélène will be taking him with her."

His mother smiled sweetly and shook her head. "No, Johnnie, no," she said, and laughed in rippling amusement, "Midnight Mass is not for children." Everyone felt that Marie Hélène was the person to sort that one out.

Inge received the "wishing almond" in her plate of rice pudding, but somehow it did not seem to placate her. "What is the good of my wishing?" she cried. "My wishes never come true."

CHAPTER FOUR

JUST before they went to bed, Kay whispered to John and Robin, "Mother's going to have a *Grossmutter* tomorrow." It was their childhood way of describing the moods of moralizing and intrigue that descended upon their mother when she felt frustrated and neglected. Her manner, at such times, became sweeter, more intimate as her fear of isolation became more desperate. Her children had decided that she inherited such reactions from their Bavarian grandmother with her *Gemütlichkeit* and her sense of persecution; this attribution to heredity at once exculpated her from all blame and made more excusable their own acquiescence in her demands. They had learned such acquiescence in childhood; their mother had been a great believer in such character-training. And, as nobody, except Inge, could remember their grandmother, it was not an explanation that could be contradicted.

As the day wore on, Mrs Middleton took her children aside one by one, and tried to reassure herself that no one and nothing came before herself in their feelings.

"Now little Kay," she said, "I am going to show you how to make a real old-fashioned turkey soup. There is no need, you know, to have poor food because one is living on the little, tiny income that my poor Kay has." She led her daughter into the vast kitchen, which, like everything else in her house, was equipped with the greatest modern simplicity at the greatest possible expense. It was the simplicity only that Mrs Middleton saw, she constantly exclaimed at the frittering and waste of more old-fashioned homes where large capital outlay had been less possible. "And all that old-fashioned way of living is so unhygienic too," she would say.

She dispersed the maids from their current tasks. "Later!" she said. "Now I am going to give Mrs Consett a cookery lesson. You see, Kay," she continued, putting herbs into a little muslin bag, "first the bouquet, so simple and so wholesome. But you are tired, my darling," she said. "Tired and sad. That is wrong. A young mother should look so happy. When you were all little babies, I used to sing and dance all day. The English neighbours would say 'That young Mrs Middleton's quite mad', and look down their noses—so! And then I would dance and sing all the more. It is not right that you should have to worry and save so."

"But, darling," said Kay, "really we're not paupers. I get £980 a year from my shares in the firm and then there's what Donald earns with his articles."

"Now Kay," said Ingeborg, "that *really* makes me sad. It is bad when you feel ashamed and have to tell lies to your mother. I don't mind that Donald does not make any money. It is not always the fine people who make money. I am only sad for him. To have no work is bad for people, and for a little orphan boy..." She left the horrible possibilities of this situation in the air.

"I don't think," said Kay, laughing, "that Donald feels unloved, if that's what you mean."

"Oh, no!" cried her mother, "you give him so much. But now there is baby." She paused and went on with her soup-making lesson, then she said, "Donald is a little shy with baby, I think. Perhaps he is a little frightened of this new stranger who has come to share his Kay with him."

"He's just awkward," said Kay.

"Oh, my dear, you need not tell me such things," her mother laughed, "I remember Gerald with little Johnnie. But Donald will be happier now that he has this work to do for Robin. I am *so* glad that I found this job for him. It will make him feel more a part of the family."

"Mummy," said Kay, "you realize he will only do this lecturing for Robin until a university post comes along. He's not going to give up his academic career."

"No, of course not," said Mrs Middleton, "but since your father did nothing for him in the university world, it was time that your silly old mother thought of something."

"Oh! I think Daddy did his best, but it's not his subject and Donald's very bad at interviews."

But Ingeborg had had enough, and, in addition, she had really become interested in the soup-making. She patted her daughter's cheek. "Always so loyal to your father," she said.

It was Robin's turn after luncheon. "Where is Timothy?" Mrs Middleton asked, finding Robin alone in the drawing-room, when the others had gone to their rooms to sleep.

"Oh! he's gone off to read somewhere, I expect."

"Robin," said his mother, sitting down, "why is Timothy so lonely?"

"Is he?" said Robin. "I should have called him unsociable, that's all. Like me."

Mrs Middleton laughed. "People don't manage great businesses who are unsociable."

"My dear Mother, I assure you, I run a mile from people unless I have to do business with them. There's nothing I hate more than entertaining. Thank God! some of the other directors like it so much."

"But Marie Hélène," asked his mother, "does not feel like that? I have heard so much of her parties."

"Oh, that's quite different," said Robin, "she doesn't have *bores* to the house. She collects all the writers and painters."

Once again Mrs Middleton laughed. "Oh, Robin. Fancy hearing *you* exaggerate! The practical man of the family. I'm sure your home is not as bad as that. The wife with her lions—her painters and writers—and the poor business husband, knowing nobody, upstairs alone. No, no, Robin, even I know enough of the American cinema to tell where you have got *that* picture."

"Did I say I sat alone?" asked Robin gruffly. "As a matter of fact, I thoroughly enjoy Marie Hélène's do's."

Ingeborg got up and altered the position of some of the plants in her long, glass "tropical garden". The drawing-room, like the rest of the house, had the mark of *Homes and Gardens* but without any touch of *chichi*. It was a taste which Mrs Middleton had acquired some twenty years before its fashion in England. Her roots lay deep in Scandinavian and German "modern" comfort. "Do you like my new curtains, Robin?" she said, fingering the long crimson velvet hangings.

"Yes," said Robin, and added with a smile, "but I miss the old ones."

Mrs Middleton, too, smiled. "Men never like changes," she said, "but things wear out, Robin, even our dear old silver curtains." Then, sitting down again, she said, "But don't think I haven't noticed that you have changed the subject." Robin look genuinely puzzled. "No, Robin, no," she said, "you know as well as I do that children are unhappy in loveless homes."

"Now, look here," said Robin, "Marie Hélène and I are perfectly good friends."

"Yes," said Ingeborg, "that I know. Oh, Robin!" she said, flinging one lovely arm towards him, "you can't expect me to sit by and see it all happening again. Your father and I made such a mistake. *We* thought that love did not matter so long as we kept the home going. You know what that meant for you children. Do you think I don't remember it every hour of the day."

Robin, touched, said, "We were happy enough, my dear."

"No, Robin, no! We should have got a divorce. Your father loved someone else and he did not have the courage of that love. To lack courage is not good. There was no reason, if we had been honest, why your father and I should not have been—what did you call it—good friends. But we were cowards, and now we are hardly even acquaintances. And every hour of the day, too, I remember that poor Dollie. She was not a bad woman, Robin, Dollie Stokesay, not even foolish. Do you think, Robin, that I can be happy to think that because of a mistaken idea, a stupid convention, that poor woman is now a hopeless drunkard?"

Robin saw nothing for it but direct opposition. "The Dollie in question," he said, "is quite unlikely to take to drink. She's a very lively, happy young woman." As he said it, he saw Elvira's laziness and untidiness slipping into drunkenness.

"She is gay!" cried his mother. "That is good. Youth has such great powers of recovery."

"Mother," said Robin, "you must get this out of your head. Even if there were a hundred more good reasons for divorce than there are, it isn't possible. Marie Hélène is a Catholic."

His mother stood over him, brushing his curly hair very lightly with her hand. "Forgive me," she said, "it's so difficult, Robin, for me to understand a religion that *denies* life. I am getting old, you know." Then she walked across to the door and stopped to rearrange some chrysanthemums. "I don't care so much for anything now except beautiful things," she said, and smiled across at her son, clear blue eyes and head high, a Nordic Ceres. "Is she beautiful, your Elvira?" she asked, "I wish I could see this girl who has made my solemn Robin lose his head. But that would never do!" And with a sly little smile, like a little girl caught kissing, she had left the room before he could reply.

By tea-time, Mrs Middleton felt restored enough to eat hot buttered scones and Christmas cake. "Look, Johnnie," she cried, pointing out of the window, "even the sun refuses to be banished on Christmas Day. Will you not come for a little walk in the garden? I have put up the Christmas sheaf for the little birds as we do at home. Come and see what sort of Christmas the birds have enjoyed. A little walk will help to keep you slim," she added. "It needs it, my darling." Only with John did she allow herself the intimacy of teasing.

As she came downstairs in her heavy fur coat and with a cyclamen silk scarf tied round her head, her complexion seemed restored to dollhood once more.

"Well, Thingy, what are *you* working round for?" John asked. His subjection to her lay on a deeper level of frankness than that of the other two.

Mrs Middleton smiled. "I am too happy for 'working round', Johnnie," she said. "Do you know it is now three times in two months that you have been down to see me. That is nice. At first, you know, I was so worried that you had resigned from Parliament. My dear father was thirty years a deputy in the *Rigsdag* and, like you, he was a good Social Democrat. That was fine, Johnnie, to stand for the clean, simple things in life, for a world of peace and good living for all. But now I am glad. You are like your grandfather, but you are also like me. We are very headstrong people, you and I. No whippings for us because we do not think what some party tells us. No," and she stood for a moment, looking her favourite son in the eyes. "I am proud of all my children, of course, but especially of my Benjamin. I will even have that awful television in my house so that I can watch him talking to people, helping them in their troubles. Only imagine, I was in the grocer's at Henley and I heard some woman say, 'That John Middleton is a good man. We could do with more like him. . . .' That's what I always knew people would say of you, Johnnie." She stopped and bent down to pick up some of the purple-green hellebores. "But I have a scheme. Yes! I would like you to come here for the summer, Johnnie."

"Oh, my dear Thingy," said John, "I'm afraid that's quite impossible. I've a full programme of radio work and speeches."

"I see," said Mrs Middleton, "what a pity! Larrie will be most disappointed."

"Larrie?" asked John in surprise. "Have you been plotting something with him?"

Mrs Middleton did not answer the question. "That's a nice boy," she said "He is very fond of you, Johnnie. He is a bit fussy perhaps. He thinks you don't look after yourself properly in London."

John laughed aloud. He pictured his mother and Larrie blarneying each other into this scheme. All the same, there were a hundred reasons why he would be glad to see Larrie out of London, if he was willing; but to stay at Thingy's was out of the question.

"Did he not tell you how much he liked the flat?"

"What is all this about?" John cried. "You are a couple of schemers." But he was delighted that one afternoon together had brought his mother and Larrie into such agreement.

"The flat over the stables," Mrs Middleton said, "it seemed such a pity that it should go begging. I thought perhaps that you would like it." She paused as though considering whether she should say more, but she only remarked. "The sun has gone now. We should go in, I think."

They walked between the box hedges that rimmed the rose garden, and Mrs Middleton said, "Larrie will be able to drive you up to London for your talks and so on."

So that was all fixed, John thought, and, as so often, wondered what his mother would not swallow to accommodate him. "Larrie never said a word of this to me," he said.

"No?" said his mother. "Perhaps he can keep secrets from you better than I can, Johnnie."

As they passed by the drawing-room, they caught a glimpse of Marie Hélène's long face bent over her needlework. "How is your secretary?" said Ingeborg immediately. John smiled at the thought of how much his mother always knew. "She's leaving me," he answered.

"I'm afraid that her troubles are only just beginning, poor girl," Ingeborg remarked. "I have always tried, you know, not to be nationalistic about the French. It is a danger for anyone with German blood. But they are so practical, Johnnie, and so proud of it. It is strange to be proud of denying the truth of life. For it is the unpractical things which are the true ones, as you and I know." John did not reply, he was not prepared to be led into a discussion of his sister-in-law. "Perhaps it is just as well that that secretary goes. You do not want everything that you do reported all over the family." Once again, John did not bite; he felt that Thingy should not accept Robin's relations with Elvira quite so easily. She was, after all, their beloved, wronged mother. It was all a little out of place.

"So now," said Ingeborg, "you will have a new secretary. I know!" she cried, "we will get Miss Totton to come over from Reading. She is a very good secretary, I believe, and a most discreet girl. But that is wonderful!"

John laughed. "I promise nothing," he said.

Mrs Middleton's spirits, however, were quite restored when they got back to the drawing-room. "Imagine," she cried, "my four little rosebuds have survived the frost. Do you know what I believe about these little rosebuds? No, Donald, you will laugh at me, but I don't mind. I believe they are four little roses that refused to grow in summer because they wanted to see that strange white world they had heard so much about. 'We are not frightened', they said . . ." Dutifully, the family listened, all except Timothy, who went on reading his book. Marie Hélène, so dexterous with her needle as a rule, pricked her finger.

As Mrs Middleton's mood of distrust melted back into her usual flow of whimsy, her children's rally to placate her dissolved and their natural antipathies came to the surface again. Gerald noticed the change and welcomed it. Apart from his unreturned affection for Kay, he could find no interest in their lives, but their united efforts to assuage their mother's ill-humour had depressed him. It recalled too vividly the whole pattern of his family life: a world of indulgent sweetness and syrupy intimacy. He had done nothing to reform it all these years; he could do nothing now. Nevertheless, the failure of his family life added to his preoccupation with his professional death and closed him round in a dense fog of self-disgust. It seemed to him that his whole life had grown pale and futile because it was rooted in evasion.

After Inge's enormous Christmas dinner, he sat in a deep armchair in the drawing-room, hunched up as far as his great height would allow him, and remote. He seemed even to have barricaded himself from the rest of the family with little tables on which were his brandy glass, his coffee cup, his ashtray.

Marie Hélène felt a special reverence for him as head of the house, university professor and *homme du monde*; but even her great pertinacity in maintaining social intercourse was no proof against his withdrawal. It was terrible that a stupid woman could age and impair a brilliant man to such a degree, she thought, but then he should not have married a peasant. In stressing her mother-in-law's peasant origin she found it easier to disregard her.

They were not origins that Ingeborg herself chose to disregard, as she was proclaiming at that very moment. "But, of course, Johnnie must defend this Mr Cressett. He is a gardener, a good man, a peasant. Don't forget, Robin, because you are now the great master, that your ancestors were peasants. My grandfather was just an ordinary small farmer. All his life, he lived on his farm in Jutland. He was very proud when his son became a deputy and he used to come to Copenhagen and point Father out to people and say 'that is my son'; but he remained always a peasant, a simple, wise man. And my mother's mother, dear *Grossmütterchen*, too. I can see her now, such a fine, old, wrinkled face. She was a Bavarian peasant, a winegrowing peasant. That is the best kind, is it not, Marie Hélène?"

Her daughter-in-law did not answer her question, but merely said to John, "I suppose you are very sure of your facts. It does not do to trust this kind of people too much. They will say anything for money, you know."

"Oh, yes, thank you, Marie Hélène," John replied. "It's a pity that Robin's hero, Mr Pelican, didn't make as sure of *his* facts when he removed the wretched man's land from him under one subsection and then graciously decided to restore it under another."

"I don't understand why you're so set against the existence of laws about these things," said Kay. Since Donald had so far made no pronouncement about the Pelican affair, she felt free to side with Robin. "If expropriations are necessary, surely it's better that they should be carried out under some carefully defined law than . . ."

"Of course, there's got to be a law," said John impatiently. "What I'm objecting to is the tyrannical, uncontrolled use of these laws by unimaginative bureaucrats. The House passes laws with a certain honesty of intention behind them, an intention that reflects a certain social truth. It's absolutely essential for the interpreters of the laws to respect that truth. Judges *do*, bureaucrats *don't*. That's all."

"It isn't all by any means," said Robin angrily. "That's a lot of nonsensical cant, John. Pelican and other useful civil servants like him have a job to do. They have to work hard. You'd know what that meant if you'd been in industry, where what you do affects thousands of people, instead of getting up on your hind legs in the House of Commons, where you can say what you like because it affects nobody."

"All the same, I was always careful to say what was true," said John.

"Oh! I've no doubt," Robin stirred his coffee furiously, "all sorts of little pinpricking, puking bits of candour that matter to nobody set against the wider truth of the situation the country's in. It's simply self-indulgence, all this John Hampdening about the place, and very dangerous self-indulgence at a time like this."

Gerald, dozing away into a blurred haze of the past, heard the phrase "the wider truth of the situation the country's in." The mist before him receded until it diminished into one clearly defined picture—Professor Stokesay, grey Shavian beard, heavy tweed suit, parrot on his shoulder, and all the rest of his eccentric's paraphernalia in the book-lined study of his old, rambling house in Highgate. . . .

"My dear Gerald," the professor said, "I know what I'm doing. Oh, don't think that I'm not grateful to you for speaking the truth to me as you see it. It's the proper function of distinguished ex-pupils. Without it, there's always the danger that the old and, perhaps I may say, the eminent, can get cut off from life and life's criticisms. But, in this case, I think perhaps the boot's rather on the other foot."

He shuffled across the great room, dragging his thin, tweed-clad legs as he had done ever since the slight stroke he had suffered in 1936. He brought a decanter of sherry and a small silver box of charcoal biscuits. "I don't know whether you take these, Gerald? They're said to be good for constipation. I find them good certainly. The bowels are very important, you know, when you get as old as I am. Yes, but that's not the point. In a sense, my dear boy—and I mean this as no *criticism* of you, you've stuck to your scholarship and done excellent things—but, in a sense, I've been closer to life than a lot of you younger fellows. In touch with people of responsibility, you know, which forces one to modify one's attitude a certain amount. That's why I took the line I did with those young lecturers who wrote that absurd letter about Non-Intervention."

Gerald laughed. "But that's exactly why I am so anxious that you shouldn't be party to the Dresden conference," he said. "You know as well as I do that it's a Nazi government stunt. There's no real historical work of value being done over there. It seems to me terrible that a man of your eminence should lend himself to what is pure propaganda."

"Ah! Now look here, Gerald," said the old man, and he bent down to allow his famous green parrot to hop on to his shoulder. "It's true that there's a lot of nonsense being talked in Germany—all this *Rassenkunde* and so on—but it won't help if reputable historians in other countries cut themselves off. Will it, Joey?" he asked the parrot. "I sometimes wonder how much that bird *does* know, Gerald," he added. "As a matter of fact, I'm not telling everyone, but the Government has particularly asked me to go to Dresden. No, no, to 'opt out' "—he repeated the phrase, as though it was peculiarly realistic—"to 'opt out' " at this critical moment would be quite indefensible. Of course you see, my dear Gerald, it's impossible for an outsider to judge of these things. I don't mean that offensively, but when I read the nonsense in the *News Chronicle* and some of these papers about a man like Simon,

for example. . . . It's been the greatest privilege to me knowing
Simon. People say 'a legal mind' as though that was a criticism. They forget the extraordinary experience of life, of men
and women, that a brilliant mind like that gets in the courts.
No, the P.M. wants me to go to Dresden and I must go."

"I see," said Gerald. "There's nothing I can say then."

"My dear boy, I take it as the greatest compliment that
you've said what you have. I wish you came here more often.
I hardly ever see you. I do hope it's nothing to do with Dollie.
Your relations with her, you know, shouldn't keep you away
from *me*. We've worked a long time together and it does me
good to see you. You were Gilbert's friend and that's the most
important thing I can say of anyone."

Gerald felt sure that Professor Stokesay no longer really
cared to see any of his academic colleagues, and, indeed, the
next moment the old man said, "Well, I don't want to hurry
you, but the motor-car's coming for me at four. You've no
idea of the busy life I lead. I've got to go and see Garvin now.
I've promised to do him a few articles on all this nonsense
about the *Entente Cordiale*. How these fellows like Churchill and
Duff Cooper manage to talk all that fiddle-faddle about Anglo-
French friendship, I don't know. Of course, only amateur
historians could do it. Well, a medievalist can tell them something about our love of the French, I hope," he chuckled.
"Shades of King Harry!" And suddenly, his quavering voice
was reciting, "Dishonour not your mothers, now attest that
those whom you call'd fathers did beget you." The tears
streamed from his red, rheumy old eyes. Then he wiped them
away with his handkerchief, and said, "But still, that's not the
point. It's a battle for *peace* we're waging now, and a very hard
battle. Don't think I can't appreciate what you feel, Gerald—
integrity of scholarship and so on. I don't at all like some of
the nonsense our friends in Germany call history nowadays
myself. But that sort of thing, one's distaste for this and that,
has all got to be set against the wider truth of the situation the
country's in."

The scene faded from Gerald's recollection in a haze of pathos and distaste. It had seemed the maundering end of a fine career. Two months later had come Munich, and, by the time the war broke out, Professor Stokesay had been paralysed by another stroke. He died in 1940, oblivious of the Battle of Britain overhead. But the rot had begun earlier, Gerald now decided, with a growing distaste for accuracy, a wider and wider canvas, a life of conferences and pious platitudes. Like one of his own heroes—Ramsay Macdonald—Lionel Stokesay had gone on and on and up and up. As though he was running away from reality. And as Stokesay's gas balloon had floated away into outer space, Gerald had found himself shrinking from his own high aspirations, refusing the wider implications of his own work, all out of distaste at the spectacle of such empty eminence. . . .

Gerald came out of his memories, disturbed to think that it was his elder son who had reiterated the old man's evasive hypocrisy. He was, if anything, more cut off from Robin than from his other two children, but with less hostility and more respect. It was Robin, after all, who had taken on the family business, on whom they all depended for their dividends. He leaned forward in his chair. "I don't imagine your grandfather would have agreed with you, Robin," he said.

The conversation stopped and they looked at him in surprise as though it were the armchair that had suddenly spoken.

"Agreed with what exactly, Father?" asked Robin.

"Something you said about wider truths," Gerald mumbled. He was embarrassed as he realized that the conversation had moved on as he had been day-dreaming.

"Oh!" said Robin, with a slight air of humouring the old. "Grandfather was a very patriotic businessman, you know."

"Yes," said Gerald, "but he never allowed the interests of individual human beings, of his workmen and so on, to be subordinated to more powerful interests."

Robin smiled. "I think that's hardly the point, Father. But in any case, that sort of patriarchal attitude was excellent enough when grandfather was in his prime, even in the 'twenties. If you number your employees in hundreds you can be a father to them. But it was getting the firm into an awful mess by the end of his time. And if the business suffers, the workpeople suffer too. No, no, that's not my sphere, that's the Union's job. And a fine job they do." He tried to put a special affection into his smile towards Gerald to efface the impression of his curt speech.

Gerald was about to reply, but he reflected that he had no right to speak about the 'business'. He had elected so many years ago for scholarship on solid dividends, it would ill become him now to criticize the source of his misspent independence. He made no further attempt to bridge the icy waste that lay between him and his family that evening, but gave himself up to the surging sea of memory, washed hither and thither by the chance currents of the conversation that flowed around him.

It was his son-in-law's voice that he heard now. That thin, precise, over-cultivated drawl that he so disliked associating with his beloved daughter. "Frankly," Donald was saying, the arrogance and bitterness, that were usually masked by shyness, apparent when he spoke, "I fail to understand why I should concern myself with the fates of Pelican *or* Cressett. I cannot find that the bureaucracy or the lower middle-classes have any particular call on my loyalty. If, of course, this country were what it professes to be—a Christian country with a Christian polity," Donald always used words like polity, "then these ethical considerations would be subsumed into a greater truth. Each Estate would have its own place and purpose. But as we've conveniently forgotten the ultimate purpose which makes *any* sense of man's being, I really must come down on Robin's side. We live in Leviathan; expediency and power must presumably be our guides. To try to cover all this over with John's sentimental, democratic sugar-coating seems to me peculiarly disreputable. It is perfectly clear that Mr Pelican may swallow as many Cressetts any day as he can conveniently keep in his pouch." He laughed a dry, prim laugh. "If your only truth is jungle law, then the greater must devour the lesser."

Robin laughed loudly. He accepted his brother-in-law as a clever man, a bit extravagant in his views, a bit absurd as a husband for darling Kay; but nevertheless a genuine, up-to-date intellectual, a fashionable piece that the family could afford to maintain. When less-informed business friends spoke to Robin of intellectuals as communists or pinks, he liked to quote Donald to show them how out of date their knowledge was. "All right, Donald," he said, "agreed it is a jungle, but I think you know that under any scheme of values, the lesser has to be sacrificed to the greater."

Once again his elder son's voice burst through Gerald's haze. Elusive shapes, blurred objects, scraps and ends of past talk swelled and merged and faded in his mind; and one image that he had driven to the edges of his consciousness filled his whole vision. Dollie Stokesay came down the stairs of the old house in Highgate, still slight and boyish, but dragging her tired, worn-out little body over the faded, hideous red Turkey staircarpet. She held a hot-water bottle in one hand, letting it bump against the banisters in listless depression as she descended. "I can't go out, Gerrie, but if you don't mind a scrap supper, we can have something here. It looks as though he's going to sleep," she added.

But to give her the lie came Professor Stokesay's voice, cracked and petulant, "Dollie," he called, "Dollie, you've forgotten my barley water."

"All right, Pater," she called back. In 1936, she still preserved with no self-consciousness much of the vocabulary of her youth.

"He never drinks it if it's there," she said, but without the smile that would once have accompanied such maternal statements about her father-in-law. "The doctor says he mustn't fidget on any account. So everything has to be just so. I'll be down in a minute."

"I'll wait," said Gerald.

"If you want to," she said, "but I'm hardly company for any-one nowadays. I go to bed very early, you know, I get so jolly tired." When she came down again, she was still dragging the hot-water bottle. "It was there, of course," she said, "all the time." She led the way into the dining-room. "Oh dear!" she said, surveying that mahogany wasteland, "it's only sand-wiches. I let cook and Staples out most evenings and they leave something cold, only I never know what it's going to be. I thought it would be tongue. I can boil you an egg in a jiffy, if you like."

"No," said Gerald, "and for God's sake, put that hot-water bottle down." It had become intolerable to him that she should be sunk in this frowsy, deadened domestic rôle. Her skirt and coat, he noticed, were grubby and creased, but it was the hot-water bottle with its fluffy pink cover that brought on his outburst of anger. "You're being a bloody fool," he said, "and a wilful fool at that. There's no earthly reason why you should live on scraps or appoint yourself inefficient nurse to the old man."

"Oh, yes, there is," she said, "he prefers me to a professional. It's important that he should have what he wants, Gerrie. The doctor says so."

"And the sandwiches?" he asked. "What are the servants for?"

"I don't like people about," she answered. "I only ask, you know, not to be fussed. I can go on quite easily as long as there's no fussing." She picked up a sandwich and began eating it where she stood. "Anyway," she said, " accounts are bound to be presented one day. And this is mine. I was jolly lucky to get credit for so long."

"Either that's just melodramatic nonsense," Gerald replied, "or you mean literally money. And if you do, you know per-fectly well that I've told you again and again that you have only to ask me."

"Thank you," said Dollie bitterly. "I suppose people who've always had a lot of money find it easy to talk like that.

I wish you didn't though, Gerrie, it doesn't fit into my idea of a gentleman. But then I'm awfully old-fashioned."

"Oh God!" Gerald cried. "Surely one thing our intimacy means is that we needn't consider stupid things like money. I owe you everything I have and more."

"I think," Dollie said, taking her second strong whisky, "that *that's* melodramatic nonsense. If you mean spiritual things, you haven't got much to owe to anyone, and, if you mean money, then you're simply saying you ought to have paid me off. Thank you. I'd rather get it from the old boy. At least I can give him this in return," and she picked up the hot-water bottle and waved it in Gerald's face.

Gerald seized it from her and threw it across the room. "I find it disgusting," he said, "that because we have ceased to be lovers, you should regard our relationship as at an end."

"Do you?" Dollie asked. With her third whisky her cheeks burned bright red, soon her speech would be slurred. "I had something to give you then, old thing. We look at life very differently. As I see it, when you haven't anything more to give a person, well, then you're on your ownio."

Gerald looked at her slim little figure, her soft grey eyes and wavy brown hair. He felt the strange mixture of jauntiness and clinging that was always so attractive to him; he was about to say something when the red, burning cheeks caught his eye and he remembered the endless scenes of the last years. " I wish in that case," he said, "that you would take a job. You're still young."

Dollie sat down in one of the huge, uncomfortable leather armchairs; she seemed lost in its depths. She began to cry. "Blast you," she said. "I was determined not to do this. Why the hell did you say it?" She looked at him. "I see. You don't want to think of your *own* age. Well, I'm sorry," she said, "but there it is. We're old. This is 1936, Gerrie. I'm forty-five. In any case, what sort of a job could I take? There's plenty of women looking for jobs who know how to do things. I was just taught to live on others. *And I have*," she added savagely.

Gerald was angry now. He resented her tears, "All right, throw it in my face," he said. "I've taken the best years of your life. Does it occur to you how boring these sort of scenes are?" He walked over to the fire and, turning his back on her, warmed his hands. "I'm sorry," he said, when he felt in control of himself. When he looked round, he was glad to see she was no longer weeping. She was instead squirting soda water into her fourth whisky. "It's just that this is all so squalid," he went on. "I can't bear to see you running round after a paralysed old man. Emptying bed-pans."

Dollie giggled. "Dance, dance, dance little lady, leave your troubles behind," she said. "You're impossibly romantic, old thing. You won't face anno domini, will you? In any case, I didn't ask you to come here." She got up rather unsteadily and came over to him. "The pater *is* absolutely hot stuff at his own game, isn't he?" she asked, looking up at him earnestly.

Gerald hesitated. "He's a very great historian," he said.

"All right then," Dollie replied. "I took his son from him. The one thing he cared for. I've taken his money, because he thought he owed a duty to Gilbert's widow. He saw me, Gerrie, as that most romantic thing on earth—a young war widow—the widow of the great Gilbert Stokesay, poet, who died for England. Have you ever heard the old boy recite 'In Flanders fields the poppies grow?' You should. And what did *I* do? I didn't even marry again. I lived with *you*, Gilbert's best friend, his own favourite pupil, a married man. But he's accepted me in his rather pompous way, poor pet, even when my own family have given me the go-by. And I spent his money. Oh, yes, lots of it, since I left you. You know how I run up bills, I've been betting a lot and losing. The old boy's never so much as grumbled. Oh! I'll give him that. He's always the great gentleman. And now he's stuck up there. He'll recover, but not for long. It's only a matter of time the doctor says before he has another stroke, and then he won't recover. You say he's a great historian. *I* didn't even keep the home fires burning. It's the least I can do, Gerald, to stick by him."

She broke off and suddenly leaned over, peering into his face. "Do you remember that scene we had with Inge at the Café Royal? Well, you're not likely to forget it. You said then something about your family life, your children and—me. I haven't forgotten *that*. You said, 'The lesser has to be sacrificed to the greater'. The lesser was me, and you were right."

She went out of the room, holding a little with one hand to the backs of the chairs, as she made her way, in order to retain her balance. In a moment she was back again with Gerald's hat and overcoat. "Look," she said, "it isn't any good, old thing. You take the high road and I'll take the low road."

They had met again, of course, but she had taken good care to see that she always got drunk on such occasions and, already before the war broke out, he had ceased to see her. . . .

Both Marie Hélène and Kay were intent on steering the conversation away from *l'affaire* Pelican; but, to John and Robin, it seemed one of the most potentially succulent of all the many bones over which they had snarled and snapped since boyhood. John's temper was hanging by a thread behind the humorous, bantering air which he more and more used in his days of celebrity when talking to old friends or to the family. He attributed all criticism from those who had known him before his success to envy; the fact that he had often been correct in this supposition was his strongest defence against self-doubt. Robin tried hard to assume the air of detached superiority which he knew from experience would break down his spoilt, younger brother's defences. Their mother, with more truth than she realized, regarded their quarrels as a sort of tribute to her.

"This is really wonderful," cried John, with extra hearty laughter, pushing back his curly hair with a carefree boyish gesture. "I wish our Communist friends were here to see it. It would warm their dear little Marxist hearts, which must always be a bit lonely on Christmas Day. What a partnership! Robin Middleton, the head of our greatest steel construction business, the champion of 'more free-enterprise houses for all', and

Selwyn Pelican, one of our top red-tape manufacturers, the champion of that rousing slogan, 'Every brick laid means a civil servant paid'. With their combined pull on the noose, who dares to say old England won't be hanged? It's Merdle and the Barnacles all over again, and, by God, we need another Dickens to blow them off the face of the country." John, watching the growing distaste on Donald's and Robin's faces, pitched the vulgar note the more loudly.

"Really, John, That's libellous!" Kay took up a teasing note. "Merdle was a wholesale swindler. We don't want Middleton v. Middleton in the courts." She realized too late that it was not altogether a tactful joke.

Robin's heavy form was sprawled in his armchair. His smooth, well-manicured hand rubbed his fleshy face to conceal his impatience to attack his brother. "My dear Kay," he drawled, "there's nothing John would like better than a family law-suit. A nice bit of sentimental Galsworthian social drama. Think of the publicity!" He chuckled. "I see our dear Johnnie dressed as Robin Hood, doing a Douglas Fairbanks leap across the court benches, defending the rights of the Common Man."

Kay tried to make up for her unfortunate attempt at humour. "I think he could still leap with a little more agility than you, Robin," she said. She felt herself young again, bringing a schoolgirl sense of fair play to her brothers' quarrels. "Well, anyway, John, if it's Dickens that's needed, that's easy." She smiled at her younger brother. "I do wish you hadn't stopped writing, my dear," she said.

Robin smiled. "I believe John feels himself somewhat out of sympathy with the world of literature nowadays. The young tread unpleasantly fast upon our heels, you know. The fashions have changed since Johnnie's *jeux d'esprit* hit the highbrows in that dawn of freedom 1945! I believe the taste for proletarian vignettes has gone out, hasn't it, Donald?"

Before her son-in-law could affirm the statement, Ingeborg had come to her favourite son's defence. "Now, Robin my dear," she said, "you don't understand anything at all about Johnnie. He is very good friends with young people." She smoothed the skirt of her silk evening dress. Above its harsh violet, her pink face and flaxen-streaked hair clashed fiercely. She shook her large head complacently. "I *know*!" she added.

"Oh, I've no doubt, Mother," Robin said, his eyes glinting angrily. "John's famous gift for bridging social gulfs is not unsung, you know."

Ingeborg turned away from her elder son and put her hand on John's shoulder, "Dear Johnnie," she said.

John moved his shoulder abruptly; whatever depth of understanding his mother's gesture implied, he felt it to be out of place. He was glad that Robin had stepped over the border of personal privacy around which they had been skirting the whole evening. If secret citadels were to be attacked, so then should "open towns". He leaned his head back against the chair and gave way to frank laughter. "Oh, my dear Robin!" he cried, "you shouldn't believe everything that *Elvira* tells you about the great world of art. She's so busy keeping up with the old *avant-garde* that she hasn't time to notice the new writers growing up in front of her eyes." Then leaning towards his brother, he said deliberately, "She's incurably romantic, of course. The *avant-garde*'s a lost cause and that's enough for her. It's thwarted maternalism really. She'll be all right when she finds some starving genius of her own age to mend socks for."

It was the flush that came to her husband's face that brought a responding flush to Marie Hélène's sallow neck. At least, she thought, he might have had the power to control his feelings before his wretched family. She turned to John, and looking down her long nose at him, she said, "*I* should not be afraid to meet John in the law courts. I am sure that we should win." Her imagination had been playing with the idea with relish ever since it had been mooted. It was an unfortunate ground to choose.

John laughed loudly. "I'm sure you would, Marie Hélène," he said, "after the way you trounced your aunt. Poor Madame Houdet! She only had her tragic circumstances to speak for her."

"The law is concerned with the truth," said Marie Hélène. She turned her wrist in a contemptuous gesture so that her emerald bracelet glittered. In that gesture, John thought, one knows the picture she carries of herself. He looked at her yellow arms and heavy green silk dress with disgust. She revived for a moment the long-since faded earnestness of his youthful dislike of the bourgeois way of life. French bourgeoise snob! "Oh, of course," he said, "I suppose the wretched woman thought that two years in Auschwitz and the loss of all her possessions were truth enough."

"Really!" Donald's prim voice was shocked out of its drawl. "Are we to be spared no sentimentality, John, even the exploded realist nonsense that unhappiness is somehow truer than happiness, or that . . ."

Whatever he would have said further was drowned in Ingeborg's enthusiastic voice. She had not followed the conversation very well, but she sensed that a deflection of the conversation would assist John. "Bravo, Donald!" she cried. "I am so glad at last that someone says so. Of course that is so. Happiness is truth. It is only when we are really happy that we know what is true."

Gerald shook himself uneasily. Old age, he reflected, seemed to have every disadvantage. It cut one off; but it also let in what had long been carefully censored. He had trained himself for years not to hear the embarrassing nonsense that Inge talked, and now it cut through his enfeebled defences. "It is only when we are *really* happy that we know what is true." Inge's sugary words, her glottal Scandinavian sing-song, flowed back through his memories until they had covered with their sticky coating one of the episodes he kept apart as sacrosanct. . . .

He was standing at the door of the hotel bedroom, looking back at the disordered bed on which lay the tray with its empty jugs and crumblings of croissants. The traces of butter were liquid now in the intense heat that stifled the room even at seven in the morning. He had been Dollie's lover for four years, but he still left any bedroom they shared with obvious reluctance. Dollie enjoyed their love-making as much as he did; but every episode in its place for her. She had always been greedy for the minutes as they came, but, since she had accepted disreputability, she devoured time.

"It's after seven, Gerrie," she said. "We must get going." She accepted foreign travel only if certain English disciplines were maintained. The "early start" was first among them. Once she was assured of these obvious symbols of continuity, she could give herself entirely to the moment. She was too much in control of herself to fall into the little superstitions and obsessive acts that had replaced religion for many of her generation and set, but certain conventions had become sacrosanct in her life. Without their fulfilment, she lost momentum.

A letter awaited them at the little hotel reception desk. Dollie opened it. "Mrs Salad," she said. "Her writing *is* odd. Everything's going swimmingly at Fitzroy Square."

"What does she say?" asked Gerald.

"You read it, darling, if you want to," she answered, and gave him the letter.

"She's been taken to 'Mr. Cinders'," he said, "but it wasn't like the old shows."

Dollie laughed. "Read it to yourself, darling," she said, and when, surprised, he asked, "Surely you want to hear what Mrs Salad has to say?" she said, "Not really, Gerrie, everything in its place."

"I don't believe Mrs Salad would be out of place anywhere," he laughed, "even in Avignon. She'd have found some way of ministering to the pleasures of the exiled popes."

Dollie did not answer directly, but as she drove the little Wolseley Hornet over the bridge to Villeneuve she looked at him with a frown. They sped past the great stone walls that still guarded the ruins and she said, "I want to go up there again."

"All right," Gerald answered, "We can go on our way back."

"*You* don't need to come, darling," she said. "You've got it all in your head. That's why Mrs Salad and things don't put the wind up you. But I need so many goes to make me feel I've really been to a place."

Gerald once more looked at her with surprise. "You know that we needn't go back for at least a month, if you'd rather not," he told her, but she shook her head. "Oh, no, it'll be quite jolly to be back once we're there," she said.

They lunched at Aigues Mortes in a little restaurant in the central square looking across at the statue of Frédéric Mistral so pitifully declaring the nineteenth century's certainty of its taste. But before luncheon, while Gerald drank his vermouth, she had insisted on walking the ramparts despite the grilling noon heat. He caught sudden glimpses of her pale-green linen dress from moment to moment and imagined her there intent on every object—a lizard, and salt pans in the distance, a Romanesque tower, some old men playing bowls. She would listen when he talked of the historical meaning of what they saw, would even ask questions, but he knew that, if she remembered anything of what he said, she kept it quite apart from what she saw. Her pleasure was direct and sensual. It was part of the atmosphere of concreteness, of certainty which she built around him. There were moments of odd, childish questioning, as this morning, but they were gone very quickly. Mostly she was just there, silent and happy. After the constant rambling of Stokesay, the eager enthusiasm of Rose Lorimer, above all, after the crescendoing whimsy with which Inge so consciously greeted each "wonderful, natural" stage in the children's growth, Gerald found his energies and confidence depleted. His interpretation of Dollie's silence as affirmation of life brought him new vigour. Without her, he would never have gone beyond cautious articles, lectures only less cautious because he could believe them to be ephemeral. She had given him the assurance needed to generalize his knowledge, to sustain the scope of his long work on Cnut. She allowed him time to find words for his thoughts, and without words he lived in a blur of distrust.

After luncheon, as they sat at a café table over coffee and cognac, the unpleasant little Englishman whom they had noticed during the meal came over to them. "Well," he said, "Snowden's had to eat his words and *we've* got to pack up and go home. I hope to God they get rid of the whole lot of them," he said. "I suppose Ramsay Mac's all right. He's had the courage to own he was wrong, at any rate. As for the rest, the sooner they go back to the board-school teaching or mining or whatever the damned thing was they were doing, the better for the country."

"Baldwin," he assured them, "will pull us through. He's a cautious old bird, but as wise as they make 'em. Just what we need. 'You can't be too careful', that's got to be England's motto. Cheerio," he said, "see you in Angleterre."

It was thus that they learned of England's going off the gold standard. Gerald, knowing Dollie's simple jingo responses to any national event—responses that had become more immediate, more violent, since she had become a "bad woman" in the eyes of her family—decided to forestall her reactions. "I'll get a paper," he said, and then, scanning *Le Temps*, he worked out exchange rates on the back of an envelope.

She sat staring across the Square with that expression he called "her forehand-drive look". She kept it, he told her, for tennis and the National Anthem. They treated her being an ex-tennis champion as one of the private jokes that oiled the machinery of their life together, and she helped in this on occasion by parodying the rôle. Nevertheless, the joke on his side was in some part defensive; he feared the "Stock Character" side of her, that it might engulf the individual person on whom he depended, and he avoided as far as he could the conventional responses she made to events she did not comprehend.

In such a situation, he spoke as now, hurriedly, forestalling her possible comments. "We've just enough to get back," he said, "and for a good dinner in Paris."

She sat smoking her cigarette for a moment and drank some of her cognac; she had never lost a manner of "being rather fast" in her smoking and drinking, although both tastes were habitual to her. "Do you honestly think we have to, Gerrie?" she asked. "I can't see what earthly use it would be to anyone for me to be back at the flat, or you, for that matter. I mean it's not like the General Strike, is it?"

Slowly he explained the financial crisis to her in very simple terms, emphasizing the plain patriotic line to which she would respond.

"Yes, I see," she said. "It's pretty serious, isn't it? But then so's this holiday to you. Thinking out this new book and so on. And it is to me, too," she added, "very important. Couldn't you wire for some money?" she asked.

"I *could*," Gerald answered.

"Well then, go ahead, old dear," she replied, "only do ask for enough to make a *good* holiday. I mean it seems so difficult, darling, to know what's enough, doesn't it, with all this pound-falling business. It's better to be on the safe side."

It was partly stupidity of course, as he knew, but not altogether, and he thought of the complaining, moralizing self-denial with which Inge would have greeted the situation—or else she would have made a terrible whimsical game of the economies needed to get home. "Are you sure?" he asked.

Dollie did not answer the question. "Pay for the drinks and let's move," she said. "I'm not going to let you off going round the wall. The view's quite stunning."

For twenty minutes or more, they leaned on the wall parapet, staring out southwards across the salt marshes and on to the Camargue.

"I've tried," she said suddenly, "but it doesn't work. The guide-book says it was a port and the Crusaders set off from here and I know what Crusaders looked like, I've seen them in books and churches, so I ought to be able to imagine it, but I can't. It isn't a port now, it's flat marshy land. Perhaps it was that heron flying by that distracted me. I like it, though." When Gerald did not answer, she said, "I suppose you can imagine Crusaders."

"I expect I could if I tried, but I was thinking."

"Oh, not about the Confessor, so far from Hastings!" She could never separate the Confessor from the Conqueror.

"No," said Gerald, "one of those things that seem so important and end up as platitudes. I was remembering the few times that I've been really happy like this and feeling that they were so much more intense than the rest of life that perhaps they were on a different plane of reality. I was wondering if it was only when we were really happy that we knew what was true. A nice bit of cosy egotism, I suppose."

"It does seem a bit goody-goody," Dollie said, "like those horrid little limp suede books Mother used to put by the spare-room bed for visitors. Full of great thoughts." She pressed her finger slowly against his temple, running down to his chin, feeling the outline of his cheekbone. "I'm very happy too, dear, you know," she said.

The shops in the Square were open once more when they came down into the town. They bought postcards. Dollie found one with a feather skirt which you could blow. "All the same," she said, when she had blown it three or four times, "it is a bit pathetic. And a bit foul," she added. It was clear that she felt it; then she laughed and blew it again.

"Do you think Kay would like this?" Gerald asked, picking up a cicada brooch. "It's very unattractive. But the taste of sixteen! You would know, Dollie, you were a girl once." She did not answer. "All right then," said Gerald, "girls have better taste than boys. They're born with aesthetic discrimination. *You* choose something for her."

Dollie raised her eyes from the tray of postcards. "No," she said, "I'd rather not," and she went on absurdly blowing at the feather skirt.

"Well, *I* think a cicada brooch. You know what, Dollie! Some of this awful folky stuff would just suit Inge. What do you think—an Arlesian doll or a quotation from Mistral in poker-work?" and when she did not answer, he said again, "which do you think, darling?"

"I haven't the foggiest idea," she said violently, and threw the feathered postcard back into the tray.

It was impossible for Gerald to interpret the silence she maintained on the drive to Arles as life-affirming. She could lose her temper on occasion at tennis or at bridge, but it was a momentary flare-up with inept partners; this was something more. He suggested that they left sightseeing in Arles for a cooler day, a day when they were less tired, any other day that she chose. Her answer was to drive to the Arena, and, without bothering to take her box camera out of the car, she made a complete circuit of the stadium with him in silence. He was not spared the ruins of the theatre or the traipse across the river and down the long avenue to the Christian tombs. Finally, the storm broke on the roof of the cloister of Saint Trofime.

"It's no good telling me about columns and carving, Gerrie," Dollie said, "I don't know Roman from Romanesque and I never will. Oh! I know you don't care, but perhaps half the trouble is that you like to pretend I'm not a fool."

"Not knowing the styles of architecture isn't my criterion for judging fools," said Gerald. "In any case, *what* trouble? I shan't say that I thought we were so happy, because you obviously aren't. But I will remind you that you said *you* were."

He was suddenly angry with her, but she was unaffected by his mood. "I shouldn't take that line if I were you, Gerrie. You pretty near got your marching orders this afternoon. No!" she said, "I mean it. But I care for you too much and it isn't as if you were to blame really. I shouldn't have agreed to it."

"Agreed to what?" asked Gerald.

"To your keeping on with Inge," she said. "I should have insisted on your getting a divorce. Even the silliest little shopgirl has the sense to try to get an honest woman made of herself."

Gerald put his hand on hers; she did not return the pressure but she did not move her hand away. "We had a very difficult decision to make," he said. "Perhaps we were wrong. If so, I'm very sorry. But we had the children to think of. And, after all, Inge behaved very decently."

"I don't know anything about Inge. I don't want to hear about her. Neither your complaints nor your praises. How do I know what's gone on between you? The rights and the wrongs of it. I don't want to know."

She walked away from him and began to descend the wooden stairs to the cloister below. She was talking now over her shoulder, disregarding the other tourists. "One thing—there's to be no more present-giving. I'm not going to choose all those damned presents for your family. Oh! I know you're not to blame. I should never have accepted the situation. With Inge ringing me up, 'I knew it must be *your* choice, Dollie, Gerald would never have thought of anything so charming', and 'the children looking forward to Auntie Dollie's gifts'. It's disgusting, Gerrie, that's what it is."

"Aren't you making rather a moral mountain of it all of a sudden?" he asked.

"Yes. That's true. It's nothing to do with morals, of course," Dollie said, "I'm past all that or superior to it or whatever you like. Anyway, right and wrong and so on never meant much to me and they don't touch me at all now. I'm sorry. I was dramatizing. It's just that so much of it has gone rotten on me, Gerrie. And Fitzroy Square and the good times together, dancing at Ciro's and Mrs Salad don't quite make up for that. I know it when I'm away from England and I know it's not going to get better. It'll get worse. It's all right for you. It's all one piece for you. That's why you're perfectly happy reading Mrs Salad's letter here and so on. Well, I can't. I can't give you up either and I don't want to. But I'm not being sweet Auntie to your family any more. No fear. It hasn't done any good. You're as much a stranger to the children as if you'd made the break. You say so yourself. And if that's how they feel about you, what do you really suppose they think of sweet Auntie Dollie? What does Inge make sure that they think? No, I've no right to say that. It's not her fault, it's ours."

As they passed down the steps of the church into the broad square, she looked backed at the carved tympanum. "Is that a Last Judgment?" she asked. "It usually is. Well, that's when I'll judge Inge and I don't want to hear any more about her until then. Oh! don't worry. I know I've got to see them and I'll behave myself, but, for the rest, you've got to keep them out of my life."

That evening in their hotel at Avignon, she drank too much and apologized again and again in a maudlin way and was very amorous. Their relationship dragged on like that for the next three years. . . .

Robin was telling a story now. "I'll give you this one for your column, John," he said, "because if you use it everybody who's ever had to do any serious business will laugh at you. I'm telling you because it's time you knew what life was like, what real moral decision means. We have a supplier," he said, "of small parts. He wasn't very important before we took on prefabrication, but he is now. A funny little man, probably churchwarden of the local church—it's a South-West suburb. He only produces in a small way, but he was an old business client of grandfather's. Father probably knew him. Do you remember Grimston, Father?" he asked, "a fuzzy, sandy-haired little man?"

Gerald made no answer.

Robin laughed. "He's asleep. Well, this chap can't produce on the scale we need, he's slow and unreliable but he's got an old-established name. We've offered him everything to buy the goodwill, a first-rate price for the business, even retirement with a good holding of Middleton shares—he couldn't possibly get them on the market. But he's an obstinate old fool; he insisted on holding out, partly from sentiment, partly from conceit. So we've busted him. We got him flooded with so many orders from important firms that he hadn't a chance of fulfilling them. I know just what you'll say about that, John, but in the next breath you'll say people must have their houses quickly. All right, what's your choice?"

He leaned back in his chair and smiled with satisfaction—he had made a confession of an action that troubled his conscience and spiked John's guns at the same time.

John smiled. "You speak as though I accepted your premises," he said. "You probably think that everyone does. I'm all in favour of removing these moral burdens from your conscience. Nationalize you. That's the answer. And when you've done that, watch the national planners—our good friend Pelican and so on—like hell to see that they don't become the same dyspeptic, conscience-racked tyrants as you and your private-enterprise colleagues." He raised his voice and smiled a little as though to a radio audience. He even underlined the naïve, self-satisfied tone of his voice to annoy Robin more. "After all," he said, "it's simply a matter of checks, isn't it? The individual conscience is an imperfect machine at the best and needs checking."

Donald smiled. "I'm glad at least to hear that the Left recognizes human imperfectibility," he said. "I've always imagined that they thought we were living in a state of grace. I must confess, however, that I'm still on Robin's side."

Robin caught Marie Hélène's eye. How right he was to have offered Donald this new job! It just showed Mother's extraordinary powers of judgment. Who but she would have thought of that solution to Kay's worries?

"You see, John," Donald went on, "in a land where centuries of Protestantism have broken down any satisfactory guidance for human frailty, I would prefer to trust myself to the decency and judgment of the educated individual than to be at the whim of the mass hysteria which you call a democratic check. I'm afraid, Robin, though," and he turned to his elder brother-in-law with a prim smile, "that some of us have a more satisfactory guide than our poor, troubled personal conscience, haven't we, Marie Hélène?"

His sister-in-law did not return his smile. She was always embarrassed at Donald's attempts at alliance. Anglo-Catholics were certainly not real Catholics, and that was that. So she said rather vaguely, "I think that anyone who is born a Catholic is bound to find all this rather difficult to understand."

Robin saw that his mother was about to spring at the rearing of Rome's ugly head, so he turned the conversation. "One of the worst will-o'-the-wisps you dogmatic Utopians pursue," he said to John, "is the idea of human consistency. No human being can hope to be consistent."

Kay was up in arms at once; her round, unmade-up face shone with high-minded, intellectual disapproval. "Oh! I don't agree at all there, Robin," she cried. "At least not for bringing up children. No woman could, I'm sure. The one thing that matters with children *is* to be consistent. It's the only kind of truth you can give them. That's where Mummy was so wonderful," she added, and patted Ingeborg's hand.

Gerald felt a little shiver of distaste, but the emotion was now so worn out it hardly touched his brooding introspection. Kay's thankless affection for Inge was the only pill in the over-stocked family medicine-chest that he still found bitter, but with the years you can accustom yourself to swallow anything. Two gulps now and he'd forgotten it. All the same, he reflected, the consistency which was one of Inge's chief prides was a somewhat doubtful legend. He wasn't prepared to give it more credence than—than, say, the Melpham burial. He rejected the simile with annoyance. It was becoming a King Charles's head. More profitable, he decided, to pursue the problem of Inge's consistency, since it seemed that the past was relentless tonight with his exhausted mind. . . .

"The one thing that matters, Gerald, with the children," said Inge, "is to be consistent. We want their little bodies to grow straight and fine like the birch trees on the mountains.

But that is not so difficult. They are good strong little animals without blemishes." Gerald wondered if she really succeeded in forgetting Kay's hand. "But it is more difficult with their little minds, their thoughts, their feelings. For these to grow straight and strong, there must be trust. And how can there be such if we tell lies?"

"That's all very well in theory," Gerald answered, "but it won't be so easy in practice."

"Is the theory good?" Inge confronted him with it. The shingle, which fashion had forced upon her corn-coloured glory, removed the majesty from her; with her giant height and ample bosom it made her oddly like a guardsman *en travestie*.

"Yes," said Gerald, "as you've put it, in the void, of course it is," and he laughed.

"Never mind about voids," Inge declared. "The theory is good. Very well. We must also make the practice good."

"Which means, I suppose, that three small children should be told that their father has a mistress and that because their mother tells them so they must love their father's mistress and pray for her at night."

"Now Gerald," said Inge, "you know very well that the children do not pray at night. 'If you do something *good*, then you are making a prayer', I tell them."

"Well, then they will be busy doing good deeds to Dollie because we want it that way." After eleven years of marriage, he met her theories and wishes with a touch of mockery: it absolved him, he felt, from full responsibility when, as was always the case, he acceded to them.

"Oh, Gerald," Inge laughed at his strange incomprehension. "How little you know your own children. They are not little slaves. If they make good deeds, it's because they are good children. Even poor little Kay. She is so much better, Gerald, now. She does not try to fight against love and life so much. You know I even believe her little hand is better."

"I doubt if medical opinion would support you there, my dear Inge."

"Medical opinion. Pouf!" Inge literally blew it away. "And so that is settled. No more of this nonsense that Dollie should not go to Kew with you just because I am taking the children there. You will tell her please to bring some stale buns. Johnnie is not happy unless he can feed the geese. I told him that they are not nice birds, that they have bad tempers and beaks that snap. 'No, Thingy, you are wrong', he told me, 'they are the good birds that saved the Capitol'. He is clever, Gerald, you know, and his little heart is so big. I think he will be a man to help humanity like Father. But he has a little will of his own, too, like me, Gerald. The other day when you were at Fitzroy Square, he asked, 'Where is Daddy?' 'He has gone to stay with Auntie Dollie', I told him. '*I* want to stay with Auntie Dollie.' You will tell Dollie this, please, Gerald."

From the broad street of Queen's Gate the sounds of "Lady be Good" came floating through the summer heat into the spacious drawing-room. Execrable it sounded on saxophone and banjo. "I'm just a babe that's lost in the wood, lady be good to me." Gerald's face twitched with repulsion and he went across to close the french window.

"Oh, no," cried Inge. "Those are the poor unemployed men. That is bad, Gerald, to try to shut them out, because they are forgotten. You cannot so easily avoid unpleasant things. You must pay for living in the past with the Vikings," she said with a smile suitable for a naughty child. "Give them a shilling, my dear." She followed her husband on to the balcony. "Oh, they are my friends," she cried excitedly. "That is the little Welshman I told you about, Gerald, who has the boy like Johnnie. Wait!" she called into the street, "wait! I come to talk to you."

Gerald saw the one man wink at the other. Such things happened too often with Inge as she got older for him to feel much about it. He tried to remind himself of what she was.

When they returned into the drawing-room, Gerald laid his hand on his wife's arm. "Give me a moment, please, Inge," he said. "*I* was shutting the windows because *you* were trying to avoid unpleasant things. It's no good, my dear, you don't see what you're involving yourself with. I repeat what are the children going to say when they're asked to love their father's mistress?"

"Gerald, really! What sort of minds do you think these little ones have. Robin is ten. Do you think he is interested in mistresses?" Inge flung out her arm as though in appeal to a greater audience than her husband—perhaps, to humanity.

"You know very well I don't mean now," said Gerald. "But in six or seven years' time, what then?"

"Then they will have good, wholesome minds. They will not think that the acts of the body are bad. What sort of children do you think I am bringing up? Listen, Gerald, shall I tell you what I shall say to them? I shall say, 'When *din lille mor* married your papa, they made *you*. Now that was a beautiful thing was it not, children, to make little seeds into three fine, strong bodies? Well that was because your papa and I loved each other so much, that we did not want to be two bodies, but just one body. But this kind of physical love does not last', I shall say. 'Some people, especially women, I think, do not need this love of the body after they are no longer young. But men do. You must always remember that, little Kay.' I shall say. 'And so it was with your papa. And *I*, what do *I* think, children?' I shall say. '*I* think it is natural, as natural as it is that one day you will find somebody whose body you will wish to look at and to touch. For *you* will grow and marry and leave me. Great big Robin and little Kay, and yes, even, perhaps, little Johnnie. Your papa's love for Aunt Dollie is as natural as that will be. And if it is natural it must be beautiful'."

"Or ugly." Gerald turned on her savagely. "Why don't you say what you mean?"

Inge's large blue eyes grew round with fright. "But I don't think it ugly, Gerald," she cried.

In face of her panic Gerald always capitulated. If anyone was responsible for her view of sex it was surely her husband.

He turned away. "You'd better not keep your unemployed friends waiting," he said.

"Oh, the poor men, I must get them beer. They will like beer," and Inge hurried from the room. She called upstairs to the nursery, "We shall see Papa and Auntie Dollie at Kew, won't that be nice?" and then, putting her head round the drawing-room door, "And no nonsense, please, Gerald, about coming back here tonight. I shall tell the children you have gone to stay with Aunt Dollie. Little Johnnie will be quite envious."

Gerald took up the telephone and dialled the Fitzroy Square number. "Look, darling," he said, "Inge insists that we keep to our plan of going to Kew. No, really, she means it. Oh and will you bring some stale buns—no, no, she said buns, for John to give to the geese. No, I shall be coming back to the flat. I don't know. As long as you like. There's no reason to keep me *here*."

The unemployed were giving Inge a tune for herself. "Make my bed and light the light, I'll be coming home tonight. Bye-bye, blackbird."

So much, thought Gerald, for 1928. And so it had gone on for four years. Freudians would probably have imputed some exceedingly unpleasant suppressed motives to Inge's behaviour. For himself, he found it easier to believe that her actions were those of a spoilt girl who had turned into a woman who was slightly cracked. It was better, of course, to remind oneself that if she had been a smaller woman, if her English had been less comic, all this whimsy and theatricality would not have appeared so ludicrous. She would simply have been thought an impulsive, lively little foreigner, at the worst, a good-hearted eccentric. But for a giraffe or an elephant to behave in that way would just do in a Walt Disney cartoon; in daily life it meant a complete separation from reality. She was, in fact, unbalanced. Mentally and emotionally unbalanced he had decided in those years to consider his wife, which was probably the same as what the Freudians would have said. In either case, what could one do about it? In fact, he had done nothing except to get used to it, forget it and live entirely in his life with Dollie. But Dollie's outburst in Provence had taught him that *she*, at any rate, could not get used to it. On their return, he had done everything he could to keep Inge and the children out of his life with Dollie. It had not been easy, but, at least, with Mrs Salad's aid, he had prevented Inge's little visits of friendship to the Fitzroy Square flat.

Inge seemed far more jealous of Mrs Salad than she did of Dollie. "She is so dirty and sly, Gerald," she would say. "But nobody else I suppose would understand poor Dollie's crazy housekeeping."

Mrs Salad, in return, resented Inge's existence in the sentimental idyll she had built around her sinning love-birds. "I know you won't mind my saying so, dear," she had said one day after a visit from Inge, "but that's not just 'cos she's foreign that Mrs Middleton has that very coarse 'air."

"But my wife's hair's admired by everyone, Mrs Salad. It's such a wonderful colour."

"Bright in colour, perhaps," she said, "but very coarse to the touch, I should think. What sort of people would 'ers have been now?"

"Her father was a Labour member of the Danish Parliament, Mrs Salad."

"Ah!" she said, "I thought it wasn't just foreign. That's very common 'air if you'll excuse my saying so." Mrs Salad was a great snob.

Dollie, too, with her increasing tippling, showed her possessiveness of him more openly. She was only just polite to Inge. In the end, however, it was neither Mrs Salad nor Dollie nor he who made the complete break, it was Inge herself. For the children's sake. And at the Café Royal. . . .

The children were now happily settled on the long red velvet sofa. "And so Robin is a big man now and he chooses smoked salmon," said Ingeborg. "Do you think you will like that? It is only red fish, you know, with lemon." But when

Robin solemnly reasserted his choice, she said to the waiter with mock seriousness, "The gentleman wants a good portion of smoked salmon."

"What about you, Kay?" asked Gerald.

Kay, in her disfiguring chamber-pot velour school hat, wriggled nervously. "I don't know, Daddy," she said.

"Little Kay will have *hors d'œuvre*," said Inge, "it is the same as our favourite *smaabrod*, you know. But not so good, perhaps," she laughed. "You will have your dear *smaabrod*, won't you, Johnnie?"

John looked primly down the menu, "I don't see the sense of having it if it's not so good," he said. "I will have plover's eggs."

"Oh you won't eat the little bird's eggs!" cried Inge.

"He'd better eat them while he can," said Gerald, "they're being prohibited after this year."

"And I should like *sole mornay* to follow," added John.

"I shan't have fish," Robin said, with the importance of the eldest child, "I will have a steak."

"And what will you have, Kay, it's your birthday. You choose what you like." Gerald looked at his leggy daughter with affection. But Kay looked at her mother.

"What shall I have, Mummy?" she asked.

"Oh! you must not ask me. Ask Papa, who is giving this lovely birthday to a lucky little girl."

Kay looked at her father obediently. It annoyed Gerald that she apparently had no views of her own, after all she was thirteen, but he guessed the agony this spotlight was causing her and thought it better to order for her. "Lobster Thermidor," he said to the waiter. "There you are, madam," he said, hating himself for the facetiousness which he could not avoid with his children "the lobster is being boiled at your command." Kay became very red in the face.

"Oh! Gerald, my dear, what have you said?" cried Inge.

"She will never eat it now. Poor little Kay! You don't want the lobster to be cooked for you, do you, dear?" Then she whispered fussily to the waiter. "I've ordered her some fried sole," she told Gerald.

"Kay's turned red instead of the lobster," Robin declared with glee.

"Shut up," said Gerald.

"Poor Robin!" cried Inge, "you were only teasing, weren't you? You mustn't tease your sister on her birthday, you know. But even so, Kay, *you* mustn't cry just because your brother makes a joke," she added to her daughter, who was now in tears.

John was waving across the room and smiling with all the charm he already put over at twelve years old. "There's Auntie Dollie," he cried. "Why doesn't she come over?"

Gerald's heart sank; any other interruption but this would have been heaven-sent. "I expect she is dining with someone else," he said, without looking round.

"She isn't dining," John replied. "She's sitting at one of those long marble-topped tables, drinking. All by herself," he added precisely. "She's talking to herself," he said. "She oughtn't to do that, ought she, Thingy? People will think she's potty."

"The French mistress in the form I was in last term talks to herself," Kay announced. "We all laugh at her." Gerald shot her a look of gratitude for the child's tact in changing the conversation; but it was clear that it was a childish rather than a tactful remark, for she added, "Let's all laugh at Auntie Dollie."

"Good idea!" cried John. They both laughed loudly, "Ha! Ha! Ha!"

"Now that is very unkind to laugh at people," said Inge. "Auntie Dollie will come over when we have finished our dinner."

"It's very bad manners to laugh out loud in restaurants," Robin announced. "I suppose this *is* rather a good restaurant," he said conversationally to his father.

Once again Gerald heralded the tact that goes with fifteen years. "Yes," he said. "It used to be very famous when your grandfather was young. All sort of writers and actors and people came here. But it's still pretty good."

"I thought so," said Robin. "Harkness said his people wouldn't come here because it wasn't good enough. Not that that shows anything. I don't think they're as rich as we are, and anyway his father has to work for *their* money." His curiosity satisfied, he sat back.

"And what do you think *your* father does?" asked Inge in shocked tones.

"He lectures in medieval history," Robin answered by rote, "but we don't get much of our money from that. We live on unearned income," he announced proudly.

"That is no reason to be proud." Inge was deeply shocked now. "We hope Robin that you will go into the business with grandfather and then all the money we have will be earned."

"*You* wouldn't be earning it just because Robin was working," said John loudly.

Inge ruffled his hair. "Be careful the trolls don't take that quick little tongue of yours."

Gerald hoped for a moment that John was going to put his tongue out at his mother, but he only put his hand in hers. "Is my tongue *very* quick?" he asked.

"As lightning," said Inge. "We shall all have to have little lightning-conductors on our hats."

Kay laughed at her mother's joke until she choked. Robin now had started to stare at Dollie and soon the other two joined him.

"Gerald," cried Inge in cooing tones, "go and ask Dollie to have a liqueur with us. Somebody has said some silly thing and now she is shy to speak to me. She looks very unhappy," she whispered as though Gerald's failure to make Dollie happy was directly answerable to her.

"I don't think that's necessary," he said. "She'll come over if she wants to." But it was too late, for Kay, anxious to please her mother, asked, "Shall I go and ask her, Mummy? After all it's *my* birthday party."

In the end, Gerald accompanied his daughter across the great dining-room.

"Good evening, Kay," said Dollie, trying to bring her fuddled senses to cope with the situation. Her mind reeled round until the centre of everything seemed to be in her mouth. This she contorted into what she hoped was a suitable smile.

"It's my birthday dinner," said Kay. "I came to invite you to join us." She could see that Auntie Dollie was "not very well" and she put all the sweetness into her little speech that the English mistress had taught her in last term's production of *Marie Rose*.

The stilted little elocutionary voice only made Dollie giggle. She was acutely aware that she could not trust herself to walk happily across the room. "Thank you," she said, "I can't come." Then she stopped dead, for she could think of no reason to give. Gerald desperately announced, "Auntie Dollie's waiting for someone."

Dollie smiled at him gratefully, then she sought for something to say to Kay, something funny. "You shouldn't wear a hat like a jerry on your birthday," she said.

Every sense in Kay was outraged—to talk of vulgar things like that in public, to make fun of her clothes, to make fun of the school hat. "It's our *school* hat," she said. Then, red in the face, she walked back to their table.

"Oh, my God!" said Gerald. "Whatever made you say that?"

"She's a silly little tike," said Dollie, "she needs a good what-for on her behind. I say, I'm most awfully sorry, Gerrie." She looked at him earnestly.

"Yes, my dear, I'm sure you are. Shall I get you a taxi?" he asked.

The scene he dreaded, however, was not to be avoided. Tears began to roll down Dollie's cheeks. "You're not to leave me, Gerrie." she said. "*You* must take me home."

"I can't, Dollie, really I can't. You had no right to come here. You knew I was giving Kay her birthday dinner."

"I tried not to," said Dollie. She had got to that stage in their relationship when she felt that she must force her prior claim upon Gerald's love and she knew that by doing so she risked losing it altogether. Either seemed better than accepting terms from him. Yet as soon as she took any action, she regretted it. "I meant to have an evening at home with a book." And she pictured with longing a series of evenings spent at home with books, anything would be wonderful that excluded all this, that excluded, in fact, Gerald. But as soon as her mind reached this point, her emotions revolted. "You had no right to leave me this evening," she said, "you know I was in a state. You ought to have stayed with me."

"You promised me that you would go out with Pamela, if you felt like this," said Gerald. "It was all fixed."

"I'm not one of your bloody children to be sent out and told to behave," Dollie raised her voice.

Gerald sat down on the bench beside her. He took her hand. "Look," he said, "you've got to understand. Some things you've got to put up with. And this is one of them. Kay gets little enough in life. You're entirely selfish." One of his growingly frequent fits of revulsion from her possessed him. "It's bad enough that I should have lost all real contact with the children. I refuse to be entirely cut off from them because of your lack of self-control. The lesser things have to be sacrificed to the greater." He spoke with deliberate cruelty. He only did so when, as now, Dollie was too far gone to respond to cold-water shock, however.

She looked at him with a face that was trembling. "It's no good," she said, "your talking. Because you're going to take me home."

"Very well," said Gerald, "but I'm not staying at the flat. You realize that."

Dollie knew, as well as he, that she had won, for she said, "Of course, this isn't really a scene, you know." They had got to the stage where "scenes" were to be computed against her in a list. "It's only because I'm drunk."

But they had reckoned without Ingeborg. Before he could make his way to the family table to explain his departure, she had borne down upon them. "You must go back to the children, Gerald. I will take Dollie back to her flat."

"*Gerrie's* taking me home," said Dollie in petulant assertion, but she was no longer shouting.

"No!" said Inge in her soothing voice, "Gerald is giving Kay her birthday dinner. *I* will take you home, Dollie," and she began to slip Dollie's coat on her.

Gerald, seeing Dollie's sudden acquiescence, held back his objections. "What on earth are the children . . ."

Inge answered his unfinished question. "I have told them that Dollie's drunk," she said.

"Was that necessary?" Gerald asked angrily.

"Yes, Gerald, it was. They must be told the truth. Besides," she added, "they must know the reason why they will not see her any more." She turned to Dollie. "You see, Dollie, what comes of behaving like a little child. You frightened my little Kay and I cannot have that. So you will not come to see them and they will not visit you."

So this, thought Gerald, is where Inge wriggles out of the position her muddled ethics have got her into; but, looking at his wife, he saw that her big blue eyes were sincerely full of tragic compassion for Dollie's deprivation. More surprising to him still, however, was Dollie's reaction. She took Inge's arm and, with a tearful voice, "Please take me home, Inge," she said. As they left the restaurant, a huge and a tiny figure, each in the fashionable black cloth coats with fur at shoulders and cuffs, they did not seem the two women with whom he was most intimate, but rather two repellent black shapes from a nightmare. . . .

Gerald emerged from his reverie with a feeling of perplexity. It had been doubt of Inge's much advertised claim to consistent treatment of the children that had led him to recall all this—so much he remembered—and yet what relation was there? If

Inge had been inconsistent it was in her treatment of *him*, he thought indignantly, but no more than Dollie had been. They had constantly humiliated him at that time. It was he rather than the children who had suffered. He, in fact, who was the pitiable child. . . . Gerald drew back with disgust from his introspection. It seemed as though some part of his mind was intent on manufacturing causes for self-distaste. The very ease with which that word "child" had slipped into his thoughts spoke of second childhood. He turned his attention determinedly to the family conversation.

An interlude of purring had succeeded the growls and scratches. Donald's adherence to the firm of Middleton was now the topic, and, since it had been Inge's idea that Robin should give Donald a job, even John was unwilling to criticize. In any case he looked forward with malicious glee to the results of the venture. A satisfied look of favours bestowed had appeared on the faces of all the interested parties. Robin had put that touch of twinkle in the eye into his mask of patronage which made clear that he knew he was acting a little quixotically, was taking one of those calculated risks that show that the industrialist is not always bounded by practical, day-to-day horizons. Donald, too, felt he was conferring a favour, but his mask of intellectual superiority was tempered by a smile that suggested the temerity of his rôle—how few academicals would have seized this opportunity to season their theory with a pinch of practice. Kay smiled with indulgence as she thought how little her family realized what a brilliant bargain they had bought in Donald. Marie Hélène just smiled as the cultured wife of a brilliant business man. But the most contented smile was Ingeborg's—once again the architect of her family's happiness. She felt that it was her place to say a few words in launching the ship.

"You know, Donald," she said, "I believe that you are going to have a wonderful experience. You will find these men and women very alive, very receptive. And you will be doing a very good deed. I remember so well how my father used to tell me of the lectures that he went to when he was a young worker just arrived in Copenhagen. They taught him everything, he said. 'Evening classes,' he would say, 'are the foundations of social democracy'." She smiled as one intellectual to another. Donald did not return the smile, but, as he had promised Kay not to quarrel, he said nothing.

"There you are," cried John delightedly, "Donald's Adventures in Webbland. I look forward to hearing how you deal with the Communists in your audience."

Robin smiled. "I doubt if Donald will find a lot of Communists at his lectures. I sometimes think half these Communists in the factories have been invented by Radicals like you, John, to make yourselves respectable. I don't know of any at the works. Oh! one or two perhaps. A lot of the bloody-minded, of course, but that's not the same thing at all. And a few natural anarchists, who I must say," he leaned back in his chair with broad-minded pride, "have my fullest respect. They'll slap into you, Donald, I promise you, if you start anything tendentious."

"Oh! Donald will confine himself to facts, won't you, darling?" Kay smiled with teasing affection at her husband.

"Selected," said John with a laugh.

"Yes," said Donald primly and a little angrily, "but selected out of respect for human intelligence, not out of a desire to please."

"Haha!" cried John, delighted at the prospect before them, "I know, 'We're not living in the nineteenth century'."

"Exactly," said Donald. "You may prefer John Stuart Mill and Robert Owen as bedfellows, others are happier with the living."

Any remark of this sort made John forget his company. "Oh! I don't think I should go for either of them if I turned necrophile." Donald frowned; he never made jokes of that sort.

"Don't get across the unions, Donald, for God's sake," Robin showed alarm. Donald smiled. He had no intention of discussing trade unionism with either of his brothers-in-law at this stage. "My lectures will be informative," he gave a little laugh, "designed to give *me* the maximum information." Robin felt relieved—that sort of witty answer wouldn't harm anyone. "Even increased information which has not been put through the usual worn-out mincing machine may do something to fill up the spiritual vacuum that threatens us," Donald added.

It happened increasingly rarely that John thought or said anything that came from the conviction of his own experience, anything that was not part of his build-up. His mind, however, had strayed to people he knew, like Derek Kershaw. "If you really care about this famous spiritual vacuum," he said, "I doubt if information is going to help. I think you will have to touch people at an unpleasantly personal level."

"We have first-rate welfare officers," said Robin.

"I wasn't thinking of welfare," John went on.

"Shame! Heresy!" cried Robin, "John Middleton turned against the Welfare State."

John laughed. "I'm sorry, I forgot my place as family clown," he said.

Kay leaned forward. "What were you getting at, Johnnie?" she said. It was not that she was interested, but that she knew a sister's place.

"Something we all guard desperately," he said. "The level at which we all prefer emptiness, because to fill it would mean facing something we prefer not to."

"If," said Donald, with distaste, "that means anything at all, it sounds dangerously like the subconscious. I'm certainly not going to Middleton's as a psychoanalytic witch-doctor, if that was what you were thinking. The Church is the remedy for soul sickness, and if they don't care to go to her, well, *I'm* not the keeper of other men's consciences. . . ."

"See the scapegoat, happy beast, from every personal sin released. . . . Am I my brother's keeper? No! lightly come and lightly go." He had come on the lines so appositely at the time, Gerald remembered, in a Georgian anthology in Dr Winskill's room. And then Dr Winskill had echoed them to him. It struck him now that Dr Winskill had been a man not unlike Donald—embittered and uncertain, masquerading as mordant and self-assured. He had thought so highly of him at the time—a young, clever doctor so different from the ordinary G.P. Life, at least, had made him a less facile judge of character. Of course, it was chance that had brought Dr Winskill to their home, and chance always gives additional distinction to acquaintances, lending them the flattering air of "discoveries".

Gerald sat in his study, marking the History Finals papers. Everyone in Oxford had said what a problem the ex-Service officers were going to create, and now that many of them were in their final year everyone was saying how they had been no problem and how difficult it was going to be to get used to having children about again instead of adults. All that might be so, but the truth remained that many of them were past the age of assimilating historical facts or, at any rate, of serving them up again as little dishes with trimmings of epigram and "original thought" cut to shape. And that was what History Finals demanded. " 'Power follows trade routes.' Discuss this statement in relation to the collapse of the Empire of Canute." " 'Feudalism is a pattern imposed upon medieval society by historians unversed in the difficulties of practical government.' Discuss this view of feudalism in relation to English society in 1100." It was all very well for him, he wanted to think about such things. But what did it mean for Wilkins, who had been a subaltern with him on the Marne and now must have a degree in order to invest his little spot of capital in a preparatory school? He wiped his small moustache with his handkerchief and noticed with annoyance that he was about to replace the handkerchief in his sleeve. All these hangovers of the war! The moustache should go. He suddenly felt the disgusting crampness of his study—no proper room for books or papers!

Inge appeared at the door. Her great height only further dwarfed the little room. "I am ready," she said. "Baby has had his bottle, and cook will sit with the children in the nursery."

Gerald looked at his watch. "My dear, it's only a quarter to four," he said.

"But the invitation says four o'clock." Inge was always particular about punctuality.

"Oh, I doubt if we need get there before half-past," he replied, "with these garden parties, you know. . . ."

She did not know and her doll's face showed her increasing irritation with English customs. She had tried so hard to cope with the university world . . .

Gerald, seeing her expression, said, "You look very nice, Inge. That's a charming dress."

Her blue eyes shone with delight. "I made it myself," she said. The cream shantung silk dress fell round her ankles in scallops edged with blue velvet, a broad blue velvet sash clung round her thighs, her broad-brimmed straw hat was trimmed with blue velvet cornflowers. "I have not quite cut rightly the neck," she said.

"It looks very nice to me," said Gerald, "but you don't *have* to make your own dresses, my dear, surely."

"Oh! but I like to," she cried. She hated to think of the lavish allowance that Gerald gave her; it seemed to make her so useless.

"We'll certainly have to get a larger house if you're going to wear hats as big as that," he said, with a smile. "They're not suited for this poky little study."

"Oh! Gerald!" she cried, "don't call your dear little study 'poky'. I am so proud of our first little house and you don't even like it."

"Yes, I do, dear, but it just seems unnecessary to live in a doll's house when we can well afford something better."

"We must not think of that. I am sure we must not think of that." Her gargling singsong accent rose to heights of distress. "You are just starting your life, Gerald, your new profession. You must live as though you were building up from nothing and not think of that money that you do not earn. And besides I, what should I do with a big house and servants to cut me off from my babies? And they to grow up as rich men's children. No, I could not bear it, Gerald, we must not speak of it."

"No," said Gerald, "we mustn't." Indeed, he thought, what would be the good, for they would surely talk of it to-morrow and the next day, as they had every day for the past year.

Inge came over and kissed him. "I love you very much, Gerald," she said. "I will go and be with the children until you call me."

"I think you're a very clever wife, you know, Inge," he said.

"I—what is it your father says?—I contrive," she said. His father's grumpy reference to "all this contriving instead of living like a gentleman" was the joke they had between them, and Inge produced it often—to please Gerald.

The room after she had gone seemed very bright and hygienic, full of that clean smell of soap and lavender water she took everywhere with her. Gerald, however, was not to enjoy its brightness for long. "We must always remember that if William brought harshness and terror to the subject English, he also brought law and order. As the chronicler says . . . ." But he did not read what the chronicler said or what the candidate said he said, for suddenly there came from upstairs a strange, high shrieking, that grew and grew in convulsive bursts, like a trapped rabbit, higher in note, more like a rat that some men had scalded for fun once in the trenches. Gerald turned sick at the memory of that.

A moment later, he could hear Inge's screams, and then, as the baby added the note of its cries, the noise became almost deafening. Gerald was half-way up the stairs before Inge's voice came to him, calling, "Gerald! Gerald! Quickly! Quickly! Little Kay is burned."

As he entered the nursery, Inge stood, staring in front of her, beating the palms of her hands on the table. Kay's small body was stretched on the hearth-rug, twitching and shuddering. Her screams were stifled now into convulsive sobs; her face was scarlet, and, stretched above her head, one small arm which ended in what seemed a gross, crimson insect against the buff rug—her swollen, reddened little hand. Gerald snatched her up and laid her on the sofa.

"Get the vaseline and bandages from the bathroom," he shouted at Inge. Her deadened, doll's face seemed suddenly to come to life again—the stony blue eyes were suffused once more with their maternal light. She stood above the heaving body of the child—six feet of majestic, cow-like, blonde calm.

"No, Gerald," she said, "we shall not touch her hand. It is too bad. Get a doctor at once." She knelt by the sofa, stroking the little face, assuaging Kay's terror. Thank God, thought Gerald, as he ran down the stairs, that I insisted at least on a telephone in this bloody house.

Dr Jacob was not there; his young partner Dr Winskill would come. Meanwhile they should apply a salt and water compress, but certainly no grease.

It seemed years before Dr Winskill arrived, years in which Gerald asked his wife, again and again, how? She could not tell—she was attending to Baby when it happened. But why a fire in June? It was not warm. Baby was cold. Where was the fire guard? She had thought it was there. Kay had been crawling around Baby's cot, she had told her not to crawl around Baby, but she *would* do it. It was impossible to let little children play with babies.

Gerald burst out in anger. "What do you mean? Kay's only a baby herself." Yes, but John was the *little* baby All this came, he cried, of her having no nurse, of her bloody obstinacy, her damned conceit. Inge gave no reply to these charges; she went on calmly tending the child. Even so, Gerald cried, it was incredible—so bad a burn. She had fallen, Inge said, it was God's mercy her face had not been touched.

Dr Winskill, when he arrived, also seemed to find it a little strange. However, he gave Kay an injection to make her sleep and within half an hour she was in hospital and remained there for over a month.

Yet it was Inge's reaction in the next few days that gave them no time to think of anything else. She refused to see any of the children. A nurse must be found at once; she had been wrong: she could not go on. If Kay's state of health was mentioned, she burst into hysterical tears.

The spectacle was at once revolting and pitiable to Gerald. At first, he was enraged at her neglect of Kay, her utter selfishness; and then he was overcome with pity for her disintegration, her utter panic. He blamed his own weakness for letting her take on too much work. At the last, however, it was physical nausea that gripped him. Inge in collapse became somehow no longer a human being, simply a mass of red, crying flesh, either too revolting to look at or else too pitiable to bear. At the end of a week she became herself again, only relapsing when Kay's accident was mentioned, her blue eyes rounded in panic, her great doll's face dissolving into tears.

At last Dr Winskill asked to see Gerald. He sat in his consulting room, his elbows on his desk, sliding a silver pencil backwards and forwards from hand to hand. "You see," he said, "it was a terrible experience for Mrs Middleton. Terrible, of course, for you too, I know. But for her—well, I think you should realize that it may be difficult for her to reintegrate herself into her family life. A young woman in a foreign country, she has reacted, I think, by feeling peculiarly alone. You may think it strange for a doctor to speak in this way, Mr Middleton, interfering perhaps; but we can no longer separate the body's function from the mind's quite so easily as we supposed. The war, you know, has taught us a great deal about those delicate mechanisms we call human beings. You probably saw a good number of shell-shocked cases yourself. I don't know that Dr Jacob would advise you like this, but times change."

He smiled, and tapped on his desk with his pencil. "You yourself have been deeply upset by it all. You resent your wife's hysteria; am I not right? Perhaps you contrast it with your little girl's bravery and the probable fact that her hand will always be affected. The fact that she is too young to speak for herself makes you feel that you must ask again and again how it happened." He leaned back in his revolving chair. "Don't!" he said. "Remember that if she's too young to speak, she is also, thank God, too young to remember for long. If you continue to question your wife, I can't answer for the effect on her mind, nor, if I may say so, on yours. You believe that there was some negligence, and since you can find out nothing, you think even worse things. You simply *must* forget about it, I beg of you. Even if Mrs Middleton *was* for a moment careless, we have all of us been so, but most of us are luckier in the results of our momentary forgetfulness. I always think," he removed his tortoise-shell spectacles, leaned forward and stared at Gerald with weak, swimming eyes, "I always think, when such troubles come upon us, we should bear in mind the old saying, 'Am I the keeper of my brother's conscience?'" And he smiled a watery smile of comfort.

And so Gerald had asked no more. Inge had reintegrated herself into family life all right. Perhaps, Gerald thought bitterly, she had overcompensated a little. He had gained his wish for servants and a nurse, and Inge had learned to accept their income, developing a special sort of 'simple' *hausfrau* form of life that was peculiarly designed to spend any money that was going. Kay had learned to accept her withered hand and to admire her mother. The unspoken questions remained, however, as a barrier of silence between him and his wife, and with them remained a certain physical nausea that would make him accept anything to avoid the sight of that great bulk shapeless with misery, those frightened doll's eyes. Even now he closed his own eyes to check the memory as Inge's voice came to him.

Inge whispered, or rather she made her lips into the shape suitable for whispering and then spoke at her normal pitch. "Oh! you don't know," she said, "how sad it makes me that he publishes nothing, and then to have retired two years before his time."

"Oh! I imagine," said Robin, "that he enjoys life. Pottering about and buying his drawings. I know nothing about them, but Marie Hélène says it's a wonderful collection."

"He has remarkable taste," said Marie Hélène shortly. She did not approve of this belittling of the head of the family in his presence, even if he had gone to sleep.

"But that is no life for a man," Inge cried, "to potter and buy drawings."

Marie Hélène's sallow face became quite flushed with embarrassment. "I should not care to make any easy judgments about scholarship," she said. "It is quite elegant that a distinguished scholar *en retraite* should become a buyer of drawings —I suppose." It was one of her few linguistic mistakes that she often said "suppose" for "think".

"I'm afraid," said John judiciously, "that he's always tried to make history a substitute for life. And, of course, it won't work."

"I should think it's much more likely that the routine of college administration and so forth killed all the energy he needed for scholarship," said Donald. "A professor's life is little better than a high-grade clerk's nowadays. It's your '*life*', John, that destroys reality, not the other way round."

"But a professor is such a distinguished position," Marie Hélène protested.

"Oh!" said Kay, "to give Daddy his due, he couldn't live on distinction. He's far too much of a lost soul for that. No, I think the truth is quite a different one. You see his work was so frightfully good, or so I'm told. You think so, Donald dear, don't you?"

"Within its own limitations, absolutely first class," said Donald primly.

"Well, there you are, you see," Kay cried. "He's a perfectionist. He daren't write anything more in case it isn't good. First class or nothing. I admire him for it."

"Well, I'm afraid that I do not," said Marie Hélène in a shocked voice. "Life consists, I believe, in accepting one's duty, and that means often to accept the second best."

Gerald with great effort withdrew his attention. When a man has sunk, he decided, to the level of overhearing the judgments of his dear ones, the least he can do is to act upon the ethics judged suitable for such a clumsy stage situation. It was, after all, the predicament which he had been preparing for himself in all these years of quietism, to use a nice word for failure and weakness. Wordsworth's old village men—the leech gatherers and what-not—had at least received encomia on their vegetable piety as they sat by in dumb, senile virtue: but then, poets were kinder than families, and less perfunctory. It was only the perfunctoriness that hurt him. It was kind of Kay, but hardly percipient, to think that he had not accepted the second-rate. If his family were a second best as he thought them, he had asked for it, because in marrying Inge, he had elected for exactly that. . . .

They made a handsome couple as they stood on the battlements of Kronborg and watched the ice breaking up in the Sound, the great snow-covered blocks floating out into the Kattegat and on to the North Sea. Handsome couples should always be tall, though perhaps they carried this a little to excess. Inge, at any rate, looked like the queen of some Northern Ruritania at the novel's happy ending. Her eyes were bright with pleasure, her pink cheeks glowed with the salt spray, her hair blew in gleaner's wisps against her sable toque. She had the rare gift of a figure at once stately and graceful. As she stood there in her long sable coat, with the tails of her muff lapping over the side of the wall, it seemed to Gerald that all the soldiers in this palace turned barracks must salute their queen, for she had that graciousness one expects of royalty, and perhaps a little of the nullity.

"I am glad," she said, "that Father got permission for us to enter the castle. Even so, I do not think you would have been allowed in if the War was not over. So even here in Denmark, you see, we notice a new world." She turned to him and smiled. "So you really and truly are not disappointed with our old Elsinore. Even after Shakespeare," she said. "That makes me very happy." She spoke to him partly in Danish, partly in a little hardly acquired English.

"I'm in love with it all," he said. "I didn't think for a moment I should be. I did everything I could to get out of it when the War Office seconded me to the Embassy here. But I am."

It was true: he had pulled every string he knew to avoid it. It was absurd and monstrous that he should be going to a neutral country, he had told them, simply because of dysentery that was over and done with, when hundreds of men with holes in their chests or one arm were being sent back to the Front. France wasn't the Dardanelles, he reminded them, or even the Italian front, to consider dysentery. And when all this proved useless, he had pleaded at least for a Whitehall job; after all, his Scandinavian languages would be just as useful in Intelligence at home. Anywhere but to the unreality of a neutral country. But, in the last resort, there was nothing for it; there were Scandinavian linguists, yes, but few who spoke as fluently as he did. He had cursed his pre-war visits to Denmark then, and cursed Stokesay who had argued him into Viking research.

Finally, however, it had been Stokesay and Dollie between them who had reconciled him to the inescapable, but even so he had come there with an ill grace. Stokesay had so evidently counted on him as his heir, not only academically but almost personally since Gilbert had been killed.

"I'm not suggesting for a minute, Gerald," he had said, "that any life should count in the titanic struggle that we're waging. A year ago, when things looked so black, I might even have spoken differently, but I really feel that 1918 has turned

the corner for us. There will be setbacks and so on, but I feel
at last that it isn't entirely wrong to think of the future. I sometimes even imagine myself a don again. No more propaganda.
It's not going to be easy for me, you know, with Gilbert gone;
but there will be an even greater task before us. I'm quite convinced, my dear fellow, that a proper study of history is going
to contribute as much and more than all your sciences to the
making of a better world, and in that study, the knowledge of
our beginnings is going to play its part. Nationalism has got
to go. And although I should be the last to subscribe to some
of the ideas of our Roman Catholic colleagues, it can't be
denied that the medieval world can teach us a great deal about
internationalism. And you, Gerald, are the best young medievalist in the country. That's all I'm going to say to you. The
decision, like every other important thing in a man's life, is
ultimately in his own hands." It had not been, of course, it had
been in the hands of the War Office, but Stokesay was tending
more and more to talk in this way.

It was Dollie, however, who had finally made the trip to
Denmark both easier and more bitter. She had so evidently
wanted him out of England.

"And now you are going to leave us," said Inge. "We shall
miss you very much." It was the sort of remark that he had
trained himself to mistrust on the lips of English girls. He had
heard it so often at country house weekends. "And now you
are going to leave us, Mr Middleton, we shall miss you very
much." It was usually said by the mothers who had their eye
on rich young bachelors; but on occasion, more coyly, by the
daughters. Inge never spoke coyly; there were times when he
had thought her remarks a little childish, oddly playful, in a girl
at once so easy in her manner and dignified, but then difference
of language made such nuances so difficult to tell, particularly
nuances of humour. And then she was the only daughter of a
doting widower who kept her younger than she should be.

"Well," she said, "you never brought little Denmark into
the war," and when he protested, she laughed. "No, I know

that was not your intention. I was trying to make an English joke, but I am not yet practised at this. You have done much to make Danes love England more. You should be a proud man."

"If I have done so at all, I am," said Gerald. "You have certainly helped to make me fall in love with Denmark."

They moved slowly along the ramparts. The March sun shone quite lustily upon them, and Gerald opened his Astrakhan collar to give himself more air. Beneath their feet the snow crunched crisply. "I like it all better that I can say," he told her, "and especially perhaps now that the Armistice has come."

"Ah," she cried, "because you will be leaving us. It is always easy to love people when you leave them."

"Perhaps it *is* a little that, but its far *more* than that. While the fighting was on I always felt a little guilty to be enjoying it all so much. Now, I should like to stay for ever."

She stopped and looked at him. "I believe that is true," she said, "but you will be leaving us soon."

"Not if I know the War Office," he said, "they've probably forgotten my existence."

"I hope so," Inge declared, "but no! I must not say that. You will do such splendid work. You have no idea of the nice things Professor Gulbrandsen was saying about you last night. He said that you know already far more of our history than we do."

"That wouldn't be difficult in some cases," Gerald laughed.

Inge sighed. "I'm afraid that is true. But there is so much to be done in the *present* here. Look at my poor father, always sitting on Committees and getting houses built. He has no time for the past. And yet I know he is proud of our history. He has spent much time working for good history teaching in the schools."

Gerald said uncomfortably, "I'm afraid my remark was meant as a joke. I'm sure you all know far more than English people do about *their* country's history."

Inge said simply, "Oh!" and Gerald felt that, as too often, he had snubbed her. They stood for a moment in silence, then Gerald pointed with his walking-stick to an eider duck seated on an ice-block that was floating out to sea. "I wonder what happens to those birds that get carried too far out to sea," he said.

"Oh! I believe that they have a special home," she cried, "where are only happy birds and . . . unhappy fish." She made a comic grimace.

Gerald was irritated at the whimsy he so disliked. "I imagine they die a rather icy death," he said.

Inge simply did not comprehend his feelings. Her face, when she turned to him, was blank and very beautiful. It was this feature that so overwhelmed him. With others, with Dollie, for instance, beauty came to them with expression, with movement, but Inge simply was beautiful, the more beautiful when, as now, there was nothing there except the shape and colour of her face. Sometimes, he wondered, if it was coldness of temperament, and yet she was warm in character, enjoying life as it came to her. He had come probably to associate passion with tension. Dollie, for all her straightforward, almost boyish manner, was always tensed; it was part of the general tension of English life that he dreaded meeting again. Inge, by comparison, was only half grown.

She put her hand on his arm. "You think I am very childish, Gerald," she said, "but it is difficult for me. Our society is a small one and so many of them are Father's friends—the trade union leaders and the Deputies—they treat me as Father wishes me to be, like a small girl. That is rather foolish when someone is so big as I am," she laughed. "I am grateful that you treat me with respect to my size."

On their return journey, the carriage stopped at Fredensborg, and in the formal garden of this eighteenth-century palace, its avenue of trees, its statues and urns all snow-covered, he proposed to Inge and was accepted. Perhaps it was the garden's declared restraint, or perhaps it was just the snow, but she showed no trace of that playfulness or whimsy, that

false warmth which sometimes disturbed him. Even though
he had to return to England, to all he dreaded, in her passive
beauty he felt that he would be taking back with him some of
the peace he had found here. He would need to commit all his
energies to work, to research, to a career, if he was to fill the
emptiness that awaited him at home. He could only do so if he
could rely on a source of protective calm. Inge, he knew,
would be that source. . . .

And that, thought Gerald, was the decision of a man already
turned twenty-seven. He shrank into the armchair with disgust. He refused the excuse of the war for his immaturity as
cant. Nevertheless, one had to be fair to people—even to oneself at an earlier age—and there was no doubt that his last
interview with Dollie had broken him. As the scene returned
to him, he felt a desperate desire to shut it off, to return to the
family's "scratchy" banal talk, but he couldn't for the life of
him see how he could avoid going through with it all now,
back to wherever it might lead. If many might have agreed
that Inge was the second best, even as she was in those days,
there were few perhaps who would have seen their first choice
in Dollie. And yet the years had proved him right in his belief
that she was his; or was it simply that an image had replaced
the woman he could not have? Later, when he had lived with
her, she had only been for moments what he had hoped for,
but then Inge had come in between. However that might be,
Dollie had made it perfectly clear in those early days that she
would not marry him, just as she had made it perfectly clear
years later that she wanted to be his mistress.

The heat was overpowering that May, and the sun's rays
refracted in an intense glare from the chalk-white cliffs and the
long line of white hotels along the front; even Dollie's white
linen skirt and coat and the white shoes and stockings peeping
from below swam before Gerald's eyes in the haze. Beneath
her white sailor hat her little, smooth-cheeked face offered
calm and coolness.

"Think of me," he said, "in a week's time in the disgusting fatness of a neutral climate." His officer's uniform gave slimness to his already heavy frame.

"Think of me," she replied, "at Hastings. It's the semifinals in a week."

"Winning all the cups," he laughed.

"Yes," she said, "isn't it disgusting? It really must be my last tournament. I'm turning into a pot-hunter. But there's such a lot of rabbits about. I miss the Canadians," she added. "Now I suppose we'll have Yanks. It'll all be over over here, 'I don't think', as Harry Tate says. All the same. I'm glad they've come in. The more the merrier, I say."

Gerald winced. "Sorry, old thing," Dollie said. "I know you don't like me to say things like that. But you make too much of words, Gerrie. Nobody, not even fools like me, really think it merry. Only we've got to see it through, haven't we?"

Gerald didn't answer her question. "I think a lot of people at home find it quite merry," he said bitterly.

"Meaning me," she said. "Oh, yes, Gerrie, you did. Or if you didn't you should have done."

"You're unfair on yourself. You've done a wonderful job nursing."

"Please, Gerrie," she said, and she lit a cigarette. "A wonderful job. And a wonderful job playing mixed doubles with the Canadians. And a wonderful job giving good times to the boys on leave. Dancing and shows and sleeping with the brigadier."

Gerald looked shocked. "Sorry, old thing," she said, "but you knew it wasn't only you. Or is it just my language that upsets you? You forget that I'm fast. Haven't you heard the old hens cackle?"

"I don't listen to gossip," Gerald said. "Besides, you've been through a lot, Dollie."

"Oh, yes," she said. "I'm a young war widow. Haven't you heard the pater talking about it? It's quite moving. Only he forgets that there are two million others. Most of them at least

kept the home fires burning. I couldn't even have the decency
to do that for his darling Gilbert."

"Your marriage was washed up long before Gilbert went
out," said Gerald. "You should never have married him. And
what's more, he treated you like a brute. I say that even though
he was my friend. Yes, even though he was killed and it was
a shameful waste."

"Yes," said Dollie, "you said it to me before. Even though
he was your friend and even though he *hadn't* been killed then.
You said it to me in bed to be exact."

Gerald seized her wrist and twisted it in his anger. "Shut
up," he said. "You're being a little fool. You can't go on
torturing yourself about that for ever."

"Can't I?" Dollie asked. "Don't you be so sure."

Gerald struck the side of his leg with his cane. Then,
calmed, he put it to her. "Look, Dollie," he said, "try to remember what happened. You were lonely and unhappy and
so was I. You knew that Gilbert wasn't faithful to you, even
on that last leave. Why should you blame yourself? We were
in love, Dollie. And we are," he added vehemently.

"Oh, yes," said Dollie, ignoring his words, "we had a high
old time all right. I enjoyed myself. But then I would. Haven't
you heard about little Mrs Stokesay? No? But then I forgot
you don't listen to gossip. You should, you know. You ask at
the club. Anyone'll tell you. Little Mrs Stokesay's hot stuff."

Gerald leaned back in his deck-chair and sighed. He stared
out where the blue was flecked with white edgings below
Beachy Head.

"Don't say *you* can hear them," Dollie cried. "Oh, they say
you *can* on a still day, you know. Even respectable Eastbourne
can't quite forget what's going on over there," she added
bitterly.

"I'm not going on this damned mission," Gerald said abruptly. He got up and stood over her. "I don't care if it means
a court martial. I'm not going to leave you in this unhappy,
bitter state."

"Thank you kindly," she said. "But napoo! I can look after myself. I didn't leave home yesterday and I'm not going *back* to the shack. I'm having a good time, Gerrie, like all the women now. You told me so."

"Oh, for God's sake!" he cried, and then, surprising the strollers on the promenade, surprising even himself, he went down on his knees beside her and took both her hands in his, "Marry me, Dollie!" he cried. "I can, I will make you happy."

Dollie's face puckered for a second and then set in hard lines. She pushed his hands away. "No, Gerrie. For God's sake, get up!" she said. "I made one man unhappy. Not another. You're brainy like Gilbert. I'm not. I couldn't help you in your career. I should only get in the way." When he seemed about to speak again, she turned away and said violently, "Oh! for heaven's sake! can't you see what I'm trying to tell you. I don't want to marry you, Gerrie. I should be bored to tears in a week."

She got up from her deck-chair and, as he rose from his knees and stood beside her, she said, "As a matter of fact, I'm bored to tears already. Do you know what I fancy? I fancy a cocktail. Let's make for the American bar. So you're to wear mufti," she said, "because the dear little Danes might not care to be reminded of the war. . . ."

Robin and John had won the day. Despite all attempts to deter them, they had brought the conversation back to Pelican again.

John, munching *marrons glacés*, looked like the spoilt, sweet-stuffed boy of their childhood arguments. As then, he answered Robin's assumptions of senior experience by the condescension of brilliant youth to dull-witted age.

"My dear Robin," he said, "I'm not entirely inexperienced in these things. I have hundreds of hard-luck stories every week. Many of them turn out to be bogus, the results of folly or knavery. I investigate them all very thoroughly. You tend to assume that you're the only one who knows how to do his job. I'm afraid that isn't so. I happen to know mine. I don't say much about it because I take that part of an intelligent man's life for granted. I investigated Cressett's claim thoroughly. It's genuine."

"Yes, yes," said Robin impatiently, "I'm sure it is." He had hoped that it might not be; but looking at John, he reflected that his younger brother was a successful careerist idealist, not a bungling, overweening small boy. He was unlikely to support a bogus claim. Robin shifted his ground. "No one doubts that Pelican or one of his staff has slipped up. I'm simply appealing to the adult in you to put side by side the small effects of his mistake and the serious consequences of your publicity—the possible ruin of the career of a man who is doing a useful job. Of course, you have to take my word for that."

"Oh, no," said John, "I know the men I'm dealing with. I've made it my business to find out about Pelican. He's a good civil servant. That's why it's all the more important to make an example of him. It underlines the fact that the executive, even the most able and conscientious of them, is responsible before the bar of public opinion."

"But Johnnie dear," said Kay, "you speak as though the man *knew* that he'd made a mistake. Surely that's very unlikely. A head of a department or whatever he is probably never sees any of these individual cases. It was almost certainly some clerk who slipped up."

"Then," said John and he pulled at his pipe, "Pelican or his successor will insist on better clerks or more clerks or whatever's at fault. Good heavens! I'm not against the civil service. I just want a good one. Besides," he added, "I don't believe that there wasn't some moment when the papers passed through Pelican's hands and, for some reason or other, because he was too busy or going on leave or what-have-you, he let a thing go by that he knew was incorrect. It may be only for a fraction of a second, you know, when it's revealed to us, but I believe that there's always a moment of truth. . . ."

Or a moment of untruth, or a moment of untruth that looks like truth, thought Gerald. His contempt for John rose to bursting-point at this piece of glibness. It was intolerable that this smart-alec son of his should follow up hunches and take action on risks, when his own life had been riddled and twisted with scrupulosity and weighed decisions. If John had been in his place, he would have been pursuing a wild will-o'-the-wisp half his life, upsetting the balance of the English historical profession, destroying the reputation of a remarkable historian like Stokesay and God knows what else on the evidence of a few words. And yet, he reflected, even if God did not know, *he* did. He had told himself all these years that these weighty results would follow any action he took; and yet, was it really so serious a matter? Was it not after all a small point of historical truth that mattered really very little to medieval specialists and nothing, but absolutely nothing at all, to anyone else? So much the more reason for taking no action on so little evidence. "A moment of truth!" What did it mean? A moment of personal conviction that may have been the result of hostility or drink or imagination or any psychological quirk.

After all these years he remembered quite distinctly his momentary conviction that Gilbert was telling the truth; but how could he estimate the worth of his own convictions when he had changed so much in the years that followed. Gilbert was only a shadow now and his own personality as it was then would seem equally shadowy if it were not for the false, absurd ideas of the continuity of human existence.

The tables he could see still, with their little pink-shaded lamps and their Chianti bottles. They were probably still there today, unless they had suddenly invested in chromium in these last years. And the ill-scrawled, purple-marked menu. The Rendezvous, had it been, or the Chanticleer, or, perhaps, Pinoli's? anyway, one of Gilbert's famous little places in Soho. And the cockney Italian waitress, she couldn't have been more than sixteen, of whose seduction Gilbert boasted, probably truthfully. But Gilbert himself?

"My dear Middleton," Gilbert affected the use of surnames even for his most intimate friends, "don't, for heaven's sake, be the prize ass of all time. Can't you see it's the greatest thing that's ever happened? We've been asking to have our legs pulled for a long time now, with our deadly tame-cat ways and our cheap little suburban civilization. A world that's come to accept the dyspeptic rumblings of a lot of City businessmen and political old women for wisdom, a world that buys its painting at a guinea a yard and takes the cheeping of a lot of constipated half-men for poetry, is asking for one thing and one thing only—a mammoth practical joke. And, by God, we've got it. The biggest practical joke of all time, that'll let a hell of a lot of blood out of an overfed world, one that'll purge our wretched constipated culture for good and all. And *you* hope that it'll be over in a few months."

His excited, high voice rose above the talk of the other diners and his hysterical laughter filled the room. His dark fringed hair had fallen over one eyebrow, and his dark eyes stared bloodshot like a racehorse in his long, high cheekboned white face. He was very drunk. "No, no, Middleton, don't, for Christ's sake, be such a chump." He reached across the little table and punched Gerald lightly in the chest. It was the affectionate, contemptuous gesture he had used since the days when he had flirted with Gerald at school.

Gerald, looking down at the thin, thick-veined hand, felt a repulsion for the friendship that should have ended with the school romance. "How soon do you think it'll be before they issue us with uniforms?"

Gilbert looked at him through bleary eyes, unsteadily lighting a cigar. "What does it matter to you, little Middleton?" he said.

Gerald, hearing the schoolboy form of address, thought, "He's drunker than I realized, perhaps he'll get us thrown out and I can send him home." But Gilbert seized the wide, braided lapel of his coat. "You've got your badge. What more do you want?" he said. "Inns of Court. You ought to be

bloody proud. Didn't you hear what the sergeant-major said?"
He called to the waiter. "Bring this gentleman a double
brandy. They're going to make heroes of us all. They're even
going to make a hero of poor bloody little Middleton."

You could quarrel with him now, Gerald said to himself,
and be rid of him. You should have done so when he came
down to see you at Cambridge; he bored and disgusted you
then, yes, and you thought he was a great man with his *avant-
garde* poems and his contributions to *Blast*, his talk of Nietzsche
and Marinetti. And now you can't because of Stokesay and
Dollie. You're tied to him, a comrade in arms, until death do
us part.

Gilbert said, "How will you like to be blown up, Middleton? Never mind. We'll go together. Let's make a compact
and seal it later with a mingling of our guts." He was shouting
now, so that the little Italian owner was looking worriedly
towards their table.

Gerald thought, "I must calm him," but in the same
moment he said in a pompous voice, "Look here, Gilbert, if
you're not going down to see your father, I shall. We haven't
got to report back until Monday. I shall catch the 10.15 tonight."

Gilbert leaned across the table. He spoke in quite a low
voice now, but with hysterical intensity. "Shut up about my
bloody father, will you?" he said. "Shall I tell you what he is?
He's a lecherous old fool. Oh yes, he is. Only he can't even do
it. He muffed it on his wedding night. Dear old unspotted
virgin dad. But he took it out on my mother all right. Made
her life ruddy hell just because he muffed it on the night of
nights."

Gerald said sharply, "You've told me all this before. I don't
want to hear it again."

"I don't want to hear it again," Gilbert mimicked him.
"But you must, little Middleton, it'll do your virgin heart good.
Do you know why he muffed it? Because he thought that
what's sauce for the goose is sauce for the gander. 'My

dear Gilbert'," and he began to imitate his father, "'when I came to your mother I was a virgin. We men have no right, my dear boy, to ask of women what we're not prepared . . .' No right, Middleton, no right! Well, he'll know about rights now. He and his sort that believed in scraps of paper. There's *my* rights and the rights of the people that have the guts and the brains. That's all the rights there are. The rest are the unwashed and the women."

Gerald said, "This is very second-rate stuff, you know, Gilbert."

Gilbert took Gerald's brandy and began to drink it in gulps; drops ran down his chin and along his tweed coat until they came to rest on a leather button. "You're a bastard and a bore with your civilization and your tolerance and your tact. You'd like to have Dollie, wouldn't you?" he asked, leering at Gerald.

"It's not fear of you that stops me," said Gerald.

"No," cried Gilbert, "it's far worse than that. You're frightened of hurting someone, her or yourself. If only you'd been a little higher or a little lower, in the social scale, Middleton, you wouldn't have minded about adultery. Think of it. You could have had Dollie, and no one, not even yourself, would have thought the worse of you for it. You'd have had me to reckon with—the injured husband. But you've said already that you don't care about that. Unfortunately, Middleton, you were born a dear little civilized bourgeois—a gentleman." He began again to mimic his father, " 'A gentleman, my dear Middleton, is, above all, gentle.' Well, that's all over since last week. There're only two kinds of women, Middleton, whores and breeding cows. Dollie's a whore, or she would be if she didn't know I'd knock the lights out of her if I caught her at it. My mother was a breeding cow, and all my dear father could give her was one son. . . ."

Gerald got up from his chair. "Look, Gilbert," he said, "I'm fed up with all this tommy-rot. I'm going."

But before he had picked up his gloves, Gilbert seized his

sleeve. "I'll tell you something that'll keep you here," he said, and smiled with a drunken, self-satisfied look of cunning. "You think my guvnor's a great scholar, just because he reads Carolingian uncials or some other farting nonsense. How could he be a great scholar? He hasn't enough imagination to come in out of the rain. How could he understand the Middle Ages with his dregs of Darwinism, his Jesus Christ who's a decent Englishman and his Primrose League politics? He wouldn't know a Giotto if he saw one, and tell him the truth about a Romanesque carving and his poor little cotton-woolled soul wouldn't sleep for nights. If he thinks about it all apart from his 'documents' and his origins of Parliament he probably sees a lot of starry eyed pre-Raphaelite women with goitre, or else a crowd of red-faced lady dons morris-dancing on the village green. As for the Dark Ages! he wouldn't know a fraud if he saw one. *I* know because I've caught him out."

Gerald, who had sat down to avoid a scene, wondered what nonsense was about to come. Gilbert, when drunk, was full of wondrous stories and elaborate leg-pulls. He decided to give him his head. "Really?" he said. "What was that?" But he need not have bothered: Gilbert in full spate heard nothing.

"The great Stokesay, and you, and all the ruddy crowd, thought that the little wooden fellow with the respectable-sized piece was part of Bishop what's-his-name's equipment for the long journey ahead of him, didn't you? Any fool with half a sense of what a man of God was like in those days would have felt the falseness of the thing. I *know*, because I put it there."

Gerald had a sudden instant conviction that he was hearing the truth. His tongue seemed enormous in his mouth; he could not speak.

"Oh yes, I did," Gilbert said. He was speaking quite softly now and with a sort of crooning pleasure. "I found the thing on the other site, among the pagan graves, where you'd expect to find it. And, with a little help, I put it in Thingummy's tomb. I just thought there was half a chance in hell that the old man was the vain fool he turned out to be. He wouldn't have believed it if it hadn't been *his* excavation, and you, you fools, took the same line. Even that theatrical old fool Portway wasn't prepared to disagree with the great Stokesay. He smelt a rat but he kept mum. After all it was *his* excavation too, *and* his land on which the great discovery was made, even if it did dishonour his Church." Gilbert shouted for two more brandies. "We'll drink a health," he said, "to the day dear father gets the knighthood he wants so much, because that's the day I shall spill the beans."

Gerald drank down the brandy and felt able to speak. "Tell me the story again, Gilbert," he said, trying to convey no decision as to the truth of what he had heard, "I didn't follow it very well."

Gilbert's face seemed suddenly to go dead. "Oh yes, you did," he said. Then he burst into a raucous laugh. "You believed every word of it, Middleton. You swallowed it whole. I fooled you completely, my father's little ray of promise, his shining pupil, the brightest jewel in Clio's diadem. You believed it," and once again he laughed loudly.

Gerald said, "I know nothing about it. It isn't my period."

Gilbert bowed mockingly. "I beg your pardon," he said, then mimicking, he added, "Of course, it isn't your *period*. How silly of me. You bloody historians and your periods, you're like a lot of women. Go on," he said. "Hop it." His eyes closed and his head slumped on to his shoulders drunkenly.

Gerald got up and went out of the restaurant, convincing himself gladly that it was another of Gilbert's aggressive drunken jokes.

And so it might well have been, for everything went according to the usual pattern. On the Monday Gerald received the usual charming note of apology from Gilbert—only this one had seemed more than usually sincere, or were they all like that? There had followed three of the happiest months of their friendship. Gilbert had been amusing, interesting, even humane. They had found a common new enthusiasm in soldiering and under its impetus Gilbert seemed to have lost his bitterness or at least the play-acting hysterical aspect of it, even when he was drunk.

It was, however, that same night at Stokesay's after he had left Soho that Gerald first had sex with Dollie. Stokesay had been in bed when he arrived there and Gilbert had been quite right about Dollie—she had been willing and eager. As to her fears of Gilbert, her answer to that had been quite simple: "Of course I'm frightened of him, Gerrie," she had said. "He's very mad, you know. But I'm not superstitious. As long as he doesn't hear of it, what's it matter?"

Even years later when they were living together, Gerald had never told her how much his tension over Gilbert's account of Melpham had given him the courage to seduce her. Melpham was not a subject that would normally interest Dollie and he had always been at pains not to arouse her sense of guilt by any hostile reference to Gilbert. If they mentioned him it was in the terms of praise they had evolved to satisfy his father's hero-worship.

Gerald's attention was drawn back to the family by the sudden sound of his grandson's voice. Timothy had finished his book, and pulling his long gangling body from the armchair, he blinked at the family through his spectacles. "I shall go to bed now, Mother," he said. Crossing the room, he kissed first Marie Hélène and then Inge. "Thank you for a very pleasant Christmas, Grandmother," he said.

Inge took one of his hands and held it for a minute, looking up at his great height. "So you have been improving your time," she said, "while we have been wasting ours in arguments. You are quite right. Life is not made for fighting and quarrels." She was depressed at the degree to which her family kept her out of the conversation. "But *you* are the one who can answer our question, Timothy," she cried. "You are the philosopher. Now *you* will tell us. How does one know the truth about something? Do we know it in a flash—So!—or does it come to us very slowly like a tortoise? Is it a big thing or is it little things? There you are. A difficult question for a very tall boy."

Gerald, remembering his children's reactions to her treatment in the past, was not surprised that Timothy did not apparently resent the immense patronage of her tone. "A difficult question?" he said. "I should have thought it was quite simple, if you know all the facts. It's just a matter of getting every detail in its right place, isn't it? Making the right pattern." His mind was still with his book and he spoke with impatience. "Well, good night," he said and was gone.

Gerald noted as some balm to his feelings that Robin had received no further separate recognition than he had. Many people in his position, he supposed, would seek an ally against the family in Timothy, whose reserve suggested so much hidden criticism. He was not sentimental enough to suppose that it would be difficult to break down his grandson's defences, to win his confidence. But what would he find except one generation's sceptical perception of its elder's follies? And what had he to offer in return? It would be pleasant to redress the balance of the old generation by calling in the new, but the thing savoured too much of Inge's emotional dishonesty, her vicarious living. And to say that the young liked her advances was no justification for betraying his own emotional integrity. Besides, he thought, young men and youths offered nothing but boredom; brash and pert, or shy like Timothy, what they had to say was ultimately callow. If there had been a granddaughter now, it would not have been necessary to listen, her presence alone would have given him life. But as it was . . . callow rubbish. Making the right pattern . . . getting every detail right. But what if there was no pattern, pray, but only a blur of half-remembered details? His arrival at Melpham, for instance, on the day of the discovery. . . .

Gilbert had written first from Melpham, "I believe I am to congratulate you on obtaining a remarkable First in Tripos. So at any rate my father has told me. He, by the way, intends to invite you here, so I give you warning. Do not feel that you have to accept. My father's admiration for your scholarship is great enough to withstand the shock of refusal; so is my friendship. However if you wish to come . . . the country is pleasant, if flat; the excavations belong as yet to the physical rather than to the intellectual disciplines, but my father seems confident of 'important finds' and I shall use all my hitherto latent historical talents to produce them. History, by the way, I now see to be even more of an artisan skill than I had supposed in my most contemptuous moments—at least as you professionals play it. You will be the guest—if you have no more rewarding plan—of the owners of Melpham House— as we are. They are rich cultural snobs who are prepared to kill any number of fatted calves—the food is only passable— in return for finding their marshy and unprofitable estates to be one of England's 'historic treasure-grounds'. To be serious, the Portways quite interest me—they show the last decadence that plutocracy has reached in our declining civilization— money without the confidence of its power. The brother, as well as being the local archaeologist, is a modern Churchman, which means, as far as I can see, an attachment to any and every belief save the dogmas of his own religion. He has revived all manner of old-world customs here—or rather invented them, for I swear that no activities of the past could be so idiotic as his. He is forever setting up maypoles, producing mystery plays and dancing on greens: and, as he has good looks of a theatrical kind, the local ladies swoon at the sight of him. There is behind all this mummery a peculiarly mischievous and foolish sort of egalitarianism based on some romantic notion of medieval society—in short the cloven hoof of William Morris. As a result of all this neglect of his proper duties, of course, he is a very respected figure in the Church, indeed a canonry is in the air. His sister-in-law, your hostess, is the 'great' Lilian Portway and very conscious of it. I thought her at first one of the most odious women I have met—an absurd example of that outdated enormity 'the New Woman'. She is a 'great beauty' in a large, willowy sort of way that would have delighted the late Sir Edward Burne-Jones (is he, by the way, dead? If not, he should be) and *does* delight the 'advanced' theatre public that flock to the plays of Shaw. In addition she has been in Holloway for the 'cause' and speaks on public platforms. Can you think of a more unpleasing combination? However, down here, it must be said, she is less of the feminist and more feminine—she plays in fact the gracious hostess with a dilettante interest in the excavations. She proves, too, to have an agreeable if uninformed enthusiasm for Nietzsche which is creditable. After all, one has to remember that these women's antics are only the product of male permissiveness. However, I get a good deal of amusement twisting both their 'advanced' tails, particularly the egregious parson's. No one of interest lives about here. So you will have to content yourself with your Fabian Maecenas hosts. There is a pretty enough girl who visits. Another enormity—a sports girl. She is on the way to being a tennis champion! However, I suspect that she is susceptible to masculine discipline. Her father is a retired colonel, whom she calls 'an awfully jolly old boy'. Apprehension of boredom has so far prevented me from putting her claims to the test. . . ."

Professor Stokesay's invitation followed hard upon his son's letter of warning. Looking back to it, Gerald felt embarrassed by the touch of Mr Collins it contained. "Mrs Portway—the great Lilian Portway—has urged me to invite you. She is a remarkable woman of extraordinary beauty, considerable personality, and, in addition, she is very cultivated. Her reception of us here has been truly magnificent, and, despite all the claims on her time, she professes and, I truly believe, feels great interest in the excavations. I do not normally attend the theatre, but I promise myself a visit when she next appears in London, for she has a notable and, I can easily believe, well-deserved reputation. She is, alas! deeply involved in the follies of women's suffrage, but with the typical tact of a great lady she has never mounted the soapbox in my presence. If only some of these raucous-voiced women would follow her example, they might do their cause more good than by their present irresponsible behaviour! I do not know how much you will see of Gilbert, for, between ourselves, he is showing a lively interest in a very charming little lady in the neighbour-hood. Despite all his Timon orations against the modern woman, Gilbert seems to have fallen a willing victim to one now, for Miss Armstrong—Dollie as I am allowed to call her —is a champion tennis player!

"I have no doubt that Mrs Portway will send her motor-car to fetch you from the station. Her chauffeur, Barker by the way, is a splendid local character, a fine specimen of East Anglian manhood, who has proved invaluable to us, both by his knowledge of the locality and by the loan of his considerable muscle power, which, in view of the difficulty of engaging satisfactory labour, has been very welcome. . . ."

Mrs Portway's Delage had, in fact, met Gerald—a plum-coloured motor-car with Barker in a plum-coloured uniform matching his complexion. Gerald, more accustomed to such luxuries than Dr Stokesay, was in the habit of making up for his father's taciturnity by a few polite observations to the chauffeur. Such replies as he received from Barker, however, were neither intelligible nor encouraging. He gave himself up to watching as much of the countryside as could be seen through the August dust. Rolling country, oak-wooded here and there among the buff-coloured corn, gave way to flat, marshy heath. Through the dust-choked air Gerald began to sense salt-freshened currents in the slight east wind that cut the morning's heat. Wilting loosestrife, its purple bruised, giant yarrows, their lace dried and buckled, were interspersed increasingly along the roadside by clumsy-headed bullrushes and bushes of feathery tamarisk, their growth twisted westwards by the strong sea gales. It was almost twenty miles from the station to Melpham house, but they had hardly travelled an hour before the motor-car turned into a drive lined by St John's wort and variegated hollies.

"There'll be no one at the house but the mistress," Barker remarked. "We turned up something to the west of Long Mile Meadow this morning. It seems that'd be a bishop's grave that they put out in the marshes in those times. Young Rammage came on the stone coffin digging there with young Mr Stokesay. But that's pretty deep laid. That'll take more than they've got down there to raise. The master's quite taken on with it though, says he must have it up. And Dr Stokesay, he says the same." He was still talking as Gerald caught sight of his hostess on the steps on the square red-brick house; his tongue once loosed, it seemed that Barker could be both loquacious and intelligible.

The sight of Mrs Portway, however, at once took all Gerald's attention. He had been famous at Cambridge for his success with young married women and widows. With his dark good looks and flushed, heavy face, he seemed older than his years and was seldom rejected as a "mere boy". In face of Mrs Portway he felt, and was convinced that he looked, even less than his twenty-two years.

She was indeed the great lady, as she came down the white steps, disconcertingly tall, embarrassingly beautiful, and a shade too striking. Gerald tried to comfort himself by imagining her on rain-swept platforms, their purple and yellow decorations bedraggled and sordid; or, being frogmarched into a police van. It was impossible to do so—she was so very elegant in her long, tight, draped dress in two shades of mauve muslin, above her massed red-gold hair a great mauve straw hat covered in Parma violets, and, held up above that again, a little parasol in the same mauve shades. By the time her wonderful intense voice reached him, he felt unsure of stepping with ease from the motor-car, and, indeed, he slipped and fell on the gravel.

If there had been any likelihood of his capitulating to Lilian Portway's charm that moment saved him. She could have been disconcerted, annoyed or amused by his sudden and clumsy fall. She was none of these things; with *grande dame* grace, she simply did not notice it.

"Welcome, Hermes!" she cried, her long arms with their flowing angel sleeves extended in lovely gesture to meet him. "Dr Stokesay spoke of you as young, brilliant, his most promising pupil. All no doubt, true, but a little mundane. I know better. You have brought sunshine where we had cloud, success where we had deep disappointment. And so, I prefer to ask you—What is the news from Olympus?" She smiled a little wry, whimsical smile.

Gerald scrambled to his feet with difficulty. One foot that had bent beneath his body as he had fallen seemed absurdly painful. He dusted himself down before he answered. All his youthful embarrassment had vanished at the spectacle of *her* shyness, *her* absurdity; from that moment she was fixed for ever outside his category of desirable women.

"Yes," he said, "I've heard the news. It's very exciting. I suppose the monks brought the body here from Sedwich. One more historical mystery solved and an important one, I should think, though it's not my period, of course."

Mrs Portway smiled sweetly. "Thank you," she said, "for your interest. It's wonderful for *us*, isn't it? that it should have been found here at our dear sleepy Melpham? But then Reggie always said it would be. I wonder what other treasures its soil will reveal now that it has been woken from its long sleep?"

Gerald could think of no answer to this question, so he smiled the neutral, polite smile that he used for mothers of friends, "I'd rather like to have a wash," he said, brushing the gravel off the palms of his hands, "and I think they'll probably be glad of a hand with the digging."

"Oh you mustn't wear those smart boots up in the marsh," Mrs Portway said, "we'll see what . . ." But before she had finished, Gerald let out a cry of pain. As he started to walk towards the house, he had put his full weight on his left foot and immediately hot needles seemed to be tearing their way through the flesh of his ankle.

This time Mrs Portway could no longer retain her composure. "Barker," she called, "don't stand there doing nothing. Mr Middleton's hurt. Help him into the house. Alice!" she called into the doorway, "Alice ! come and lend your father a hand. All the men are down on the marsh," she said in explanation to Gerald, as though his evident pain would only make him more socially critical of any defects in the household management.

"I'm so sorry, so frightfully sorry," Gerald could do no more than mutter.

"My dear Mr Middleton, it is *you* we have to be sorry for," she said, but she looked furious.

An ample young parlourmaid, ribbons flying from her cap, came to assist Mr Barker. "Now," she said, "easy does it, sir. Go gently, Father, with the gentleman's arm."

With difficulty, supporting Gerald on each side, Father and Daughter Barker hoisted him up the front steps. Mrs Portway folded her parasol, lifted Gerald's hat from the drive and followed them indoors. "On the sofa in the morning-room would be best, I think," she said with a certain distaste. She did not care for furniture removals, fuss on hot days, attention distracted from her, illness, or cowardice; she felt an unpleasant mixture of all five in Gerald's accident.

Alice began to unlace Gerald's boot, but the ankle was swelling. Her firm handling caused him obvious pain, but this did not deter her.

"If you don't want the motor-car again this day," Barker said, "I'll put that away, ma'am."

Mrs Portway did not answer. She looked at Gerald with roguish sadness, shaking her head. "Not Hermes at all," she said, "but Phaethon fallen from his golden chariot."

There was no saying what other parallels from classical mythology she might have found, but as she spoke a fresh-complexioned, light-haired young girl of seventeen or so came into the room. "I say, what's up?" she asked, then seeing Alice Barker's efforts with Gerald's boot, she rushed forward before Mrs Portway could explain.

"Oh, do be careful, Alice," she cried. "Let me. Have you a penknife, Barker?" She began at once to cut away the boot. "Get me some bandage, Alice," she said, "and a jug of cold water, as cold as you can find it."

Alice clearly left the room with a very bad grace, but Gerald was too taken up with the pain to mind the moods of those around him any more. He closed his eyes. The girl said, "It's a very bad sprain, Lilian." Mrs Portway said nothing, but he could guess at her expression of annoyance, for the girl's voice had a soothing note as she said, "Oh! It'll be perfectly all right. There's no need for a doctor."

Gerald felt the cool of her fingers and the icy tightness of the bandage as she began to bind his ankle.

"He'll have to lie here for a while yet. I'd like to have him here all day if possible," and then in reply to a murmuring of Mrs Portway's, "Oh that's all right. I make a top hole nurse."

"Mr Middleton," Mrs Portway said with dramatic urgency, "you mustn't move on any account. We can't think of it. Miss Armstrong will look after you. Don't hesitate to ask Alice for anything you want, Dollie. And now, I think the less people fussing round you the better," she said and was gone.

At first the day passed in pain and enchantment with Dollie Armstrong; later it passed in enchantment with twinges of pain. Neither mood, however, inclined him to wish for any contact with the members of the household. He could hear a great deal of coming and going in the hall outside, and once, Dollie, who sat in an armchair reading a number of *Nash's Magazine*, said, "They're all in a great fuss about this coffin they've found. I suppose it *is* jolly exciting, but I can't see the point of it myself."

Gerald agreed with her. He would have agreed with anything that this attractive girl, so cool in her white linen dress
with its huge sailor collar, might say to him.

As the day passed, they were interrupted more frequently.
Professor Stokesay was the first to come in. He had talked over
the wonderful discovery with all the other excavators and he
could not bear any longer to deny himself a further audience
in Gerald. He looked taller than usual in his tweed knicker-
bockers and woollen stockings. His face was fresh and weather-
beaten, his brown beard trim and neat.

"My dear boy," he said, "what an unfortunate accident,
and today of all days." He paused as he saw Dollie, "Ah! but
you're well looked after." He did not quite like the idea of a
young man and a young woman shut up all day in the morning-
room like this, but Mrs Portway's position as lady of the manor
and famous actress reconciled him to her advanced ways. "How
is the patient, nurse?" he asked.

"Oh, he'll be up and walking by tea-time," she answered,
"I don't think . . ." She stopped, for Professor Stokesay was
no longer listening. He knew now that this embarrassing in-
commoding of their hostess would not last and he felt free to
talk of the excavation.

"A most wonderful find," he said. "Now be prepared for a
great shock. I can hardly believe it yet. We've discovered
Eorpwald's tomb. Those loyal monks brought him here to
Melpham. Stone coffin with inscription in an excellent condition. We've moved it to the outhouse. Some trace of the
skeleton. . . ." And then as Gerald was about to speak, he held
up his finger for attention. "But wait a bit! That's less than
half. In the coffin with its Christian inscription, the remains
and the well-preserved remains of a wooden figure. I don't
know what to make of it; if it wasn't too extraordinary I
would say it was a pagan idol. I've only seen sketches and poor
photographs of the Anglo-Saxon gods found in Friesland and
on the Baltic coast, but I'd swear it was the same. After all
there were many of them in the country. It might be. Nothing

like it has been found in England before, it's true, but there
must have been many of them, and the lucky chance of a pre-
serving peaty soil. . . . But, in a Christian tomb! Well, I have
my ideas, though it's too soon to speak yet. All I hope, my
dear fellow, is that Portway doesn't rush . . ."

His voice tailed off and, in a rather artificial note, he said,
"Ah! Portway! I'm just telling this young fellow of our remarkable discoveries and adding a word of caution about
rushing to conclusions. But I forgot, you don't know each
other. Mr Portway, my promising pupil, Middleton. Promising
that is if he doesn't make a habit of damaging his ankle when
visiting other people's houses."

Reginald Portway's handsome dark eyes seemed to give
Gerald a faint wink. "Don't regard Stokesay at all. You break
your ankle whenever you come to a country house party. The
more demonstrations against landed property we have the
better, and breaking your ankle's a novel one. You might
suggest it to my sister-in-law for the Suffrage campaign." It
was a feature of his support of advanced causes that he wore
them all with a smile and a touch of humour. He saw, he always
said, no reason to offend by shouting one's convictions in an
unmannerly way. It had given him a most useful reputation in
the Church world as one of the powerful-thinking, progressive
clergymen with a sense of humour and decent manners. "I
only hope you're feeling better," he said, and Gerald realized
his charm from the immense conviction of personal solicitude
he gave to the conventional inquiry. "But I'm sure you are,
with so charming a Florence Nightingale to attend you."
Gerald saw a slight look of hostility in Dollie's eye and decided
at once that Portway's charm was very meretricious.

"As to caution, my dear Stokesay," he went on, and once
again he seemed to wink at Gerald as he addressed Lionel
Stokesay—he was clearly always on youth's side against the
absurdities of middle age, "I agree with you, but I doubt if
we shall have to be cautious long in this case. I admit it gave
me an unpleasant surprise at first, and so it should have done

to a good Churchman. But the Church has always had its odd fish." He laughed. " Some people would say you see one before you. And Eorpwald was clearly one of the oddest. After all he came of pagan stock. We aren't surprised when some poor fellow in Africa or Asia gets confused between the true God and his idols. Don't let us condemn poor Eorpwald too quickly."

His mobile, handsome features took on a look of understanding compassion, then changed to lively interest. "No, Stokesay, what of course engrosses me is the way that this confirms the anonymous chronicler writing in his monastery up here six centuries later. I've been looking up the passage. There it is as bold as life—charges of sorcery, and I think we know *now* what the sorcery was. But no mention in Bede, of course. So much for your national historian, it's the local man and the local tradition that get there every time. You see my parochialism, Middleton," he said with a smile.

"You may be right," said Professor Stokesay, "but after all the *vita anonymi* is a piece of very late special pleading. He wanted Rome to canonize Eorpwald."

"All the more extraordinary," said Portway, "that he should have put in the story of the charge of sorcery. The answer, of course, is that he had to. It was too well known locally even after all those centuries for him to dare to leave it out. And judging by the complete failure of the plea at Rome, Innocent III knew something of the story as well." He did not seem to notice that he was contradicting his defence of local tradition as the *sole* repository of truth.

"That may be so," said Lionel Stokesay, "but I made a search some years ago in the Vatican Library for a deposition against Eorpwald, when I was working on Wilfrid, and could find nothing. That's what makes me doubtful of the value of the anonymous life."

"Well, you can't be doubtful now," Reginald Portway said heartily, "and as to the manuscript not being at the Vatican, that doesn't surprise me." He gave a worldly look. "I know

Church politics too well. Ah! come in, Frank," he went on, as the head of a Botticelli cherub surmounted by red-gold curls peered round the door. "I've just been defending our local traditions against those Londoners."

The owner of the angel's head appeared as a stockily built youth of between sixteen and seventeen, his muscles already suggesting a future fatness. He was dressed in a neat pepper-and-salt cloth suit. "I'm just going home now, Mr Portway," he said.

"Yes, yes, Frank, but look in again this evening. I've written down that song the old chap sang in the workhouse at Great Yatsley. I'd like to hear you sing it. Frank has a fine alto voice," he told the company. "This is Mr Middleton, Frank, who's just won high distinctions in his Cambridge finals. We don't despair of Cambridge ourselves, do we, Frank? Or rather, our preference is for Oxford. Frank is our local scholar, Middleton, with a nice old-fashioned taste for the classics. But we may see you an historian yet, Frank, after your part in our discovery. Frank was with Gilbert when the coffin was uncovered early this morning."

"No," said Frank, "that was Barker. I didn't come until later."

"Oh, I understood it was you. Never mind, you've done stalwart work. Well, don't forget, come about six."

When the boy had left them, Reginald Portway said dramatically, "He talks of going home. But he has no real home, poor boy. He's an orphan brought up by an old woman in the village. I have great hopes for him. He's got a good brain, a fine musical sense, and he's a charming lad. I intend to see that he has education too. Education, you know, is the one road by which the simple people of this country may come into their own once more."

Gerald exaggerated his exhaustion so that he might be alone with Dollie again. He closed his eyes, and after a little conversation among themselves Stokesay and Portway withdrew. Lilian Portway came in once or twice and expressed the hope that he was better.

At lunch-time Alice Barker brought a tray and Dollie went to get her own lunch. Gerald, feeling that he had annoyed the hefty parlourmaid, said, "I hear your father was first on the scene with Mr Gilbert Stokesay."

Alice looked at him suspiciously. "No," she said, "that was that Frank."

When Dollie returned she brought Gilbert with her. "I have not visited you earlier, Middleton," he said, "because I have a wholesome dislike of pain. However, now that I understand that you are convalescent I can ask you the conventional question, 'Are you better?' I shall equally conventionally not wait for your answer. It is obvious that with Dollie to wash you, or whatever these nurses do, you've had a delightful time. I shall not also tell you about 'our discovery' since my father has already been here. However, it's nice to think that the un-diluted milk of the Nazarene gospel was not strong enough diet for the good old Anglo-Saxon episcopal stomach. He had to have this little wooden fellow as well, and a very priapic little fellow at that, I may tell you. Alas! without the faintest aesthetic interest. The Christmas Islanders do better. *This* is merely primitive, and admiration of the primitive for its own sake is a Rousseauish sort of romanticism I very much dislike."

Gerald could remember little more about the visit, except that the next day he had the pleasure of seeing Gilbert lose innumerable sets of tennis to Dollie. She was very good, it was true, but Gilbert was always very bad at games. . . .

So that, he thought, was the whole of it. Suspicions engendered by the words of a drunkard and the actions of a hysterical woman. He had never dared to confront Gilbert with his words again nor face Inge with his suspicions about Kay's hand. And from these slender foundations it seemed he had woven a great web of depression and despair to convince himself that his chosen study of history was a lie and the family life he had made a deception. Even if these suspicions had proved true—and he had carefully let them lie in the hinterland of his mind until it was too late to test them—what then? An odd freak of Anglo-Saxon history was faked. What did that matter to the general study of the subject? An hysterical, unhappy woman had been guilty of an act of cruelty to a small child. It had not made the adoration of the girl and young woman for her mother any less. It seemed to him suddenly as though he had come out of a dark narrow tunnel, where movement was cramped to a feeble crawl, into the broad daylight where he could once more walk or run if he chose.

Inge's voice came to him. "Now there is your father, who has slept all through our wonderful talk."

"No, I hear you, my dear," he said.

"We have been talking about truth. But you are the one who can tell us. The great scholar!" Her voice was sarcastic. He got up and, walking over to her, he kissed her on the cheek. It was an action only a little less sarcastic than her words.

"You know all about the truth, don't you, Gerald?" she asked.

"Yes, my dear, I think I do," he answered, "but I'm going off to bed."

When he got upstairs to his room, he sat down and wrote to Sir Edgar, accepting the editorship of the *History*.

PART TWO

CHAPTER ONE

SIR EDGAR IFFLEY lived in a large late-Victorian Italianate House near Holland Park. The manservant who opened the door to Gerald was as old as his master. The hall, though spacious, was dark and smelt of port wine and roast beef. Sir Edgar's study, into which Gerald was shown, was also a large room, but light, with french windows looking on to a trim garden, bare and grey in the feeble February afternoon sun. The study smelt of cigars and *pot pourri* rose petals. Two of the high walls were covered in books, but against the third wall was a cabinet overcrowded with objects. A tenth-century ivory chessman, a twelfth-century wooden virgin, two Romano-British tiles, a stone Romanesque demon with fish-scale body, a late medieval green earthenware pot: the excellence of Sir Edgar's collection contrasted oddly with the bad Edwardian reproductions of Italian primitives—the gold too bright and the red too dull—that hung on each side of the cabinet.

"You took your time coming back from Vienna, Middleton," said Sir Edgar gruffly, as he rose from the chair behind his long desk that filled the window recess with its card indexes and files. "You look very well, anyway. I hope you've come back ready for some hard work, because that's what awaits you."

"I stayed until the Exhibition closed," said Gerald. He did not care to tell of how he had pored over every drawing, spun out every hour, like a smoker, committed to abstaining, with his last packet of cigarettes. He would not reveal with what reluctance he had returned to the task which he had promised so earnestly to perform. Seating himself in one of the deep leather armchairs, he drew out a sheet of paper from his inside pocket and handed it to Sir Edgar. "This is a tentative list of contributors for the *History*," he said. "I wrote to them last night when I got back to London."

The little old man seemed more than ever like some beetle, humped over the long desk, peering at the list with frowning brows. "Well," he said at last, "I shan't repeat all I said to you in my letter. It's the greatest relief to me, of course, that you've agreed to take on the job. You're so essentially the only one who can do it that I never believed you would let us down." He looked at the list again, "You've cast your net wide," he said. "And rightly. Roberts, Stringwell-Anderson. I'm glad you're making good use of the young men. Do you think you can trust Lavenham not to be tendentious on the Orders in England?"

Gerald smiled. "An *English* Benedictine?" he queried, "and Lavenham is *very* English. A touch of nationalist schism is more to be feared, I should think."

Sir Edgar laughed. "Oh! We're not concerned with his relations with his spiritual directors," he said.

The old manservant brought in a tray of tea. Anchovy toast was covered by a steaming silver cover as it had been in Sir Edgar's undergraduate days. Two sorts of cake were by custom provided—a rich Dundee and a Genoa profuse with crystallized cherries. Gerald remembered too late that the tea was poured out according to Sir Edgar's taste—a strong russet brown.

After the old servant retired, Sir Edgar sat back, intently stirring his strong, sweet tea for a few moments, then he said, "A lot of these people are impossible to deal with. You're in for a number of battles that'll bring you down in sorrow to the grave. But that's nothing to do with me. Anyway, you may do better than I did with the last *History*. That was forty years ago when the academic world prided itself more on prickliness. Besides you use tact; I never did. You'll need all your tact with Clun, I can tell you. He wrote me a very unpleasant letter after the news of your appointment as editor appeared in the *Bulletin*. I don't propose to show it to you because that sort of thing doesn't do, but he's not fond of you to put it mildly. I dislike the man, you know, but I think he sincerely feels he could have done the job better."

"Oh, as a one-man job he undoubtedly could," said Gerald, "but I doubt if the contributors would recognize much of their work by the time he'd done editing it."

Sir Edgar looked up for a minute from under his bushy eyebrows. "I hope you're not going to be too soft with them, Middleton," he said.

Gerald ignored the remark. "I must have Clun's contributions. I want him on the Anglo-Saxon constitutional stuff *and* on the growth of towns. I'm prepared to use all my charms."

"You'll need to."

"I've asked him to lunch at the Athenæum on Wednesday."

Sir Edgar laughed abruptly. "I doubt if that'll impress him." Then noticing a shade of annoyance on Gerald's heavy face, he added, "Anyway, I wish you luck. He knows that his co-operation with you will score him a good mark with me for what that's worth. There's something more important than Clun though. You haven't included Rose Lorimer in this list. It's an odd oversight, isn't it?"

This time Gerald did not control his annoyance. "I should have thought you knew my concern and my personal fondness for Rose too well to have supposed that I'd overlooked her. It has cost me a great deal to omit her name. In my view, the *History* must override all personal considerations. Whatever Rose *may* have been, she is not now a responsible scholar." Gerald's habitual flush had now a dark, almost black hue and his drawl a slight braying note.

Sir Edgar disregarded these things. "Have you seen her since you came back?" he asked.

"No, of course not. How could I have done? I only arrived here last night."

"Well, you will in about a quarter of an hour. I've asked her to come here." Sir Edgar overrode whatever protest Gerald was about to make. "You'll find her changed, I think," he continued. "One doesn't like to be dogmatic about such things, but I believe she's cured of whatever was wrong with her. Perhaps," he added, "it was something to do with her age."

"Hardly that, I think," Gerald said.

Sir Edgar detected a touch of patronage towards his bachelor state in Gerald's tone. "Well, I don't know. I'm not a medical man," he said irritably. "It was probably Pforzheim's information. She seems to feel that she's been vindicated or something. At any rate she's shed all the insane fringes of her theories. She's back where she was ten years ago, and, in my opinion, that means that she's one of the best medievalists in England." He paused for a moment and smiled to himself. "I think," he said slowly, "that when she comes you should ask her to do the article on the English conversion for the *History*."

Gerald's hands trembled with anger. "I happen to have written to Wainwright already," he said. "And in any case I shouldn't care to take the responsibility of what you suggest."

Sir Edgar smiled again. "Yes, yes, my dear boy," he said, "I know what you're thinking. Nevertheless, I think you should ask her. I'll take the responsibility involved."

"I hate to remind you that I'm the editor."

Sir Edgar's little wrinkled face was set in complacent lines, his beady eyes looked at Gerald ironically. "You do what I say, my dear fellow," he said in his most authoritative tone.

Gerald hesitated for a moment, then he swallowed with a gulp of the throat. "Very well," he said, "but please understand that I resent your interference." The casual laugh with which he palliated the remark did not make it the less direct.

He felt increasingly resentful when Rose was announced, yet he had to admit to himself that her appearance was vastly improved. Her hair no longer straggled across her face, the powder on her cheeks was less noticeably splodgy, she was wearing a dark blue woollen dress which was neither stained nor dependent on safety pins; only her hat with its little bouquet of pink and pale-blue woollen flowers was faintly absurd. He reflected, however, that Rose's hats had always been a slight embarrassment.

"Well!" she said brightly, "so the prodigal's returned. I suppose you spent a huge fortune on some drawing or other."

Gerald laughed. "I would have had to have done so to have bought the Leonardos in Vienna," he said. "It was an exhibition not a sale, Rose."

"Oh! I don't suppose that would deter you if you were out for spoils," she said. He remembered that this arch manner towards men had been habitual to her before her "illness". The little "daring" smile with which she accepted the glass of sherry offered to her by the manservant equally recalled the past.

"Anyway," she said, raising her glass, "here's all success to the *History*. I'm so awfully glad, Gerald, that you accepted the editorship. But then I knew you would. You men always need wooing." In a more straightforward, comradely tone, she added, " I look forward greatly to working for you."

Gerald blushed scarlet, then with an exaggeration of his usual drawl that betrayed his embarrassment, he said, "I wanted to talk to you about that. Sir Edgar was suggesting that you might do the chapter on the Conversion of England for me." He shot a sharp look at Sir Edgar, but the old man was watching Rose intently.

She fumbled in her handbag for a moment and then spoke in a hurried, squeaky voice, "Oh, I don't think so," she said. "I've given the Church far more attention than it deserves for so many years. Besides, one of these young Anglicans ought to do it. What about Jack Wainwright? I'm all in favour of hearing from the young people. I've got my own ideas, of course, but they'll come into their own in time." She sipped at her sherry, and then looked up at Gerald with a coy look. "You know how I told you that I was bored lecturing on Exchequer administration. And you said," here she giggled, "that my pupils might be equally bored with the same old lecture. Well, of course, you were quite right. I'm thoroughly ashamed of myself. I've completely neglected my later medieval studies. After all," she said grandly, "I was one of Professor Tout's most favoured pupils."

Gerald frowned. It was all a little too good to be true. "You were Stokesay's pupil for many more years than you were Tout's," he said sharply.

"Oh, I know, but I've been rather silly lately, thrusting Lionel Stokesay's views down everyone's throat. He was far too great an historian to need my canvassing for him. Anything he did that's disputed will be vindicated sooner or later without my help," she smiled roguishly at Sir Edgar. "No, Gerald, I would like to do the chapter for you on the development of royal administration down to the fourteenth century. I'll limit myself to the Exchequer, if you prefer that, but I'd like to do the whole bag of tricks really—Exchequer, Chancery, Wardrobe and all. I've got a demon in me to get down to some really hard work." She paused for a moment and then looked at Gerald. "I think you'll find I'll do good work for you," she said. "You mustn't judge by the last few years. I haven't been at all well, you know."

It was Sir Edgar who answered her. "It's wonderful to see you yourself again," he said. Gerald felt that he had failed in not replying first, so he tried to make up the deficiency by the warmth with which he said, "My dear Rose."

Rose Lorimer fumbled again in her handbag for a moment and both men were horrified lest she should start to cry. Gerald said quickly, "Why don't you dine with me, Rose, and discuss the details? It's far too long since you were my guest." "Oh dear! how I should have loved to." She turned to Sir Edgar. "To have to refuse one of Gerald's magnificent dinners! But I'm going to supper with the Robertses. Have you been there, Gerald? They have such a pleasant little flat in Cromwell Road. Betty Roberts has been so kind to me. They've told me to make it a second home. Of course, we've been brought together by our common interest in Pforzheim's work, and now that Jasper Stringwell-Anderson has gone over to Heligoland, I hear all the new developments through the letters he writes to Theo Roberts. . . ."

Gerald interrupted her excited flow. "I can't think what's possessed Jasper to go flying off to Heligoland of all places at this moment. In term too. I particularly wanted his help in compiling the editorial rules."

Sir Edgar raised his eyebrows. "The poor chap *has* got a Sabbatical and the work there is rather important on any grounds," he said. "For the English historian it must have peculiar importance because of the possible new light it throws on Melpham. By the way, Middleton, Pforzheim wants to get your first-hand account of the excavation there."

Gerald was perplexed by all these references to the Heligoland excavations, but he had determined resolutely not to open the question of Melpham to his conscience, so he said rather grimly. "Maybe. I don't know. I can't tell him anything anyway. My ankle was sprained."

Rose was deterred by his expression from questioning him further; she contented herself by saying, "Well, it doesn't really matter now. Everything's going along so nicely. I'm convinced that we're only at the beginning of even more extraordinary finds." She, too, seemed to have agreed with herself upon censored topics, for she pulled up short and remarked with a cosy smile, "But what's so wonderful for me is the way that it's brought me into touch with people again, especially the young people. I'd got badly cut off, you know. But they're so awfully kind, Sir Edgar. Mr Stringwell-Anderson took me to a restaurant in Soho. He knows almost as much about food as you do, Gerald. Do you know *Shaslik*? Well, we had that. Rather highly seasoned, but then it's oriental. Theo Roberts said he preferred a good mince." She laughed in reminiscence of the unwonted world of wit and sparkle in which she now lived. "They took me to see this new Italian actress Magnani. Such a wonderful film about peasants. It took me back to my holiday in Assisi. Of course, I used to love the cinema, but I'd quite stopped going. It's all new names now and cowboys. I used not to like cowboys but they do take one out of oneself. But this evening I'm taking the Robertses to something *they've* never seen—Duvivier's 'Joan of Arc'. I do so hope they like it, because I shall certainly weep myself. Theo's coming here to fetch me in his little Austin. Is that all right, Sir Edgar?"

The old man came to suddenly from a half-sleep. He reflected that the price of Rose's return to normality was inevitably tedious. Gerald, too, was wondering, as he had so often in the past, how so childish a mind could be so accurate, so painstaking and, yes, so intelligent when it came to the study of the Middle Ages.

A moment later the manservant announced that Gerald's car was waiting for him. "I'm sorry to miss Theo," Gerald said. "Tell him to get in touch with me as soon as he can. Why don't you lunch with me on Friday, Rose?" He had no engagement that prevented him from waiting to see Theo, yet he felt unwilling to witness the material evidence of Rose's new found friendships. He suddenly knew envy for the easy happiness with which she had returned to life, while his own return was so lonely and uneasy.

As the Daimler was held up in a traffic block near the Brompton Oratory, Gerald saw with pleasure a tall dark girl walking ahead of them towards Knightsbridge. He followed the curve of her hips beneath her tight black skirt, and her thighs as they rubbed their vigorous way forward.

It was only when he had put his lust aside with vexation and regret, telling himself in compensation how unattractively fat she would soon become, that he realized that it was his son John's secretary, Elvira Portway. He leaned forward and told Larwood to draw up beside her. He peered out into the cold, darkening air, "How are you?" he asked. He enjoyed for a moment the trembling of her body as she was jostled from abstraction and the cold stare with which she evidently met cruising wolves.

"Oh it's you," she cried, "I thought you were in Vienna or somewhere heavenly."

"I was wishing I were still there until the evening rewarded me by meeting you," he said.

She took the compliment as though its stilted conventionality had brought her face to face with old Q or Prinny or some other long-dead satyr. "Oh it's just the same here as it always is," she said. "Nobody has anything new to say and everybody's going to bed with the same boring people as usual, or, if they aren't, it's worse."

He wondered for a moment what the circle of society could be like that failed to entertain her. "No one I know is going to bed with anyone," he replied, "but that's because they're so old." Then feeling that perhaps he was being a little comically sophisticated for an old man, he asked, "How is my son?"

Elvira paused for a moment as though uncertain of what the words meant, then she cried, "Oh! *Johnnie*! I've left him, you know. But I think he's all right. At least, as all right as he'll ever be. He's in the thick of this boring Pelican business still. There's a ghastly article of his about it in this evening's paper."

There was a moment's silence, then Gerald said, "I suppose you're full of engagements this evening." He regretted the choice of words instantly but knew that any other would have been as bad.

"Oh! no," she cried, "Mondays are one of the evenings when we . . ." She stopped and said, "No, I'm going home to read the new Compton Burnett."

The allusion was only vaguely familiar to Gerald. "Would you care to dine with me?" he asked.

"I'd love to," she answered directly, and, when he asked her to choose a restaurant, she said, "No, you do that thing. I'd much rather it was your choice." He suggested Scott's, and she said, "But that sounds absolutely the right thing." He hoped that she was not going to put him in his place the whole evening. She rejected Larwood's offer of a fur rug and settling herself beside Gerald, she said, "Do you do a lot of this picking up?" He wondered if this meant what he hoped, but when he looked at her face, her expression was entirely perfunctory. He felt depressed, flattened. "I don't often get such pleasant opportunities," he said in a dulled voice.

"I believe it's usually salesmen," she said, "The gowns must get in the way so." She pronounced "gowns" in a comic cockney accent. He felt tired at the prospect of an evening's such superior, amusing talk.

When they got to Scott's, he dismissed Larwood for the evening. "We can take a taxi," he said. He saw her look of annoyance and regretted his action. He might, he supposed, have guessed that these intellectually snobbish young women would also be snobbish about money and social superiority.

"I wish you'd kept the car," she said, as they sat down at their table, "I like everything to be as luxurious as it can be. It's such a bore when people do things they don't have to." Once again he warmed to her.

She chose oysters and lobster Delmonico. "I suppose you'd better tell me now what's your attitude to Robin and me," she remarked, picking at the torn quick of her thumb. Gerald looked blank. "Oh God!" she cried, "how boring! That's what I always do. I suppose it's being English. The English are the most ghastly egocentrics aren't they?" She took the evening paper from where it lay with her bag. "I think perhaps it would be better if I read Johnnie's article to you in a funny voice. Do you like people imitating? I can do Johnnie rather well." She began to read: " 'I am delighted to hear that some Members of Parliament of both parties are to ask questions of the Government about the unfortunate mishandling of Mr Cressett's market-garden. More power to their elbow, I say.' " Elvira read the phrase in a parody of John's schoolboy manner. "Oh God!" she cried, "isn't it hell?" She continued reading: " 'As a late member of the House of Commons, I welcome any movement that will reduce the danger of the oldest of all representative bodies becoming a mere rubber stamp. But make no mistake, this is not just a party matter. Those Labour members who use this issue as a stick to beat the Government are as much in the wrong or almost as much so as those tireless Tories who seek to use it in their selfish battle against national- ization and their self-interested attack on the Civil Service. The British are proud of their Civil Service and they have reason to be so. It is one of the finest instruments of govern- ment in the world today, but it is an instrument not an agent. It is wrong that successive governments should have allowed civil servants the power to order the lives of citizens without redress. It is wrong of the citizens to permit it. It is unfair to the hard-worked civil servants to place them in such a position of power. The redress of Mr Cressett's ills is not an attack on individual civil servants, it is a demand that the Civil Service shall once again return to those traditions of service which have made it so respected. But we must never forget that behind all these matters of principle there lies the story of an individual. Cressett has no wish, I am sure, that his already trampled-upon market-garden should become the battleground of party politics. He wants only, in the words of Voltaire's Candide, to cultivate his garden or so much of it as is left to him.' Oh! God!" cried Elvira, "Candide! Isn't it squalid?"

"I don't care for John's language certainly," Gerald replied, "but as to the rights and wrongs of the case I haven't enough knowledge to judge."

"But that's the whole *point*." Elvira was almost shouting, "There *isn't* any knowledge. It's just one of these awful British occasions for moralizing. You take up something where somebody's in the wrong and make an arbitrary de- cision about the goats and the sheep and then start making moral noises. It's just an English parlour game," she said, twisting her hair with her fingers, "and what's so *ghastly* is that it's got into our literature. It's all there in Morgan Forster and those people."

Gerald noticed that, the more vague the content of her words became, the more emphasis she laid on them. "You seem very much against English things," said Gerald.

"But *of course*, I am," she cried. "Any ordinary person who wants to lead a civilized life and who's even reasonably aware of literature and painting and so on *has* to be. It may be all right for scholars, I really don't know. And, of course, it's wonderful for geniuses. We all know about English Philistinism forcing geniuses into rebellion, killing Keats and all that. But for ordinary civilized people like me it's simply ghastly." She waved her fork at him menacingly. "It's easy enough to make fun of the intelligentsia of Europe, their earnestness and their cafés, but at least they aren't provincial. *Every single* English intellectual is *provincial* and bloody," she ended savagely.

She leaned back in her chair, her breasts swelling with indignation. That's the part *I* like, Gerald thought.

"Don't let's say any more about it. It's *too* ghastly," she said. "Can we have another bottle of wine?" The arrival of the second bottle seemed a signal for her to relax. She lit a cigarette, turned sideways in her chair and crossed her legs. Gerald decided that he would at least allow himself the pleasure of staring at them.

"I think really I'd better tell you all about Robin and me," she said, blowing a cloud of smoke as though she were retreating in battle. "You're almost certain to hear sooner or later. Though, goodness knows, I probably only say that because I can't conceive anybody not living on the gossip of my own little circle. It's probably some other reason entirely really—some awful English thing about my needing a father figure to confess it to. Anyhow, I *do* rather hope we may get to know each other, and there's a limit to hypocrisy, isn't there really? At least, I mean, now it's not the nineteenth century, there is, isn't there? The awful thing is that it's almost impossible to say it in English, because the English always divide up sex and love so much that they haven't got any real words that do for both. All the awful people I know would say 'going to bed with each other', but it isn't that only and anyway that's an awful genteelism. In any respectable language I could say

I was Robin's mistress and leave it at that, only in English that would mean either something commercial or a lot of nonsense about France and *l'amour*. Anyhow that's what *I have* been for two years."

Gerald could find no words but "I see."

"Oh, for God's sake, don't say silly things," cried Elvira. "Of course you can't see. Nobody can unless they're one of the two people concerned."

Gerald sought for words. "I meant," he said slowly, "that I've never been very close to my family and therefore I'm not used to confidences about them. What they do is their own concern. I hope you and Robin are happy, and, for the rest, I have nothing to say."

Elvira stubbed out her cigarette angrily on a plate. "I think all that's rather awful really. That sort of outdated modern thing about parents and children not being connected. I don't see any point in a family if you go on like that." She paused for a moment, then added, "I suppose if I really cared about families, I should think of Robin's. I would, I believe, if Marie Hélène was a real person, but, thank God, she isn't. But as to being happy, if you mean it as a portmanteau word for all sorts of 'goods', then, thank you, yes, we are very happy."

Gerald, looking at her profile, could not discern much of this emotion in her tense mouth and the strained look about her rather hysterical blue eyes. He felt that to remain silent would be less friendly than to risk impertinence, though the information had left him with a certain repugnance which he preferred not to define. "You've met my daughter-in-law then?" he asked.

"Oh God! yes. Before I met Robin. She's the most awful lion-huntress, you know; so she was always trying to get Johnnie to her parties, but he saw pretty soon that they were no use to him and then she tried to suck up to me. The woman in Johnnie's life! She's crassly stupid, you see. Actually, poor thing, she's probably quite a good ordinary French bourgeoise, only like all of them she's a colossal snob and money's

gone to her head. She gives these ghastly parties and poor
Robin has to tag along—British Council people and the most
minor politicians and all the bad writers and painters who
aren't even best-sellers. She thinks she's a sort of cultural link
between England and France, and every now and again she
gets hold of some French writer whom nobody would *touch*
over there and does an enormous thing about him. Actually
she's just about heard of Montherlant. I do hope you don't
like her, but I can't imagine anyone would bother to think
about her unless they happened to be in love with her husband.
I don't like her at all."

Gerald laughed; "I realized that," he said.

"Well, would *you* in my position?" Elvira cried.

"No, certainly not." Gerald replied, "Robin's very intelligent," he added.

"Yes, I suppose he *is* in a way," said Elvira, "only he's
awfully badly educated and doesn't know anything about
anything worth knowing about. Anyhow, that's not why I'm
in love with him, but I think we won't discuss that. The awful
thing is that he's so sensible, and with Marie Hélène being a
Catholic and a bitch and refusing to divorce him, *we* have to
be sensible. I'm not *really* very good at it. Because Robin thinks
he has a duty to Timothy, and, of course, he's right. So we only
meet four evenings in the week and Marie Hélène has to know
and give her tacit consent, which means that she can't do
anything about it but one feels she's there all the time. And
then what's so awful about me is that when I know it's an
evening to be with Robin, I feel I want to do something else;
and when it's like tonight and I can't see him, I have the most
hellish pain in my stomach and want him awfully. But still
that's part of being in love and the price one pays for being so
madly happy and so on, isn't it?"

Gerald looked at her to see if she was speaking ironically,
but she was completely serious. He wondered if it was fanciful
to hear Dollie's voice once more through all the years in this.
Fanciful or not, he decided, it really was his duty to try to

help for once. "I think, you know," he said, "that you should tell Robin all this. These sensible arrangements can upset things badly and they can always be rearranged if they have to be. I know something about it because the serious love of my life came to me after *I* married and it was broken up by things of this sort."

"Thank you," said Elvira, "but I don't really want any advice. Besides, I've heard about your girl-friend. She was a tennis player, wasn't she? So it's hardly the same thing."

Gerald smiled, "I doubt if such distinctions matter much in love affairs."

Elvira gulped down her coffee. "Oh no, not in the absolute basic part of it, of course," she cried, "but it must matter whether you're a person with any *real* relationship to life or not." Gerald felt angry at her tone of superiority. "I'm sorry," she said. "I don't mean to be superior. And anyhow, even if I don't want advice, I do really want a father figure, however English and awful it is of one to do so. What I should like is if Robin and I could visit you sometimes."

Gerald was appalled at the prospect. However, "I should be delighted," he said. "I doubt if Robin will care for the idea much though, we've never been on very easy terms."

Elvira rather inexpertly brushed some crumbs off her skirt. "Oh! *that*!" she said. "I think all that's rather silly."

It seemed to Gerald that he heard a voice condemning the whole complicated machinery of his past life without seeing even the remotest necessity for examining its structure. Nonsense of this sort from an attractive girl had at least the merit of making one try to defend the indefensible.

Any defence of his conduct as a parent that he intended to make was prevented by Elvira. "I must go now and get on with the new Compton Burnett," she said. "But before I go, since we've got on to this confessional basis, I think I'd better say something about Johnnie. I couldn't go on working for him, you know, because he's got so impossible and bogus, but I *am* very fond of him. Oh! not," she added, waving her cigarette in the air, "because he's a queer. I'm not that sort of a girl. . . ." She stopped and looked at Gerald in alarm. "Oh, my God! You didn't even know that. Well, it's time you did. He is," she said savagely.

Gerald stirred uneasily in his chair. "I'm not quite sure if I know what you mean," he said.

"He's homosexual," Elvira went on in the same angry voice. "That's what 'queer' means. I hope you're not going to be stuffy and difficult about it."

Gerald answered slowly. "I didn't know that John was a homosexual," he said. "I know very little about him really, and even less about the subject we're discussing. I've only come across it three or four times in my life, among people I actually knew, that is. It revolts me rather, I think, but I'm not violent about the subject. I'm just not interested."

"Well, you should be," said Elvira, "or at least, I don't know. Perhaps not. I'm bored stiff with it myself, but that's another matter. Anyhow, I don't want you to think I'm a queer's woman. I don't like a lot of them—all that cosiness and being martyred. But I *was* very fond of Johnnie. He used to be so discreet—he's that secret kind, you know—but since all this awful publicity-seeking has taken hold of him, he seems to have lost all his sense. His new boy-friend Larrie is the most awful little crook, I'm sure, and I'm worried about it. I think you should do something about it."

Gerald raised his eyebrows. "You have very exacting views of a father's functions," he said.

"I suppose I have," Elvira replied. "My own father was a very responsible person."

"I see," Gerald observed, "but I doubt if I can do much. John is hardly likely to listen to me on any subject. And on this one, as you've already heard, I'm ill-equipped to speak. His mother is far closer to him than I am."

"Oh her!" Elvira snorted.

"You know my wife?"

"No," said Elvira, "but I've heard enough about her from

Johnnie and Robin. Besides, she's having this awful boy down to her *house*. He's Irish and he's probably blarneyed her or whatever they call it." Gerald raised his eyebrows. "It's no good doing *that*," said Elvira, "you must do something about it." Her tone was quite governessy. Even later, when he dropped her at her Hampstead flat and, tired, refused the drink she offered, he heard her last words shouted after his departing taxi—"Promise you'll deal with that Larrie business."

That same night was the last that Larrie was to spend at Frank Rammage's before moving to the flat over the stables at Marlow. He was entertaining Frank and Vin Salad now in Frank's large room. As he talked he moved restlessly about, stubbing out half-smoked cigarettes, whittling a piece of wood with a penknife. Someone had once told Larrie that "his Irish soul danced through life," and with his histrionic temperament he believed that his restlessness and his untidiness were part of this dance.

"If it's dreams and visions that could make an artist," he would say, "I'd be the greatest poet of them all. But I had never had the education . . ." and then he would launch into one of the many versions of his "hard" childhood to which most of his conversation ultimately led. His roguish look, his ever so Irish dancing eyes would change to a sad little urchin look, and then, if the audience proved unreceptive, would settle into the sullen, depressed look which was his natural expression in repose.

But this evening he was not putting over a story to an un-tried audience, and his mood, though hectic, was in a different key. For Frank he was defiant, the boy who was blazing a trail through life, his cheeks aflame, his blue eyes glowing at the future before him. But for Vin, there were winks and the tongue stuck in the cheek, the wide boy who wasn't to be taken for a ride by anyone, the boy who knew all the answers and was going places that Mr Vin Salad would only see at the pictures.

"It's a wonderful house, Frank," he said, and his nicotine-stained fingers made gestures to try to describe its limitless size and wealth, "with great gardens ablaze with all the colours in the rainbow."

"That's not likely in dead of winter," said Frank, and his little mouth pursed tightly.

"Conservatory flowers that come from all the parts of the earth, from Asia," Larrie said, warming to his subject, "and Africa and China too. It's a beautiful house for a grand old lady. She's like a queen as she moves about the great rooms, and she treats me like a prince. Nothing's good enough for Johnnie's friend. It's peaches they must bring in and grapes, and if I don't like them then it's something else. All for little Larrie. There'll be maids to wait on us, and nice little bits of skirt they are, I'll tell you. But I'm not to notice, for I'm the guest in the house. 'Get Mr Rourke this and get Mr Rourke that' it is all the time. She's the grand lady all right and speaks to them as if they were no better than the muck in the stables."

Inge would have been disconcerted to hear this description of her careful social democratic treatment of her maids, but Larrie was not concerned with fact or observation in life.

Vin Salad lay back on the divan and looked at his ornate wrist watch. "She sounds a proper cow," he drawled.

Larrie winked at Vin. "That's right," he said aside, "but the old bitch doesn't see that there'll be someone else to play the grand lady now." He flashed a grin of his white teeth.

Vin raised a manicured hand to his mouth and yawned. "Get you," he said.

Going straight was getting Vin down a little. He was a good waiter and kept his job, but regular hours and hard work gave him no reward but a sense of self-righteousness. A vinegary, spinsterish note had already crept into his lazy drawl. "I notice," he said, "that you're not sleeping in the palace. It's the stables for you, isn't it? You may be the great Johnnie's new little friend but that doesn't mean they're having any common little slut smelling their grand house out." Vin's idea of abuse was that of his grandmother. Larrie's departure from the house laid the way open for him to rule over Frank's little island of washed-up flotsam, to assuage his discontent on the other, less favoured, less quick-tongued lodgers; nevertheless he was jealous. Larrie knew this, of course; he did not answer Vin's abuse.

"I was telling Johnnie," he smiled, "that we must come to Giacometti's. He's not forgotten his meeting with you, Vin. I'll see that he leaves you a proper good tip." Very slowly he began to walk across the room, his handkerchief over his arm, his legs bowed, his feet hitting the floor flatly. He was in a minute the image of a depressed, worn-out old waiter.

Frank pointed a fat little hand towards a chair. "Sit down, ducks," he said. "That would be better if you were to work hard and earn an honest wage like Vin." He turned towards the elegant lolling figure on the divan, but even he found Vin Salad's epicene languor an impossible example of simple thrift, and his sermon ended in mid-air.

Larrie was at once all boyish fervour. "But it's just that I'm going to do, Frank," he cried, his eyes ashine, "I'm to drive the car and work in the garden. Oh it'll be a fine life, a decent man's life. I know you meant it for the best, Frank, getting me that job in the pub, but it was killing me, Frank, honest it was, the smoke and the smell of it. It's the fine, clear air I need and the early rising." He ran his hands through his scurfy, brilliantined hair in the excitement of the picture he was forming of himself. "I've not had much education and I don't know much about things, but it seems to me a fine thing when people believe in you. I've been no good, Frank, I know that. Lying and fiddling, that's all I've been good for, it's all I was brought up to." The little urchin face was near to tears at the thought of all the injustice. "But I know this, Frank, it's grand when people believe in you like Johnnie and the old lady believe in me. You've been good to me, but you've never done that, Frank, never believed in me, and a bit of trust is worth all the sermons that ever were from the beginning of the world."

Vin Salad stirred for a moment in his reptilian stillness, his long dark eyes flickered, "I believe in you," he said, "bloody crap." He rose slowly from the couch and settled his coat around his hips, then he looked Larrie over very slowly, taking in the dirty, crumpled suit, the scruffy hair and stained fingers. When he spoke again it was not in his usual cockney, but in his occasional Kensington drawl. "I should think these Middletons could be very elegant people," he said, and then he added, "But of course I forgot, living amongst all those lovely flowers, they probably can't recognize the smell of shit any more."

Larrie's face flushed and his eyes blazed. "You're not going to take the mickey out of me, Vin Salad, I'll spatter you," he cried.

Frank's fat little body bobbed up immediately. "That's enough of that," he cried. "You get off to bed, Vin."

Vin Salad paused by the door a moment and yawned, "I should think it'll cost you a fortune in fumigation, Frank, after this lot's gone. The Council don't take kindly to harbouring vermin."

If there was an element of direct jealousy in Frank's attitude to Larrie's relationship with John Middleton, as Vin had once suggested, it was not conscious. What Frank felt more deeply was the wound to his philanthropic pride. He had recognized Larrie from the start as the most feckless, unreliable material that had ever come into his reforming grasp; that this prize among irredeemable material should be snatched from him was a dreadful blow. He saw it all so clearly—the hard way, the grind, the moral lesson, duty, all were losing out to the easy way, money, charm, a well-known name, for, without knowing John Middleton, he dismissed his appeal as no more than these. The easy way was Frank's horror in life, and he felt justified in his fight against it, for did he not confine himself to one bed-sitting-room in his three houses? Did he not leave untouched one half of his money and devote the other half to helping the unhelpable? Did he not do all his own housework? And here was John Middleton using philanthropy, unconventional philanthropy—and it was the unconventional approach to mission work that was Frank's peculiar pride—to make himself a celebrity, vaunting it on the radio and in the press. That Larrie should leave the narrow path for the broad highway was bad enough; nevertheless, had it been some obvious debauchee who was guiding him astray, Frank might have been able to accept it; but that John Middleton, the well-known doer of good, should act as Larrie's guide down the primrose path, was more than he could endure. There was, too, beneath all this, an aspect of Larrie's relationship to John that mirrored distortedly Frank's own past, that raked over all the ashes he had so carefully tidied away, that touched the deepest guilt in his conscience—the guilt whose expiation was the basis of his whole carefully constructed Sister of Nazareth existence. Even with Larrie's bags all packed, even when he knew that there was nothing now he could say to prevent him leaving, Frank was determined to make one more effort, was prepared to bring out into daylight that part of his own life that was so securely locked away. Characteristically he set about the task in his particular "broadminded" moralistic way. He went to the corner cupboard and took out a bottle of whisky. It cost him much to dispense expensive drink in this way.

"Well, Larrie," he said, "we mustn't part on hard terms." He poured out two very large whiskies. "It doesn't do any harm to get drunk now and again, dear," he said. He paused for a moment and stared into the gas fire. His voice lost its usual snappish quality and took on a slower, more fatherly tone. All unknown to him, perhaps, there was something of Canon Portway's note in his voice as he approached this hidden subject.

"It's strange," he said, "how things bring back old times. You see that photograph," and he pointed to the handsome features of Canon Portway, "I don't hold much by religion. In my experience there are better ways of carrying out Christ's gospel than turning your collar round the wrong way, but there are saints in all walks of life and that man was one of them. He was a father to me, Larrie, in the village where I was born. It happened I was a bit more clever than the other lads thereabouts, I fancied book study and I dreamed my dreams like you do. My folk were simple folk, good enough, but they didn't understand me. That man did and he helped me. He gave me self-respect. It might have happened I'd have gone to the university, thanks to that man, but the war came along— the First War, you know—and I had to go for the Navy. When I came back, I went into that man's service. It was too late for study then, but I was secretary and general helper to him and he treated *me* like a prince. But after a while, Larrie "—Frank's voice grew more solemn—"I felt the need to be free, the burden of that man's affection was too great for me. Oh! it wasn't what you're thinking. Those were simpler times in those days and men were simpler too. Don't think I'm moralizing upon your relation with John Middleton. I don't go much, as you know, for regarding those things as important. I measure a man's heart rather than his actions. But there was nothing of that kind in the Canon's mind, he'd have died if he'd thought it so. For all that he was a lonely man and he loved me, but that was more than I could bear for, Larrie, that seemed to take my freedom away. I reckoned it like that and I was right. If I'd stayed I couldn't have grown. So I left him, and I left him to folk that I knew would treat him badly, and they did."

Frank had so often rehearsed his story in his mind that it came out perhaps a little too glibly. He realized it, perhaps, for a note of his usual asperity came into his voice again. "Well anyway I went. And when he died he left me his money. That wasn't so much as it should have been, for the folk I've spoken of had bled him over the years, but it was enough to keep me in comfort. That's how I have these houses."

He bobbed up and, waddling over to Larrie's chair, he re-filled the boy's glass with whisky. "To my way of thinking, this whisky and everything else I have has been badly got. But it would have been worse if I'd stayed with him, for I'd have lost my own will. There was no choice after I'd started the business, except between bad and bad. I don't say the cap fits you and John Middleton. I don't know. I've not met the man. I've tried to but he wouldn't see me. But if you do decide to cut and run, you'd best do it early before he and his mother have got into the way of you."

Any narrative as histrionic as Frank's met a ready response in Larrie. "It's the very thing that's been in my mind, Frank. If you take their love, I've said, then you can't hurt them. Can you live up to it, Larrie boy? I've asked myself, and before God, Frank, I don't know. Now if I could think I could come and talk it over with you, Frank, if I was puzzled in my head what was right to do?"

"I'd keep your room for you," said Frank, "only I don't believe in something for nothing."

"I wouldn't ask it," said Larrie, and his eyes took on a dreamy look. "It's bad enough going away owing you rent, but it's got to be. Johnnie would pay it and be glad, but I'll not ask him for money, no more than what I earn in the things I can do for him and the old lady. But I'll be paying, you'll see, one of these fine days, just when you've given me up, for I know it's a point with you to be paid what's owed you."

"Only from those that have got it," Frank snapped. "For that matter, if you care to leave some of your things, duckie, there's no such shortage of rooms that you shouldn't keep yours for the time being."

Larrie broke into such a tender smile. "Well, now, Frank," he cried, "I'll accept that. It would be wrong not to. And there *are* old things I'd not care to take down there. It'd certainly be wonderful to come back to the old place when I need to think and see where my life is going to. And who knows, Frank," he cried, and he came over and slapped the fat, little man on the back, "the grand ways may not suit old Larrie boy after all?"

They finished the bottle of whisky that evening in talk that allowed Frank's underlying sentimental nature to break through his hard-baked crusty surface. The drink freed Larrie too that evening, so that when he bade his host goodnight he let a sharp edge of his hard-baked soul appear through his usual treacly surface. "Now wasn't that a wonderful thing?" he asked. "And don't I envy you? You getting all the old Canon's money and not giving a bloody thing in return?" If Frank reflected on this later, it only confirmed him in his feeling that in Larrie he had lost a real hard case for his mission of reform.

"No, no, Middleton," said Professor Clun, "I don't care for any wine."

Gerald asked, "Are you sure?" before dismissing the wine waiter.

"Yes, yes," said Clun irritably, "I am not prone to make parades of polite refusals. If, that is, such nonsense can be counted a politeness."

The luncheon was not going well. Arthur Clun had decided to be "at a loss"—he was "at a loss" to understand Gerald's acceptance of the editorship; did he feel so satisfied that his work on the Confessor was advanced enough to assume this further responsibility? "I doubt," he said, "if the exacting work of an editorship of this kind will prove compatible with the active pursuit of your hobby. I imagine that that sort of connoisseurship tends to become a full-time pursuit, if, that is, a man has the means to indulge such interests." He was at a greater loss to understand the inclusion of so many inexperienced, younger scholars in a great work of this sort. He was the last to wish to stand in the way of new ideas or fresh talent; indeed, as far as the *Bulletin* went, he often felt that Sir Edgar was not open enough to, well, he would not say progress, because such abstractions were inapplicable to the study of history, but to change. He had been seriously vexed once or twice when Sir Edgar had incalculably refused remarkable contributions by brilliant Ph.D. pupils of his own. But the *History* was quite a different matter.

"As I see it," he said, and he cut his roll into four equal pieces and placed on each of them an equal share of butter, "the *Medieval History* will remain the principal repository for secondary statements for a decade or two. It will certainly be used extensively at home and abroad for university standard teaching. I can imagine only one, or, at a pinch, two qualifications by which the contributors should be judged. For myself, the primary, I would almost say, the sole requisite is depth of scholarship tried over years of organized research work. I cannot feel happy that men in their late twenties, assistant lecturers like Roberts, or even recently appointed lecturers like Stringwell-Anderson, have the length of experience necessary, the historical background required for such important work. I shall be told that they are brilliant, it may be so, I have never been a very happy judge of brilliance *in vacuo*, but, of this I am certain, brilliance that has not been tempered by the discipline of long years of apprenticeship to research will not give the *History* what it requires. We shall get flashy stuff, Middleton, brilliant, unsustained flashes in the pan, unsupported guesses. Such contributors will be straining to prove themselves—I don't blame them, they are not yet established as scholars, they have their future to make; I would have run the same risks at that age if it had not been for a climate of established opinion, now alas vanished, which discouraged such displays of pyrotechnics. The *History* is the last place for such things. British scholarship will be judged by it abroad for many years to come. In short, Middleton, I can only say that I regard many of your selections as little short of disastrous."

Gerald's face had flushed deeper as Clun spoke, but he exercised great self-restraint. "Are you sure that you really want that trifle?" he asked, for his guest had struck the pudding once or twice with his fork and regarded it no further.

Professor Clun wiped his little moustache with his napkin and stared at Gerald with his hard green eyes. "I imagine so," he said. "Is there some reason for not eating it? If so, please order whatever is appropriate. I am indifferent to these things." And when Gerald smiled, he went on. "As I was saying, there is, I suppose, another qualification which might be held valuable in the compilation of the *History*. It is one which is highly prized today—the selection of yourself as editor bears witness to the regard of Sir Edgar and the Syndic for it. I refer to that general standard of culture, that breadth of humane study which commands literary ability, worldly experience and all the other penumbra of scholarship. It is indeed a most valuable temper to possess, and those who have had the time and means to cultivate it are lucky indeed. It is hardly, however, by definition, an attribute of the young and inexperienced. No, on every ground, Middleton, it seems to me that some of your selections must be judged deficient."

He paused and carefully placed two pieces of angelica on the side of his plate. He smiled a watery smile. "I am past the age," he said, "when an unfamiliar diet appeals. Much of my best work must be done in the afternoon."

"I've never been troubled with dyspepsia," Gerald drawled untruthfully.

Professor Clun looked at him sharply, "No?" he said, "I'm inclined in general to regard it as the inevitable malady of any serious or lengthy application to study."

It was over coffee, as Professor Clun obstinately blew clouds of smoke from his pipe into Gerald's face, that he revealed the greatest degree to which he was at a loss. It had seemed to Gerald that, having allowed the little man to vent his spite to the full, he might now begin the process of persuading him to co-operate.

"Look," he said, "you've told me all you disagree with, but if you will look at the list again you will see that the chapters you complain of are not the principal ones. I'm not going to give way over them. You wouldn't if you were editor. But I *am* going to say that if you don't contribute, you will produce exactly the result you warn me against. If this *History* goes to

press without at least two major contributions by Arthur Clun
—and I should like more—then indeed we may count on being
a laughing-stock to foreign scholars. I cannot believe that one
who has given so much to the study of English history as you
have will allow that to happen. I have made no pretences to
you, I make none now. I shall edit as I see fit, but I appeal to
you not to sabotage this important work. I ask you, not as a
favour to myself, but because the *History* should be all that you
believe it should be, to give me your help."

Arthur Clun removed his handkerchief from his sleeve and
once again wiped his moustache. He stared at Gerald. "You
claim to be honest with me," he said, "I will be equally honest
with you. I heard today—I shall not say from what source—
something which I find it hard to credit, an action of yours
which if it is true I am at a total loss to understand." He
paused, and pulled at the ends of his little moustache, blowing
his cheeks out in a self-important way. "I was told that you
had asked Dr Lorimer to contribute the article on the Conversion of England," he said.

"I did," Gerald answered, "and she refused."

Professor Clun banged his pipe heavily on the ash-tray.
"Well," he said, "the Lord indeed mightily preserveth fools."

Gerald felt a throb at his temples. "I think I should tell you,
however," he drawled, "that she accepted a general commission
to write on the administrative growth of Plantagenet England.
We are to discuss details at the end of this week."

"I see," Professor Clun's fox-terrier nose was quivering,
"there remains very little then for me to say but to wish you
luck with your editorship. You will need it. And now I must
leave you."

"Wait a minute," Gerald said, putting his hand on his guest's
rough tweed-clad arm. "Have you *seen* Rose Lorimer lately?"

Arthur Clun gave out a little bark of derision. "Dr Lorimer
and I do not seek out each other's company in Vacation. It is
bad enough that I should be forced to listen to her absurdities
at Faculty meetings."

Gerald's heavy face now had a lop-sided look, almost as though he had had a stroke. From the dark, flushed mass of flesh one brown eye glared at Clun. He was very angry. "Normally I should not discuss an old friend like Rose Lorimer with anyone who had spoken slightingly of her, but this occasion demands peculiar forbearance. It was the greatest regret to me that in my original list—the one that you saw— I did not feel able to include her name. She has not been herself for so many years. However I *have* seen her since my return and it is clear to me that she is well on the road to recovery. Naturally, as soon as I saw that, I instantly invited her collaboration. That and no suppression on my part is the reason why you did not find her name on the list I gave you."

Professor Clun took out a handkerchief and began to clean his spectacles. "I see," he said. "I'm sorry if I doubted your honesty with me, but there's been such a conspiracy of sentimentalism built around that woman. . . . Well, I'll say no more about that. I made no secret at the time of efforts to get her retired on grounds of health. I make none now. But when you talk about her recovery in this light way, Middleton, I'm afraid I must answer quite simply—fiddlesticks. People do not recover from insane delusions overnight. Oh!" he cried, waving a tough, sinewy little hand, his signet ring glinting in the air a moment, "I know the supposed reasons. This story of Dr Lorimer's recovery is not new to me. Sir Edgar met me with the glad news some weeks ago. I preferred to make no comment then. If the Heligoland excavations prove to be as Pforzheim thinks, we know—that is the sane among us—that another interesting example of a Christian missionary relapsing into some semi-pagan, semi-Christian rite will have come to join the story of Eorpwald at Melpham. Interesting, perhaps even suggestive of certain tendencies to relapse among ardent converts of forceful men like Wilfrid and Boniface. Nothing more. And by the way, we still await Pforzheim's final verdict. To be given us, I believe, at Verona. This has nothing to do with the absurd views of Dr Lorimer about the virtues of the

Celtic Church. Views which, in my hearing, Middleton, have hovered on the edge of some paranoiac delusions about a general conspiracy to suppress historic truth by the Romanists. The fact that the possible discovery in Heligoland has quietened Dr Lorimer's mania may be satisfactory to her friends, it may be of interest to an alienist, I really don't know. It does not make her a fit contributor to an important historical work."

Gerald frowned. "I admit," he said, "that there have been moments when I have felt that Rose Lorimer was in danger of losing her reason under the stress of scepticism rightly shown towards her extreme views about the Celtic Church." He stopped and, for a moment, he appeared to have lost the thread of his remarks. Clun's statement about the Heligoland excavation threatened to loose once more the flood of his disquiet about Melpham. In the effort of securing the dam which he had so resolutely built up, he found it difficult to concentrate. "But as I said before," he went on rather vaguely, "that danger is now over. In any case, we must surely give greater latitude to absurdities in a considerable scholar than . . ."

His voice tailed away. If the Heligoland discovery was as Clun described it, then Melpham . . . He should have asked for full details of Pforzheim's work from Sir Edgar. To what end? To distract his attention from the work he had taken on?

Professor Clun waited for his host to finish his sentence, then, raising his eyebrows slightly at the silence, he said, "I'm afraid I don't think so."

Gerald started into attention. He smiled. "You would be surprised," he said, "at the change in her. She confesses that she has given too much of her attention to ecclesiastical history. Indeed, as I said, she refused to write on the Conversion. I feel sure she is anxious not to give way to her obsessions again. Even if she were not a great scholar, I should feel it my duty to encourage her. She wants to resume the work she inherited from Tout. Do you remember at all those brilliant articles she did on the Exchequer in the mid-thirties?"

"I remember them perfectly," said Arthur Clun, "as much other excellent work that she did. All a very long time ago. Perhaps we may now expect some ridiculous *parti pris* theory about the Privy Seal," he laughed, "some sinister conspiracy by historians to conceal the importance of the griffin seal in administrative development." He got up from his chair. "I'm afraid, Middleton, that your decision to include Miss Lorimer must clinch my decision not to be a contributor."

They stood on the steps of the Club as the snow fell thickly around them, incongruous in height, contrasting in costume. Gerald disliked talking to Clun from his superior height; he guessed rightly that it increased the little man's antagonism. "Look," he said, "nothing's settled yet. May I ask you to reconsider your decision."

"You may," said Professor Clun. "I will give it further consideration. I seldom change my decisions, however." He refused Gerald's offer of a lift in the Daimler. "I shall walk through the Park," he said. "I have promised Mrs Clun to make some purchases at the Army and Navy Stores."

"I hope she is well," said Gerald.

"Yes," said his guest, "she has no reasons for ailing, I am glad to say." As they waited for Larwood to manœuvre the car into position, he seemed to search for some domestic comment that would soften the effect of his intransigence in the professional field. "Both my wife and I," he said, "are admirers of your son's remarkable articles about this disgraceful Pelican business. We have so few such independent fighters in the country today."

As the car turned round the Crimean Memorial, Gerald caught a glimpse of the minute determined figure in battered felt hat and dirty raincoat dwarfed to a speck beneath the towering column of the Duke of York.

A letter from Inge was not what Gerald would have chosen to find on his return to Montpelier Square. He stared at the sprawling handwriting, the Continental script, for some minutes before he could bring himself to open it.

"Dear Gerald," he read, "I am sorry that I have always to write nasty things to you, but life is not all so agreeable as Vienna and wonderful drawings. It is my fault anyway that I did not speak to you at Christmas, but you were so strange and quiet and I know you do not like to talk private things with me any more. Yes, you were most sad for a Pappi at Xmas time! But then the children are used to this, God knows. But I do not write to complain at all. You are always the scholar and I the practical one of the family, so I shall not mind to tell you quite straight—*I do not feel the need for secrets after so long a time*. Well, then, I received my allowance for January 1 (first quarter), but we are agreed October 1st (last quarter) that I shall need £100 more. We are agreed price rises in England are quite dreadful—perhaps it is having a bad Conservative Government, how can England do such a thing?—and this is a general reason, I thought you will know this must be £100 1st January (next quarter) also and indeed all quarters. I despair when I think of working-people, for I live always in a simple housekeeping like the people—plain, good things are my way of life as you know, not waste and show—and how can they manage, these poor working-people? Perhaps there will be revolution. So please arrange £100 more for all quarters.

"Here we are very happy, for happiness, as you know, Gerald dear, is always what I think for in life. The snow makes everything so beautiful, but it is not beautiful for the birds, so that we are always reminded there are some not so fortunate as ourselves. I have now here Johnnie's friend Larrie, a sweet Irish boy. He has had so sad a life so that he needs much love. Johnnie who works so hard will now have his Thingy's care and for Larrie I must love him too for he loves Johnnie. So we are all loving and happy and busy so that we do not care if it snows so hard in all the world outside. There are so many things I can give to this unlucky boy who has not had the advantages of our little children. He is happy and smiles when I give to him. It is like when Johnnie was young, but here is Johnnie too, so we have all . . . "

Gerald sat down and instructed his lawyers to increase his wife's allowance by £500 a year. The extra one hundred pounds was typical of the many gestures he made to salve his conscience about his treatment of her. It depressed him that they were always monetary and therefore cost him so little. At least, he reflected, he never allowed himself an overt criticism of the hypocrisy of her absurd "simple" housekeeping. Larrie's name recalled his conversation with Elvira. He had shelved the problem of John's private life, convinced that his intervention would be as fruitless as it would be resented. The presence of this young man at Inge's was, however, a different matter. He had decided that Elvira's intellect was as inadequate as her body was desirable; nevertheless, she had some experience of the more disreputable aspects of modern life and her distrust of the young man could not be completely dismissed with the rest of her muddled talk. The image of his wife's huge body came to him and as usual her clumsy size lent pathos to her foolish life. The clumsiness of her written English, too, recalled their early days together when her spoken English had been as imperfect. Here, at least, was something not entirely easy, not connected with money, that he could do for her. He would go down to Marlow to see this Irish fellow for himself; if necessary he would talk to John. He was suddenly very angry with his son—his private life, however unsavoury, was his own affair, but he had no right to take advantage of his mother's foolish adoration to involve the poor creature in such squalid things. He set about cancelling his appointments for the next day.

He was all ready to depart the next morning when Mrs Larwood announced a visitor. There was one appointment he had forgotten to cancel. "Miss Crane to see you, sir," she said.

"At last we meet," cried Clarissa. "I've had audiences of the Pope, I've been received by the Queen, I've met Elsa Maxwell, but that's child's play to getting hold of you, Professor Middleton. But how right you are to make yourself rare! The awful accessibility of everyone nowadays! And how delightful of you to have invited *me*! And for what my charlady calls elevenses! My favourite meal!"

Gerald remembered his invitation with horror, but he saw in her last remark a means of escape. "The embarrassing thing is that we shan't be *able* to have more than a brief meeting. I have to go down at very short notice to my wife's." He crossed the room and pressed the bell.

Clarissa had decided to look a little absurd, a little out-rageously smart; she felt sure that "her Scholar Don Juan," as she already called Gerald, would like the *outrée*. Alas! Gerald paid no attention to ornament once he had decided against the basic structure.

"Your wife's Scandinavian, isn't she?" she asked. It was so fascinating; she knew Dollie and her "Don Juan", and now this wife. For some it would just be the eternal triangle; but she knew that every such relationship had a hundred over-tones, a thousand nuances that made it unique and utterly fascinating.

"Danish," Gerald replied shortly.

"I'm terribly interested by the Danes," Clarissa cried, before she had given herself time to think why, so she ended rather lamely, "they're such a completely separate people."

"Oh," Gerald demurred. "I think they're rather more imitative than the other Scandinavians."

"Do you?" Clarissa asked. "In a sense, of course, you're right." She was unwilling entirely to relinquish her improvised opinion. "And how was Vienna? Wonderful, of course, as always, but a little less able to hide that sad, defeated look in the wintry landscape. But, of course, you didn't go to see Vienna. You went to see Leonardo. Oh, how I envy you!" She accepted only the smallest home-made scone with her coffee, then leaning forward a little, she said so seriously, "I can't, you know, Professor Middleton, forgive so many bad novelists for having written about him. Wonderful many-hued Leonardo! I know *I* could have brought him to life. But there you are, what's done cannot be undone." She laughed a little bitter laugh. "So they've found another Melpham!" she cried, "and you missed Professor Pforzheim's dramatic revelation." She had only subsequently learned from Rose Lorimer the importance of the Heligoland excavation. "We were all sworn to secrecy. I haven't told a soul." She knew no one who would be in the faintest degree interested. "You, of course, are of the inner council."

This, thought Gerald, is where I begin to stonewall. "Yes," he said. "Nothing's known exactly yet."

"I thought at first," Clarissa said, "that *I* might use it too in my novel, but I've looked up some things about Boniface, and I hardly think it would do. All about Germany, you know. . . ."

"Unless some of your characters are *very* long-lived, it might be difficult certainly," Gerald said.

Clarissa laughed embarrassedly. "I'm impossible about dates," she said, "but now you must tell me about Melpham. Give me the atmosphere of the discovery, the excitement of it."

Gerald smiled, "I arrived after the discovery was made," he said, "and in any case my whole memory of Melpham is rather clouded by pain. I sprained my ankle badly on my arrival." He felt that he was being a little brusque. "The most exciting thing for a young man was my hostess—the great Lilian Portway. A wonderful actress, you know."

But Clarissa was not interested in Lilian. "Surely," she cried, "that can't be true. Even for a young man the presence of the brilliant Gilbert Stokesay must have been a thrill."

"I'm afraid not for me," said Gerald, "I had known Gilbert for many years—since schooldays, to be exact. In any case I was a scholar, you know, not an intellectual. And then Gilbert kept the two sides of his life very much apart. I knew, of course, indeed I'm afraid I must say he made sure that I knew, of his acquaintance with Wyndham Lewis and T. E. Hulme, but, for the rest, I was completely ignorant. Now that his essays and poems arouse so much interest, I get numerous letters from Ph.D. students and others. I can tell them almost nothing; apart from his admiration for a painter named Wadsworth and his detestation of Roger Fry, I can't recall any of that side of his life. The awful truth is that I've never read his work."

Clarissa thought for a moment of looking amused, but then she reflected on how little she had learned from her host, how much time she had wasted; she decided to look shocked. "You're as bad as Dollie," she said.

Gerald did not reply to the charge. He gave her a cigarette and lit it. Then he asked as casually as he could muster. "Have you seen her lately?"

"Dollie?" Clarissa queried without interest. "Yes, about a fortnight ago."

"Is she well?"

"Oh, I think so. She doesn't change much, you know." Clarissa was not prepared to expand to someone who had proved so fruitless.

"Does she go out much?" Gerald asked. He could not ask directly how much she was drinking now.

"Oh, yes," Clarissa replied, "as much as her little hobby allows her."

Gerald was revolted. He had thought Clarissa affected, but now she seemed heartless also. He could not bring himself to discuss Dollie with such a woman, however much he longed to hear news of her. There was a silence, then Clarissa said, "I'm sure you're bursting to get away. Actually I've got an appointment. Thank you for the lovely coffee."

As she moved to the door, her passion to be liked overcame her. "And I've said nothing of your enchanting room," she cried. "For it *is* enchanting. I have known many men who had rooms of great beauty, but a man's room that is beautiful and somehow does not embarrass—*that* is rare!" Gerald did not answer. She felt quite angry at the lack of response, and in a mischievous mood, she said, "You know, of course, that Dollie's affection for *you* is something quite fantastic still."

She had no idea if this was true. It seemed to her probable that poor old Dollie *would* be unlikely to forget such a Don Juan in her dreary life; in any case it was fun to watch old flames rekindle.

"I too," said Gerald simply, "am very fond of her."

Gerald was very late for luncheon. In his mood of sentimental remorse towards Inge, he had remembered her pleasure whenever the children paid surprise visits and he had given her no warning. He still found it difficult to realize that his wife's reaction towards their children's behaviour was no guide to her response to his. A surprise visit from her husband was only irritating to Inge; a surprise arrival late for luncheon brought a puckering frown to her broad forehead, a sulky pout to her baby mouth.

"No, Gerald, this is too bad!" she cried. She seemed a giant Diana the huntress in her winter tweeds. "No, everything is finished. No service today! Is that not so, Johnnie? We had a very nice meal, didn't we, Larrie? Steak and béarnaise sauce which I made myself. But that would not have been enough for Gerald, especially as the wine was only an ordinary white table wine—the same that I used for the sauce. Oh! that would not do for your father, Johnnie, that is just peasant food. But we live like peasants. And what about Larwood? Of course, you have not thought of him. Poor Larwood!" She ran from the room and her cooing noises to Larwood could be heard from the drive outside. His embarrassed responses were less audible.

John said, "I don't think you've met my friend Larrie Rourke, Father. This is my father, Larrie."

Gerald shook hands and sat down by the table with its remains of pineapple and Brie. Larrie, however, did not resume his seat. He walked about the room excitedly, cracking walnuts and devouring them with evident relish. He was all the excited and shy Irish boy and his eyes gleamed with delight. "Well, now this is a big day for me," he cried. "I've never met a real live professor before. I've heard of them, mind you, I'm not that ignorant. At school they would say to us, 'You'll never grow to be a professor'. And to be honest I didn't much care. But now that I've seen your father, Johnnie, I see what they mean. There's a grandeur—well, I'll not flatter you, Professor Middleton. Is that right, Johnnie, do I call him that? I'll just say that I can see it's a grand thing to be."

Gerald sought desperately for something to say to stop this outflow, which embarrassed him so deeply. He tried to tell himself that the embarrassment was not for what he was hearing, but simply because of his new knowledge of his son's life. He saw clearly, however, that John was equally unhappy; his usual cocky manner was replaced by a look of peculiar sadness. He seemed like a small bedraggled bird.

Larrie's quick eye caught the situation, his expression changed to one of timid thoughtfulness. "You know, Johnnie, there's a strange thing," he said, "I hardly like to say it. Your father doesn't know I'm just ignorant and uneducated. But Johnnie'll tell you, I have strange ideas. I don't know how they come to me and they're daft enough all right, but Johnnie doesn't always think so. Shall I tell you what it seems to me? And there's no disrespect to your father. Yet it seems to me there's a strange power in words. When I saw your father, Johnnie, I won't say I was disappointed, but there was something broke in me. I'd thought of that word 'Professor' often and often, it had a kind of magic power for me, and now it has gone. The word and the reality, the dreams we have as children and what comes after—it's a mighty gulf all right. But now Johnnie's ashamed of me—aren't you, Johnnie?—for talking so 'daft'."

To Gerald's amazement, John's depressed expression gave way to a look of pride. "No, I'm not, Larrie," he said, "there's a lot in what you say."

So this, thought Gerald, is the effect of the love that dares not speak its name. He would have expected Inge to respond to such sentimental, insincere nonsense, but John . . . He looked at Larrie's immature features, his calculating, boyish smile, with real distaste.

Luckily the tension was relieved by Inge's return. "Larwood is so happy. He is sharing the maid's meal," she cried. "I think he has quite fallen for Trudel." She gave a "spooney" look at Larrie and he replied with a wink. "But what are we to give this big man?" she continued, looking at Gerald with mock sternness. Her good mood was almost restored. "I'm not going to disturb the maids at their meal," she said firmly to Gerald, as though he had requested this piece of tyranny.

Larrie came over and put an arm round her large waist. "Let me go into the larder, Mrs Middleton. I'm an old hand at scrounging. I'll find something, never you fear. There's sure to be some delicious tongue in your well-stocked pantry."

"A tongue!" Inge cried, "but this boy has such good ideas. I will tell Trudel to boil a tongue in some red wine with some onions. No! I must do it myself, she will always put too much onion."

"A sandwich will do me perfectly," Gerald intervened. "There's no need for you to do a lot of cooking."

"A sandwich," Inge cried. "Now isn't that like a man? To cut sandwiches, my dear Gerald, is far more troublesome than to cook tongue."

"She's right, you know," Larrie said. "There's a great deal of trouble in sandwiches," and he winked at Gerald, who looked the other way in annoyance. "But don't you worry yourself with it, Mrs Middleton," Larrie went on. "Aren't the maids fighting to do things for you, with all your kindness to them? And if it's a bit of charm they're after, I'll go and talk to them."

When he returned with a plate of cold tongue and salad, Inge was still lecturing Gerald on his selfishness in arriving so late, and announced, "You're very lucky to get anything at all, Gerald. We have a very sick little invalid in the house who needs a great deal more care than you deserve."

"And how is the darling little bird?" Larrie cried.

"Thingy found a little owl in the snow," John explained. "She and Larrie have been fussing about it trying to force brandy down its beak all the morning." His voice showed a certain impatience. "You know really, darling, you'd much better put it out of its misery. Its wing's injured, and even if you get it to take some food, it can't fly again."

"Oh no!" Inge cried. "What a terrible thing to say, Johnnie! It's such a wise little bird." She rounded her eyes, and called loudly across the room, "Ee-wik, ee-wik, ee-wik. It goes so, Gerald." She looked more like a great Scandinavian eagle owl than the little owl. She may have sensed this, for she said very patiently to Gerald, "Not the big kind that goes Woo-Woo-Woo. The *little* owl."

"Yes, I had understood, Inge," he replied. He disliked Inge's sudden animal imitations; before Larrie they seemed intolerable.

"Very well," John got up from his chair and looked out of the window, "I wash my hands of it. If you and Larrie want to fuss over the wretched bird, do." He turned quite savagely upon Larrie, "Only I hope to God the damned thing isn't still here when I get back tomorrow. I shall have to start soon, by the way, if I'm to get to town in time with these slippery roads."

Gerald said, "I can give you a lift back, if you like. Larwood's very reliable, even on roads like glass."

John was still very short-tempered. "No, thank you. I shall need the car to come back tomorrow. You rich people always have very inflated ideas of chauffeurs' driving."

Larrie had been watching John's mood and he seemed to make a sudden decision. He crossed the room and put his hand on Inge's arm, "Johnnie's right, you know. The poor little thing would be better out of the way."

Inge turned great frightened doll's eyes upon him. "Oh! no, you mustn't say so. I couldn't kill anything."

"Why, Mrs Middleton, who'd wish you to do such a thing? No, it's I'm the one for that."

John looked round from the window and said abruptly, "Do it quickly, mind, Larrie."

"Oh no! no!" Inge was still saying, but Larrie had gone from the room.

Gerald walked over to John, "Do you think I could have a few words with you, John?" he asked quietly.

John looked up at him. "It'll have to be very few words, because I must go," he said.

"Is there a fire in the morning-room, Inge?" Gerald asked. "I wanted to have a short business talk with John on his own."

"Business that I mustn't hear? What can it be, Gerald? That is not very polite."

"I'm sorry, my dear, I have no other chance of seeing John. By the way," he added, "I've written to Thurstan about that little business of yours. I should have done it before, but I've added a little yearly present which I hope you'll like."

"Now you are trying to bribe me," Inge cried, but she was smiling. "All right. Go along with you. If the central heating is not enough, you can put on the electric heater."

Before they had left the room, however, Larrie returned. Gerald felt that he could almost hear him purring. All the wistful, orphan lines of his face seemed to have filled out in a fat-cat contentment. "The poor little thing's out of the way," he said.

Inge sighed. "Oh dear! I *never* have anything killed in this house. I do hope you're not going to bring me bad luck, Larrie."

The boy went up and kissed her. "How can you say that?" he asked.

"No, I don't mean it," Inge smiled. But Gerald, who could see that she was genuinely distressed, said, "I'm sure the little bird died very quickly, dear."

"Well now, it did and it didn't. . . ." Larrie began, but John broke in abruptly. "You can spare us the details, Larrie," he said. He turned to Gerald with a mock schoolboy expression. "Let's get the pi-jaw over, Father," he said, "or is it to be six of the best?" As they went out of the room, Larrie shouted after them, "Make it a dozen, Professor."

As they entered the long morning-room, so grey and empty in the dying February light, Gerald felt desperately that he had bungled the whole thing. He should have contrived the interview by chance; as it was, it reflected exactly the pattern of those few, clumsy, ill-managed "talks" he had suffered with John in his early boyhood, any effect of which had immediately been undone by Inge's blandishments.

John sat on the arm of a large chair, swinging his legs, boyish once more in the absence of Larrie. "What on earth is all this, Father?" he asked; but his careless smile did not entirely hide his annoyance.

Gerald, desperate to avoid the central topic, said, "I'm worried about your mother, John."

"Thingy, but why on earth? She seems in cracking form."

Gerald forced himself to sit down and face John. "Do you find it cold in here? Shall I turn on one of those heaters?" and, when John replied with an impatient gesture, he continued, "Oh yes, she's very well, I think. I'm just worried about her making a fool of herself over your friend, Larrie. You know how fond she gets of people."

John raised his eyebrows. "But good heavens!" he cried, "it's the best thing in the world for her to have someone to be interested in. For one thing it stops her fussing over her children so much. Surely you know that." He took out his pipe and began filling it. For the rest of their interview, he was busy lighting it, sucking at it and throwing away matches in a manner that doubled Gerald's nervous annoyance.

"We know nothing, at least I know nothing of your friend," Gerald said.

John roared with laughter. "I'd like to know when you've ever known anything about any of our friends," he said.

Gerald flushed, but he added determinedly, "They didn't come to live with your mother."

John stared at Gerald with an ironical smile. "I could say a lot about your sudden solicitude for Thingy. However, I prefer to behave as though you had the ordinary husband's right to ask questions. Very well. Larrie's an orphan, an institution boy who's been in a lot of trouble, he's had three convictions for petty thieving and he's been to an Approved School. Thingy knows all that and she has welcomed him here as my friend. Do you want to know any more?"

Gerald's growing resentment made him bolder. "I don't think that's the answer," he said. "You know as well as I do how vaguely warm-hearted Inge is and the difficulties it gets her into. You have a perfect right to befriend anyone you choose. . . ."

John's dark eyes narrowed in anger. "Thank you, I have," he cried. "I know," he went on, "somebody's been getting at you. You came down here expressly to spy out the land. I think I know who it was too. Robin! Blast his eyes. He's got a bloody nerve to interfere, with his own little dreary double life."

"I haven't seen Robin. . . ." Gerald began, but John was carried away. "I don't believe you!" he cried. "Well, you can tell Master Robin from me there's one little thing he's not getting away with, writing letters to *The Times* about 'radio demagogues'. His beloved protégé Mr Pelican is on the out. . ."

"This has nothing to do with it," Gerald interrupted. "I haven't seen Robin."

John looked sulky. "All right," he said. "It was someone else then. His *chère amie* perhaps, anxious to save me from myself. Hell hath no fury, you know. I suppose she 'told' you about Larrie and me, and you're 'deeply shocked'."

Gerald tried to curb the anger generated in him by the growing atmosphere of a "scene", he set his features in a look of friendliness. "I know about it, yes," he said. "I'm not saying how. I don't know *what* I feel about it really. In any case my feelings aren't relevant. If there's any blame going I must receive a large part of it as an inefficient father." He smiled across at John. "I should be very upset, you know, if you got into any trouble, but you must manage your own life. And I'm sure you do." So much, he thought bitterly, for the part I've played in warning him that he's taking risks and he spurred himself to say more. "You're a very well-known man now, John," once again he smiled, "and well-known people can't always afford the same life as others. However," he hurried on, "*I'm* purely concerned to protect Inge."

John rose to his feet. All the bitterness generated in childhood, all Inge's teaching coalesced in him for a moment. "Your past success in that respect gives you every reason to be confident this time, I'm sure," he said with heavy sarcasm. He jumped up from his chair. "I'm afraid I must go," he said, "or should I ask your permission to get down?"—Gerald looked away—"I've no objection to your talking to Thingy if the curious workings of your conscience demand it," John added patronizingly as he left the room. Gerald, trembling with anger, shouted after him, "Thank you, I have every intention of doing so."

Tea—one of Inge's most lavish teas to make up for Gerald's small lunch—was a gloomy meal for him. He sat silent while Inge and Larrie cooed away at one another. At about five, Larrie became restless. He walked up and down, opened newspapers at random, whistled, gazed at the clock, then suddenly he went up to Inge and putting his hand on her arm, he said wistfully, "I know I promised you and Johnnie to stay home this evening, but let me take the car and go into Reading. It's only to go to the pictures. I won't be late. But it's Marilyn Monroe, the girl of my heart."

Inge sighed, "Oh Larrie! What will Johnnie say? You know what has happened all this week. Nobody wants you to stay at home, but you have done such naughty things."

"I had a few too many beers in me," Larrie said. "Now that's being honest with you, isn't it?"

"They must have been very strong beers," said Inge in coy reproof. "Look what has been broken—all the furniture in the bedroom I furnished in the garage, one mudguard smashed, the maids frightened in their bedrooms. Bad boy!" She wagged her finger.

Larrie looked dramatic. "Oh, when will I ever be rid of this beast in me? You'll help me, won't you? But it's not by staying in and getting restless that I can do it. That's no victory. It's by going out and coming back the same as I went that I'll win, isn't it?"

Inge smiled. "You are determined to go, I can see. But you will not be too late, will you, Larrie?"

"Cross my heart," Larrie said. His look was playfully shy. "I'll just be going to the pictures and back again. With Marilyn Monroe in my mind, I won't be thinking of much else."

"All right, I give way," said Mrs Middleton. "Have a lovely time."

"Thank you," said Larrie, and he gave her a big hug. "It's been wonderful to meet *you*, Professor Middleton," he said. "I've heard talk of you so much from Johnnie. He's so proud of his father." Gerald looked away.

Inge got up. "I'll arrange for some sandwiches to be put in the flat," she said, and went out of the room. To Gerald's surprise, Larrie came and stood by his side. His eyes blazed with hysterical rage. "You'll not get me out of this house," he said softly. "You just try." The next moment he was gone.

Inge was quite gay as they drank their sherry. "You must stay and have dinner, Gerald," she said. "I have told them to make one of your English steak and kidney pies and I have a bottle of Châteauneuf du Pape—that you will like." She moved round the room, banging cushions and rearranging chairs as she loved to do. "Soon the snow will go away and there will be my snowdrops and then my little irises. You remember the *Iris reticulata* that I brought you last year to Montpelier Square. Does Mrs Larwood cook all right?" In such a mood, she did not wait for answers. "Isn't he a charming boy that naughty wicked Larrie?" she cried. "Already he is responding to kindness."

"I didn't find him very charming," Gerald said, seizing the opening.

"No?" Inge cried, wide-eyed. "Oh, Gerald! you don't know

him. He is so full of jokes and fun. He keeps me young. But also he can be very serious. He has Irish blood, you know, they are dreamers. I think perhaps he will die young, poor thing. All the more reason to make him happy now."

"I wish," said Gerald, "that the mission hadn't fallen to you. I don't like his being here at all."

"Oh! Gerald, how can you talk like that. I am glad of his company. I am very much alone, you know."

"That's just it. You're isolated down here with only the maids. A long way from the nearest house. It's not the place to have an ex-Borstal boy as a companion."

Inge stopped and stared at him. "Johnnie told you that. It is very naughty of him. How can the boy change his life if everybody talks about this? Besides he is not a Borstal boy, he was at an Approved School. It is quite different."

Gerald picked up the decanter and poured out two more sherries. "I only had to hear what was said to know that he's drunken and violent," he said. "And I watched him too. He's probably got good somewhere, but it's terribly laid over, my dear. He's dishonest and deceitful, and I'm inclined to think that he's a malicious hysteric." He reflected that this was also Inge's character in her bad moods. All the more reason that they should be kept apart, he thought.

Inge stood over him and shook her head. "That is very uncharitable, Gerald. It comes with living too much with old books and not enough with people." She dismissed his views. Then, "And what would Johnnie say if I would not let his friend live here?" she asked.

"He's got on all right up to now without it," Gerald said. He was determined not to use his knowledge of John's life to assist his arguments.

"He has got further and further away from me, that is why I like Larrie so. He is the *first* friend of Johnnie's who has brought us together."

Gerald looked at her with a new interest. "Have you met many of Johnnie's friends?" he asked,

"Oh, many, many, Gerald. But they are always trying to take him from me. They tell him I want to possess him and other cruel things. That man Derek Kershaw said dreadful things about me."

Gerald smiled at her. "And weren't they right?"

His disarming smile robbed the words of all seriousness for Inge. "No, Gerald," she said in mock anger, "of course they weren't. You are a pig."

He gave it up as hopeless. "Will you promise," he asked, "that if I'm right about Larrie, you will get rid of him? And if I'm wrong, I'll give you ten pairs of nylon stockings."

Inge laughed with pleasure. "I promise," she said.

They ate an enormous meal together with more real friendliness than they had felt for years. There was only one moment of annoyance, when Gerald asked if Inge had heard from Kay. "Yes, Gerald," she cried, "and I am very angry with little Kay. I have written to tell her so. All that trouble to make that good arrangement for Donald to lecture in the firm and she now writes that he finds Robin rather superior. I don't know what he expects. Robin is the boss. Besides, I do not like to make arrangements for people and then they are not quite pleased." It was so simple a statement of her attitude to life that Gerald could not dispute it.

Despite the unusual ease of the occasion, Gerald went away feeling that he had entirely failed in his purpose; it vexed him, too, that he had no idea of what Inge knew or guessed about John's life.

February brought untimely fogs that year, but to Gerald it brought a clarity of mind that he had not known for years. He corresponded and lunched with possible contributors each day. He met young historians from the provinces for the first time and picked up old friendships that he had almost forgotten. He astonished himself with his energy and the lucidity of his expositions. He began a scheme for the editorial preface; he even organized some of his notes for *The Confessor*. There were,

it was true, occasional mentions of Pforzheim's work in Heligoland and some consequent remarks about Melpham which he
had to meet. In general, however, the topic awaited a full
statement at the forthcoming historical congress at Verona.
May seemed in yellow February a long way off. The family, too,
had receded from his life after the unwonted intimacy bred of
Christmas. At times Gerald had to admit to himself a carefree,
even happy temper.

It was in the first week of March, when endless rain had
driven off the fogs, that Elvira telephoned him, reminding him
of his promise to let her bring Robin round. "He'll be horribly
shy," she said. "He's always kept his private life from his
family. Not that that matters, but it's bad because he's so
conscious of it."

Gerald reflected that his son Robin's life was getting all too
like a parody of his own. "I shall be shy too," he said. "But
don't drop in. Come and have a proper dinner." Somehow an
informal visit from his eldest son seemed more unthinkable
than a formal invitation to a meal.

Robin, it was true, was shy with his father, but his happy
absorption in Elvira's presence overcame it. Gerald was surprised to find how delighted he was to see Robin so happy. His
feelings for his children, though equally unsuccessfully expressed, differed greatly. For John, he felt a guilty and jealous
dislike; for Kay a deep love which made him always criticize
her, for he knew that inevitably she would reject his advances;
but for Robin he had great respect that was only held from
becoming strong affection by a certain awe.

It was soon apparent that Elvira had no such awe. She
treated Robin with a little-controlled impatience for his ignorance of the cosmopolitan values reigning in her circle of
London intelligentsia. Her awareness that there were other
criteria only made her more assertive of those she was accustomed to. Robin, it was clear, did not help himself by
trying too hard to please her. It had taken him some years
to acquire the brand of cultural talk demanded by Marie

Hélène for her parties, it was too late to learn quite another for Elvira.

"This is a lovely room of yours, Father," he said, looking at Gerald's long dining-room, very plain, formal and grey, intended primarily to show off the John drawings that were hung there. "Not quite enough colour for my taste, especially as it's so beautifully proportioned. I like a dining-room to be rather splendid, you know. I should have thought a Regency couch and one of those mirrors with eagles—Empire aren't they?— would give it a sort of grandeur. . . ."

Elvira said, "Oh, Robin, please do stop!"

Robin looked surprised. "Well, don't you think a touch of gold or yellow here and there . . ." he began.

"No, I don't," said Elvira. "I can't think of anything more ghastly than all that fake Regency."

"I like the Regency style," said Robin doggedly.

"Yes, darling, you don't know anything about it, but you know what you like. I've told you again and again that's no reason for saying it." She turned to Gerald. "It's the awful effect of Freud on the middle classes, you know, they think they've a moral duty to say whatever dirty thing comes into their minds."

Robin laughed quite happily; nevertheless he persisted. "Well, what would *you* have, darling?"

"Oh God!" cried Elvira. "This awful idea that one has to 'have' this or that in a room. The influence of the women's magazines on the business classes!" Then, softening, she said to Gerald, "I wouldn't bully him like this, only it's the only way to learn. As a matter of fact, he knows it all quite naturally if he didn't get hold of all these awful middle-class ideas. I'm right, aren't I, darling?" she appealed to Robin, who merely smiled. Gerald noted that she did not openly attack Marie Hélène. "Surely, darling, you see," Elvira went on, gesturing with wild abandon, but speaking like a headmistress. "When anyone's got these wonderful drawings," and she waved her arm round the room, "they don't want Regency tat."

Gerald thought, she knows nothing about it. He said, "I suppose it may be said that I 'have' the John drawings. In any case, I'm not sure that I don't fancy a bit of gold to brighten the room up here and there."

"Oh, don't give way to him," Elvira cried.

The same pattern of tentative cultural feelers from Robin and snubs from Elvira went on all through dinner. Yet Gerald noticed that she never took her eyes off her lover. She's physically obsessed with him, he thought, and then—a lot of this snubbing is an attempt to get her own back on him for possessing her so. His own feelings rather alarmed him. I should like to beat her for her treatment of Robin, he decided, and yet I'm not jealous of Robin for having her. He's welcome to so much pretension if he wants it.

After Robin had rushed in very unwisely to assert that abstract art, like everything else creative, deserved careful study, Elvira pushed her dessert plate away and, lighting a cigarette, said, "Let's talk about something we *know* about. Personalities. Have you done anything about Johnnie and that Larrie yet?" she asked Gerald.

He glanced sideways at Robin, then, smiling at the situation, he said, "I went down to my wife's to spy the land out. Indeed, I tried to raise objections to the situation but it was no good. He's Inge's white-haired boy. I agree with you," he added, "he's a nasty piece of work."

"Oh! he's hell. But it's no good just *talking* about it. After all, we can't just go about having hunches," she said very fairly. "You must try and find *out* something about him. Whether he's just awful, in which case it's John's affair not ours, or whether he really *is* a crook, in which case we must *do* something."

Once again Gerald suddenly found himself liking her. "I'm afraid," he said, "that he *has* a criminal record, but neither John nor Inge are prepared to allow that to stand in their way of helping him. And, of course, they're quite right."

"Oh yes," said Elvira, "it's the best thing I've heard about your wife. It's one of those awful cases where one has to save one's friends from doing the right thing because they're the wrong people to do it. At least John is. In any case, his is a doubtful example of right-doing. *We've* got to be the bastards," she added, "and to push Larrie out, reformed jail-boy or not. Anyway, I'm *sure* he's not reformed. If only we could find out that he's still in with some crooks or something," she said vaguely. She reflected a moment. "I must be very fond of Johnnie, you know, to argue something so utterly disgusting and against my principles as the persecution of a wretched boy who's been in jail."

"I don't care for the job," said Gerald, "but we ought to know the truth if we can. I have a possible connection," he said, "and I'll follow it up."

Mrs Salad's mysterious sibyllic words clicked into place. He would write to her and find out if her grandson knew anything to the point.

Robin pushed back his chair noisily. "Do you mind if we don't discuss John like this?" he said. "His sex-life is surely entirely his own affair."

"Don't try to be broad-minded, darling. Nobody supposes it isn't. But if we can't disapprove of our friends' sex-lives these days, at least we can discuss them to our heart's content." She paused. "It's the new liberalism," she said.

That must be a *mot* she's picked up second-hand, Gerald thought, she's a cultural magpie. He noticed, however, that she made no attempt to continue the discussion after Robin's objection.

"Did you see my letter to *The Times*?" Robin asked.

"I heard something about it," Gerald replied.

"I had to do something," Robin said, "John's behaved abominably. The ghastly thing is that he's got a lot of M.P.s on their feet, and since they're technically in the right, Pelican'll probably get a large raspberry."

"I've heard something to that effect," Gerald said, then stopped short. I'm beginning to sound like the wise old owl, he thought.

"I've got an idea of offering Pelican a directorship if the bloody Civil Service push him around too much," Robin said, and as he leaned back with his cigar he seemed to Gerald to be once more the usual self-assured man. "It'll be a bit tricky with my dear brother directors. Pelican'd be the hell of an asset but they can't see beyond the end of their footling little noses. However, I'm on very good ground there at the moment. They can't eat their words fast enough about Donald. I must say he seems to have been very tactful all round. His first lecture was a howling success with the shop stewards *and* with my dear co-director Simpson, who's such an old diehard he makes Sir Waldron Smithers look like a red."

He paused to savour his brandy. That's all right, Gerald thought, there's a lot of bluff goes with this act; he knows nothing about brandy.

"I wish," Robin went on, "that Donald was a bit more tactful with *me*. He seems to have no sense of time or place. He comes into my office about nothing at all. It's frightfully bad when everyone knows he is my brother-in-law. He doesn't seem to see that there has to be some hierarchy in the place."

"You must put your foot down, darling." It was clear that Elvira's admiration for Robin in his business life was unmodified.

"I shall," he said, "but I don't want to lose my temper."

Gerald accused himself afterwards of watching for tension in their relationship. He was very conscious of an ambivalence in his own attitude, yet unable to perceive its exact nature. He tried to dismiss the whole thing by telling himself that this self-analysis was an adolescent activity unsuitable for an old man of his years, yet he knew that this attempt bluffly to dismiss his doubts was only a hypocritical evasion. At any rate the tension came entirely to the surface before the evening ended.

"Are you going abroad this summer, Father?" asked Robin as they sat round the fire after dinner.

"I've got to go to a congress at Verona," Gerald replied, "otherwise I shall be too busy. I've agreed to edit the new *University Medieval History*, you know."

Robin said, "Oh?", and Elvira, "I suppose those sort of things are fairly stereotyped."

Gerald smiled to himself. He did not, however, press them to show more interest in his affairs. "And you?" he asked Robin.

"Oh, Marie Hélène still insists on the usual Arcachon holiday. It's supposed to be for Timothy, though he's bored stiff with it by now. Anyway, this year we're at least to motor down through the Dordogne. By the way, darling," he said, turning to Elvira, "have you found those guide-books?"

Elvira looked at him, her round, soft face suddenly heavy and dead. "No, I haven't," she said, and then she added violently, "I'm not going to look for them. I don't see why you asked me to."

"It was only because Marie Hélène was talking about what we should see and what we shouldn't, and I immediately thought of you because you'd been there. It's perfectly simple."

"It's simply awful," cried Elvira, "I wish you *wouldn't* talk to her about me."

"I think it's good for her to face the facts since she's been so bloody about the divorce."

"Oh, I don't mind about *her*. I just don't want you to discuss *me* with her *and* I don't want to hear about the holiday not *ever*, not ever. Not now before you go or when you come back. Oh, I know how you've got to go and how we've got to be sensible. All right, I will be. But that doesn't mean I shan't hate every day of it."

Robin tried not to look at Gerald. "Aren't you being a bit unreasonable, darling?" he asked.

"Of course I am," Elvira shouted. "Somebody who's obsessed with somebody else always is unreasonable. Oh, can't you explain to him?" she cried, turning to Gerald.

Robin was very embarrassed. "I really don't think we should drag poor Father into this," he protested.

"Oh, that's all right," Gerald said, getting up. He turned to the now weeping Elvira. "Have a spot of whisky," he suggested, "it's a great help at such times."

Her hair falling over her face, she shook her head, then, "All right, I will," she said. "I'm sorry. It's all this bloody being in love."

"I'm in love with you too, my dear," said Robin.

Elvira looked up at him with eyes blazing, "Oh, for God's sake let's talk about something else!" she cried.

In the end, they got through the rest of the evening with remarkably successful conformity to good manners.

It was some weeks before Gerald got any reply to his letter to Mrs Salad, and when it did come it was not in the form he expected. "There's a Mr Salad on the telephone for you, sir," Mrs Larwood said one morning before he had risen from bed.

"Well, I can't speak to him now," Gerald called to her.

"I told him that, but he says it's very important. It's about his grandmother."

"Oh very well," he answered. This comes of refusing to have an extension in my bedroom, he thought, as he pulled on a heavy dressing-gown. March gave no promise of relief from the cold wintry weather.

"Middleton speaking," he called brusquely into the telephone.

It was obvious that his caller was put out, for an adenoidal voice said in nervous, though carefully refined tones, "Oh! How do you do? My name's Vin Salad. I'm afraid it's frightfully early."

"Yes," Gerald said, "it is. What do you want?"

"I'm ringing on account of Mrs Salad. She's my grandmother."

"Yes," answered Gerald. He was getting angry.

The caller's spirits seemed to be recovering from the original impact of Gerald's tone. The voice changed at a lightning speed from refined to cockney. Gerald could hardly hear the refined words, they were so swallowed; on the other hand, the cockney tones hit his ear somewhat painfully. "My grandmother's been taken up," came the cockney.

"Taken up?" Gerald queried. And then refined came the explanation. "Yes, she's been arrested. On a charge of shoplifting, it seems."

Gerald was horrified at the prospect of Mrs Salad in the hands of the law. It hit his sentimental centre very hard. "Poor old thing," he whispered. "Can I be of any help at all?" he asked.

"Well, I think you might be. I'm going up to the court with a friend. We're taking her up there together. But I think it might help if someone respectable was to speak for her. On her behalf," Vin corrected himself.

Gerald, remembering what Mrs Salad had said, saw that Vin might not be altogether "respectable". "Oh, certainly," he said. "I've not been her employer for many years, of course. But I've always kept up with her. Anyway, I'll do anything I can."

"Well, actually, in my opinion, they'll only fine her. But I think it would do her a lot of good if you were there." The combination of the telephone, Gerald's masculinity and his professorial rank had put Vin on a mettle of refinement that he seldom attempted. "My friend Mr Rammage saw a solicitor last night and he's talking to one of the Welfare Officers this morning." Gerald would have been surprised if he could have heard Vin's name for all these assisting people, including Gerald himself.

"Well, that all sounds very good," said Gerald. "What about her daughter Gladys? She always seemed to rely so much on her and her husband."

Vin's voice took on its normal hard, deadly note. "Oh did she?" he asked. "Well, that's a mistake she won't make no more. Gladys 'as come out of this a proper cow, as could have been told from the first." Vin broke into a high-pitched imitation of his aunt: "Can she say anything on behalf of her mother? Well, no, that she can't. Her living with them was only a convenience like to the old lady, and she doesn't see her way to being able to accommodate her no more, not after this has happened. Respectable neighbours, they've got. As for Mr Health and Strength—he stands by his little woman, which he may well do for no one else can when the wind's set in the wrong direction."

Gerald recognized Mrs Salad's personality in Vin and felt warmed towards him. "Do you mean they've turned Mrs Salad out?"

"That's right," said Vin. "C—— bitches."

"It's disgraceful of them," said Gerald. It was as though stone after stone was being thrown at his life with Dollie, shattering and breaking the edifice of memories which he had built around Mrs Salad. "Of course, she can come here until we've fixed up something more permanent."

"Well, thank you, if I may say so," Vin replied, "but there's no need to go to the trouble. My friend Mr Rammage has a room available which will suit the old lady nicely." And then, surprising Gerald, came that occasional Kensington hostess's swallowed contralto of Vin's. "I must say, all things considered, I think we shall get along quite marvellously once this little bit of trouble's over."

"How is she?" asked Gerald.

"Taking things very bad," said Vin, then he added, "Well, if you'll pardon the reminder, time's going by," and he gave Gerald directions to reach the North-West London Court.

The solicitor announced, as Gerald had expected, that it would serve no purpose for him to go into the box. "As it's a first offence," he said, "I think she'll get away with a fine. It'll be a heavy one though, the magistrate'll aim at frightening her. I've persuaded her to plead guilty, though I'm by no means sure that she knows what she's saying. The great thing is to see that this doesn't happen again. I should like to impress that on you," he said sternly to Vin. "If she comes up again, they'll send her to prison."

Vin was a very muted figure in the court-room, despite his chic dark suit. Court-rooms had no happy memories for him. "I'll do my best," he said.

Frank fussed and comforted Mrs Salad. Although she seemed hardly to understand what he was saying, she held to his hand tightly. Gerald patted her shoulder. He could find nothing to say but "Never say die, Mrs Salad. It'll be all over soon." Vin added, "And then we'll be quit of this bleeding lot."

Mrs Salad fumbled with her old vanity bag and her eyes blinked up through her eye-veil. She took in all the four men around her. "All my gentleman," she said. Even through her terror and tiredness, she preserved what she called her "artful ways".

She made a little, black, trembling smudge in the prisoner's box. The magistrate was known to Gerald at his club as a professional *bon viveur*, intelligent and sharp, but given to over-elaborate, unsuccessful witticisms. The glance that he gave Mrs Salad seemed perfunctory, but Gerald guessed that long experience made it sufficient.

"Emma Adeline Salad," read the clerk, "you are charged that on the fifteenth day of March . . ."

Gerald found himself taking refuge from the scene in marvelling that all these years he had not known her Christian names. He stirred himself with the reminder that it was his duty to follow closely. Mrs Salad's cracked old voice produced a hardly audible plea of guilty. Gerald whispered to the solicitor, "Does she give any reason why she did it?" The solicitor held his finger to his lips, then scribbled on a piece of paper "They never know why." It seemed curious to Gerald that a man who dealt with such cases day after day should not have evolved some theory of their causes. He wrote on a piece of paper, "Why do *you* think she did it?" The solicitor frowned in annoyance. "So many possible reasons," he wrote, and folded his arms as though defying Gerald to question him further. The dreary case went on.

The evidences of the shop detective—a tired, pleasant-faced young woman—and the inspector from the police station were taken. It all seemed so small an affair—some artificial violets valued at two and sixpence and a packet of gift wrappers valued at sixpence, but Gerald thought of Mrs Salad's habitual bunch of Parmas. He noticed that she was not wearing them in court and then saw that the fat, red-faced little man called Rammage had them on his lap. He seemed to be a sort of universal help. Indeed, Frank sat there like a kindly but determined mental nurse ready to receive her charge after a routine examination by the doctors. Vin had replaced his usual languor by an attempt to sit in an erect, military position. The effect of the police court had brought him back to the efforts he had made to impress as an ordinary, straightforward young citizen during his own trials. All the reptilian, passive intelligence that usually showed in his hard face was replaced by a negative, dull stupidity. With his sallow skin and his adenoidal open-mouthed expression, he looked not the plain young chap he hoped, but constipated, almost cretinous.

To Gerald's irritation, what seemed a cruel length of time was taken up by the magistrate's enquiries about the nature of the gift wrappers. What purpose did they serve? Were they sold separately from the gifts they were intended to accompany? How had they acquired this name? He examined the small packet itself at length. Eventually it became apparent that the packets were placed in each stall so that customers might buy them with any articles they chose to send away as gifts. "I see," he said, "then they are hardly a separate article," and he refused to consider them separately in the charge.

At last Mrs Salad was asked if she had anything to say in exoneration of her action. It was difficult to make out the meaning of the trembling croak that came from her and she was asked to repeat her remark more loudly. This time, to Gerald at any rate, the words were perfectly clear. "I never took up with the trash," she said. To Gerald, too, the meaning was perfectly clear; it was simply an affirmation of her social code, necessary, no doubt, in her mind because of the socially humiliating position in which she found herself.

The magistrate interpreted her words differently. "You will have to learn," he said, "that you cannot wilfully take things that do not belong to you, however little value you may attach to them. This is a very serious offence, for which I *could* send you to prison. I am counting it in your favour that you have not attempted to deny your actions. On the other hand, I see no particular sign that you are sorry for what you have done. However, as this is your first offence and you are an old woman, I propose to fine you the sum of ten pounds. But listen very carefully to what I have to say. If you appear here again before me on a charge of this kind, I shall have no hesitation whatever in sending you to prison."

They all drove back to Earl's Court in Gerald's Daimler. They made a light-hearted party. Mrs Salad, it was true, was very shaky and still a little tearful. However, she pinned her Parma violets back on to her coat and dabbed a little lavender water behind her ears with a lace-edged hanky. "I didn't intend to make no statement," she said, "I told 'em. I don't intend to make no statement, I said. But I never took up with the trash in my life." She mumbled these sentences to herself so often that Gerald began to wonder if her ordeal had disturbed her mind.

Vin lay back on the cushions of the car as though he had at last come into his own again. His customary drawl was quite restored when he spoke. "Well, ten quid's not going to put us on Assistance. I don't know what sort of class 'e thought we were." He seemed aggrieved at the smallness of the fine.

Gerald felt he must remonstrate at this interpretation. "I don't think that's quite the point," he said. "These fines are fixed by law, you know. But you shouldn't think that because he only fined your grandmother ten pounds that he didn't mean every word he said about sending her to prison if it happens again."

Frank Rammage clucked appreciatively, but he was too happy to have another unhappy charge coming under his roof to say anything. He kept looking at Mrs Salad as though he had purchased a peculiarly satisfactory antique—one absolutely guaranteed fake.

Vin listened respectfully to what Gerald said. "I see what you mean," he said. He was not only impressed by Gerald's wealth and position, but even more by his elegant, military-style good looks. It must also be said that he was genuinely grateful for Gerald's kindness to his grandmother, of whom he was very fond. "That lawyer friend of yours is on to a nice, easy thing," he said to Frank. "He did bloody all for his money. Not that *we* should worry. It's not as if we were going to pay," he added with a pleased smile.

"I've already paid Mr Levett," snapped Frank.

"All right." Vin lay back and closed his eyes. "If you like to be the Muggins." He did not feel the same admiration for Frank as for Gerald and he saw proportionately less need for gratitude.

Mrs Salad was enough recovered when they arrived to grumble at the large room Frank had provided for her. He had distempered it mustard in a fit of decorating enthusiasm. "I shan't sleep in the yeller, dear," she said. "There's them that's made their bed of gold and I'm not one of them."

Gerald said embarrassedly, "I think it's a lovely room, Mrs Salad. Look, you can see into the gardens of the Square."

"Ah!" she said, peering dimly through the window, "and nice goings on there'd be, no doubt." She felt the mattress. "I don't know 'ow I'll lay on that," she said, "I've always slept on the feathers. Mr Salad wouldn't have me sleep on nothing else. Light I was when 'e married me. 'Is little featherweight 'e called me and feathers it was I'd to sleep on. And 'ave done to this day." She poked the bed with one of her gnarled, ringed old fingers. "Is it one of them new cork mattresses?" she asked Frank.

"Horsehair," he said, his little mouth pouting in his determination to endure her petulance.

"Ah!" she said, "coarse 'air more like. That don't do for the sensitive skins like what I've got. Now Mr Salad's sister, she'd got more the rough skin, like emery paper it was, as 'er own *'usband* said, and 'e'd touched it often enough."

Even Vin's affection for his grandmother had been tried long enough. He turned away from the wardrobe mirror before which he had been arranging his hair. "Shut up," he said in a hard voice, "you're lucky to be in a decent bed at all. Personally," he added in more delicate tones, "I should advise you to put your feet up and sleep it off." Vin's government of his grandmother, it was clear, was to be an autocratic one.

Mrs Salad, however, did not demur; her recent experience had, temporarily at any rate, fitted her for a more obedient rôle. Her hands trembled, so that she had the greatest difficulty in removing her toque and veil.

"Oh! Let me do it," said Vin, irritably. "I'm sure I don't know," he went on as he removed the little, battered object, "when veils like this were last worn, short of the Chelsea Arts Ball. Well, say goodbye to the Professor and thank him for all the trouble he's taken."

Once more Mrs Salad took refuge in a general coy glance at all three men. "My gentlemen," she said again. She seemed unable to address herself to Gerald directly in the new circumstances.

"Don't get into any more scrapes," he said, "and come and see me when you feel inclined. I think you're going to be very happy in this nice room."

Mrs Salad gave him a look which was not encouraging.

As soon as they were outside on the landing, Vin took up his grandmother's complaints. "You'll have to find another room for her, Frank. I said that mustard would be cruel to the old lady's looks. I can't say I liked what I saw in the mirror myself with that background, which shows you chose wrong. You can move that little bitch Mona from the pink room. Pink'd be more kind to the old lady."

"I'll see," said Frank.

Vin gave him a sharp, sidelong glance. "Yeah, you'll see to it right away," he said.

Frank did not answer. He opened the door to his room on the ground floor. "Well, I think we can all do with a drink," he said. "I waited till now because I didn't think that would do the old lady any good in her present state."

"I think I've got to go," said Gerald, looking at his watch.

Frank's fat cheeks shook slightly, he had seemed shy of addressing Gerald from the first moment they had met, but now he gobbled at him. "I believe you wrote Mrs Salad about Larrie Rourke. I'd like a word with you about that, if you please. Won't you sit down."

Gerald was about to sit down on a little hard, scarlet-upholstered bentwood chair, but Vin motioned him to the large scarlet armchair. "Sit there, Professor," he said. "You sit on that one," he ordered Frank to the hard chair and then stretched himself out on the divan. "Well, get the drinks," he said.

"I've just sat down," Frank replied.

"Yeah, we saw that," Vin yawned, then he turned to Gerald, "Have a drink," he said. "He's saved one on Gran already. Don't let him get away with another."

"There's no occasion for waste," Frank asserted.

"Well, that's all right then, 'cos there's no opportunity for it here."

"I don't like to say anything personal against your son," Frank began, but the door was half open and a blowzy red-haired woman of forty-five put her head into the room, "I'm busy now, Mona," Frank said. "Will it do later?"

"That's all right," Mona said, "I only wanted to say that I'm taking those six glasses off the bill that you charged me. They were cracked when I borrowed them."

"All right, duckie," Frank answered. "By the way, I'm thinking of moving you into the big room on the first floor."

"Well, think again," Mona said.

Vin slithered to his feet. "I'd like a word with you, Mona dear," and he followed her out of the room. Their voices could be heard in the passage as Frank spoke.

"That'll be the best way," he remarked, "Vin knows what to do." Then to Gerald's surprise he got up and stood over him, arms akimbo like a caricaturist's washerwoman dressing someone down. "As I say, I don't ever speak personalities. That doesn't help in life to my belief. But your son's doing wrong, Professor Middleton. I've tried to see him to tell him so, but he won't stoop to hearing the plain truth from a common man like me. I'm casting no aspersions on his feelings for that young chap, there's a good deal too much of that talk these days to my mind."

Gerald said sharply, "No, I don't think I should do that if I were you." He did not know where to place Frank and was anxious to tread carefully.

"What I do say is that it's wrong to take him out of his own sphere," Frank went on. "That's a grand house I daresay where your wife lives and he'll learn not to do without while he's there. And then when he has to, he won't know how. Add to which," he went on. But Vin came into the room.

"She'll move tonight," he said, and settling himself on the divan again, he lay motionless while Frank was talking.

"Further to which," Frank continued, "the boy's got a bad record and I've worked hard to help him. I'd got him a job in a pub around here. I don't say he'd have stuck it, but he might have done. I don't like to see good work ruined." Frank, his cheeks almost purple with protest, resumed his seat.

"Well," said Gerald, "all that's really got nothing to do with me, though you may be right, Mr Rammage. I'm simply concerned to protect my wife from the possibility of being exploited. When I heard this fellow had a criminal record, I didn't like it, but if, as you say, he's trying to reform, I shouldn't like you to suggest that my wife's influence couldn't help him."

"You've got to help people to help themselves," said Frank, "that's what. He needs hard work that boy and a kind word but no spoiling. If that's what he gets there's no reason why he shouldn't turn out as decent a citizen as you or I, he's got all the makings of it."

Vin rustled very slightly on the divan, then, "Get you!" he drawled. "He's got all the makings of a bloody little twister, our little black-eyed 'colleen' from Killarney. He'll never go straight, and if he wanted to, the lot he goes around with wouldn't let him. I know."

Gerald said, "You mean that he still keeps up with his criminal associates?" He felt himself stuffier and more pompous every minute in this improbable setting. Vin began to manicure his nails.

"Yes," he said, looking up for a minute, "that's what I do mean. You don't want to let 'im stop down at your wife's place." His accent seemed more cockney and glottal as he got more worked up. "I should think your son must be a fool to pick that one up. But you get 'im out of your wife's place. That's what I mean."

Frank grunted disapproval. "You've no right to talk of the boy that way," he said.

Vin disregarded him. He put down his nail-file and, folding his hands in his lap, he stared at Gerald with his great dark eyes. "I tell you what. I know the places 'e goes and the crowd 'e goes with. If there looks like trouble, I'll let you know. 'E'll get into trouble all right sooner or later, but you want to get 'im out before it 'appens."

Gerald said, "I hardly like . . ."

Vin interpreted Gerald's hesitation as a fear of bothering him rather than of any scruples about having Larrie spied on. "That's quite all right," he said, once more very refined, "I'm only too glad to help someone who's been so marvellous to Gran." He looked at his very expensive watch. "I must go," he cried, "I told Giacometti I'd be late, but not this late."

"Can I give you a lift?" Gerald asked.

"That would be marvellous," Vin replied, "but I hardly care to arrive at work in a Daimler." When he had gone, Frank seemed to relapse into his original shy silence.

"I must be off too," said Gerald.

Frank made no reply, but he arose and opened the door. "That was right," he said, "what Vin did. The old lady'll sleep better in the pink."

Before he had reached home, Gerald felt a revulsion from the whole subject of John and Larrie; he cursed Elvira for pushing him into the sordid business; Inge for getting herself into such a situation; himself for having such a son. He reflected that it was unlikely that he would hear any more about the matter; if Vin telephoned he would choke him off.

In the next few days, he plunged deeply into the preparation of the *History*, compiling the editorial rules for footnotes, discussing format and map reproduction with the printers, he even began to sort through his papers for the substance of his own contribution—"The Impact of Norman Feudalism upon Anglo-Saxon Society." He succeeded in forgetting John's affairs altogether, but he could not so easily get Elvira out of his thoughts. The last days of March brought bright days with high winds and beautiful sailing clouds. He interspersed his work with walks in the Park; he felt twenty years younger in a new light-grey tweed suit and a new loose buff spring overcoat. He spoke to children by the Round Pond and engaged in quite a long conversation with a Pole who asked him for directions; he stood and gazed at the mauve and white streaked crocuses, reflecting that he had thought of them only as yellow or purple; he observed the steel-like claws of the crane that scratched in the little stream behind the Serpentine. He bought pots of hyacinths and daffodils for the house and spent a pleasant half-hour ordering wine. In all this, for the first time for many years, he did not feel lonely, but he constantly found himself wondering what Elvira was doing. Probably talking a lot of pretentious nonsense over coffee or cocktails in some smoke-filled room, he decided, or more likely in bed at noon. It would do her appearance a world of good to get out of doors more.

He was quick to check these speculations, and gradually they were replaced by a growing concern for Robin's relations with her. He thought over her hysterical outburst that night, Robin's surprising freedom and happiness, her obvious physical passion for him. It was an explosive situation that reminded him too easily of his own life with Dollie. *He* had allowed conventional ideas about the family, Inge's possessive interest, to ruin that; it was his duty, he decided, to give Robin a warning tip. Here at least was something he knew about, not like that peculiar business of John's; besides, Robin was an admirable chap. Gerald had no compunctions about Marie Hélène, he thought her a selfish, snobbish sort of woman. Besides, what good was the present situation doing *her*? What sort of life would she have with Robin if she destroyed his relationship with Elvira? What sort of life had Inge had? As to Timothy, Robin himself knew how far general happiness helped children in the end: besides the boy was sixteen. He rang up Robin and suggested lunch. He would call for him at his office, he said. Robin seemed friendly and pleased on the other end of the phone.

Robin, indeed, sat in his large comfortable office overlooking the Thames and awaited his father's arrival that morning with more pleasure than he ever would have expected from such an event. The truth was, that for all the embarrassment of Elvira's little outburst, he had enjoyed the dinner at Gerald's. It was satisfactory to have a father whom Elvira liked; it was pleasant to be able to take her to dine with that father and know that the occasion would be a civilized one. His father had proved friendly but not interfering. Robin here contrasted the occasion with any at which Inge would have so happily presided in the same circumstances. He had had quite enough of women lately; he somehow rather liked the situation of man, mistress and elderly but experienced father. It had a worldly flavour, and worldly flavours tended to flatter Robin's somewhat starved soul. Of course, as the eldest son, he had seen what his mother had been through far more than John, who had only been a kid; he would always admire her and be grateful to her; he would always remember how rottenly his father had behaved, but it had to be faced that Gerald was rather pathetic—a washed-up, lonely old man.

Robin did not exactly compare his own marital behaviour to his father's, but in avoiding the comparison he sought refuge in a broadminded determination not to judge him too harshly. After all, it was natural that he should get on with his father, he was essentially a man's man, not like John, a mother's darling. Robin had been very impressed by the views of an Oxford don who had been brought to one of Marie Hélène's parties recently. It seemed that his father was really a very eminent historian, even if he had not quite fulfilled his original promise. When Robin heard this, he remembered with pleasure how interested his father always was in what he said, how he deferred to his opinion on politics or economics. His father's respect for him seemed somehow doubly gratifying now that he knew how eminent he was in his own field. He decided that he would take Gerald out and give him a really good lunch.

Perhaps if Gerald had been a poorer man, had needed the good lunch a bit more, Robin would have looked forward to the occasion even more. Even as it was, he was in very good spirits. He had lunched with Pelican a few days earlier and suggested that, if things went wrong, it was possible that Middleton and Company could do something about it. Would Pelican think it over and let him know what he felt about the idea? And now Pelican had written. Reading between the lines, it was obvious the poor chap was desperately anxious about the future. Robin's handsome, fleshy face was gathered in lines of pleasure. He loved helping people. He read the letter over again. ". . . in these circumstances, and in view of all the publicity that has been given to the incident, I suspect that the Minister will be driven to take what is called disciplinary action. If so, it is more than likely that I may find myself sent to one of the branch offices. Apart from the general disinclination that anyone in middle age feels for such changes, the situation would be peculiarly unfortunate in my case. My two boys are at St Paul's. It would be a serious dislocation to their education to move them to another school at this stage, even if this were possible, which I very much doubt. My wife, too, sets great store on the boys being at home. She is a great opponent of boarding schools. So that if the blow does fall, I fear it will be a choice between a number of very uncomfortable evils. I confess that I am dearly tempted, in any case, after all this, to resign from the Service, but to give up my pension at forty-five with a family to consider would be an impossible luxury. If, on the other hand, there were an opening . . ."

Robin rang for his secretary. "Miss Rodmell," he said, "take a letter, will you, to Pelican. You'd better not send it to the Ministry. Send it to his home address. He lives somewhere out Elstree way. 'Dear Pelican'," he began, when the door half opened and Donald's long white face, so like an intelligent sheep's, peered round it.

Miss Rodmell looked horrified at this sacrilege. Robin said sharply, "Yes?"

"There are one or two points . . ." Donald began.

"I'm busy now," Robin said. "Put them in writing."

Donald came into the room. "Oh, I should hardly care to elevate them into the importance of a written memorandum," he declared primly. Robin sat back in fury. Donald took his silence for permission to proceed. "I'm not entirely happy about the hour appointed for my next lecture," he announced. "I've been talking to Mr Ferguson down at the Works and it's quite apparent to me that Grant here has rather unfortunately only considered the clerical staff in fixing . . ."

Robin suddenly shot forward in his seat. "Look!" he cried. "I think I told you that I was busy. What is more I seem to remember that this very situation has occurred far too often.

Perfectly good machinery exists for making appointments to
see me. Please use them, Donald." It was all he could do to
soften his speech by the use of his brother-in-law's Christian
name.

The result was unfortunate. Donald's success so far with the
staff of Middleton's, due to factors of which he had no compre-
hension—desire by some to curry favour with Robin, determination by others to let him have a rope and hang himself—
had removed his doubts about his ability to deal with people.
It was only the academic world, he had decided, that from
jealousy disliked him. All his natural conceit had been released.
Robin's use of his Christian name reminded him of their
family relationship and of Inge's assurance that, when her
eldest son was angry, he could always be teased out of it.
Donald had somewhat vague ideas of the nature of teasing, but
he set out nevertheless to tease. "I find it so difficult," he said,
his watery eyes gleaming with a pale, flickering light of
humour, "to remember the various cabbalic passwords and
devices with which I should approach the Holy of Holies,
Robin. You should devise something more simple, like 'Open
Sesame'."

Robin glowered at him. "If you don't mind," he said, "this
is not an occasion for misplaced facetiousness." He had decided that he must strike heavily and put an end to these in-
trusions for good and all. "If you wish to see me, you should
telephone Miss Rodmell, or in her absence my other secretary,
and state your business. They will no doubt be competent
to decide whether it requires my attention. I would remind you,
though, that they are both very busy people. Please don't
bother them with petty questions that can perfectly well be
decided by reference to someone else, if, that is, you feel
incompetent to decide them yourself. As I said many times
before you joined us, we are on a business not a family
footing here."

Donald was both alarmed and angry at the failure of his
jocular approach. "Certainly," he said, "I shall have no

occasion to forget an order made in those terms. I may add, however, that I have hardly been tempted to recall any family relationship. I have received the greatest help in work from everyone in this place except you."

Robin looked at him for a moment, then he said wearily, "Please sit down, Donald." He turned to Miss Rodmell. "I'll let you know when I'm ready for that letter," he said.

He was beginning to fear that his brother-in-law might turn out a bad investment, but he felt that he might be able to swing the market if he took the right steps at once.

"Now, Donald," he said. He found it difficult—as indeed it was—to look neither stern nor amiable. "I think we *must* get a few things straight. I'm appreciative of the success you made of your first lecture. The whole idea of these lectures was a pet one of mine carried through in the teeth of a good deal of opposition, so that I'm naturally grateful for the good start you've given them. But that doesn't mean that I think them other than a small luxury to the firm, a little up-to-date side-line." He smiled at the possibility of Donald's supposing them to be more. "In any case, you must not think of your job here as anything but a stop-gap. Your proper sphere is the university world, where I have no doubt you'll have great success. But I would like to say something to you that may be of general help. Wherever you work and whatever you're doing, you'll need to have a more realistic assessment of people. You've been very pleased with the praises here for your lecture, the praises of Kennedy and Hollett and Jim Straker. I've no doubt they were pleased, but there are a hundred other reasons why they should have chosen to make a fuss of you. You simply must not take these things at their face value. For example, every time you come in here—and we won't go into the undesirability of that again—you retail a bit of gossip. First of all, let's get this clear, I never listen to it. But neither should you. If you're going to be elated or depressed by every chance remark or mood of the people you work with either here or elsewhere, you'll never get anywhere, which would be a pity, because I'm quite sure you could have a fine career ahead of you." He sat back in his chair and smiled.

Donald got up and walked to the door, then he turned and said, "I think it would be much better for everyone if you ceased to think of these lectures as your peculiar possession, particularly as you did not see fit to come to the first one."

Robin smacked the arm of his chair. "Oh, for heaven's sake!" he cried. "Surely you saw that I stayed away so that everyone should have a free hand."

Donald's thin lips compressed, "If that really is so," he said, "you might consider how far your present attitude is due to a dislike of your protégé acquiring wider loyalties to the firm."

As he went through the secretary's room, his white face was suffused with pink. He did not trust Miss Rodmell to be discreet, the story would be all over the office by tonight and common talk at the works tomorrow.

Robin looked at his watch and saw that it was nearly the time of his appointment with Gerald. He rang. "Miss Rodmell," he said, "I'm expecting my father at any moment— write to Pelican for me. Tell him that I anticipate no opposition, perhaps we'd better say no serious opposition here, to my proposal for his joining us in a situation satisfactory to him. And add that I look forward to making him an official proposal in the event of his wishing to leave his present work."

They lunched at the Savoy Grill. Gerald chose a Château-briant and a Mâcon, because Robin remembered that this was his favourite lunch, though he did not share the memory. He was a little uneasy at having so much fuss made of him, although it pleased him. Robin talked at great length of John's misconduct in the Pelican affair and of the surprise his brother would get when Pelican was made a director of Middleton's. "I have some connections with the newspaper world," he said. "Not John's ghastly rag, of course, but the more reputable papers. I shall see that it gets into print and not only in the financial column." He saw that his father was a little bored with the topic. "I shall be glad when it's all over," he added, "it's getting to be rather an *idée fixe* with me, and a boring one for other people." He laughed self-deprecatingly.

Gerald asked after Donald's progress, but Robin was short in his answer. "He's got a very bad manner sometimes," he announced judicially, "but I think he's learning." Recalling the Oxford don's praise, he asked his father after *his* work.

For a moment Gerald was quite nonplussed, he did not remember his family ever showing an interest in his studies. However, in his new happiness, he soon warmed to the subject and told Robin about the new history. "It's a very large affair really," he said, "four or five volumes. Heaven knows if I shall live to see it finished!"

"My dear father, it's just the thing to give you a long life. I'm frightfully pleased. But, of course, you're the obvious man for it. Everyone says you're right at the top of your tree."

Gerald wondered who "everyone" could be, but instead he said, "I'm very grateful to your girl-friend for bringing us together, Robin."

"Oh! trust Elvira to do the right thing. She likes you very much, Father."

"I like her." He paused and chose a little colloquialism which he remembered hearing somewhere: "She's got it very badly over you, Robin." The phrase sounded strangely on his lips.

Robin said "I hope so. I'm in the same boat."

"Not quite, I should think," Gerald commented.

"Oh! you mean her little outburst the other evening." Robin shrugged it off. "She's very highly strung, you know, and then the crowd she goes about with never go to bed as far as I can see. At least not to sleep." He was very impressed with the easy promiscuity of Elvira's friends.

Gerald tried another tack. "Do you remember Dollie at all?" he asked.

"Dollie Stokesay?" Robin blushed involuntarily; he had not expected quite this degree of intimacy but he determined to cope with his new rôle. "Yes, of course," he remarked with what he hoped was a casual air. "I was fourteen or fifteen when you cut loose from her."

"I didn't," Gerald said firmly, "she cut loose from me. I've never ceased to regret it. Oh, don't think I'm going to say anything that is critical of your mother. I'm fully conscious of the fact that I'm entirely to blame for the whole thing. I don't know that I should ever have married Inge. I did so, you see, on what they used to call the rebound. From Dollie's refusal of me, to be exact." Robin was more and more appalled. He gave himself grimly to breaking up his rings of rum-soaked pine-apple—"But having met Dollie again, we both knew that everything else was unimportant. I believe romanticism of that sort is unfashionable. Indeed, it was not very sophisticated in the 'twenties. We tried to be much more sensible, and Inge tried too. In fact everybody tried. Your mother and Dollie used to meet. Well, you remember how she was Auntie Dollie in your childhood. It worked at first because we were so much in love that we didn't notice how impossible it was. It went on working for some years because Dollie disguised from me how much she hated it. In the end neither she nor Inge could keep it up. I lost Dollie. She became a 'dipso', you know. And I lost all the respect and affection of my family too, and any right to it. I'm very much against being sensible in these things; as a result I don't think one has any right to impose that strain on anyone one loves." He had told the story so badly, indeed he wished that he had never told it.

Robin wished this too. He said, "My case is a little different, you know. Marie Hélène can't give me a divorce, she's a Roman Catholic."

Gerald quickly said, "Yes, yes, I know. You'd have to work it out in your own terms. I only wanted to warn you against putting too much strain on Elvira."

"Thank you," said Robin. "I think we'll manage all right."

There was a pause in their conversation as they were given coffee. Offering Gerald a cigar, Robin said, "Don't take this in the wrong way, Father, but ours is a very new acquaintance. I think we ought to take it slowly, you know."

Gerald had determined that he would pay no regard to the various rumours that reached him of the Heligoland excavations. He admired Pforzheim and he would wait for the congress at Verona to hear his report. The spring weather at the end of March brought May too often into his mind, but, on the whole, he was so absorbed by his current work that he suffered no more than momentary anxieties. After all, even if the Heligoland burial proved similar to that at Melpham, the two things were not one. Certainly, at this stage, he had no right to influence Pforzheim's views with what were only suspicions—and suspicions in no sense based on historical scholarship. He had allowed the incident with Gilbert far too much influence in his life as it was; he could do far more for his chosen profession in getting on with the job in hand, than by interfering in the detailed scholarship of a period that was not his own. If Pforzheim expressed any misgivings himself about Melpham, then he would report what he knew—but privately, in a way that would take the decision out of his hands. But the decision was put firmly back into his hands before May or the congress had arrived.

It was in April, on a morning when Gerald had noted the first primroses in the Park, that Jasper rang him up. He was in England for a short interval, he said, to check some facts at the B.M. He proposed to go to Verona and then to spend the rest of the summer in Italy finishing his book. He would like to discuss the articles for the *History* that Gerald wanted from him while he was here and to tell him of the very fascinating time he had had in Germany. He could come round whenever Gerald chose. He would like a little relief from early medieval Church and State.

He came two days later to tea, suave and a little vulgarly elegant as always. Gerald was somewhat perfunctory in his expressions of interest about Germany and insisted on getting

down to business at once. However, even his protracted discussion of the editorial rules and his minute discussion of the
nature of the articles he had requested had to come to an end.

Jasper had, indeed, become a little restive. "You promise to
be as great a tyrant as Clun in your editorial supervision," he
said, laughing. "I suspect we've avoided King Stork to be
landed with King Stork. Oh, no," he protested, waving a well-
manicured, somewhat thick hand, "I'm delighted, Gerald, delighted. I haven't seen you so animated for a long age. I look
forward to your reactions to what I have to tell you of Pforzheim's work." He fitted a cigarette into his holder and lit it.
"Is it too soon after tea for a drink?" he asked. "Just the
Vermouth, no gin."

Making himself comfortable, he began his story. "Pforzheim's work was a revelation to me," he cried, "the neatness,
the clarity. I doubt if any English historian or archaeologist
could turn technique into art in that way. But he's rewarded.
It's Aldwine's tomb without a doubt. The remains of the coffin
are fragmentary, but they're enough. By a miracle a part of the
inscription came to light at a slightly deeper level; it must have
been broken off and sunk in a softer part of the peat. What's
held up the report, of course, has been the idol. Pforzheim
spent a long time with Cuspatt and Fish at the Museum and
they've been over there. It's very worn down and fragmentary,
but it builds up well to fit all the Baltic and North Sea Coast
idols that have been found. Of course, that wouldn't have been
enough to admit it as such in such a place, but for Melpham.
It's really a fantasy how something which seemed so much a
fascinating oddity should suddenly become so important. That's
why the Museum people here were in such a pother. It appears,
believe it or not, that Cuspatt insisted on subjecting the
Melpham idol to Geiger laboratory tests. Of course, it's a bit
recent to respond to most of these things, they can only answer
for such enormous periods of time. It was utterly unlikely
anyway, as Pforzheim said, that the thing could have been a
fake. Apart from Stokesay's reputation, it would have been so

utterly pointless to fake such a thing at that date. Anyhow, there's no doubt now on that score. Actually I think even he was a bit worried at one point. He'd been through all the reports of the Melpham excavation, including some unpublished papers of Stokesay's and of Portway's, which Cuspatt had, and apparently the whole thing was wildly haphazard. Of course, we didn't think that a 1912 excavation would have stood up to modern tests, but even so, I think, Pforzheim was a bit shocked considering Stokesay's reputation. However, the less said about that the better, especially if Rose Lorimer is anywhere about, she'd get into such a state if criticism were made of Stokesay."

He smiled, "We must be considerate of our Rose now. After all, there's a certain reason in her madness. She sees the pagan hidden hand in every Christian action, and even those of us who are good old-time agnostics would not care to go that far. Nor do I think many people will follow her in her back-to-Iona movement," he smiled and finished his drink. He was so interested in what he was saying that he hardly thanked Gerald when his glass was filled again. "All the same this dual cult wasn't simply a personal roguery of Eorpwald's. Cuspatt and Pforzheim are both very keen to start other excavations that might throw up the same thing, though it's a very long shot, of course. We're all wondering how Lavenham and the Roman Catholics are going to react." He gave the nearest to a chuckle that elegance would permit. "By the way," he said, "Pforzheim tried hard to get in touch with *you* but you'd gone off on some jaunt to Vienna. He wanted any first-hand impressions you had of Melpham. I told him you could only have been in long clothes or whatever they put babies into in 1912, but apparently you *were* there. You look so distinguished, Gerald, one can't tell what age you are."

"I *told* him I was simply an undergraduate staying there who saw nothing."

"So it seems he realized when he read the reports and your name wasn't mentioned, and then Sir Edgar wrote a few weeks

ago to say that you'd had a sprained ankle throughout the proceedings, so that put you out of court. I hope you haven't any
vital evidence to contribute, because if so you'd better speak
now or for ever hold your peace."

Gerald smiled and gave Jasper another drink. "How is your
book getting on?" he asked.

It seemed hours to Gerald before Jasper left that evening,
although there was time before his dinner engagement in
which to begin the desperate brooding over Melpham that was
to take hold of him during the coming week, breaking his new-
found ease, flattening and fading the spring colours of the
Park. In the end he was driven to the decision that he had
avoided aimlessly for so much of his life, more determinedly
since Christmas night. Even so, he would not perhaps have
been committed had it not been for the advice of three
people; and two of these had no relation to historical scholarship at all.

It was seldom that Kay came to see Gerald. It was seldom,
to give her her due, that the housekeeping and baby care
allowed her to come up from Reigate. After two years there
she had found two or three other intellectually inclined young
married women and they made a sort of social existence out of
lamenting how little they were able to keep in touch with what
mattered. She had arranged her life to revolve round Donald,
baby and home, and she was, in fact, almost entirely content,
however much she followed the fashion of this little group.
Yet, like many people, she was very conservative about her
dentist. She had been to Mr Yeats for many years, ever since
she was a child, and so when her teeth ached badly, she found
someone to look after baby for the afternoon and came to
London. Even so, had there been more time to spare after her
visit, she would not have spent it in going to see her father,
but Inge's lack of sympathy with Donald's difficulties at the
office had put her into a very rare hostile mood towards her
mother, and this mood in turn had given her an equally rare

feeling of conscience towards her father. Nevertheless, such an access was hardly enough to accommodate her to a *tête-à-tête* with Gerald; she banked upon his being out if she called unannounced. She could salve her conscience by leaving a note. He was, however, in.

Gerald was delighted and terrified at seeing her. He cleared his mind of criticism of her dowdiness by putting it down to the visit to the dentist and fussed unduly over her extracted teeth until she said rather softly, "Oh, for heaven's sake, stop, Daddy. Anyone would think I'd had *all* my teeth out." Gerald tried to hide his soreness but not so successfully that Kay did not feel irritated both with herself and him. She really wished she could return his affection even if she could hardly be expected to respect him.

She tried to treat him to her confidence by telling him about Robin's treatment of Donald. "It's absolutely incredible, isn't it? It just shows how we can grow up with someone and know so little about them. But then I've always been so fond of Robin that I probably didn't notice. I knew he'd got a bit pompous, of course, but I put that down to Marie Hélène. I'd no idea he'd turned into a sort of petty Caesar. Donald says everyone there complains of it." She stopped and waited for Gerald's comment, but as none came, she went on. "It's so frightfully shortsighted too. Donald's obviously cut out for the job. All the other directors saw it at once. And he likes it. He even thought at one moment of suggesting that he stayed with them permanently, but, of course, he wouldn't think of it now. The meanest thing is the way Robin pretends that the job isn't important when he'd made all that fuss about it himself. Of course one ought to have realized. He's always been eaten up with jealousy. Look at the way he goes on with John." She paused, and wondered if she should mention Inge's monstrous attitude, but even her annoyance at it could not bring her to criticize her mother to Gerald, so she ended, "Well, I only hope Robin doesn't go too far. Donald can be a very dangerous hater."

Gerald felt deeply embarrassed. He would have loved to curry his daughter's approval by siding with her, but he reminded himself of his new friendship with Robin. In the end he contented himself by saying that he had never viewed the scheme with favour.

It was the worst thing he could have said. "Oh really, Daddy," she cried, "isn't that typical of you? Why on earth didn't you say something at the time? But no! let everything get in a mess and then say, "Well, I never liked it but I didn't dare to say so!' No wonder we've never been able to regard you as the proper head of the family."

There was a very uncomfortable silence as they both reflected that she had gone too far. Gerald determined to make a desperate effort to retrieve the occasion. She had given him her confidence and he had failed, the least he could do was to return it. He told her of his problem over Melpham. "It's not for public consumption, of course," he said.

"I doubt if I know the public who could digest it," she laughed. Nevertheless, she plied him with questions, and intelligent questions too. She remembered that Donald greatly respected her father as a scholar; here, at least, there was a matter in which she could talk to him without overtones of family history.

In the end he told her the whole story in far more detail than he intended and she listened respectfully. It was only when he got on to personalities—to his fears for Rose Lorimer, to his desire not to damage Professor Stokesay's reputation, to his memories of Gilbert's friendship—that she became impatient. "But these are personal things, Daddy," she cried. "You simply can't take them into account. It's a question of intellectual honesty"—and her voice rose high—"Oh, a small one maybe. But you say yourself you don't know where it may lead, what accretions of untruth—if it *is* untruth—may gather round it. This is a matter of historical truth, of course you must speak up." Her round face had all that head-girl earnestness that had so moved and so frightened him when she was a child.

"But I haven't got any proofs," he cried.

"Oh, I can see that," she said. "But you must go on searching until you've found them or until you're sure that they don't exist." She smiled. "It's a strange sort of task for *you*, isn't it? I doubt if you . . ." she was about to say "if you have the guts," but she checked herself and added, "I mean pertinacity's never been your strongest suit, has it?"

The visit of Elvira was not unannounced. She called up and asked if she could come round for a drink. "Oh, no special reason," she said. "Do people have to have special reasons for visiting you? It's one of Robin's home-days and everyone else seemed so ghastly. So I thought of you. At least you've got good pictures on your walls."

That, at any rate, thought Gerald, was not the incentive. She clearly didn't know one drawing from another.

She looked older and more blowzy. It came into Gerald's head that a less scrupulous man could turn her growing devotion to him into something less platonic; and immediately there followed the thought, "Well, she'd better hurry, if her looks go downhill as quickly as this I shan't be interested." He shut off the thought savagely, and then smiled as he realized that psychologists would probably say it had only come to him through repression.

Elvira accepted a drink, surrounded herself in clouds of cigarette smoke, and then said, "You talk about something, please. Something that will last a long time. But not about me and Robin. I've got one of those awful obsession things that he's been killed in a motor smash and I want to ring up to prove it's only an obsession, but of course I mustn't." Before Gerald could speak, she went on, "Oh God! it is all so boring. Any fifth-rate psychology student can tell you that when you're always imagining your lover's death like I am Robin's, it means you really want to get rid of him."

Gerald said, "Isn't all that a bit far-fetched? There are so many possible explanations of these things. Why shouldn't it be the simple one?"

Elvira curled up in her chair. "No, of course not," she said. "The Freudian explanations are quite obviously the true ones. We've just come to distrust them because a lot of silly people repeat them parrot fashion."

There was a silence which Gerald broke by saying, "I'm not at all happy about all your 'sensible' arrangements with Robin. I told him so the other day."

Elvira stubbed out her cigarette angrily. "I know," she cried. "It made me *frightfully* angry. I had so hoped you were a nice, uncomplicated person. It was very silly of me, of course, because we none of us are."

Gerald braced himself to deal with her annoyance. "Why does my talking to Robin show that I'm not uncomplicated?" he asked laughing.

"Oh, of course, it does. Freud again, so you won't like it. But you couldn't have acted like that just out of a straight motive. I've thought a lot about why you really did it," she frowned. "I *think*," she said judicially, "that it may have been because you were attracted to me and felt you shouldn't be and so you tried to compensate by being frightfully altruistic. I hope it isn't that though, because although I like you very much, I've got an age limit. Anyway, I'm madly in love with Robin, so I don't want to go to bed with other people. Only, of course, I can't expect you to see *that* because your generation were all muddled up about love and promiscuity."

From anyone else, Gerald thought, I couldn't have taken that: but with her, at any rate, directness proves very disarming. Elvira drained her glass, and cried, "Oh dear! What a nuisance! The one thing I *asked* was that we shouldn't talk about me and Robin."

Gerald told himself that it would be indiscreet to talk to Elvira of Melpham. In the end, however, he did so. She was hardly more likely to speak to anyone to whom it mattered than Kay was; it would be a helpful means of taking her mind off Robin; and, anyway, he wanted to talk to her about it. No doubt that was a sublimation, he reflected, and then smiled as he thought what a cosy exchange of Freudian motives they could have made of any *affaire* they might have had.

Elvira, perhaps, was a little less quick in grasping the historical significance of what he told her than Kay had been. It was clear that English history was not included in her view of culture. She was no less attentive and interested, however, and no less adamant in her view that he must sort it out. "Sort it out," indeed, summarized her approach, for she saw Melpham simply as a symbol of a conflict inside him that needed to be resolved. Unlike Kay, she disregarded the historical facts and concentrated solely on the personalities involved.

For her, Gilbert's alignment to the Wyndham Lewis anti-Bloomsbury group was quite enough to mark him down as a probable culprit. "Oh! don't think that I don't *know* the faults of Bloomsbury," she cried, "but they had a kind of hard core of intellectual integrity. While all these others are what John and his generation would call crypto-fascists. Of course, it isn't really a question of politics but of basic mental honesty. All the same, Gilbert Stokesay's exactly the sort of person to hate scholarship or anything like that. Have you *read* his essays? He's the most ghastly egotist and he'd think that sort of practical joke was cosmic or something equally pretentious." As to Professor Stokesay, she wouldn't hear a good word for him. "You can call all that pro-Nazism plain vanity, but it wasn't. It was intellectual dishonesty again. Like father like son. I bet you he knew all about it." On the other hand, likely as the Stokesays seemed to her to be culprits, she was most convinced of her own grandmother's guilt on personal grounds. "Now *her* vanity," she cried, "is limitless, and look at all the kudos she got out of it, and I expect my great uncle was quite as bad. On the other hand, she's frightfully weak. *I* know what you've got to do. You must go to Merano and bully the truth out of her." And then rather illogically, she added, "I'd rather like someone to go and see her anyway. I couldn't possibly bear it myself. But I did hear from Robin, who'd got it from those relations of Marie Hélène's, that she had a sort of stroke after Christmas. Of course, she's made her bed and she's got to lie on it. But all the same, it would be rather good to get a first-hand account from someone dependable."

Gerald was not finally convinced as to the course of action he should take, however, until he had seen Sir Edgar. It was not going to be an easy interview for him, he knew. Sir Edgar would recoil with disgust from anything smelling of scandal, particularly scandal that touched Lionel Stokesay; for, since he had always disliked the showiness of the great historian and was perhaps a little jealous of his powerful influence upon younger scholars, he did everything he could to disguise his antipathy, to dissociate himself from criticism of the dead man. In any case, his shyness, his strong conviction of moral rectitude and his cautious approach to life, would all be affronted by the story of troubled conscience that Gerald had to tell him. Yet Gerald also guessed that the old man would criticize him for not having acted sooner. Sir Edgar was slow to judge, but, his judgment once made, nothing would deter him from a speedy execution of his decision.

The interview proved as Gerald had prophesied to himself. Before Gerald was half-way through his story, Sir Edgar, like a tortoise feeding, shot his wrinkled old neck out of the hunch he had made of his body at the prospect of unpalatable words. "Look here," he said, "before you go any further, if you've got it into your head that the Melpham idol was a fake, you can forget it at once. I saw Cuspatt the other day and it seems they've made all the possible tests in the Museum laboratory. They're not tyros, you know. There's no doubt at all that the thing's genuine."

"I'm sure," said Gerald. "As you will see from my story, that isn't the point. I have no doubt that the figure is a genuine Anglo-Saxon idol. The only one to be found in English soil. That's what makes the whole thing so ironical. But it may very well not belong to Eorpwald's tomb. If what I suspect is true, it was found at Bedbury in the pagan cemetery. Gilbert Stokesay, incredible though it may sound to our modern ears, was practically in charge there. Stokesay was only too flattered that his beloved son should want to take part to interfere with anything he did. I suspect that when Gilbert told me he had placed the idol in the Melpham tomb he was speaking the truth. He brought it over from Bedbury and put it there. I have such a strange conviction of having thought so at the time he told me."

"My dear Middleton, you're trying to tell me now that Stokesay's son was a lunatic."

"No," said Gerald, "only a particular kind of man at a particular time." He tried then to explain to Sir Edgar, as far as he understood it himself, Gilbert's outlook on life. He spoke of his hatred of his father, his wild devotion to his mother, his hostility to contemporary culture, his Nietzschean idea of a practical joke.

A film of weariness crept over Sir Edgar's eyes. When Gerald had finished, he said, "I see. Gilbert Stokesay was killed in the war, wasn't he? I can't help thinking, you know, Middleton, that a lot of that generation were lost souls from the day of their birth, poor fellows." It was clear that a full appreciation of the point of view of Gilbert Stokesay was quite beyond him. "But even if what you suspect is true, with Stokesay's son dead, there could be no evidence now."

"I don't know. There may have been people who helped, or who found out afterwards and for one reason or another kept quiet. That's what I must find out," Gerald said.

Once he was convinced that Gerald had a case worthy of consideration, Sir Edgar's criticism changed its tack. "I'm afraid I simply don't understand, Middleton," he said, and his eyebrows beetled over his bright little eyes, "why you haven't spoken before. You owed it to Pforzheim and even more to our own Museum chaps to give them some warning of this. Thank heaven Pforzheim hasn't made his report on Heligoland yet! You've run the risk of putting him in a very awkward position. Quite frankly, I think your behaviour's been indefensible."

Gerald tried not to look resentful, he strove to allow his real desire for the old man's understanding to be unclouded by the irritation that he felt at its not being immediate. "I have so little evidence," he said, "and so many people that I care about are involved in the repercussions—Stokesay himself, Rose Lorimer, the general reputation of the English historians. Do you think it's been easy even to reach this point? Besides, how far would Pforzheim listen to what is only really a personal hunch?"

Sir Edgar's face softened. "I understand, my dear boy," he said. "It all explains a lot to me about your attitude to things in these last years. All the same you *must* say something to Pforzheim. It's all too likely he'll dismiss the story. These Huns are very obstinate, you know. But he'll probably modify his statement at Verona. If you like, *I'll* have a word with Cuspatt, just to alert him, you know."

"So you think I *should* pursue the matter?" Gerald asked.

"Yes, Middleton, I'm afraid so. It's an unpleasant business. More like some detective's job. But you say there are people who may know more—Portway's sister-in-law and others—you must see them. They may not know just how important the matter is. Laymen are very ignorant. Let me know how you get on."

"It's damnable," Gerald said, "all this coming when I want to get on with editing the *History*."

Sir Edgar smiled. "For a man of your years you have a curious expectation that life runs smoothly," he said.

Before Gerald left, he tried to hurriedly excuse himself again by speaking of the family difficulties that beset him. He started to speak of John's double life, but Sir Edgar checked him. "My dear fellow," he said, "your private affairs don't concern me. I don't mean that unkindly, but these things are better kept apart. In any case, I can't help you in anything like that. I have only one answer—my trust in God. And you're old enough to have considered all that for yourself. I will say one thing though: as historians we've got to tell the truth about the past as far as we know it, but that's quite a different thing from searching into the truth of people's lives here and now. All this prying and poking about into what other people prefer to keep hidden seems to me a very presumptuous and dangerous fashion. But then I'm a very old man. It doesn't much concern me any longer."

CHAPTER TWO

PROFESSOR PFORZHEIM listened respectfully to Gerald and agreed to modify his report to the congress. It was clear that he did so more out of deference to Gerald's authority than out of any weight that he placed upon the evidence that Gerald gave him. It was hardly to be expected that a German historian would be much influenced by a story so dependent for its conviction upon nuances of personality—of personalities, too, so very English. The report that he gave to the congress laid emphasis, then, on the dependence of the conclusions drawn from the Heligoland discoveries upon the earlier discoveries at Melpham. For anyone who doubted Melpham, Heligoland would have seemed quite unestablished; but as no one *did* doubt Melpham, Heligoland was acclaimed. It was the most Gerald could hope for. The interest of the congress, in any case, was not so much aroused by Aldwine's dual faith as by the addition of Aldwine to Eorpwald and the exciting promise of more to come. Two or even one and a half have always a disproportionately greater power of suggestion than one.

It was an intensely hot May in Verona. Even the seemingly tireless throng of local bourgeois who in the evenings passed and repassed between the cafés and the amphitheatre seemed robbed of their usual Italian high spirits. Gerald welcomed this, for he found the Italian character, so beloved of his English colleagues, childish, noisy and inane. He fought steadily a desire to remain in his hotel bedroom and read; he denied himself the easy excuse which the intense heat would have given to fulfil this desire. The congress would soon be over and he would be on his way to Merano and the first step of the quest for which he was now so impatient. He had written to Mrs Portway, recalling her hospitality of long ago and asking if he might visit her when he was in that neighbourhood. He had received an answer in a shaky, but imperious hand, telling him that no old friend who came to Merano and did not visit her would ever be forgiven. He had not mentioned Elvira, but he had presented the compliments of Marie Hélène to Madame Houdet. In addition to Mrs Portway's reply there came a very formal letter in purplish ink returning the compliments of Madame Veuve Houdet and her son, M. Yves Houdet, and begging that the father-in-law of their dear niece and cousin would present himself to them on his visit to Merano.

Meanwhile Gerald went on all the expeditions provided by the congress, so securing a reputation for friendliness and a deal of cool air on the motor-coach journeys. It was thus that he found himself at Mantua, screwing his neck upwards to gaze at the curious behaviour of horses and goddesses portrayed by Giulio Romano on the ceilings of the Palazzo del Tè. With him was Father Lavenham, who soon ceased to contort his neck and peered instead through the windows at the little formal garden outside.

"I hope," said Father Lavenham, "that I don't seem ostentatiously puritan, or rather, for once, I don't mind if I do, but I confess that all this Renaissance paganism is very antipathetic to me. I have neither an aesthetic inclination towards it nor a Warburgian interest in the development of myth. The vulgarity of Imperial Rome is unsavoury enough, this sort of imitation is insufferable. It makes me glad that I am a medievalist. If I am forced to choose a pagan spirit, give me that of the Gracchi rather than of the Gonzagas. But then I'm very English." It was a perfectly true and obvious statement, yet he never failed to find a necessity to repeat it to combat his colleague's distrust of a Roman priest.

Gerald said politely, "I'm largely in agreement with you." Professor Clun was so intent on the intricacies of mythological monstrosity that he heard nothing around him.

"Do you know," said Lavenham, "I think I shall escape to the small amount of shade offered by that oleander."

"A very good idea," Gerald agreed.

"Are you coming, Clun?" Father Lavenham asked loudly and with a certain distaste.

Professor Clun came to, and, fearing that his obsessive interest might have been remarked upon, he said, "The trouble with these congresses is that there's a great deal too much fiddle-faddle attached to them."

With difficulty they evaded the guide and sat on the grass in the half-shade of the oleander—three elderly English scholars with no real communion of feeling except their nationality, which in the circumstances was a very powerful one. Lavenham's goat face seemed in happy keeping with the pagan world he so disliked. Gerald could not forbear to say, "You have a curiously Pan-like look yourself, you know."

The priest looked seriously disturbed. "I hope not," he said. "I always incline to think that the Nonconformity into which I was born is the most depressing thing in life, but it only requires a small dose of paganism to make me count my Methodist upbringing as a blessing. The Chapel at Stoke-on-Trent was a gloomy place but it seems as nothing whenever I am confronted with the desert waste of the pagan world. To play at paganism as these people did," and he waved his hand towards the imitation Roman bath-house, "seems to speak such weariness of soul that I feel stifled by its presence."

Gerald turned an ironical eye towards him. "Of course," he said jauntily, "you can't lump the whole of Olympus together with the idols of Melpham and Heligoland like that." In the determination of his new quest, he felt free at last to speak of Melpham.

Father Lavenham smiled. "I make little of varieties of terror and despair," he said. Gerald thought, what a theatrical way of talking these R.C.s have.

It was evident that Arthur Clun reacted similarly, for he said sharply, "Well, that may be, Lavenham, but Pforzheim's report's left you with a little explaining to do about your missionaries."

Father Lavenham laughed heartily. "You're the fourth of my colleagues who's told me that," he said. "I believe even the most civilized of Englishmen still think that Catholic historians falsify or deny whatever doesn't suit their book. Apostasy's not exactly a new problem you know. Readmission of apostates was one of the burning questions for the Early Fathers. And as for sorcery! Why, my dear Clun, even in the small experience of a priest like myself these things are not new. In the life of the Church . . ." he waved his hand to suggest a limitless range—"I doubt if the Church will boggle at Eorpwald or Aldwine, or a few others if they turn up for that matter, in her infinite variety of experience. No, it's my chauvinistic pride as an Englishman that's been dealt a salutary blow there."

"It's just as well it's all an open historical question now," Clun remarked. "The whole thing's safely in the hands of reputable scholars. It's no longer the playground of cranks."

Lavenham smiled. "If you mean Dr Lorimer," he said, "it looks to me as though her crankiness is on the wane. I'm glad, for she's a good soul and, as a matter of fact, I'm peculiarly glad because there was a moment when her crankiness seemed to be involving me in a most unpleasant fashion."

Gerald turned to him. "In what fashion?" he asked.

Lavenham now appeared anxious to retrieve what he said, for he remarked with studied casualness, "Oh, I think she's got it in for all of us Romans, you know, as part of the great conspiracy the poor soul imagined was formed against her. She wrote me one or two rather foolish letters." The other members of the party came streaming from the palace headed by a voluble guide. "This looks like relief at last," he said abruptly and joined the crowd.

The intense heat did not diminish as Gerald's train climbed up from the Italian plains into the foot-hills. He had refused to take Larwood on his European trip and would not even make use of hired cars. He had not made a train and bus journey of any length for many years, but one side of him had turned his new quest into a youthful adventure, though the other was filled with foreboding and anxiety. He read an Everyman copy of Gilchrist's life of Blake. He had a pious devotion to Blake's life which was in some degree an atonement for his poor opinion of his drawings. As he read, memories of the adventures of the heroes of John Buchan's novels came irrelevantly into his mind. Such self-mockery was his talisman against the hubris he so dreaded in life. At Trento the storm broke overhead; and by the time his taxi was carrying him to his hotel, the little arcaded streets of Merano were filled with jostling umbrellas of bedraggled Italian holiday-makers.

The rain continued so heavily that he telephoned to Mrs Portway to ask if he could postpone his visit until the next day. Madame Houdet answered the call and her heavy French accent was difficult to interpret. After consultation, however, she asked him to luncheon. She enquired after Marie Hélène, but on the whole she seemed preoccupied with a story of a local family of peasants whose house had been struck by lightning. The bedridden grandmother, it appeared, had been hit by a chimney brick and had died before a priest could reach the house. "And terrible burns," she cried, rolling her r's with relish, "terrible burns."

After dinner, he took Blake's life to the American bar. The only other occupants were two stout, hiking schoolmistresses, whose voices suggested that they had been strangely washed up there from Manchester. As Gerald ordered his drink, a tall, broad-shouldered young man came or, more truthfully, strutted into the room. With his coat draped over his shoulders, his flashy wrist-watch, his faint whiff of perfume and his sensual black eyes, he was all that Gerald detested in the Latin male. He pictured such men forever swaggering in front of women in cafés or bars and wondered if his great distaste for them was due to jealousy. Before Gerald could bury himself in his book, the young man turned from the bar, glanced at the cover of Gerald's book, and said with an American accent, "What's your guess about all these storms we're having? Do you think it's the A-bomb?"

Gerald said abruptly, "No, I should think that was most improbable."

"I don't know," the young man's American accent seemed almost a stage one, "there's a lot of experiments going on we don't know anything about." He addressed the room when he spoke. "And if we do know, we can't say." He left no doubt as to which of these categories was his. "You heard about the guy who talked?" he asked, looking round the room, "No, Well, you never will now, 'cos he's not talking any more." He laughed loudly at this joke, which suggested an imperfect understanding of the language he spoke so fluently.

Gerald read his book, but the schoolmistresses laughed politely. The young man devoted his svelte, overdressed person to them.

"So you're from England," he said. "I've got relations over there. Pretty big people, too. Robin Middleton, ever heard of him?"—Gerald looked up in horrified amazement—"Yeah, he's on the Market," the young man continued. "You know the sort of stuff. Money talks and so on. I'm going over to their place to stop this summer. My cousin's quite a bit of a hostess. All the big people—Churchill, Eden, all that crowd, T. S. Eliot, H. G. Wells."

One of the ladies mentioned that Wells was dead, but the young man was quite unperturbed. "Yeah. He may be too," he said. "He *certainly* burned the candle at both ends. Of course, it doesn't mean anything to me," he said, ordering another whisky sour, "I've been around too much. I'm the cosmopolitan type, you know. Born in France, lived a good deal in the States, as you can hear from my accent, or so they tell me. But Italy's good enough for me now. That's where you get the *real* aristocracy—feudal estates, starving peasants, all the works. You heard about that big ball they had in Venice?" One of the ladies thought she had. "Yeah. That was the real thing. Champagne poured in the canals. Of course, the Commies screamed their lungs out. I was there. I had a pretty good time, too. But still you can't play all the time."

Gerald closed his book and left the bar. If he was fated to meet M. Yves Houdet, tomorrow seemed quite soon enough. Sensual and elegant though Gerald was, he detested the flashy smartness of such Latin womanizers.

The heat next day was once more stifling, though the sun was hidden by low clouds that hung around the mountain-tops and threatened further storms. Mrs Portway was sitting in the garden when Gerald arrived at the villa. Although he would not have recognized his former hostess in the handsome old woman who came across the brown, dried lawn to greet him, there was something in the pale mauve parasol, the wide-brimmed lavender linen hat and the violet tulle at the throat which recalled his arrival at Melpham to him, so that unconsciously he took peculiar pains to avoid falling on the gravel path.

It was Lilian, however, who had need of such care; since her stroke, her walk was tottery and her head shook more often. She still carried herself as erect as a young woman. Gerald wondered if she would greet him with classical allusion as she had in 1912, and sure enough, "Welcome! Professor Middleton," she cried. "We meet as shades on the other side of the Styx." Such allusions were, perhaps, her stock in trade for academical visitors. "Though why *you*, who do not have to do so, should wish to plunge yourself into Stygian gloom, I cannot imagine."

"I was at the Historical Congress at Verona and . . ." said Gerald, working towards his fabricated excuse for being in Merano, but he had no need of it.

"Ah!" Lilian Portway cried, "Verona! *That* is Italy. Not Tuscany, but still Italy. While this . . ." She turned her lovely swan neck in disgust.

"I didn't see much of it last night because of the rain," Gerald said smiling, "but it seems very attractive this morning. Don't you like it?"

"*Like* it!" Mrs Portway beat in the air with her hand. "I hate it! I detest it! *That*," she said, pointing southwards with her parasol, "is where I should live. But the doctors forbade it. Ah, how well G. B. S. understood those doctors. They hate the arts. They killed Dubedat and they'll kill me."

It seemed a little illogical to Gerald but he did not contradict her; already, indeed, Madame Houdet—her only concession to the heat the crêpe-de-chine material of her black dress—was at their side. "You must not excite yourself, Lilian," she said. "Poor Mrs Portway has been ill. She is always so brave when she is *souffrante*."

Lilian Portway waved her aside. "They would have me live as an invalid," she said scornfully. "But if I live, I *live*, not crawl upon the surface of the earth."

Conversation with the two ladies did not prove easy. Madame Houdet talked of Marie Hélène. So *distinguée* and so clear-headed—Gerald must be so sad to be apart from his dear ones, it was always sad to be apart from one's dear ones—and of the old peasant woman killed by the lightning—"Imagine! pinned beneath a beam for nearly an hour and one arm completely charred, but completely!" She made no clear distinction between the two topics, so that when she said, "*Et toujours si dévote.* Believe me, sir, Notre Dame de la Misericorde knows those who honour her," Gerald was not sure whether she referred to the old peasant woman or to Marie Hélène.

Mrs Portway, on the other hand, determined to exclude Stéphanie from the conversation by restricting it to reminiscences of English life. She took it for granted that Gerald shared her memories of the great. "Oh, they were brave men, Mr Asquith and his colleagues!" she said scornfully. "They thought they could break the women's spirit by forcible feeding. They could ruin the beauty that God had given to women like Constance Balfour, but they couldn't break their spirits, as you and I know, my dear old friend." She called him to share intimate laughter over Tree's vulgarity and intimate honour for Granville Barker's high projects for the theatre; yet, in and out of her ramblings, came clear threads of memory. "What a day," she cried, "to sprain your ankle. They made the greatest archaeological discovery of the age, my dear Stéphanie, and what did this fellow do—he sprained his ankle!" She turned to Gerald. "And now they've all gone, my dear friend. Reggie and Stokesay and his brilliant son killed in that senseless war. And only you and I are left. Oh! and Dollie, dear English Dollie,"—and she looked scornfully at Madame Houdet—"But you and she had an *affaire de cœur*!" she cried to Gerald.

He was astonished that she should know this and horrified that she should shout her knowledge abroad.

"Oh yes, you did! Don't deny it! You sprained your ankle so that you should be nursed by that pretty English primrose." Gerald breathed again.

They had finished their apéritifs before Yves appeared. "This," said Mrs Portway with disgust, "is Stéphanie's son Yves."

Gerald had feared that Yves might be embarrassed after his boasting of last night, but it was an unnecessary fear. He shook Gerald's hand vigorously. "Well, I certainly should say they're right about the English modesty," he said. "Here's this guy," he said, turning to his mother, "sat there last night when I was talking about Marie Hélène and didn't say a word. Yes, that's modesty all right. Mind you," he said confidentially to Gerald, "it doesn't do to be *too* modest. You can pass a lot of business up that way."

"Professor Middleton has no connection with commerce," said Lilian contemptuously, "He is an historian."

"Well, you've certainly come to the right place." Yves was in no way abashed. "Italy's chock full of history. Have you been to Florence? That's where you ought to go, you know."

Gerald supposed that such brash naïveté should have disarmed him, but it did not. "I have just attended the historical congress at Verona," he said rather huffily.

Madame Houdet meanwhile had exchanged some sharp words in very bad Italian with the maid. "The *déjeuner* is ready," she said. It was clear that her hand directed the menu of the household. They were presented in turn with underdone *gigot*, *haricots verts*, a salad, and *beignets* in a custard sauce. She apologized for the wine, which was local.

Gerald could have given more attention to this pleasant bourgeois meal if he had not been asked to listen to three conversations at once. Mrs Portway got on to the Shaw-Patrick Campbell correspondence. "Nobody understands," she cried. "They say 'egotism'. But this was a love affair of artists, so of course it was a war to the death between two egos. G. B. S. made some ridiculous declaration to me after the first night of 'Candida', but I simply laughed at him and said, 'You're not in love with me, man, you're in love with your own creation'. He . . ."

Madame Houdet meanwhile had gone on from the current market price of vegetables to the economy of M. l'Abbé Tartaglio's housekeeper. "The money goes into her pocket and nothing goes on to M. l'Abbé's plate," she confided in Gerald, "And *quelle mauvaise langue*, that woman! I told the poor man . . ."

It was Yves' voice that was loudest and hence his conversation that most battered Gerald down. "Do you know Etruscan?" he asked, and when Gerald shook his head, he laughed. "No," he cried, "I don't suppose you do. *No one* can read it."

Gerald suggested that some words in Etruscan had in fact been deciphered.

"You're right there," Yves said, "*I* ought to know. I gave them a few hints. I know all those guys. They showed me the inscriptions. It's all mathematics really. I did codes and cyphers in the war. But I'm not talking about that."

"Yves was with the American Air Force," Madame Houdet said proudly. "He has still many American friends."

"I should say I have," Yves declared. "If this cold war blows up hot, which it may any minute, I've got *my* orders.

But I'm not talking *there*, either," he announced defiantly to Gerald.

"Oh! please don't." Lilian cried, furious by now at his continuous interruption of her reminiscences. "We don't wish to be burdened with the barbarians' secrets—Russian or American."

Yves smiled patronizingly. "The barbarians sacked Rome," he said. "The Professor'll tell you that."

"Of course," Lilian was saying, "they don't train them to *speak* nowadays. When I started at the Court Theatre we were told that even when we were whispering we were expected to be audible to *every* single person at the back of the pit. . . ."

"But then what are they, these Tyrolese? Simply dirty pigs," Stéphanie cried. "The poor little girl had already been *violée* by her own father before she was twelve years old. *Mais oui, c'est vrai, Yves*," she affirmed, mistaking the interested light in Yves' eye for incredulity, "*par son père. Je l'ai entendu de M. l'Abbé lui-même. Quelle cochonnerie!*"

"Well," said Yves, stretching back in his chair, for an expansive man-to-man talk with Gerald, "how do you feel about Europe? Do you think it's decadent? No, no," he cried before Gerald could answer. "I agree with you. It may be new to the Yanks, but we know it's all as old as time. Incest, rape, they've happened before. It's not news to us. I don't say a word against the Yanks, they're our friends, yours and mine. They're grand guys. But it's a new civilization. They've got a lot to learn. The art of life—that's what we've got to teach them. Good food, good wine."

Madame Houdet here nodded vigorously, "*Mais c'est affreux, ce coca-cola*," she said.

"And," Yves continued—his gestures seemed to become more exaggeratedly French as his accent became more absurdly American—"the art of love. Why do you think these American dames are so frigid?" he asked Gerald.

Mrs Portway winced.

"Because," Yves answered himself, "they've never been woken up. Their men don't know how to make love, they just know how to go to bed." He paused, for this was usually one of the most successful remarks in his repertory. On this occasion, for varying reasons, none of his audience responded. "It's not the same thing," he said.

The lack of sympathy in his audience had a curious effect on him, for, suddenly, without any bridge in his conversation, he began to take up the opposite point of view. "Yeah," he said. "Europe's decadent. She's finished. And why? Because she's living in the past. Look at you all now. What are you talking about? The past. What have you come to Italy for? The past." His eyes flashed malignantly at Gerald. His manner had changed from loud to offensive. He turned on his mother, shouting at her. "France is finished. Do you understand me?"

Madame Houdet's rouged cheeks trembled a little, her lip-sticked old mouth twitched. "*Jamais, Yves, jamais,*" she said.

Her son leaned across the table. For a moment Gerald thought he was going to hit her, but he only flung his arm towards her in contempt. "*Tu es folle,*" he cried, "*on lui a déjà tordu le cou, ton coq.*" He imitated the quick turn as the bird's neck was twisted and then he let out a hideous crow. He got up and flung his napkin across the table. "I've got an appointment," he said. "What do you use for money?" he asked his mother, and picking up her bag from the table he helped himself to some notes.

When he turned to Gerald, his manner was once more ingratiating, though brash. "Pleased to have met you," he said, shaking Gerald's hand. "If you want any introductions to the big people in Florence or Rome, let me know." Draping his light grey coat across his shoulders, he swaggered out of the room, his buttocks swaying under his tight trouser seat as he walked. Madame Houdet, with tears in her eyes, excused herself in order to superintend the coffee-making in the kitchen.

Mrs Portway had closed her eyes. She sat rigid in her chair, her head shaking slightly. Then, opening her lovely eyes and turning them on him, "I'm so terribly sorry, Professor Middleton," she said, "for all this."

Gerald made a deprecating gesture, "I'm only concerned for you," he answered.

"Oh! *I've* seen too much bullying and vulgarity to mind by now." She shrugged her shoulders wearily. "It's not what I should have chosen for my last years, but one no longer makes one's life when one is old. Life is made for one. An unpleasant return to the nursery. However, it helps Stéphanie my being here and she is a good soul. Narrow, you know," her voice was redolent with the drawing-rooms of high social comedy, "but we have been through the same horrors. It is another of the prices of age—our bonds, our companionships are those of sorrow. I always hated sorrow and pain or anything ugly."

She rose from her chair and motioned him away as he moved to assist her. "Let us go into the garden," she cried. And as they walked on the veranda, she said, "That vulgar young man is disordered in his wits."

Looking at her, Gerald saw that she meant this literally; and reflecting on Yves' behaviour, he was inclined to agree with her.

It was amid the cloying scent of the dying lilac, its purple and white horns turning an ugly brown in the hot sun, that Gerald told her of his doubts about Melpham. He spoke tentatively at first; and it was clear that he had need to do so, for he had not proceeded far before she waved him aside with her hand. "No! no!" she cried. "Lying and deceit! That's not the colour of *those* days. It's the present that is a perjurer, not the past."

"It's to clear the past of a lie that may have been laid upon it that I am asking these questions," Gerald replied. We're not going to get very far if we talk in Delphic oracles like this, he thought. "You spoke just now," he went on, trying a different tack, "of that young man being disordered in his wits, I am suggesting that Gilbert Stokesay too was capable of freakish, insane actions."

"I don't know, I don't know," Mrs Portway cried. "I only know that I want those days at Melpham left alone in their rosy glow. You've seen something of my life now, surely you don't want to poison the memories I live in. Reggie, above all, is my happiest, my finest memory."

Gerald raised his eyebrows. "I was not for one minute suggesting that Canon Portway had any knowledge of the fraud, if fraud it was. No, if it happened, Gilbert regarded it as a genius's joke on the dead world of scholarship; and I'm afraid that included your brother-in-law as much as his father, or shall I say, it was intended to make his father look a fool, and if anyone else was caught in the net, so much the more amusing. Stokesay, you know, even in those days, was looking forward to a knighthood, and if my guess is correct Gilbert was looking forward to that day too as the occasion for revealing the fraud. Only fate decided otherwise."

Mrs Portway sat with the palm of her hand pressed against her temple. Gerald was not even sure if she heard what he was saying. "The whole thing seems very fanciful, I know," he continued, "only I can't get away from the conviction which has stuck with me all these years that Gilbert Stokesay was telling the truth that night in Soho."

Mrs Portway looked up. "Does it matter now?" she asked. "He's dead and we're old. Heaven alone knows who lives at Melpham now! The last time I heard anything, there was talk of making it an Eventide Home for old people. And very fitting too."

Gerald felt a moment of impatient anger. "I'm afraid it isn't a question of what happens to Melpham House. It's a far larger question of historical truth. This lie, if lie it is, has become the cornerstone on which a whole false edifice may be erected. And even if it wasn't so, even if it was just one single historical oddity, I see now that I've been wrong all these years in treating it lightly. If an historian has any function at all, it is to maintain honesty. The study of history can't be the plaything of the sort of egoistic mockery that I'm suggesting Gilbert indulged in."

"You make a lot of your conscience," Mrs Portway said bitterly.

"It's not *my* conscience," Gerald cried, "it's the good faith of a humane study in a world rapidly losing its humanity."

Some spark seemed to catch Mrs Portway's feelings. "Yes, I see," she said. "If I could help you. But I don't see why you come to *me*. What do you think *I* could know of it?"

"Nothing, I suppose," Gerald replied dully. "It is only that I have always thought that when people do things secretly there is usually some slip up, some suspicion, some talk. I only hoped that you could remember a word or a deed that would suggest a dissatisfaction or a doubt. For example, you knew the servants at Melpham well, the men who assisted the 'dig'. Gilbert had great hauteur towards the lower orders. He would not have hesitated to enlist the help of one of the workmen, he would certainly not have bothered to conceal things from them with the care he would have taken with regard to the others. They might have seen things of which they didn't even realize the significance. No, I see now, it's hopeless. I must allow the negative answer of the dead to tell me I am wrong."

There was a silence, then Mrs Portway began to trace lines in the grass with the ferrule of her parasol. "I am not sure that you are," she said. "Oh! I don't know. What I can tell you is again no more than a surmise, only it's one that makes me happy because it removes a far more awful belief from my mind."

She stopped for a moment and seemed intent on the scratchings of her parasol. "Understand this," she cried, "Reggie Portway was a great and good man. Nothing I say alters that. There was only one thing on which we did not agree. He had a foolish, a deeply foolish affection for a lad in the village, a deceitful, smooth-tongued boy who'd got above his station. Reggie thought him brilliant, he indulged him, talking of sending him to Oxford. The war, which did so many foolish things, at least put a stop to that. The boy went into the Navy. But the connection, I'm afraid, did not end. Oh! don't mistake me. Reggie did nothing wrong. It's I who have been wrong in allowing myself to suspect such a thing for many years. That is why what you have said today relieves my mind, for I see that

the whole thing has quite another explanation. I've wronged
Reggie deeply all these years in my mind. The boy came back
to him after the war as a sort of secretary. I had lost touch.
My place was in Italy when Mussolini made her strong again."
She waved her hand to dismiss anything he might say in
disagreement. "We will not argue about that. There was no
coldness between Reggie and me, but we let time draw us
apart. I cannot regret it too much." She smiled bitterly, "It's
a habit of the Portways. I've let myself be cut off from my
granddaughter in the same way."

Gerald was about to speak to her of Elvira, but he reflected
that he would do nothing by such an intervention except distract her from her story.

"I felt deeply unhappy at the association being renewed. I
wrote and told Reggie so, but he ignored my letter. I comforted
myself with the thought that our old servant Barker and his
daughter were there to look after him and I knew that while
those loyal souls were with him he would come to no harm.
Some years before Reggie died, Alice Barker wrote to tell me
that this vile creature had left the house. My brother was no
longer at Melpham, you know, he had been made a Canon at
Norwich and lived in the Close. I read between the lines of her
letter that she had driven him out and I rejoiced. But far worse
was to come. When Reggie died, he left every penny to this
dreadful man, for man he was by then, I suppose, if he ever
deserved the name. Oh! it was shameful. He had no reason to
leave money to me. I had my own. But to have left the Barkers
unrewarded after all those years of service! I did what I could
to make up for it." She paused and smiled. "Not that they need
any help now. Alice is in the news. She married that Mr
Cressett whom your son—it is your son, isn't it?—has been
writing about so much in the papers." She shook her head.
"We live in a topsy-turvy world when good simple people like
Alice Barker are pushed into the headlines."

"The Cressett of the Pelican affair?" Gerald asked in
surprise.

"Yes," Mrs Portway replied with a laugh. "But that absurdity doesn't alter the way Reggie treated the Barkers. That was bad enough, but what upset me so was the fact that the money left, though far more than a creature like that could possibly know what to do with, was only a small part of what my brother-in-law once had. It was obvious to me that this man had been bleeding poor Reggie for years. I've told you what I allowed myself to think. Oh! I didn't blame Reggie even then, though I abhor anything unnatural. I thought that a moment's foolishness had been paid for by a lifetime. The creature had wiles enough and Reggie had always insisted on the very false notion that a clergyman should be celibate. Men should be men, Professor Middleton, whether they wear cassocks or not."

She was silent and Gerald could hear Madame Houdet's voice coming from the house. She was scolding the maid.

"But now," said Mrs Portway, and her long body relaxed in its cane chair as though she had thrown off the weight of years. "I see now what it was. Reggie must have learnt of this fraud and it was for *that* that the wretched Frank Rammage blackmailed him."

Gerald jerked with surprise. "Rammage!" he cried. "Oh! but it can't be the same. I remember the boy you spoke of. He came into the room the day I sprained my ankle. An angelic-looking youth with red hair."

"Angelic!" Mrs Portway spat the word. "A mollycoddle! But, yes, he had red hair."

"This man I know called Rammage is a fat little creature with a bald head. I suppose it must be the same. He's got reddish tufts. Do you know if he lives in Earl's Court Square?"

"He has the impertinence to send letters from that address." Mrs Portway would commit herself no further on such a subject.

"In any case," said Gerald, "I'm afraid this is all the wildest guess of yours, you know. How could Rammage have known of the fraud?"

"He *committed* it, no doubt. He was very quick to make up to Gilbert Stokesay that summer. A great London poet! Frank Rammage didn't let the grass grow under his feet. I thought Gilbert Stokesay was making fun of him. He called him 'Little Mr Self-Educated'. But perhaps I was wrong. Rammage was probably his assistant in this fraud as well as in other vilenesses. Indeed, I remember that they were together when Gilbert Stokesay made the discovery." Mrs Portway seemed to be releasing a lot of pent-up emotion.

Gerald smiled. "I really think you had better not let your imagination travel too far. You've already done your brother-in-law an injustice of that kind."

"Frank Rammage was capable of anything vile," she cried. "I hated him. He was the only person I ever felt jealous of with Reggie. And there seemed to be no way of getting at him. He was so meek."

Gerald laughed. He hoped that a humorous attitude might lower the tension. "Well, *Gilbert*," he said, "whatever his faults, was completely normal." He paused and shook his head.

"No, it just won't work, you know," he said. "It's kind of you to try to find an answer for me. But if Canon Portway *was* blackmailed—and I do suggest to you that there may be a hundred other reasons for his money disappearing — he wouldn't let himself be got at on a thing like this. He had only to speak his knowledge at any time. Indeed, it was his duty to do so."

Mrs Portway protested. "Oh no, you're asking too much of him. The Melpham discovery meant such a lot to him. He believed it had done more than anything to increase the prestige of local historians and of local traditions too. And then he had to think of Professor Stokesay. It's not like now, you know. He was still alive. What a terrible thing to say of his son! Oh no, Reggie would not have done a thing like that. He was a great Christian."

Gerald looked at her in amazement, but he saw that it would be useless to explain to her what Canon Portway's duty as a *scholar* would have been, "In any case," he said, "all this is pure guess-work. We have no evidence at all that he ever doubted the genuineness of the excavation."

Mrs Portway smiled. "Ah! That's what I'm coming to. It was while you were talking that I remembered something he once wrote to me. Oh! it was during the nineteen-thirties. He did not write often then. We disagreed over Abyssinia. Reggie was so easily misled. He wrote to me, 'It may be that we have no real right to much of our money. My conscience is not clear about this yet, but you must not be surprised if I write some day to tell you so.' I thought it was some Socialist idea of his, you know. He lived by the gospels and he did not see that others could not be so good. But now I wonder. Perhaps he referred to the money we were paid for the Melpham treasure. Of course," she said proudly, "if this proves to be true, I shall do my best to refund it."

"Oh, that would hardly be necessary. The Melpham idol, even if it came from elsewhere in East Folk, as I suspect, is unique so far in English archaeology. That's why the fraud— if fraud it is—could not have been the work of a real scholar. It would have been too senseless."

Mrs Portway had closed her eyes; she looked a very old woman.

"I have tired you," Gerald said. "Thank you for being so patient with me. I'm afraid we haven't got very far but you have been very kind. May I come to see you tomorrow, not as an investigator but just as an old friend in search of a chat about the past?"

Mrs Portway raised her great eyes to him. "I should like it very much," she said. "Meanwhile I shall write down all this and anything else that occurs to me. It will give you some evidence."

Gerald doubted if such ramblings could be called evidence, but he thanked her and left her sitting with her eyes closed, her wide-brimmed linen hat slumped to one side on her thick coiled hair—an old woman asleep beneath the lilac bushes.

It was late that night—a little after midnight—when Yves drove into the villa garage in his Lagonda—the only trophy left to him from his *affaire* with the industrialist's widow. She had finally kicked him out just before Christmas; and he had made little protest, for she had it in her power to send him to jail for quite a long stretch. He had forged her signature on one too many cheques. Since that time he had been forced to stay in Merano. His mother had only enough cash to keep him in current pocket money, and Mrs Portway would produce nothing. He had thought for a few days that he had found an American woman to take him to Venice but in the end she had gone without him. He had tried to get into the racket of smuggling watches from Switzerland through the mountains, but neither his physique nor his intelligence nor his trust-worthiness had commended themselves to the gang-leader. He had just enough cash from Madame Houdet to keep him in a bad temper and periodic bouts of drunkenness. He was drunk this night when he returned and he severely dented the mudguard of his car on the garage door. He entered the house in a rage.

Already the intense heat of the day had once more given place to ominous rolls of thunder. Lilian Portway lay awake in her great walnut bed listening to the thunder and watching the long procession of memories called up by her talk with Gerald. A louder clap suggested that the storm had broken overhead, but a moment later she heard Yves' voice bawling drunkenly in his mother's room. She guessed the thunder-clap to have been in fact his banging of the front door. She was so used to these scenes that she smoothly slipped back into her reverie. They usually ended quite soon, with Yves fumbling his drunken way to his bedroom. Tonight, however, the shouting seemed to go on for longer—first Yves' manly oaths and abuse, then Stéphanie's tearful but shrill protests. Lilian had acquired a hatred of the French language from hearing it so often abused.

Madame Houdet, it was clear, had got out of bed, for Lilian could hear the patter of bare feet. Then suddenly there was a sound of a blow and then another, and a third as something or someone fell to the floor.

Lilian got out of bed with difficulty; her legs so quickly became stiff now after a few hours' rest and she was liable to giddy fits on rising. She sat for a moment dangling her long legs over the side of the bed; then putting on her mauve muslin dressing-gown and her lilac quilted slippers, she made her way across the corridor to Stéphanie's room. Already, in the passage, she could hear Yves shouting, as he loved to do, that the Nazis were bunglers, that they had botched their work —what were their famous ovens for but to get rid of such unwanted rubbish as his mother? Lilian was too used to this to be horrified any longer, but she was still repelled by the thought that the son who shouted such things really loved his mother, and in other, more maudlin moods, would fondle and caress her. The door stood open and huddled on the floor lay Stéphanie, in her nightgown, moaning.

"Go to your bedroom, Yves," Lilian cried, and she ran to raise his mother from the ground.

A combination of self-interest and fear usually made Yves obedient to Mrs Portway's orders. The situation unfortunately had gone on too long; familiarity breeds contempt. He was, too, very drunk. He raised his fist and had she not stumbled out of his reach he would have hit her in the face.

"Shut up, you old cow," he shouted, "they ought to have finished you off too. The Fascists had no more sense than the Nazis." Suddenly he began to roar with laughter as a joke worked up inside him. "Say, you old dames must miss your camp exercise," he laughed. "You don't want to get out of training." He leaned down and pulled his mother by the arm. She tottered to her feet. "Come on both of you. Get moving. Left, right, left, right," he shouted. Then he began to bawl oaths and abuse at them in German and Italian. The two old women shuffled behind one another to the door, Stéphanie pushing at Lilian to avoid her son's blows. As they passed through the door, Yves collapsed on the bed in howls of laughter.

Madame Houdet slumped on to the floor in the passage and began to pray; but Mrs Portway ran past the door of her own room and down the stairs. She had only the thought that she must run, she could not let them keep her in that place again. She must get away before they shut her up once more behind barbed wire. Through the garden she ran with tottering steps and out into the road. Her hair uncoiled and streamed around her shoulders, a slipper fell from her foot, but she still kept on. It was a moonless night, but even had it been twice as light, she would not have known where she was going. She reached a little path that ran down the hillside—a walk made in the eighteen-eighties with rustic wooden railings and planted ever-greens, a road to take tourists to view the "panorama"—on she kept and then stumbled and fell, rolling a few feet on to a grassy bank below. She lay there cut and bruised. For a while she was stunned and when she came to her senses, her mind was clouded and she could feel no life in her right arm and leg. The thunder and lightning died away in heavy rain and her mind too faded away in vague confusion. She was not found until six that morning, when some workmen were making their way into the town. They knew the strange *Englische Witwe* by sight and carried her back to the villa.

Gerald had been kept awake by the storm and he almost thought in his tiredness the next morning that he would present his excuses to Mrs Portway and leave Merano. There was nothing to be gained by stirring up the old woman's memories. He would tell Elvira, when he got back to England, that he did not think she should be left with the Houdets; but he did not believe that Elvira was likely to take any action. The whole visit had not only been fruitless but depressing. However, by half past ten he felt more refreshed and reflected that it would be selfish not to pay the promised call. At sixty, he had a superstitious dislike of disappointing the hopes of old people of seventy.

Madame Houdet opened the door to him. She looked old and exhausted, but her make-up was complete as usual. "Mrs

Portway is very ill," she said. "She can see no one. She met with an accident. She has a stroke and pneumonia. No one can help her now but the *bon Dieu*."

Gerald attempted to get some details of Lilian's accident from her, but her answers were confused and vague. "*Il faut prier le bon Dieu de lui pardonner*," she said.

As he turned to leave, a priest came up the path and Madame Houdet's full attention was given to welcoming him as Gerald walked slowly away. When he reached the gate, Yves came running after him. "My God," he cried, "this is certainly a big responsibility for me. The only man in the house." Gerald offered to stay, but Yves would have none of it. "I guess I must go through with it alone. But thanks a lot." He did, however, borrow six thousand lire to deal with urgent expenses until he could get down to the bank.

Gerald returned to England immediately, flying from Innsbruck. He was being packed into his car by Larwood at London airport when he saw a woman getting on to the bus for the passengers from Paris. Her walk and the trim neatness of her figure were familiar to him. As the bus moved off, she turned to look out of the window. It was Dollie. She looked, of course, much older, but more than that, her face was white and puffy and her hair was slipping untidily from beneath her hat. She looked, as he expected, a confirmed drunkard. He waved, but she did not recognize him.

John's face contorted in the series of grimaces that he knew by experience appealed to his viewers. He leaned forward in his chair and smiled with peculiar intimacy. "I've had a great number of letters from you asking me to discuss the results of my investigation of the Ministry's treatment of Mr Harold Cressett. It is certainly very pleasing to see the extraordinary and very sympathetic interest that this affair has aroused. It does after all mean that the defenders of our liberties are on their toes. I wish I *could* talk to you about it this evening, but, as you may have read in your daily newspaper, the Minister has now ordered a full inquiry into the conduct of the Government servants concerned. I'm sure you will understand that in these circumstances it would be most improper for us to discuss it."

Professor Clun turned to his wife. "Very remarkable chap, you know. Unusual to find a sense of responsibility with such a gift of the gab," he said. John Middleton had become the outlet for all the rather naïve enthusiasm in him which the years had buried so deep. He would praise remarks from John's lips or pen that he would have snapped at from anyone else. He settled himself in his chair and smiled at his wife. Mrs Clun felt an unusual sense of well-being. She loved John Middleton's half-hour; it was the only time when her husband smiled upon her passion for television.

John, too, was smiling now—the smile of an indulgent parent who has a pleasant surprise up his sleeve. "All the same, I don't want to disappoint you just because of a point of legal etiquette." He grinned at the viewers as though to say that if the trip to Whipsnade was off, they might at least hope for Regent's Park. "*You're* interested in Harold Cressett. You have a perfect right to know more about him. Neither Mr Cressett nor his wife sought this publicity. I'm sure they'll be only too glad when the fuss is over and they can get back to the comfortable days when they could open their daily paper without the embarrassment of seeing their name in print. But, as I've told them, once a man's in the news, well, he's in it. You've found in Harold Cressett a symbol of your daily fight against petty tyranny. However little he may relish the publicity, Mr Cressett is proud of being at the centre of that fight. I think you'll see all that for yourselves when I ask Mr Cressett a few questions this evening. For that's what I'm going to do. The first people in this evening's interviews will be Mr and Mrs Harold Cressett. We shan't, as I've told you, discuss their little trouble with the Ministry, for which I may say they expressed heartfelt thanks; but we shall have a few words about their daily life and especially about what it feels like to be in the news."

John glanced quickly towards the studio door through which the Cressetts were to appear. After meeting them, he had felt the gravest apprehension about bringing them before the public; he had even felt, beneath all the thick layers of his skin, a certain doubt about the value of the whole Pelican affair. However, there was an increasing stream of letters demanding more of the Cressetts, and John never believed in denying the public what they wanted.

Mr Cressett came in wearing a very tight navy blue suit and a stiff collar, he was greatly embarrassed by the powder that had been put on his face. Mrs Cressett, in ample puce lace, had refused all but the minimum of make-up. She appeared very large, he very small. . . .

"Oh, my God," said Maureen. "Poor Dad!"

"Your stepmother looks very imposing," said her hostess.

Maureen did not answer, but Derek said, "She's every sort of a cow." Their hostess looked a little shocked.

"I could kill Johnnie," Maureen whispered to Derek, "for getting Dad into this."

"I'd like to know what that old cow's leading poor old Johnnie into," he whispered back.

Their hostess frowned and put her finger to her lips for silence. It was all very well the Kershaws having all their friends and relations on T.V., but to pretend that they didn't like it was a simple show-off. . . .

"I believe you come from East Anglia, Mrs Cressett?" John was asking now. He gave an encouraging smile, as though she might fear that if she answered the question a lion would swallow her up. But Alice Cressett had no fears. "That's right," she said. "I was born at Lowestoft. We lived twenty-two years at Melpham. That was with Canon and Mrs Portway. She was his sister-in-law, you know, a well-known actress. Then we were at Norwich and then we came to London. I married Harold Cressett late." It was not very interesting to the viewers and she did not try to make it so. They had asked her to tell them the facts and she did so. However, they had also told her to look cheerful, so she attempted a smile upon her comfortable features.

Many viewers remarked on what a simple, ordinary, pleasant-faced woman she was. Gerald's host at a West End club, peering into a darkened room, whispered, "That's the television room."

Gerald, seeing John was on the screen, was about to move on as quickly as possible when Mrs Cressett's name was spoken. He looked at her with great interest. It may have been an unconscious memory of her harsh treatment of his sprained ankle that made him uneasy, but he thought, "She doesn't look the good, simple soul that Mrs Portway described. I trust I shan't have to interview *her* about Melpham."

"Good old soul," said his host with a laugh, and they went on to the coffee room. . . .

"Father was a coachman," Mrs Cressett was saying.

"Well, that certainly takes us back a bit," John remarked, "but I believe it was once his lot to take part in an important archaeological excavation. Not the usual duty of a coachman, I must say."

"Yes," said Alice, "Father helped with the digging. They discovered the grave of an old bishop in the grounds of Melpham Hall where we worked." She had wanted to say "the tomb of Bishop Eorpwald," but for some reason Mr Middleton seemed to think she ought not to know its proper name.

"Ah, yes," John smiled, "the tomb of Eorpwald, Bishop of Sedwich, I believe. He died in 695. Quite a long time ago. I suppose the discovery caused a good deal of talk locally," he said breezily.

"Oh, yes," said Mrs Cressett, "and in London. Scholars came from everywhere. But *we* didn't make much of it." She brought out this last sentence with evident reluctance. Once again she had been *told* to say it, though why it should be supposed that the villagers of Melpham would not have been interested in a local event that got into the London newspapers she couldn't imagine. . . .

"Trust her to do all the talking," Derek whispered.

"Anything is better than poor Dad making a fool of himself," Maureen replied. She spoke too soon. . . .

John turned to Mr Cressett. "I suppose *you* were very interested when you found that your wife had been associated with an archaeological excavation, whatever *she* may have thought about it. I believe you're a very keen reader of history and indeed a great reader generally."

"Yes," said the little man in a sad, slow voice. "When I am not gardening I always have my nose in a book"—Mrs Cressett's eyes narrowed with hatred—"Archaeology in particular," he went on, "interests me greatly." He paused, and John, knowledgeable in such things, feared that he was about to dry up. Indeed, Mr Cressett was overcome with terror and could not remember a word of the script they had rehearsed. Suddenly, however, the article on archaeology in one of his favourite encyclopedias came back to him and, just as John was about to intervene, he began to recite it.

"Archaeology," he said, "is yearly proving itself to be one of the most valuable handmaids of human knowledge. Year after year treasures come to light revealing the past in all its day-to-day detail—treasures unearthed from the very ground on which we take our evening stroll or from which we get our annual harvest. Mesopotamia, the birthplace of civilization, has revealed its mighty temples, its rich carvings and its strange writing cut in stone known to scholars as cuneiform. . . ." John shifted uneasily and began to mumble, but Mr Cressett went on; "Perhaps no single discovery has so excited the imagination of the man in the street as the discovery of the tomb of Tutankhamen, the Pharaoh of Egypt. . . ."

Maureen seized Derek's arm, "Oh, my God!" she said, "I can't bear it. I'm sorry," she turned to their hostess, "I knew something awful would happen. I can't face it, Derek. We must go."

Their hostess looked quite annoyed. "*I* think your father's marvellous. Fancy being able to reel all that off!" She turned to rebuke Maureen for her unfilial attitude, but her visitors had fled. Into the darkness of the room Mr Cressett's sad, weak face peered from the little screen. . . .

"It was archaeology, too," he went on, "that revealed to us that one of the earliest ancestors of man once trod our own familiar island. Piltdown Man . . ."

It is doubtful if John's two dearest ones—Inge and Larrie— would have realized any more than the mass of viewers how near the programme had come to disaster, so instant and powerful were the geniality and charm with which he burst in at the first hesitation in Mr Cressett's recital. In any case, as it happened, they were spared the spectacle of Johnnie's discomfiture and of the wretched market-gardener's sudden attack of automatic memory.

They had fully intended to view the programme together in the drawing-room. Indeed, they had promised John that they would do so as a pledge of their agreement not to quarrel any more. As time had gone by, their quarrels had grown more and more frequent until their ominous echoes had penetrated even John's egoistic world. It had needed all his charm on his last visit to heal the breach. His visits had come recently at increasingly greater intervals. It was one of the causes of their quarrels. Inge saw less and less charm in a Larrie who did not keep Johnnie at home; Larrie found his new home more and more irksome unrelieved by Johnnie's presence, while with Johnnie's supplies of cash coming at longer intervals, he was increasingly imprisoned within the four walls of Inge's capricious hospitality. John had been forced to promise that he would make a long stay there in order to reconcile them. The Cressett television programme which they should watch together should be his last engagement for a fortnight. To impress them further he sat down and cancelled his other appointments on the spot. When he was alone with Larrie, he promised the additional reward of a motor tour in Europe in the coming month.

After dinner Inge produced a bottle of Irish whiskey as an earnest of her sincerity in the reconciliation. It was a noble gesture, for a large part of their quarrels had arisen from Larrie's getting drunk. Inge, perhaps, marred the effect a little by underlining her broadmindedness. "You see," she said, "Old Mrs Middleton is not always a spoil-sport."

Larrie put his arm round her waist and dug his fingers into her stiff corseting. "Sure, and you're a darling, sporty old woman," he cried. They would have gladly welcomed a return to their former sentimental pictures of one another, for they both loved life to be sweet and happy.

Inge ruffled Larrie's tousled head. "It is nice to have my *good* little Irish boy back again," she said. "We have had such a nasty little boy staying here all these last weeks, not a bit like my nice Larrie."

Larrie wrinkled up his nose at her. "It's your own Larrie that's here to stay for good and all now," he said.

Neither of them felt any embarrassment at this nursery style of talk, though Larrie might have done had a third party been present. He almost promised not to do anything naughty again, but when he remembered his last naughtiness he decided not to mention it. He had been short of cash and had relieved the monotony of his life there by having the German maid over to the stables flat at night. Inge, taken with a sudden romantic wish to look at her early roses at midnight, had caught Irmgard coming back to the house. Clean sex was one thing, but sex with the maids was quite another. It was an interpretation of her precept that servants should be treated as though they were friends, which did not fit in with her picture of Larrie as a little orphan boy. He did wisely not to recall the incident.

"Now take the whiskey into the drawing-room. I must go and make myself look splendid for John to look at," she said.

"And don't you come in rustling your lovely dress after he's begun to speak or he'll not forgive you," Larrie replied. It was one of the favourite whimsies of their friendly times that John could view them from the television screen as they could view him.

Larrie poured himself out a strong whiskey, sat down in a large oatmeal-coloured armchair and made his head comfortable on a silver satin cushion. He thought of his holiday with John and of how best to ask for a sports car of his own. He was so overcome by the charm that he intended to use that he already saw John paying out the cheque in the motor sale-room. This in turn filled him with gratitude to the man who would give him foreign holidays and cars. Sure, he thought, the mother of a pal like that was bound to be a grand old lady. And so she was; for all her funny ways, she had a heart of gold and a soul of kindness. When he thought of the alternatives to being at Marlow—beds where and how chance brought them, or the hard work at the pub which Frank Rammage's help represented—it seemed well worth putting up with Inge. He clenched his fist and stiffened his lip and decided that he would "go straight" to show Johnnie what stuff he had in him.

Inge, too, went upstairs with a light step. Johnnie would be home tomorrow for a whole fortnight. That fortnight seemed to stretch indefinitely in her mind. But she would need Larrie's help. Johnnie's other friendships had been taking him further and further away from her, she must not allow this opportunity to disappear. She reminded herself that she had no right to expect perfection of Larrie. If she had brought an ex-Approved School boy into the house, she had no right to complain if he behaved like one. Hostility and criticism would not reform him, she would show patience and kindliness. She was proud of this determination. Also, if Johnnie did not object to Larrie's drunken fits and his other naughty ways—this covered in her mind the unpleasant episode of Irmgard—it was not for her to complain. Better an unreformed Larrie who brought Johnnie home than no Johnnie. Of this chain of thought she was less proud. She began to tell God that she had not really meant that part of her thoughts; if only Johnnie were to stay longer than the fortnight—a week longer, no, four days would be enough, no, perhaps a week—she would honestly and truly try to help Larrie.

Suddenly it came to her that she had not thought of her mother for more than a month. Mutti, whom she had never loved as much as her father. That was why Johnnie was not coming home as much as she had hoped. Looking at herself in the mirror, she decided that she would wear Mutti's old amethyst brooch. No wonder her luck was against her—leaving her mother's jewellery in the silver box in the wardrobe. She would wear a different piece every day now and keep Mutti's memory alive and then her luck would come back. She took out the silver box and laid it on the dressing-table. When she opened it, it was empty.

Superstitious fright rapidly gave way to rage. She knew at once who had taken it. She had shown the jewels to Johnnie and Larrie some weeks before, saying that she never wore them. At that moment even Johnnie's devotion would not have saved his friend from her fury had the boy been in the room. To take *her* property, to bring *her* bad luck was not the mark of an ordinary criminal, it was an act for which there could be no mercy. Her more considered train of thought, however, was too recent to have altogether left her. She must not risk Johnnie's love by a rash action. She sat down on her dressing-table stool and made such an effort to control her anger as she had never made before. The sheer physical spasm of such self-control made her great body shake all over and tears welled up in her blue eyes. After a minute or so, however, she realized that she had won. She descended the stairs with a sad look of reproach and a bitter little smile. She had brought a thief into the house and she must pay the price. It was her duty, her sad duty, to make the boy ashamed, to make him tell the truth.

Larrie gave her a great big, loving smile when she came into the room. "Just in time," he said. "And won't Johnnie be proud of his old lady?" He looked for the heart of gold and the soul of kindness in those big blue eyes but they did not seem to be there. "Now, Mrs Middleton, darling," he cried, "you must sit down. We'll be missing Johnnie's introduction and then what'll we say to him?"

"I don't know what *I'm* going to say to him," she said, shaking her head in solemn reproach, "I don't know how I am going to tell him that his friend is a little thief."

Her discovery was a nasty blow to Larrie. He had, of course, expected it sooner or later; but neither sooner nor later ever meant now in his scheme of things. He had told himself in his heroic moods that he would tell the old lady the truth; but he had always anticipated her rage, and this unexpected mood of soft-speaking sorrow reminded him too easily of the many kindly, moralizing people he had met in his life of institutions. For such old fools he had only one reply—evasion, lying, soft-soaping. And so he said, "Now whatever do you mean, Mrs Middleton, darling?"

"No! no!" Inge cried, shaking her great head to and fro and rounding her great eyes. "No! Larrie. That is not good enough. You know very well what I mean."

"I do not," he cried. "I swear I do not. If you'll not tell me what you mean, how can I? Even if I've been in trouble, I've the right to defend myself."

"I want to give you the right to tell me the truth," she answered with a little bitter, disappointed smile. "I can't help you, you know, if you won't help yourself."

Larrie had heard it all so often before. "Indeed I want to," he cried, "and yet you say these wicked, cruel things to me." His eyes began to fill with tears, he could only remember all the unfairness he had met in life.

Inge, too, had now completely assumed the rôle of the trusting woman who had been let down. She sat on the arm of his chair and stroked his unruly hair. "Now, Larrie," she said in a soft, cooing voice, "shall we try to see if we can remember the truth? Perhaps I can do it for you. You've tried to fit in here, to live the happy, good life I offered you. But it's not easy to throw off the wicked, black troll who has sat on your shoulders for so long."

"Indeed, that's the truth," he said, gazing up at her.

She smiled and twisted a lock of his hair around her finger.

"Well," she said, "the little black troll won, didn't he? You spent all your money on silly, bad things and you wanted some more. That stupid old fool Mrs Middleton wouldn't give it to you—I'm afraid she wasn't darling Mrs Middleton then. And you remembered that old box of jewellery which she had told you she never used and so . . ."

Larrie jumped from the chair. With his tousled head and his flushed cheeks, he was the picture of frightened indignation. "It's not true, it's not true," he cried, "I've not taken a thing that isn't mine. God strike me down! I wish I were dead if it's always to be this way. People suspecting me, hating me because I never had a chance in life." He was shaking all over and his voice came shrill and hysterical through his tears.

Inge sat monumental, patient and sad. "The jewellery has gone, Larrie," she said. "Who has taken it?"

"How do I know who's taken it?" he cried, and then suddenly he turned to her, his bright tear-glistening eyes awake with a new idea. "And yes, I do. Indeed, I do. It was that Irmgard, Mrs Middleton, you can be sure it was. She's a lying, deceitful bitch. Don't I know it from the wicked lies she told of me?"

Inge's splendid, Valhalla neck flushed scarlet. She arose from her chair, an avenging goddess, "No!" she cried, towering over him, "you cannot be helped. You are wicked and bad all through!"

The accusation against one of the maids touched deeply all her social democratic morality, but further still Larrie's reference to his exploit with Irmgard brought back all the disgust she had felt at the time. It had only been Johnnie's pleading that had made her pass over the incident so easily at the time and the suppressed distaste came surging up. "You are filthy too," she said, "to use your position here to make the poor girl do *that* with you. It was vile and disgusting."

Through all Larrie's fright came a wave of anger at her bullying and a fury of hurt vanity. "Made her!" he cried. "She was glad to get the chance to do it." He turned to Inge, laughing and pointing his finger. "And so would you too, for all that you're old enough to be my grandmother. That's why you hated it so, you old beast!"

The idea was horrible to Inge, indeed for many years any idea of sex had been revolting to her. Now indeed she was the thunder goddess. "How dare you?" she cried. "There is only one thing to do for this. I shall telephone to the police. They will know how to deal with such filthiness."

Larrie clung to her dress, but with greater strength she moved on, erect, determined. He began to whimper at her. It was true what she said, but didn't she see what his life had made of him, an institution boy; and not only that, his physical health, hadn't he been turned down for National Service, though he'd wished to serve and him an Irish boy. Inge's heart was stone.

Suddenly Larrie's tone of voice changed. "You'd better not be telephoning to the police. Johnnie wouldn't be liking that at all," he said.

"I can't help Johnnie's feelings," Inge said, "this has been too bad."

"You'd best be careful or you'll be sorry for what you're doing," Larrie shouted, and in crude words he began to speak of his relations with John. "That'll not sound so good," he said, "in a police court."

Inge turned towards him a doll's face of horror. Then she put her hands over her ears. "Don't speak such things. Go away! Go away! It is terrible." The thing that she feared most was happening to her, that she dreaded most. Someone was telling her things that she could not bear to hear and she could not stop them. She met the attack with the hysterical panic that had seized her in the old days of Kay's burned hand. "Go away! Go away!" she screamed.

"I'm going all right. I don't want to stay here. You needn't worry," Larrie said. He found easily the tough, hard tone which he had so often assumed in such scenes in the past. Although he had always been too frightened to blackmail, he had no such fears about a little threatening and bullying. "I'll just be needing a little money. That's all." Going over to where her bag lay on the table, he opened it and took out the notes. He counted them. "Twenty pounds," he said, "I'll take that."

She had sunk on to a chair by the door and, with her elbows on her knees, she covered her face with her hands. She would not look.

Her fright increased Larrie's bullying and a very genuine resentment of the rotten deal he felt he had got from the Middletons. He remembered how some men he had known, who had broken into a flat in Knightsbridge, had told him that they had urinated on the lady's bedroom carpet, "to teach the old tart a lesson". It seemed to him that this would be the tough thing to do, yet surveying the spacious drawing-room awe overcame him. He contented himself by shoving his hands in his pockets and, as he slouched across the room, spitting on the polished parquet skirting. Even then he was seized with shame, he scraped the spittle with his foot. "I apologize," he said, "I shouldn't have done that."

Inge saw nothing of what he was doing, she repeated, "You must go. You must go away."

He went down to the stables flat and packed his bag. Then taking her car, he drove off to London. He guessed rightly that once anything had been stolen, she would make no attempt to recover it.

John, driving out of London on the sunny June morning of the next day, decided to visit the Kershaws once again. He was beginning to find his new career a strain. Elvira was no longer there to give him support. The Marlow set-up had removed Larrie from him and had only made his visits to Inge more difficult. The little that he had seen of the Cressetts had told him that he was easily carried too far into things without examining them closely enough to see where they would lead him. He had only extricated himself from graver self-mistrust

by refusing to look any further into the matter. When everything went smoothly on its own impetus, he felt himself master
of his own fate—the strong, individualistic social reformer
with cynical good sense enough to make a nice career out of
his genuine mission. When there were mishaps or setbacks or
close shaves like the Cressett affair of last night, he saw himself
as the artist caught up in a web of other people's trickery,
chicane and selfishness, by the unfortunate fact that unlike
other artists he had a social conscience. He would write again,
but not among the carping, little-minded cliquey literary world
in which Elvira lived. He would go away with someone simple
and ordinary—somebody like Larrie who needed help—*that*
would take care of his social conscience. And he would realize
himself as an artist. All the same a certain canniness told him
that he could not easily get off the celebrity big wheel. It would
be as well to find out a little more about the Cressetts, for example; not directly, but from Maureen. After all, with Derek
there, she would not tell him anything "too disturbing".

Derek was busy at the garage when he arrived and he was
left to a *tête-à-tête* with Maureen. He did not feel easy. She
produced coffee and home-made coffee-iced cake. "We saw
your television programme," she said, "or as much of it as we
could stand. Honestly, John, you drive me up the wall. What
sort of a mess have you got poor Dad into, or yourself for that
matter?"

John swallowed a draught of coffee too quickly, but his
choking fit allowed him time to compose his face in an innocent
boyish look of surprise. "What do you mean 'a mess'?" he
asked grinning. "I look like getting your father his compensation after all and you call that a mess?"

"Have you seen Dad's market-garden?" Maureen asked.
"No, well I shouldn't. The compensation would be difficult
to assess. But that isn't the point. Dad's a wretched creature in
some ways, but he doesn't deserve to be made a fool of like
this. Heaven knows what sort of nonsense he'll get up to if
he has much more of this publicity. Or the awful Alice. She'd

be as much a fool in things like that as he is, if she wasn't such a tough nut."

John decided to probe further. "As a matter of fact, Maureen, I was a bit taken aback last night," he said candidly. "I thought I'd never stop the old boy."

"You shouldn't have put him there," she said. "But he won't do you any harm. My stepmother might. She's ignorant, but she's as hard as nails and pretty sly. Don't you let her in on your private life! Not that she can get you into much worse of a mess than you're in. What sort of a circus clown are you making of yourself, Johnnie, with all this radio racket? You were a ghastly reactionary in the Labour party, but at least it was some use, but this sort of nonsense is *bound* to make you look a fool in the end."

John said huffily, "I happen to think there are more ways than one of effecting social changes."

"Oh! Johnnie. And you've got education. *I* don't know."

"We'd better not argue about it."

"No," said Maureen. "You're right there. Have some more coffee." When she had poured it out, she added, "All the same, it'd be more respectable to be a crooner."

John held up his hands in mock surrender. "All right," he cried, "you keep Nye Bevan for your pin-up boy. I'm not competing."

"A lot you care if I pin you up or not," Maureen laughed. "All the same, some of the fans you do care about will be taking your picture down from the wall soon. Derek, for instance." As soon as she said it, she felt ashamed, but could only cover her embarrassment with gaucherie, "Look!" she said, "it was lovely seeing you, but I've got Derek's lunch to cook. Go round and see him at the garage." She went into the kitchen.

John drove round to the garage and had a few words with Derek between customers. The garage did a good summer trade. "I honestly think I'm going to pack the whole racket up, Derek," John said, "and go back to writing stories."

Derek glinted his best advertisement smile at him. "I don't say you'd be wrong there," he said. "And while you're about it, Johnnie, I'd pack up that Larrie. *He* won't get you any-where."

He went to serve another customer and John drove off without waiting to say goodbye.

He was very annoyed to find Larrie out when he arrived at Marlow. Inge said she had no idea where he had gone, but she had no doubt that he would be back later in the day. She was beginning by now to hope that he *would* return—anything rather than having to recount last night's scene to Johnnie. She fussed around him all day, pretending that she had watched the television programme with Larrie as she had promised. Luckily he did not seem very keen to discuss it. She told her-self sometimes that a chastened Larrie would return and all would be as before. He would tell her that the dreadful things he had said about himself and Johnnie were lies and she would tell him that she had not heard them. Then again she told herself that Johnnie would give Larrie up for ever when he heard her story; indeed, would stay with her for a long, long time to comfort her for what she had been through.

As the day wore on, neither hope seemed likely to be realized, Johnnie grew more and more restive over Larrie's absence; his picture of the boy as the simple devoted soul who would keep him company in his simple life devoted to letters, took stronger hold of him. Derek's remark, coming on top of all the criticism of Larrie that he had been forced to listen to in the last months, had clinched his decision that here was his true friend. John was always a fighter against criticism.

At last, after dinner, Inge could not keep back her story any longer. She told him nearly all, only omitting the dreadful remarks about his relations with Larrie. She was too unsure of the new relationship that her knowledge would entail. Johnnie, she felt sure, would prefer her never to have heard and she set about convincing herself that she had not.

John's reaction even to her bowlderized version was instant and fierce.

"Why the hell couldn't you wait until I got home?" he demanded. "You knew Larrie had been in trouble for thieving before, you shouldn't have left the bloody jewellery lying about? Anyway, you never wore the damned stuff." He had never used abusive language to his mother before, but now it flooded through the broken dam.

Inge tried to defend herself. "What have *I* done? You should ask, 'What has *he* done?' Threatened your mother and stolen. I wish I had gone to the police."

John seized her wrist. "Don't you dare, do you hear! Don't you dare," he shouted. "I asked you to look after him and you promised. And this is what has happened. You knew how much it meant to me, but you didn't care. You've never cared for anyone but yourself in your life."

"I have cared for you, Johnnie," she said. She stood there, huge, flat-voiced, motionless; she was too unhappy to be hysterical.

John shouted at her more violently each minute. He had rehearsed this scene so often in his life when her possessiveness had threatened him that now the words poured out before his sense of shame could stop them. "You'd better get wise to yourself, Thingy," he said. "You've never considered anyone else but yourself for a minute of your life. Your affection for me! You've tried to strangle me with your selfish love." He laughed hysterically in her face. "If you don't care for my friendships you can thank your own unhealthy, greedy love for them." He was horrified to hear himself speak all these stock, case-book sentences.

Inge's great round mouth opened wide, but she only mumbled, "It was not a good friendship, your friendship with Larrie, Johnnie."

He stared at her for a moment, "That bloody swine your husband's been talking to you," he said.

"I have not seen your father," she said.

"Don't call him my father," he shouted. "If you'd had any decency you'd have got rid of him long ago. It was filthy the way you both lived when we were children. Yes, and you wanted it both ways. To keep that man in the house and then come whining to us about him. Do you think it was nice for us to have an old lecher for a father and a ridiculous clown for a mother?"

Once again in twenty-four hours Inge sat down on a chair and began to weep. John turned away in horror. In all the scenes he had rehearsed in his imagination her tears had led him to a reconciliation. He was determined that it should not happen so in reality.

"Understand this," he shouted, "if I lose Larrie or if he gets into any trouble, I'll never speak to you again." Slamming the door he left the house.

She heard his car start up in the drive and listened as its purr faded away into the distance. She walked over and looked at herself in the mirror. Her reflection seemed some monstrous, red-cheeked doll that was melting in great rolls of fat, white wax. She went upstairs to bed and cried herself to sleep.

Although it was after midnight when John got back to London, he went straight to Earl's Court Square. He rang and knocked loudly for some minutes before the door was opened by Frank in a heavy camel-coloured dressing-gown and lamb's-fleece bedroom slippers. Below his shining bald head, his little pink face scowled angrily. "There's no need for that noise," he said, "whoever it is."

"I've come to see Larrie Rourke," John said.

"Well, you've come to the wrong house. He doesn't live here any more."

"It's John Middleton," John went on, peering into the dimly lit hall.

"Oh," Frank snapped. "Well, that'll be the same answer." He was about to shut the door, when John put his foot on the threshold.

"He's run away," he said desperately.

"I'm not surprised," Frank answered. "I wrote you that no good would come of his living like that but you didn't have the courtesy to answer my letter. Good night."

John put a hand on Frank's arm. It was roughly shaken off. "If you're a friend of Larrie's, you'll try to help me find him. He went away in a hysterical state. He took a lot of mother's jewels and her car. Of course, I'm not thinking of that. . . ."

"I daresay your mother is," Frank interrupted.

"Yes, she's very upset, but she's not trying to prosecute or anything."

"That's wise."

"I'm only frightened of what trouble he'll get into," John pleaded.

"He probably has already," said Frank.

"Good God!" John cried. "I understood you were fond of the boy. If you had a grain of my feelings of affection. . . ."

"I don't go for affection," Frank said. John thought, what a disgusting little hypocrite; but he said nothing for fear of causing offence. "I go for compassion," Frank added. He spoke as though it was a stock article of trade. "Affection tends to muck up the works."

"At least you'll help me find him," John said.

"No!" said Frank shortly. "I'll have a search for the lad myself, but I shan't tell you if I do find him."

This time he did not say good night, but simply pushed John's leg out of the way and shut the door. John could hear his slippers slopping along the passage. He turned and made his way to the West End to continue his search in the all-night cafés.

It was about a week later on a morning towards the end of June that Gerald Middleton presented himself at Earl's Court Square. The promising early spring had turned to a wet summer, and the continuous rain seemed only an extension of the depression that had once more settled down upon him. His interview with Mrs Portway and the dismal close of his visit to Merano had made his Melpham quest seem not only fruitless but ludicrous. He felt suddenly that he was playing a childish game. On his return, he tried to resume his work on the *History* as though Melpham had never existed, but his concentration had gone. Disgusted at himself, he decided that this was only further proof that he was too old for serious work, fit only for dilettante hobbies. He resumed his visits to the dealers. But Melpham would not leave him. Despite his English ironic temperament, he had not got the usual English worship of the sense of the ridiculous. Perhaps marriage to Inge had taught him that the ludicrous was too often only a thin covering for the serious and the tragic. The fact, then, that his Melpham quest presented itself as ridiculous did not in the end deter him from resuming it.

Frank Rammage came to the door this time with a duster in his hand. A huge white apron covered his round, little belly. "If you've come about Larrie Rourke," he said, "I've nothing to say. I told your son so. If he's anxious, you can say I haven't found him. But that's all I'm saying."

"I know nothing about Rourke," said Gerald. "I thought he was down at my wife's."

"He was," Frank said. "But he's left. Taking her motor-car with him." He chuckled.

"Good God!" Gerald cried, and then added, "Oh well! I suppose it's a small price to pay for getting rid of him."

"It's a small price to pay for ruining the lad's chances of making good. I've no doubt at all he'll get into worse company now."

"Hm," said Gerald shortly. "Well. Maybe. Anyhow, I haven't come to talk to you about Master Rourke. You don't remember, Mr Rammage, that we've met before—a long time ago. To be exact at Melpham in 1912 on the day Eorpwald's tomb was excavated. I sprained my ankle."

Frank peered at him with his little piggy eyes. "That's a long time ago," he said, "you've aged and so have I."

"All the same," Gerald smiled at the little man, "it's about the Melpham tomb that I wanted to talk to you."

"The Melpham tomb?" Frank's tone was amazed, but not, Gerald thought, anxious. "I don't know anything about that. I haven't read a word of history for years." He laughed. "Fancy *you* coming to me about an Anglo-Saxon tomb."

"I want to reconstruct the circumstances of its discovery if I can," Gerald said. "Do you think I could come inside and have a little talk with you about it?"

"That'll have to be a *very* little talk then," Frank said, "because I'm doing the housework. But come inside." He led the way to his bed-sitting-room. "Sit down," he said.

"How is Mrs Salad?" Gerald asked.

"Complaining, poor old dear!" Frank answered, "but you didn't come here to talk about her."

Once more Gerald told his story, but this time he was careful to give no leads by particularizing his suspicions. He merely suggested that Gilbert Stokesay might have done it as a practical joke; and even this he put forward as a youthful folly rather than the trick of an embittered man. In fact, he made light of the whole episode.

Frank was in no way deceived; his turkey face gobbled as he listened. "That'd be no joke if it were so," he said. "Scholarship means truth as you ought to know, Professor Middleton." He looked reproachfully at Gerald. "It might have been young Stokesay's way too," he said. "He was a bad type of man. I was a young lad then, hungry for knowledge, and he made mock of me."

Gerald could not help smiling at the Victorian note of this. "You're a very old-fashioned person, Mr Rammage," he said.

Frank looked most offended. He stared at his room, indicating the scarlet anchors, the Danish lampshades. "I favour the contemporary," he said simply. "Young people find me very up to date."

He sat down on a tubular chair and crossed his fat little hands over his large aproned stomach. "That's be a terrible thing if it were true," he repeated. "It's a mercy Canon Port-way's dead. He hated a lie, and a lie in a scholarly thing like that would have about killed him after he'd given his name to it." He sat motionless, his little mouth pursed in thought.

"Mrs Portway thinks her brother *did* know. Oh, after the event, of course," Gerald added hastily, as he saw the little man's face twitch with anger. He told Frank of the letter from her brother-in-law that Lilian had quoted and of her belief that he had been blackmailed.

"Ah!" said Frank, smacking his fat little lips, "she'd have put that on me—fraud, blackmail and all."

"She doesn't care for you certainly."

"No, no more than I care for her. I shan't speak ill of her, but I shouldn't wish to see her again."

"I don't think you will," Gerald observed, and he told Frank of the state in which he had left Lilian.

"She'll recover," Frank said sharply. "She's very tough." He leaned forward, his little eyes popping lobster-like out of his red face. "I said I'd say nothing against her. But I will. She's eaten up with jealousy—always has been—and she's got a vile tongue. I don't doubt she said unfitting things of her brother-in-law and me."

Gerald gave no answer.

"Ah!" said Frank, " I thought she would have done. Well, that wasn't true what she said and, if it had been, that'd have been no business of hers."

Gerald hastened to leave this topic and return to the excava-tion. "But you *were* with Gilbert Stokesay, Mr Rammage, when the coffin was first uncovered," he cried.

Frank folded his arms and leaned back in his chair. "No, I wasn't," his little mouth snapped shut like a turtle's.

Gerald flushed slightly. "Oh come!" he said, "I distinctly remember what was said that day."

"Oh that was *said*," Frank replied, "but that wasn't true. Barker was with him. I didn't come up from the village until near ten o'clock. Alice Barker always said I was there, though what she knew of it, I *don't* know, except that she knew everyone's business." He shook his head, then suddenly he jumped from his chair and stood over Gerald's chair, arms akimbo as though about to deliver him a "talking to".

"That'll be it," he cried, "Barker would have helped that Gilbert if help be needed. Most likely for a few pounds. There's nothing the Barkers wouldn't do for a few pounds, though they'd got plenty put away even in those days. They'd not understand the meaning of it, but if Gilbert Stokesay was fool enough to part with his money to play a joke they'd not refuse it. Besides Barker would welcome Mr Portway making a fool of himself. A joke on the gentry paid for by the gentry. That'd just appeal to them. And then, in case there was trouble, Alice'd make sure they weren't blamed. It'd be that Frank Rammage that Mr Portway was so soft on that'd have been there. Likely enough Gilbert Stokesay agreed to that, he didn't care for young chaps that went out for education."

Frank became more and more excited as he put forward his theory. He began to trot round the room, dusting the ornaments, as he spoke. Gerald was forced to turn round in his chair to speak to him. "Steady on," he cried, "you're as bad as Mrs Portway. She doesn't like you so she pinned it on you. You're doing the same thing with the Barkers. You've said nothing to suggest that anyone was involved in a fake, nothing odd even, except for Alice Barker's insisting that you'd made the discovery when her father had." That, he thought, could be read two ways, but he said no more.

Frank stopped short in his little trot. "There's a little more to it than that," he said. "I left Mr Portway—Canon he was by then—because he wouldn't get rid of those Barkers. So you'd better consider all I say in the light of that." He paused to let Gerald make his allowance for bias, then coming close to him, he shook a fat forefinger in his face. "Mrs Portway was nearer right than she thought; for the old man was blackmailed, and by the Barkers, I'm sure of it. When I got back from the war, they'd got such a hold on him, I wouldn't believe my eyes. Well, we all settled down together. It didn't take me long to see how they treated him. Bullying the poor man. He couldn't even have what he liked to eat. Alice took a real pleasure in feeding the man on eggs although she knew he couldn't abide them. And cheating him of his money, not large sums, but a bit here and a bit there. He was scared of them all the time, scared out of his life. He was still the same fine man in public, but at home he was an old man even before he left for Norwich. After I came there, it was quarrels all the day, for I couldn't stand for their goings on. In the end it came to it that life wasn't worth living. I was sick of it, duckie"— in his excitement, Frank dropped into his usual endearments even with Gerald—"so I told the old man it was them or me. He cried and begged me to stay. But it was no good. I reckoned the choice had to come, and even if he chose them, at least life would be quieter for him. All the same I didn't believe he'd let me go until it happened. In some ways I was glad, for I couldn't go on taking from him and in any case I had work to do, my dear. I couldn't let my life pass in Norwich, though there's misery enough there too, and crime. But when that man chose to keep the Barkers and to let me go, I knew there was something badly wrong. He loved me as much as he could love anyone and he was a loving man by and large. Oh not as Mrs Portway chose to think and as the Barkers were quick to tell anyone. But he did love me. The Barkers must have had a hold on him for him to do a thing like that even though he cried to ask me to stay. I often puzzled what that could have been. None of the ordinary things, that I knew, for the Canon was a good man, a bit too good perhaps. Oh yes! they took a lot off him, that I know. You see, duckie, when he died, he left me all his money. A nice little bit it was and I felt very bad about it, though I've tried to spend it in ways that would do him justice. All the same, it wasn't what he'd once had. The Barkers had had a good cut, you mark my words." He snapped his mouth shut and began to dust the lamps vigorously.

Gerald got up from his chair and began walking up and down. "That's all very well," he said. "I'm sure you've given me a true picture of what happened, but there's nothing to connect it with Melpham. It was Portway's duty as a scholar to speak out at once if he found out that there had been a fraud. As it was, you suggest this man, who you say was a very good man, submitted to blackmail in order to hide up what it was his duty to reveal."

Frank turned on Gerald irritably. "Goodness isn't all of a piece," he said, "any more than badness. Canon Portway was a very good man. He'd never admit he was wrong. Not even in little things. If he was faced with it he just walked out of the room. And this which was a public thing, that touched his scholarship. No, duckie, you don't understand people very well. Besides, he had to think of old Professor Stokesay. That'd have been a terrible thing for him when he loved his son so. No, Canon Portway would have done anything rather than that."

Gerald went to the window and stared at the trees of Earl's Court Square. "There's nothing to connect it with Melpham, nothing," he said, and turned round sharply to face Frank.

"There's a thing I *do* remember," said the little fat man. "He wouldn't talk of Melpham. I asked him once. In Norwich it was, I remember. He was getting old then long before his time. He'd come in from his sermons complaining of rheumatism and the cold. There'd have been no fire either if I hadn't made one and given him crumpets as he liked them. He'd talk then, a bit rambling but always clever. I asked him about Eorpwald once, how that pagan god fitted in with the Church in those days and so on. I gave up all my book-learning when I went into the Navy and I never went back to it. I found more important things to do, but I always liked to learn things. He snapped me up then. He said the whole thing was a mystery and he hoped it'd remain so. It wasn't a thing he saw any good in discussing, he said. And then he asked me a strange thing. Never to talk about the Melpham burial to the Barkers. I didn't make conversation with them anyway and I'd no more have mentioned a learned thing to them than flown. I thought he was wandering. But perhaps he wasn't, duckie, after all. Anyway, you'd best go and see the Barkers. Mrs Cressett she is now. I should see the old man on his own. He's a hard man, but he's old, and the old wander in their talk. You'll get nothing out of her, nor out of him if she's by."

Gerald sighed. "I suppose I must," he said. "Well, thank you, Mr Rammage, for all . . ."

Frank cut him short. "If you've no more to ask, I'll say good day to you. The cleaning and polishing there is to do!" He showed Gerald out.

As Gerald was getting into his car, a voice came from the front steps behind him. "Can I have a word with you, please, Professor Middleton?" He saw Larwood's eyebrows rise slightly and turned to find Vin Salad standing on the steps in black crêpe-de-chine pyjamas, a jade-green silk dressing-gown, held tightly, draped round him. His face was covered in vanishing cream.

Gerald's back stiffened slightly; he'd had about as much of that sort of thing as he could take. "Oh, good morning, Salad," he said in his most officerly voice, "I'm afraid I can't stop now. I'm late for an appointment."

"It won't take a sec.," said Vin. He looked down at his costume. "I hardly cared to call out to you in this negligee," he added. "You asked me to keep an eye on that Larrie Rourke. Well, he's liable to be in bad trouble any day."

"Yes," said Gerald, "he appears to have stolen my wife's car. But since he's left her house, I don't know that it matters."

"Oh, I don't know anything about that," Vin said, "but he's in with some Irish boys now. A very bad crowd. Burglars and things. He'll be taken up any day I should think."

"Well, since he's cut loose from my family it's hardly my affair," Gerald answered.

Vin flounced his head. He was hurt at the Professor's manner. "Oh well, I'm sure I don't know," he said, "I was only anxious to oblige. I should tell your son to keep away from him if I were you."

"Thank you," said Gerald. He started to get into the car, then turned and said. "How's Mrs Salad?"

Vin smiled. "Ever so lively, thank you. She's always hoping to see you."

"Oh," Gerald answered, "I'll look in one of these days."

Vin's eyes narrowed. "That's nice," he said. "It's lucky she's such a patient old lady." He turned and went indoors.

Gerald looked out of the window of the Montpelier Square house some days later. The rain running down the panes blurred his vision. Despite the summer season, he had been forced to turn on the central heating. Inside the house everything seemed warm and snug. The first contribution to the *History*—Hilda Ferguson's chapter on the influence of the Crusades on English social life—had arrived. It looked most interesting. It seemed to Gerald that he could start the chapter of *The Confessor* on Stigand's relations with Rome. The words were already formed in his head. A catalogue of the Wroxesley sale lay on the table—there were notes on two Guardi drawings he had never seen. Nevertheless, he rang and asked Larwood to have the car ready in five minutes. He gave the address of Harold Cressett.

It would have been less depressing, he thought, to have left some warm, sunbaked merchant's house in Pompeii to set sail for Ultima Thule or the bright Lords' hall for the darkness of the voyage to Vinland. Indeed, the hideous hybrid terrain of the by-pass seemed more monstrous to Gerald when he reached it than all the fantastic lands of medieval travellers. Mr Barker's huge, motionless red face stared out of the window at the ruined glass-houses. One rolling eye was fixed on Gerald as he came up the path. So, Gerald thought, must Polyphemus have looked out at the voyagers from his cave.

Mrs Cressett answered the door—comfortable, neat, but ready to bar the way. The compensation money now seemed assured. Numerous well-wishers had sent them substantial cheques. The time had come when she would keep out intruders, snoopers, reporters and other busybodies. Alice Cressett has never believed in knowing people—strangers, neighbours, family or anybody else—you could never tell what they were trying to get out of you. A small kingdom ruled by herself with a rod of iron was what she liked, and all this contact with the great public tended to undermine her sense of omnipotence. It seemed also to have undermined Harold—he was getting out of hand. The sooner they got away from the small-holding and established the boarding-house in Cromer, the better she would be pleased. A nice little kingdom with ten or twelve chosen subjects—preferably old people—would just suit her natural talent for ruling.

She was not over-friendly to Gerald then, although her eye took in the car and chauffeur. When she learned that he was John Middleton's father she felt constrained to ask him in.

"I saw you on the television," said Gerald, "and I was so interested to learn that you had been at Melpham. You probably don't remember it, but I was there the day the discovery was made. You very kindly bound up my sprained ankle."

"Oh yes, I remember, sir." Alice's expression remained fixed and comfortable, like a mother doll carved out of wood. She led him into the parlour. "How do you do, Mr Barker?" Gerald said. "I remember well your driving me up to Melpham Hall. We had a very interesting little chat." He seemed somehow impelled to lie about the events of that day.

Alice Cressett chuckled. "Well, you won't have another," she said. "Father's paralysed. He's lost his speech. But he understands very well. Don't you, Father? You'd be surprised how much he *does* understand, sir."

Gerald felt quite downcast at this check to his inquiry. "I'm writing a book about Melpham. I'm a history professor, you know. I was hoping perhaps your father could have told me a little about the exciting circumstances of the discovery."

Mrs Cressett looked more satisfied than ever. "He could have done," she said, "but he can't now."

"Oh I expect he told you most of what he knew," Gerald said. "He was with Gilbert Stokesay, wasn't he, when they first came on the coffin?"

Mrs Cressett went to the sideboard and got out a bottle of beer and glasses. "You'll take a glass of beer won't you?" she asked. Then she said, "He couldn't have told me that because he wasn't there. It was one of the village lads that was with young Mr Stokesay. Father only came later when they needed all hands to raise the coffin."

"How strange," Gerald said, "I could have sworn that someone told me he made the discovery."

"They told you lies then," she said.

Gerald sat puzzled for a moment, then he took a long chance. "Oh! I know. I got that impression from your father himself when he drove me up there that day."

For the first time Mrs Cressett shifted her ample bottom a little uncomfortably on the chair. "Oh!" she said. "Well, if you know so much there's no occasion to ask me."

There was an awkward silence. Gerald thought of the paralysed mother in *Thérèse Raquin* and wondered if Mr Barker too might give a sign. "I always hoped Canon Portway would publish his reminiscences. It would have been most valuable to have had *his* first-hand account of the excavation. I believe you were in his service a long time, Mrs Cressett."

"More than twenty years, sir. And Father? Let me see. I believe he was over forty years with the family. You was more than forty years with the Portways, weren't you, Father?" She waited a moment to register the unspoken and then said, "Ah! I thought so. More than forty years Father was with them, sir."

"Did Canon Portway ever say anything to you about why he hadn't published more on Bishop Eorpwald's tomb."

Mrs Cressett looked at him very straight. "We were servants, sir," she said.

"The best in the world according to Mrs Portway," Gerald went on.

Mrs Cressett seemed now to be anxiously listening for something. "*She* was a very good mistress, sir," she said. "Ah, Father knows you're talking of her. He worshipped Mrs Portway, sir. Do you know how she is these days?"

"I'm afraid she was very ill indeed when I left her at Merano last month. They didn't think she would live!"

Mrs Cressett clicked her tongue. "I don't know how Father'll take that," she said. However he took it, Mr Barker still gave no overt sign. "Did she speak of us on that day?" Mrs Cressett asked.

"Oh, yes," Gerald replied, "a great deal, and most warmly."

"Ah!" said Mrs Cressett with satisfaction. She even filled up Gerald's glass.

"*She* seemed to think her brother-in-law was worried about some aspects of the excavation," Gerald said. Mrs Cressett looked at him with an expression of polite but blank failure to understand. "And Mr Rammage agreed when I saw him."

He watched carefully to see the effect of Frank's name, but Mrs Cressett said rather strangely, "Ah you know all the lie of the land, sir. *You* spare no trouble."

Gerald was about to follow up his remark, when there was a noise at the back door. Mrs Cressett's listening attitude seemed to relax. She got up from her chair. "Excuse me, sir," she said and was gone.

Gerald looked at Mr Barker's red moon face and his staring eye. The eye looked back at him and once it swivelled round. No sign, however, came.

From the kitchen Gerald could hear the voices of Mrs Cressett and her husband. She was examining the groceries he had been sent out to buy. Suddenly her voice was raised. "Danish butter?" she cried. "What's that butter doing there?"

"I thought we'd have a little butter now," Mr Cressett mumbled.

"Oh did you?" Mrs Cressett said. "You'll get butter when I choose to give it to you." Then her voice became slow and soothing again. "You'll take it back and change it for marge," she said. "No, not now. John Middleton's father's here and he'll want to talk to you."

As Mr Cressett came in, he smiled feebly at Gerald. "We're very grateful," he said. He was so used those days to being expected to feel grateful that he did not particularize.

Gerald laughed. "There's nothing to thank me for. I've nothing to do with my son's good works. I'm only glad it all looks like turning out so well for you."

"It looks like turning out badly for Mr Pelican," Mrs Cressett said with relish.

Gerald said, "I was talking to your wife about the old days at Melpham. I suppose Mr Gilbert was backwards and forwards most of the time from Bedbury, Mrs Cressett. Did Mr Barker ever work over there?"

Mrs Cressett got up and, taking a handkerchief, she blew her father's nose. "We don't know the half of what you did, do we, Father?" she asked. Then she said, "If you'll excuse me, sir, I'll leave you to talk to my husband. He brought the wrong things back from the shop and I must go and change them." Mr Cressett seemed about to speak, but she gave him a look and was gone. Gerald was left to talk uneasily to Harold Cressett and to pray in vain that Mr Barker might be miraculously revived to give a sign.

After five minutes or so, Mr Cressett found his self-confidence, which under the spell of his own voice became considerable; he embarked upon a lengthy and very factual discourse upon the government of the British colonies. Coming from one of Mr Cressett's outdated sources, it would have been most valuable to a student of the Empire before the Statute of Westminster; for seekers after contemporary knowledge, it would have been nothing; for Gerald with his preoccupations it was irritating beyond measure. After a quarter of an hour, he managed to excuse himself and depart.

The day after his return to England, Gerald had telephoned to Elvira, but he could get no reply. He felt it his duty to inform her of her grandmother's condition and he tried again each day. At the end of a week he was answered by the charwoman, who told him that Miss Portway was away on holiday. He left a message asking her to telephone him as soon as she returned.

The morning after his fruitless visit to the Cressetts she rang him up. "I was told that you wanted to speak to me." Her voice sounded edgy and unfriendly.

"Yes," Gerald replied, "I was very anxious to let you know how I left your grandmother. She was . . ."

"I don't know how she was then," Elvira said, "but she's dead now."

Gerald said, "I see. I'm very sorry. I was afraid it might happen."

"Oh God! what a silly thing to say," Elvira's voice became deafening. "Why the hell didn't you send me a telegram?"

Gerald found it difficult to explain why he had not. In truth, he had feared getting a raspberry from Elvira after the way she had always spoken of her grandmother. "I didn't want to give you a shock," he said.

"Oh!" Elvira answered. Her voice was exaggeratedly flat now. "Well, I got one. Three telegrams from the Houdets waiting for me and a letter telling me the news in full." Gerald did not like to point out that there would apparently have been no point in any telegram he might have sent. "Naturally *they* think I've behaved like a bitch," Elvira said. There was a pause, then she added, "And so I have."

"I shouldn't take too much notice of their views," Gerald said.

"Oh! Why?" Elvira asked snappishly.

"The impressions I got . . ."

"You seem to get a lot *too many* impressions," Elvira interrupted. "*They've* had to put up with all the trouble. If you're going to tell me that they're ghastly, I'm sure they are. But

that isn't the point, is it? It's a matter of decent manners."
Gerald could think of no reply, but Elvira spoke again. "The
most ghastly thing is that she's left her money to me and
nothing to those frightful Houdets. It's a completely bloody
situation. In fact the poor old cow has bitched everything up
after her death just as she did when she was alive."

Gerald said, "Don't be too bitter about it all, Elvira, she'd
had her life. I don't think she was sorry to die."

"Thank you for your views," Elvira said. "*You* don't seem
to have helped to keep her alive. The Houdets as much as say
that your fussing her about that Melpham business brought
the stroke on."

"Good God!" Gerald cried, "What absolute nonsense!"

"It sounds like quite good sense to me. Oh! I've only myself to blame. I urged you to go and bully her over all that
ridiculous Melpham business. As if it mattered about that
damned bishop. I *would* fall for all that scholarship guff. Oh
God! the boredom of it all."

Gerald controlled his anger. "I'm sorry," he said.

"It's a habit your family have," Elvira replied. There was a
big pause. Gerald thought she was about to ring off, but
suddenly she said, "I've broken with Robin. So pat yourself
on the back. You were quite right. I couldn't stand all this
'sensible' business any longer and, of course, *I* was quite right.
And Robin's got into a mess and can't get out of it. And anyhow I accepted it and he can't put everything on to Timothy
because our love-life's gone wrong. In fact, Robin's got to stand
by his family, so *he's* quite right. Hooray for him! You see I know
the right bitter note to take. And it's all absolutely bloody!"

Gerald said, "So that's why Robin's so elusive since I came
back. Look, Elvira, I'll go and see him."

"Would you mind," Elvira cried, "not doing that? I know
it's asking an awful lot when you have all that perfectly wonderful worldly experience ready to give away for nothing, but
if you could just leave my affairs alone for a bit I would be
grateful." Gerald suddenly felt that he might cry, but he

accused himself of self-pity and prevented the tears. "I think," he said, "it might help if you tried to keep your temper." As usual, however, he had found courage to dash cold water a little too late. This time Elvira *had* rung off.

He decided that the strain of talking to people at luncheon would be less than the strain of having no one to talk to. He set out to walk to his club. July had brought one of the rare sunny days of that summer; after the heavy rains, the Park gleamed with fresh colour. He saw neither trees nor flowers. Only as he was crossing to the gates of Hyde Park Corner did he notice a bed of his favourite ragged, pink and green parrot tulips. He wondered with disgust how many more revolting flowers these horticulturists were going to cultivate; those damned things looked like that marbled linoleum second-rate people had in their bathrooms. He decided that he would send Elvira some flowers—not these sort of things, decent, conventional dark-red roses. She could throw them down the lavatory if she liked, but he would have done the conventional thing. He would go to Fortnum's for them. He was sick of meeting the sort of people he didn't usually meet in his life and hearing about the sex lives of people who had nothing to do with the sort of life he led. He hailed a taxi. All this walking about and thinking was quite unsuitable at his age.

The first person he met at Fortnum's was Marie Hélène. When Marie Hélène went out shopping, she dressed as though she was going to lunch at Fortnum's, and did, in fact, lunch there. She was wearing a bottle-green watered-silk coat and a monstrous little hat of bottle-green feathers. Against it her faced looked peculiarly yellow. If I was Robin, Gerald thought, I'd see to it that she had a dose of salts every day. It always annoyed him that she insisted on shaking hands. Good God! he thought, the woman's been in England long enough to learn not to do that.

"How pleasing to meet one's father-in-law in the morning," she said. "Pleasing" was one of the English words that she believed to be elegant. Gerald supposed that he should answer,

"Pleasant to meet my charming daughter-in-law at any time of the day," but he thought I'm damned if I will. Faced with Marie Hélène, he began almost to enjoy his mood of ill-temper. He asked, "How's Timothy?"

"Beginning to fall in love at last," she said. "Thank heaven! He's already asked me to give two theatre parties for him next holidays. Imagine, Timothy asking for a party," she curved her thin mouth and dilated her camel's nostrils in amusement. "I was really beginning to despair. Nothing but books. Not, of course, that I want him to grow up a barbarian, but there are limits even to culture." She paused for a moment and gave her father-in-law a searching look, for she suddenly remembered that someone had suggested to her that "culture" was not an elegant word. However, Gerald did not appear disturbed, so she went on, "In any case I longed for his first love affair. It's so amusing to see them in love at that age."

It was a view that Gerald could not share, so he asked, "Do I know the girl in question?"

"The Jevingtons' eldest girl?" she queried, and, when he shook his head, she told him, "Quite charming people. He's a barrister. She sculpts. Rather lovely things. Thank heaven, it's nothing disagreeable," and when he did not seem to appreciate the good fortune enough, she added, "Oh but it can be, Father. Sometimes boys of Timothy's age fall in love with the most unsuitable girls."

As she was talking, Gerald decided not to send Elvira flowers after all. It's none of my business, he thought.

Marie Hélène meanwhile had decided how pleasing it was to have so elegant, so distinguished-looking a father-in-law. I shall cultivate him, she thought, I shall take him up. As a start she decided to ask him to lunch with her on the spot. She had an idea that to give one's father-in-law lunch would be somehow amusing and she sought constantly to do things that could be classed under the heading of that elegant word "amusing". "Come and lunch with me. It's delightful here at luncheon-time."

Gerald was appalled. First Robin, now Marie Hélène. What did they think he was, a pauper? He pleaded an urgent engagement. She looked so put out that he felt he had been rude.

"Then you promise to come to my evening party on the 20th," she said. He saw no escape from acceptance. "Good," she said. "Now write it down," and she craned her long dingy neck over him until he had entered it in his engagement book. "Black tie," she said. Black fiddlesticks, he thought. "That will be quite perfect," she remarked, "because I have Armand Sarthe coming. You know him, of course."

Gerald remembered the name as something unpleasant. "By name," he said.

"But he's a most distinguished historian," she cried, "and a medievalist too. He's written about Héloïse and Agnes Sorel. I'm amazed you don't know him." Gerald recollected what he knew of Sarthe. He was one of those ghastly French writers of *biographies romancées*. He had seen copies of his books in Paris shops—*Onze grandes maîtresses* and *Les causes célèbres du moyen âge*. He was horrified.

"Oh!" said Marie Hélène, "I quite forgot my aunt Stéphanie and my cousin Yves will be here by then. They wrote so charmingly of your visit to Merano. You quite won my poor aunt's heart—'*un homme bien distingué*' she wrote. And Yves, too, said you had so much in common with him. How unfortunate that you had that disagreeable business while you were there. I really can't feel sorry that that old woman has died. You know that she left nothing at all to my poor aunt after all these years."

Gerald made no reply.

Marie Hélène gave him a sharp, mischievous look. "At last Robin has stopped seeing Elvira Portway. I am so glad, because it was making him so unhappy." When once again Gerald made no comment, she said, "You were quite naughty, Father, to encourage it. But I forgive you." She gave him a little *mondain* smile, shook hands once more and went upstairs to the restaurant.

Gerald took a taxi back to Montpelier Square and demanded luncheon from a surprised and rather annoyed Mrs
Larwood.

A few weeks later as Robin was leaving the Works after a
flying visit from the London office, he met Donald, neatly
dressed in a blue pin-striped flannel suit and carrying a brief
case. "You'll never forgive me this time, Donald," he said.
"Here I am, actually down at the Works on the day of your
lecture and I'm not staying for it. I really had intended to, but
something's turned up at the last moment which means that
I must go back to town."

A fish seemed to flash momentarily behind Donald's glasses;
it was the nearest he ever got to a smile. "Perhaps we may hope
that you will put in an appearance at the last lecture," he said.
It might have been a reference to the gracious presence of
royalty or a don addressing an absentee undergraduate. In
either case, Robin suspected sarcasm, but Donald's face
showed no trace of hostility.

"I hope I shall see you and Kay at Marie Hélène's 'do'
tomorrow night," Robin said. "She's insisted on inviting
brother John, but I hope to have a bit of news to take the
wind out of his sails over the Pelican business."

Donald's thin lips expressed satisfaction. "I doubly look
forward to the occasion now," he remarked, and hurried
fussily into the Works entrance.

Robin, as usual, took the wheel, his chauffeur beside him.
Time enough to be driven about when he ceased to be the
youngest director. He wished that Donald wasn't quite so
prim. Of course, it was his background. No one respected these
lower middle-class chaps who won all the scholarships more
than Robin did, but inevitably it took them a long time to
shake off their background. Donald was bound to be a bit
genteel for all his cleverness. All the same, Robin reflected,
he'd taken that bit of advice he'd given him very well; he
seemed to bear no resentment. He dismissed Donald from his

mind with the comforting thought that there was another human being who had responded to the right sort of treatment.

He turned his thoughts to Pelican. It looked pretty certain now that the poor fellow was going to take the rap, but he'd pretty near brought his fellow directors round to accepting the idea of offering that executive post, with a few shares to give the chap a bit of incentive. John would be sure to crow over his disgraceful victory at the party; and then, Robin thought, he'd be able to announce Pelican's new appointment. Not that John would care so much, but it would be a moral triumph. With this sense of moral glow upon him, Robin turned and asked the chauffeur after his wife, but he did not hear the answer because he suddenly remembered Elvira. Robin was always suddenly remembering the fact that he had lost her, suffering a sense of void and defeat; nevertheless, though he hardly cared to admit it to himself, he felt a strange, new sense of ease in no longer having a divided life. The last few weeks of the *affaire*, with their accompaniment of scenes and tears, had proved very disagreeable. He had no talent for *Sturm und Drang*. Not, he reflected, that his passion had been less than other men's; he had suffered and was suffering deeply, but he supposed he was a bit of a fatalist, or, without boasting, a little more adult in his adaptation to life. Timothy would never know how much he owed in stability to his father's basically integrated character. Once again he glowed and asked the somewhat surprised chauffeur after his wife.

The Middleton Hall in which Donald gave his lectures was a large Lutyens Georgian building presented to the firm by the family in memory of Gerald's father. It served for all forms of communal entertainment. A bust of Gerald's mother stood on the platform by the side of an old grand piano. On the walls hung photographs of works dances and works football and cricket teams. At the far end of the room there was a large portrait of Gerald's father in rather bad modern Academy style.

Donald's audience was not so large as it had been for the first lectures, but even now there was a fair number—those who, in the manner of Cressett, thirsted for knowledge of any kind whatsoever; those who thought that their presence at the lectures of Robin's brother-in-law would be noticed and earn them promotion; and those who had hoped that they might trap Donald into some mistake and earn a reputation for standing no nonsense from the powers that be. There were still a few of the managerial staff and of the trade union officials who attended from a mixture of all three motives.

Donald's theme this evening was Industry and Ethics. He spoke first in praise of the medieval world in which industry and commerce, like all other human activities, found their place in an ordered scheme. He mentioned the ban on usury, and the fair wage. With gathering sarcasm he described the greater freedom, the more individual ethic that had come with the Reformation. He mentioned the blessings of exploitation, child labour, slum dwellings and so on that had accompanied the free expansion first of commerce and then of industry—the substitution of man as an economic unit for man as an immortal soul. It was clear, competently told and unashamedly partisan. His irony, however, grew deeper as he went on to speak of the liberal and socialistic ethics by which competitive man had attempted to palliate the results of his destruction of the Christian order. His greatest scorn was reserved for the sentimentalism of welfare ethics.

The smiles on the faces of those who hoped for some mischief from these lectures grew broad. One director pointedly walked out and a shop steward began to talk audibly to his neighbour. Donald paused and blinked at them through his glasses.

"I am not normally in the habit of indulging in homely stories. Nevertheless we have the best authority, that of scripture, for using the simple anecdotal illustration. So I will this evening tell you of a little incident with this very firm which demonstrates most neatly the points I have been trying to make. Christmas," he said, and he gave an ironic smile, "has tended as you know to change in this country from a feast of deep spiritual significance to a sentimental occasion vaguely suggestive of family good will. My own family is no exception to this prevalent spirit. Last Christmas my brother-in-law, Mr Robin Middleton, your director, had an argument with my other brother-in-law, Mr John Middleton, whom you probably all know well, if only for his remarkable performances on the radio and on television. Now it so happens that the points of view taken up by these two men, both so eminent in their respective fields, coincide very exactly with the two main social philosophies which I have been describing to you. Mr Robin Middleton is the very able defender of the business ethic of free enterprise and open competition. Mr John Middleton is the no less expert standard-bearer of the liberal or radical attempt to palliate or remove the less attractive features of that individualist social order. Your director instanced, as an example of the necessary workings of modern industry, the means which a large firm—Middleton and Company—had been forced to use in order to put out of business an old-fashioned small manufacturer whose obstinacy and inefficiency were holding up the supply of goods. This man—Grimston I think his name was," he looked up as though in faint surprise at the whispering which had begun in the audience, and continued, "this Grimston was flooded with orders for various parts which Middletons knew he could not provide in the time allotted to him. In consequence he was forced into liquidation. When your director told us this story, Mr John Middleton immediately attacked the unethical, as he called it, nature of such behaviour"—Donald smiled to himself as he thought that this part of his reporting of the conversation was not entirely fair to John. It represented more what a radical reformer should have felt than what John actually did feel—"He suggested various social remedies by which such unpleasant actions could be avoided. Mr Robin Middleton liked what he had been forced to do no more than his brother, but he correctly pointed out that it was necessary. If Mr Grimston's old-fashioned obstinacy had been allowed to persist, far more harmful results would have followed. Orders would have been lost, men thrown out of work, England's industrial prosperity weakened for the sake of one man. He argued from the head, Mr John Middleton from the heart. But the point that I wish to make, of course, is that the whole of this controversy could only arise in a system which has no moral foundation. . . ." He led the lecture back to its general theme, but he noted with satisfaction that his audience's attention was still riveted upon the homely little illustration he had used.

The story of the Grimston deal travelled rapidly through all grades of Middleton and Company, so that when Robin went to the office next morning he was greeted by very irate co-directors. He sent at once for Donald, but was told that he had not come to the office that morning—he had booked a day's leave some weeks ago. Telephone calls to Donald's home received no reply.

As an immediate result of the little indiscretion, the proposal to employ Mr Pelican was turned down by a large majority vote at the board meeting. It was therefore in no pleasant mood that Robin returned home for Marie Hélène's evening party. He almost thought of telling his wife that he would not be present, but with the collapse of everything else, his relations with her were becoming of paramount importance to him. Anyway, he reflected, he was never expected to play a large part on these occasions, simply to see that the domestic wheels went round without any grinding while Marie Hélène did the talking and entertaining. This time, he decided, the Houdets could take on his job; they'd been at the house now for a fortnight and showed no signs of departing; they could at least do something useful for their keep.

It was hardly a fair judgment of poor Madame Houdet. From the very first she had set herself the task of becoming indispensable to Marie Hélène's housekeeping. The household, it was true, was already run with true French economy, but even so Tante Stéphanie had a great deal of pleasure in discovering odd extravagances or minor acts of waste. In this way, she had soon quarrelled with Marie Hélène's servants, but as they were all either Italian or German, they did not give notice but preferred to skirmish out their days. For Madame Houdet it was simply her old life on a larger scale, and the Hampstead house rang with her bad Italian and worse German as had the villa at Merano. She soon found a Catholic church and a priest or two into whose housekeeping she could pry. Her veil, her smart black and her make-up became as familiar on the slopes of the Heath as they had on the picturesque Tyrolese walks of Merano. At first she deplored the lack of objects of charity in welfare England, but at the end of a fortnight she met a slightly dotty colonel's wife in the Vale of Health and from her she heard something of the difficulties of the retired and the old. After that, she was entirely content, and retailed to the household in the evening stories of ex-officers unable to leave their rooms for lack of shoes and ex-headmistresses shivering in coalless bed-sitting-rooms. It was not the sort of talk which either Robin or Marie Hélène cared to hear, but with a good deal of courage she made them listen and even on occasion part with money for her objects of charity.

For Marie Hélène, *chère* Tante Stéphanie came as a godsend. She was too frugal by nature to relinquish domestic economy entirely, but for some time she had been finding that housekeeping interfered sadly with her new rôle as a hostess of culture and elegance. Now she could hand over the keys and know that, if anything, more cupboards than ever would be kept locked from the servants.

Mother and son had both arrived with the fixed determination of not leaving unless and until either of the two women—Marie Hélène or Elvira—who had profited so greatly at their expense, should have paid handsomely to secure their departure. Indeed, the Houdets were hardly in the position to leave, for they had realized most of Stéphanie's little capital and all of Yves' Lagonda to equip themselves suitably for the visit. Madame Houdet had found her niche; Yves' rôle was a more difficult one. He had determined in advance that there were various possibilities open to him: he would become Marie Hélène's well-paid lover, he would acquire a rewarding sinecure in Robin's firm, he would turn Elvira's sense of guilt into good hard cash or, perhaps, if all then failed, he would become Elvira's well-paid husband. As it seemed likely that all these offers would be made to him, it was only a question of seeing that they were accompanied with the maximum monetary reward.

By the eve of Marie Hélène's party, he had been in London for three weeks and he had received no more than his board, two cheques for ten pounds from Robin, one for fifty pounds from Elvira, and three ties from Marie Hélène with the suggestion that they were more suitable for England than the ones he at present sported. If for a moment his vanity had been hurt, he soon found reasons for the delay of his schemes. Marie Hélène, in a moment of cosiness bred of admiration for her aunt's economies over the maids' food, had confided the story of Robin's *affaire* with Elvira. Yves then attributed Elvira's failure to make due restitution of her grandmother's money to her hatred of Marie Hélène. He saw in Robin's neglect of his business abilities the jealousy of a failed lover and husband. The slowness of the women's response to his advances he attributed more generally to the hypocritical climate of the country. He looked to time and continued effort to repair all the omissions. To these schemes he added possible money-making projects connected with spying on Robin and reporting to either his wife or his ex-mistress; and certain pressures that he might apply to Gerald, whose disturbed manner at Merano gave promise of some rewarding secret. Meanwhile he invested his seventy pounds in taking out an elderly, rather tarty stockbroker's widow from Bromley. He had met her on the boat and her conversation suggested that, although she would need playing slowly, she would prove, once landed, to be as comfortable in *rentes* as she was in figure.

Both mother and son regarded the coming *soirée* with awe; but while Tante Stéphanie, splendid in black satin and appliqué jet, with one of Mrs Portway's lilac chiffon scarves to cover her *décolletage*, proposed herself a retiring rôle in seeing that none of the food was eaten by the servants, Yves, superb in midnight-blue *smoking*, a legacy of his Italian widow, saw every opportunity to shine.

He addressed himself aggressively to Robin as they awaited the arrival of the first guests. He was one business tycoon to another. It was not at all what Robin cared for in Marie Hélène's lovely gold and white Regency drawing-room, where the arts were intended to exercise a rather genteel, flattened out, *convenable* supremacy.

"What's your wastage, Middleton?" Yves asked, and before Robin could inquire the meaning of this somewhat cryptic question, he followed it up with a machine-gun fire of searching business questions intended to flatten Robin out, lay him stone dead with their ruthless drive, their dead-hit punch, their incredible grasp of detail. "What do your absentee figures show?" he asked. "What's your pension load? Have you got a record of your pay-out in widows' benefits? Where's your man-hours production graph taking you? What's your loss in toilet time?" These and many other questions which had once so depressed him from an American colleague in the air force he now worked off on Robin and, without waiting for a reply, he cried, "Good God! man, a guy's *got* to ask himself these questions. You need an efficiency expert to give your place the works." And when Robin looked dejected, he patted him on the elbow. "That's all right," he said, "your worries are over. From today you're going to be lucky. I'm going to save Middletons thousands."

Marie Hélène, tightly swathed in crimson velvet, her bosom deadly yellow as a Japanese corpse's beneath the fires of her opal necklace, held up her hand in horror. "No business talk, Yves, please," she cried. "You will ruin my *soirée*." And in hard flat tones, she said, "Do you think that Anouilh is *passé*? I find a terrible lack of *esprit* in his last play. I'm afraid he has quite lost his elegance." She gave it to him as a copy-book model for the evening.

Yves looked her over. "*Mais tu es ravissante, ma chère cousine*," he said, "*absolument ravissante*." He took her hand and, raising her arm, he planted small kisses all the way up its scrawny, yellowish inner side. Marie Hélène had only just time to snatch her arm away before the first guests were announced.

Thick and fast they came, filling the Hampstead double drawing-room, covering the gold-and-white couches, sitting bolt upright on the little Empire chairs, staring over each other's shoulders into the gilt mirrors, leaning on the two un-used harpsichords and the hardly used grand piano, threatening the bad Sèvres with their elbows, swallowing quantities of champagne, gobbling up lobster patties and *vol-au-vents* from Fortnums, debouching in elegant pairs into the little garden with its walnut tree and its iris pool.

The more cultured of Robin's business friends were im-pressed by the representatives of British Council and Arts Council and Institut Français and a hundred other councils and institutes; all these bureaucrats of modern culture were equally impressed by the business friends; and everybody was im-pressed by the odd French or English poet or sculptor or violinist. Dotted among them here and there were B.B.C. officials—programme-planners, features-producers, poetry readers—and an odd publisher or two; these had a profes-sional appearance of not being very impressed. Only perhaps Mrs Jevington, at once wife of a wealthy barrister and an "interesting" sculptress in her own right, floated about in a haze of impressing and being impressed until she was silly with conflicting emotions. But impressed or impressing, every-body was superbly flat and dead; even when they had drunk a great deal of champagne and had begun to cut the air with that peculiar harsh sound of cultural voices—English, French, competent English-French and grotesquely incompetent French-English—raised in conversational competition, they never betrayed themselves into saying anything that could possibly mar the tedious triviality with which they clothed

serious subjects or the deadly heaviness with which they discussed the trivial. Marie Hélène's bony shoulders quivered
with the success of it all.

Gerald, on arrival, edged towards the french windows to
get some air, but Madame Houdet, seeing him alone, thought,
Ah! the poor man, he is old and knows no one, and, as there
was a lull for a moment in her surveillance of the servants, she
came over to him. "Ah! you are sad, Mr Middleton," she said,
"you are thinking of your dear Lilian." Whereas Yves had
attached the most dubious motives to Gerald's visit to Merano,
his mother has ascribed it to the flickering embers of an old
romance.

Gerald started. He had been watching young Caroline
Jevington talking to Timothy and admiring his grandson's
taste. A little unripe yet, he was thinking, but she would
develop; already she showed none of that ugly, flat-breasted
boyish nonsense that spoiled too many of these girls. Oh Lord!
he thought, as Madame Houdet talked, what a dirty old man
I'm getting to be, but, looking at the dead-pan faces of Marie
Hélène's guests, he added, and thank God for it!

"Poor Lilian! she found it hard to die. *Mon dieu! comme elle
a lutté!* She loved the world so much. She would not give up
fighting for life. No never! You and I, we are different, Mr
Middleton, we are willing to be old, we are ready to go."

Gerald thought, I'll be blowed if I am, you speak for yourself old Madame Sanctimonious.

"But I was so fond of her. Oh! I will not pretend that she
was not very difficult and hard. Oh! so hard! It is terrible
when suffering make us hard. *Et elle a souffert, la pauvre!* But we
were old, and although she talks and I do not listen, I do not
like her to die."

Gerald looked at the ravaged, old rouge-flecked face and
thought, Good God! the poor old thing's genuine. He said,
"I'm sure it must have been a terrible shock for you. I could
see how much the villa meant to you even in the short time I
was there."

It was not the most tactful choice of words. Beads of caked lipstick trembled on Stéphanie's lips in her agitation. "Oh, I do not mind, believe me, that Lilian left me nothing. I am old and, after all, a granddaughter is a granddaughter, however little she did for Lilian. But, for Yves, I mind—yes, very much. It was not so nice for a young attractive man to spend his time with an old woman. But he was always willing to stay and give the pleasure of his young company to Lilian. She knew that life had not been kind to my boy. She should have left him something."

Yves' visits, however painful at the time, had been a source of such pleasurable anticipation and remembrance to Madame Houdet that she truly had come to think that Lilian had been ungrateful for all the pleasure he had given them. Gerald, catching sight of Yves leaning over some woman guest with fatuously self-satisfied gallantry, could hardly believe any longer in Madame Houdet's sincerity. Nevertheless, he made no comment. Despite the vexatious failures of his Melpham quest, despite John and Inge and Robin and Elvira, he felt somehow so light-hearted that evening that he could not bring himself to criticize. His recent adventures into life after his long seclusion had revealed such complicated webs of muddled human activity—the Barkers, Rammage, Mrs Salad, this old woman. And all I feel is, he realized, let them get on with it. I can't praise or blame. It's because I've done my best, he said to himself, and then laughed at the awful priggish words. No, it's not that, but I've had a chance to look at it all a bit from the outside and I'm simply not going back into my own tortured web. I feel free.

He said, "I say, you've got no champagne," to Madame Houdet. The words and the accompanying smile came from the behaviour of his youth.

Stéphanie was shut tight within her own web. She did not hear his words. "Lilian thought too little of others altogether. She saw so little of the poor people who had not got lovely villas. She thought only I am no longer young and beautiful, she did not realize that there were many poor girls—yes, in Merano, at her own door—who have never been beautiful, who were poor and crippled. And it is the same here, Mr Middleton," she said. "Only today I have heard of a Miss Rowton-Riversby,"—the rolling of r's invested the name with a terrible ferocity—"*Ah! cette pauvre dame! Quand je vous raconte quelle est sœur d'un général, et maintenant...*"

Gerald said at the end of her story, "Yes, that's certainly jolly sad," and, before he knew where he was, he had given her a cheque for the dispensing of charity. It was an ostentatious gesture connected with his wealth that would normally have horrified him.

Attracted, perhaps, by the sight of the cheque-book, Yves walked over to him. "Pretty big people here tonight," he said.

Gerald looked round the crowded room. "Yes. That woman's enormous," he said.

Yves was only momentarily disconcerted. "I'd like a word with you, Middleton." His tone was strangely sinister.

Gerald smiled. "If you can make yourself heard above the din, the future is yours."

Yves slowly lit a cigarette, and then, puffing a cloud of smoke into Gerald's face in a carefully insolent manner, "Rather a strange meeting that of yours with Mrs Portway, wasn't it?"

Gerald looked at the stupid conceited face, the flashing dark eyes and beautiful white teeth. Through his carefreeness he remembered that he had intended to be very angry with Yves. "Oh! yes. Look here!" he said, "you've been making a fool of yourself. What's all this nonsense you've been telling Miss Portway about my causing her grandmother's death?" He found it impossible to sound really annoyed.

Yves smiled cynically. "Is it nonsense? I'm not so sure. There was something pretty strange going on between you and the old lady. Something it seems to me you wouldn't like the world to know." He paused and smiled again. "And there is no reason why it should know. Only I shall want persuading that it would be better that way."

He stopped, for Gerald appeared not to have heard him, so he took out his wallet and produced a sheet of notepaper. "Perhaps you don't know that I have this," he said, and handed it to Gerald. "It was lying on Mrs Portway's desk."

"My dear friend," Gerald read the shaky handwriting, "What you and I discussed this afternoon is a terrible thing. And perhaps more terrible still is the fact that we have both kept silent all these years, for I fear that we have both guessed that something was wrong and we have acted very wickedly. . . ."

Gerald handed the paper back to Yves. "You seem to be the prize ass of all time," he said, using unconsciously the language of the past, of Dollie and Gilbert. He walked away.

As he took a glass of champagne from one of the hired waiters, he saw with horror that Marie Hélène was leading a tall, grey-haired Frenchman towards him. It was as he feared, the distinguished author of *Les causes célèbres du moyen âge*, Armand Sarthe. Oh, well, he thought, the chap must be a cynical journalist who's written the stuff for money; he may well be quite a pleasant fellow in real life. But when Marie Hélène moved away in grave deference to the esoteric bonds of scholarship that united them, M. Sarthe's first words were not promising.

"Woman," he said, and he waved his hand towards Marie Hélène's sharp shoulder-blades protruding uglily above the flowing folds of her crimson gown, "defies the historian's art. We can catch her differences, the change in her art. We can catch for a moment the turn of Aspasia's head as she delights Pericles with her wit. We can bring to life again the harsh note in Xanthippe's scolding voice. We can turn with horror from the cruelty in Messalina's eyes or with shame for ourselves from the innocent love with which Héloïse looks at her lover. We can stand with the Maid as she scorns her judges. But the essential woman—the woman that was there in the caves at Lascaux and is here in this room today—eludes us. Do you agree?"

Gerald had some difficulty in following the rapid French, so he contented himself by saying "Yes."

"And you," M. Sarthe went on, "the medievalist, have the greatest mystery of all to explain—the world of Sacred and Profane love, the world of Beatrice and Laura, the age that could produce both Isobel of Bavaria and Catherine of Siena. . . ."

It seemed to Gerald that M. Sarthe would never make an end, he had hardly realized that so many Famous Women had passed through History's pages.

"And what strange thing happened," M. Sarthe asked, "to bring the Montespan to those sordid rooms, to take part in those revolting rites?"

Gerald gave no answer, for his ear had caught the sound of Kay's voice. "Yes," she was saying, "I thought the success of Donald's last lecture gave us the right to a day off. So we simply parked Baby with the people next door and had a day at Brighton." Marie Hélène made a sort of shocked sound, though whether at the irresponsibility of parking babies or the choice of Brighton for a day's outing was not clear. Kay took it as the latter, for she said, "Oh! but Brighton's so beautiful. Especially in midsummer with all the crowds." She had all the intellectual's reverence for that town.

Marie Hélène turned to Donald. "I'm glad that your speech was so successful. You've quite found your *métier*."

Kay laughed a little annoyed explosion. "Oh! hardly that, the poor darling. He doesn't want to be chained to industry all his life. But it's all rather fun."

"Don't make me appear too irresponsible, dear."

Gerald could just imagine the little prim deprecating smile with which Donald would accompany this remark.

"She had played so often at being a shepherdess at the Trianon," M. Sarthe was saying, "now she was called upon to play a rôle before a world audience."

Gerald heard no more, for John's voice sounded in his ear, boyish and triumphant. "We've won," he was telling the little family group. "The report's found against Pelican, and the

Minister's told the House that he's to be sent to a branch office at Bangor."

"Ovid among the Scythians," said Donald.

Marie Hélène must have seen Robin approaching, for Gerald could hear her voice desperately trying to break up the family knot before he arrived to hear John's bitter news. "Now, Kay, I want you to meet Bill Stillingfleet, the painter," she was saying, but it was too late. Robin was greeting his sister with warmth. He spoke no greeting to the males of his family, but Gerald imagined his curt nods.

Robin, in fact, had not looked at Donald at all. He had made up his mind that he would not mention the subject of the lecture at Marie Hélène's party. Even if someone else raised it, he would pass it off as easily as he could. Business was business, and nothing to do with his home. He had treated Marie Hélène badly enough already without intruding his impossible family further upon her.

Passing from group to group at the party, Robin had felt the respect for his wife, which had been surging up since his break with Elvira, burst in one huge wave of reverence. He owed all this genuine culture and elegance, he thought, to his wife—and he had considered leaving her for the neurotic, raffish, "clever" bohemianism of Elvira! He could never make amends. Seeing Donald in the distance, he had thought, you'll get the push tomorrow, my lad, but you'll not have the satisfaction of spoiling my wife's party. So now, when Kay said, "Isn't it nice that Donald's won the heart of all your workers?" he simply replied, "Very."

"Well, Robin," John announced, "your Mr Pelican's got to brush up his Mabinogion." And when Robin said nothing, he went on, "He's been severely censured by the Commission and the Minister's transferred him to the Bangor branch."

Robin's stomach turned. He thought of Mrs Pelican and her wish for the boys to remain at St Paul's. Poor old Pelican! he thought, and his cheeks blushed scarlet as he remembered the promises he could never fulfil.

"If I remember rightly," said Donald primly, "they shot an admiral named Byng *pour encourager les autres*. I doubt if it had that effect." He smiled at John through his spectacles. "But I believe Robin has schemes to save Mr Pelican from the firing-squad on the quarter-deck. When are we to hear of the brilliant administrator's adherence to the firm of Middleton, Robin?" he asked.

Robin's head swam. He plunged headlong. "Never," he said with violence, "thanks to your crass tomfoolery."

Donald started; he had expected an attack, but not at that moment.

Kay asked, "What ever do you mean?"

"Only this," Robin said. "Your bloody fool of a husband has undone all my work over the last two years. He's alienated the shop stewards, upset the directors, and effectually prevented my offering a job to Pelican." He was shouting now. Gerald came over.

"A little quieter, my dear boy," he said. "Whatever it is, we don't want all the guests involved. What's Donald been up to?"

Robin mumbled now. He would have given anything to be a small boy once more who, by saying "Take back what I said" or "As you were," could erase a whole conversation. "Parading my confidences made to the family before the whole factory!"

"My dear boy, what dark family secrets could possibly interest the employees of Middleton's?" Gerald tried to give the quarrel a lighter tone without annoying Robin by face-tiousness.

Robin noticed nothing of this. "I *told* John about the Grimston liquidation in confidence."

Gerald raised his eyebrows, he had not cared for that story at the time. "You choose your dirty linen with care," he said to Donald, and tried once more by his smile to relieve the tension.

Kay turned on him. "I really don't see that it has anything to do with you, Father," she said. But John intervened. In view of his Pelican victory he felt the need to be magnanimous to Robin; also he prided himself as a public commentator on never using confidential material.

"That's all very well, Kay," he said, "but Robin made it perfectly clear that he was speaking in confidence. Heaven knows Thingy's Christmas occasions are ghastly enough without feeling that what one says may be taken down and used against one."

Gerald looked at his younger son with surprise when he heard the bitterness with which he spoke Inge's name.

Kay's face showed alarm at this family unity against her husband. "I'm sure Donald didn't realize the importance of it," she said.

"I'm not in the habit," her husband said, "of making public utterances without weighing their consequences. I chose my material very carefully; if it doesn't put Robin in the benevolent light in which he normally likes to dispense his patronage, that is unfortunate. Egotism tempered with benevolence is likely to break down as an ethic of conduct; and when it does, it's liable to appear as hypocrisy, as the Victorian exponents of so-called individual morality found to their cost."

"Look here! this is awful balls," said John. Despite all his enmity to Robin, he had always stood up for him if some other boy at school attacked him.

"What I can't forgive," said Robin, "is that you committed this indiscretion quite deliberately."

"How strange!" Donald replied. "I should have thought it far more unforgivable if I had blundered into it." He moved close to Robin and when he spoke his voice came through his thin lips almost as a hiss. "I fail to see why you should have expected that your arrogance, rudeness and complete lack of consideration towards me should have gone unanswered."

Robin was amazed, he simply could not conceive anyone acting with such deliberation. "But you never showed . . ." he began.

"I am not given to the emotional exhibitionism of your family," Donald said. "When I act, I act after full consideration."

"I hope you took into consideration the fact that your services will no longer be required by the firm."

"Don't let's rush too far, Robin," Gerald said, but his son brushed his words aside. "No, Father. I've considered carefully, too. I had every intention of sacking the swine tomorrow. It's only the occasion I regret."

"There's no need, I think," Donald said in his most governessy voice, "for abuse. On my side, I assure you, I'm only too glad to bring to an end a very absurd piece of patronage which, but for Kay's feelings for her mother, I would never have considered accepting. I wish I could bring the whole family connection to an end as easily."

"That's not very kind, Donald," said Gerald.

"Oh, I have no quarrel with you, Professor Middleton." The remark seemed to reduce Gerald's family status to that of an honoured old servant.

"It's very unkind to Kay was what I meant," Gerald replied rather grimly.

"I can look after myself, thank you," Kay cried. "Come on, Donald, we'd better go." As they walked away self-consciously, Kay turned a crimson face on her family. "I think you've all behaved abominably," she said. Nevertheless, as she went out of the door, Gerald could hear her saying to Donald, "Why did you have to do anything so childish? It's unforgivable."

Yves was now talking to a cultured stockbroker's wife. "Did I know Colette?" he was saying. "I certainly did. What a grand old lady and what a great writer! Mind you, she had some very funny ways. She certainly embarrassed me once or twice. Not that I'd have minded. When a lady's a great artist like that, I'm always willing to oblige, no matter if she's a hundred. I just didn't want her to get hurt, that's all. Love can be pretty painful when you're old."

Madame Houdet, flushed with a few glasses of champagne, had lost much of her shyness of the English. She talked on rapidly to a B.B.C. lady producer, who was under the impression that she was an "important" French guest.

"And all along one side of the leg there are," Stéphanie paused, "how do you say? ulcers. Big ulcers. Red!" She rolled the words out in the astonished lady's face. "And he is so young, this boy, only fourteen years. *Ah! comme il a souffert, le pauvre petit!* But never a cry. And he has his reward. *C'était Notre Dame de Lourdes qui l'a guéri.*" As the lady producer said afterwards, there was no doubt that the influence of Claudel in France at the moment was colossal.

Marie Hélène sat rather stiffly on one of the striped couches and talked. "Do you think that Anouilh is *passé*?" she asked. "I think he has lost his elegance. I find a terrible lack of *esprit* in his last play."

Timothy was having a very familiar argument with Caroline Jevington. "My mother's quite as embarrassing as yours," he said.

"Nonsense," said Caroline, "you just listen to Mummy now."

Mrs Jevington, large and blonde but dead and elegant—the English version of Marie Hélène—was holding forth from another sofa. "Well, I think anyone who's experienced the creative process . . ." she said.

Timothy turned to Caroline. "Yes, you're right," he said.

Gerald, overhearing this, smiled. They're both quite right, he thought. Nevertheless, he decided to say nothing. To be confidential with the very young would be unbecoming in a man of his age. He decided to go home. As he collected his hat, he whistled "A Room with a View". It was a tune he and Dollie had often danced to.

Coming out into the moonlight to find Larwood and the car, he suddenly saw Elvira standing there by the front steps. Her dark hair was more tousled than ever and she was staring through puffy eyelids. She's been crying or drinking, or both, he thought. When she saw him she deliberately looked the other way. He was about to go on with the thought that other people's business was not his; but he rebuked himself for his selfishness. She was clearly unhappy to a mood of desperation; Robin had suffered enough for his pomposity for one evening. If I'm as frightened of the security of my own happiness as this, he decided, it isn't likely to be very durable. He must not allow his new-found acceptance of life to degenerate into a patronizing, passive compassion. However much I involve myself, I'm quite free from them, he reassured himself.

Going over to Elvira, he was about to speak, when she turned on him a set, hysterical face. "Oh, good evening," she said, "were you just leaving?"

"Yes," Gerald replied, "can I give you a lift anywhere?"

"Thank you," Elvira replied, "but there's no need. I'm quite under control, you know. I don't need your old-world gallantry. I haven't come to break up the party or anything. I want to see Yves Houdet. I've decided to make them some restitution for all they did for dear Lilian. Silly of me, isn't it?"

"No," said Gerald, "I think it's very kind of you."

"Oh, do you? How funny. I think it's very stupid. It's a kind of superstition really. If I give them the money, Robin'll come back to me. Freud, you know. Only I think we've discussed all that."

"Why not let's discuss Freud again?" Gerald asked. "Let's have supper over it. Houdet's very much involved in this party. You can see him tomorrow."

Elvira laughed hysterically, "Do you mind if I say no?" she cried. "I mean to any more suppers with you. I can't really think they've helped much." She turned her head away and began to cry. "Oh God! This is so bloody. It won't leave me alone. I'm so unhappy."

Gerald took her arm, but she shook him off savagely. "Do you mind not being such a bore?" she said, "because it would help if you went away."

He turned to go and she ran up the steps into the hall. He turned and followed her. "At least let me bring Houdet out here to you," he said.

She sank down on a bench among some late-comers' hats and cloaks. "Perhaps it *would* be better" she said, and began to repair the ravages of weeping with make-up.

Yves was rather drunk by now. He greeted Elvira with a passionate kiss on the lips. To Gerald's horror, he then took her arm. "Come along in, Miss Portway. There's plenty of big people here. People you ought to know." When Elvira drew back, he cried, "What the hell? You and Robin have quarrelled. So what? There's nothing like a party to make up quarrels."

"I suppose not," Elvira replied, laughing hysterically, and she allowed herself to be led in. At the door of the drawing-room, she turned towards Gerald. "Oh God!" she cried, "what absolute hell it all is!" Gerald felt compelled to follow her.

As Elvira came into the room, Timothy said to Caroline Jevington, "That's her."

"Who?"

"That Elvira Portway person."

"Oh!" cried Caroline, "I don't think I've ever seen anyone's mistress before. She's rather old. She must be about thirty. And rather fat too. I can't see why your father should want to have her."

Yves led Elvira over to Robin. "Here's a little girl come to say she's sorry," he said. Robin went white with horror.

"I hear you've got all the big people here," Elvira cried. "Do let me see them. Where are they?" Then, looking round, "But these aren't big people at all, Yves. These are frightfully, frightfully unimportant people. Darling Marie Hélène, she always manages to get the really unimportant people. It's her great social gift. They're what are called stuffed shirts, Yves. You'll understand that. You speak American so perfectly."

"Sure I understand it," Yves said, but he moved away as he saw what he had brought about.

Robin turned on Gerald angrily. "What the hell do you mean by bringing her here?"

"I didn't," said Gerald.

"Oh! the absolute bliss of old-world chivalry," Elvira cried bitterly, then seeing Marie Hélène, she waved her hand and called out, "Hullo, Marie Hélène, I see you've got all the gang here." She turned to Gerald and said, "It's rather enchanting to think of them as the gang, isn't it?" she asked.

Marie Hélène's yellow face was flushed with pink as she came over to them. "I don't think you should be here, Elvira," she said. "Please ask her to leave, Robin."

"Oh, Robin darling, do," Elvira cried. "It would be such absolute heaven for me to be able to say no. Hullo, Johnnie!" she called. "Are you here talent-scouting? I didn't know you interviewed corpses in your little shows."

"How delightful to see you, Elvira," John said, all tact that evening. "And how unexpected."

"Yes, isn't it? Because Robin and I aren't lovers any more? We're washed up, as they say on the movies. But I just miss hearing him talk about his dear family so much, I had to come and see them." She burst into tears, but resisted all attempts to lead her out.

Suddenly Timothy came over. He bent his lanky height down upon her. "Let me take you home, Miss Portway," he said. Whether it was that she shared in the general astonishment or not, she did in fact let him take her all the way to the door of her flat. She cried all the way. Timothy's worldly sang-froid won him Caroline Jevington's deepest admiration.

The B.B.C. lady was transfixed by Madame Houdet as by a gorgon. Stéphanie spoke in French now. "*Ah! mon dieu! Comme il était courageux, le pauvre homme! Mais, quand même, qu'est ce qu'il pouvait faire avec ses deux jambes paralysées et sa sœur qui était phtisique? Le bon dieu seul...*"

"Sure I know André Gide," Yves said to a wealthy stock-broker. "He was a great artist and a great man. Of course, he had his funny little ways. Well, you know. But it was pretty embarrassing for me sometimes. I didn't happen to have been born that way. All the same I wouldn't have refused him—I'm always ready to oblige a great artist—but I didn't want him to be hurt, that's all."

Gerald was once more making his way out when M. Sarthe buttonholed him. "Now," he said, "here's an Englishman who can tell us what was in the old queen's mind as she lay there dying on her cushions. I will tell you," he went on, "she was not thinking of the young Essex. No! no!" he shook his finger in Gerald's face—"Her heart was with Leicester, the only man she ever really loved."

There seemed no possibility of getting away from M. Sarthe's obsession with women in history. Gerald stood there, trying to make his mind a blank, but fragments of the discourse insisted on breaking through. "Ah, those little beauty-spots with which our grandmothers sought to enchant, how poorly they imitated nature. Moles! There you have something really piquant. What a charming little book it would make—the moles of famous women. The little star-shaped mole on the *belle cuisse* of Diane de Poitiers, the mole like a little black pearl on the *gorge superbe* of Olympe Mancini, the strange heart-shaped mole of la Dubarry, known only to her most intimate lovers. . . ."

Gerald's sensual nature was repelled by this arch treatment of women's bodies. "And don't forget the mole on Oliver Cromwell's nose," he murmured.

"Excuse me," said M. Sarthe. But Gerald's attention had been drawn to the door.

He heard a familiar voice coming from the hall. "I must see him, I tell you. I must see him. Will you say it's his friend Larrie Rourke?" The voice was a plaintive whine. Larrie, like Elvira, was in tears.

Oh my God! thought Gerald. Well, this *is* nothing to do with me. He then remembered Vin's admonitions. "Damn," he said in M. Sarthe's face and walked out into the hall.

Larrie was sitting among the hats and cloaks. His great eyes looked appealingly out of a thin, white little face, locks of his curly hair were plastered to his forehead with sweat. "Oh, Professor Middleton," he cried, "do you know where Johnnie is? I must see him. I'm in terrible trouble."

"I'm afraid John is not here."

"Oh Jesus!" Larrie cried, "they told me at his flat I'd find him here."

Gerald, embarked on a lie, decided to stick to it. "He's gone," he said. "Do you want some money or something?"

Larrie looked up at him. A cunning look came into the orphan eyes. "I don't believe you," he cried. "You're not telling the truth." He rushed into the drawing-room, a bizarre figure in his dirty old T-shirt and his slept-in jeans. Some of the guests looked at him in surprise. Robin came over. "What do you want?" he asked sternly.

"I'm looking for Mr John Middleton," Larrie said, but, before Robin could answer, he saw John and rushed across to him. "Johnnie! Johnnie!" he cried.

Robin walked up to his brother, his mouth trembling, "I'd be grateful if you'd keep your street pick-ups out of my wife's house," he said in a whisper of rage. John seemed not to notice, he took the boy's hands. "Larrie, this is wonderful," he said.

Larrie smiled wistfully at him. "Oh, I'm in such trouble, Johnnie. Can we go somewhere where I can talk to you alone?"

"Of course," said John, "I've got the car outside." He took the boy's arm and led him from the room.

"You didn't believe what *she* said about me, did you?" Larrie asked.

"I didn't care about anything," John said, "only to see you again."

As they passed through the hall, Gerald put a hand on John's arm, "Do be careful what you're doing, John," he said.

Larrie looked up at him with hatred. "*He* told me you weren't here, Johnnie, he tried to send me away."

John turned and stared at Gerald. "I wish," he said slowly, "that you and my mother were both dead." Then he led Larrie down to the car.

Strangely enough, the dead bourgeois elegance of Marie Hélène's party had been little ruffled by these family scenes. The guests were too absorbed in their habitual interchange of cultured nullities. Only perhaps here and there someone, pausing for a moment to recover their strength before ordeal by chatter, was aware of some slight strain or disturbance in the atmosphere. It was not unusual, however, at parties for the odd guest to break through the general glaze, which increasing consumption of champagne set upon the company, with a moment's aggression or hysteria. If Kay or Elvira or Larrie were noticed at all, they were accounted among such weaker heads. Indeed, Marie Hélène's *soirée* would have been a complete success had it not been for a jarring incident at the end of the evening. Yves by this time, though not as drunk as he used to be in Merano, was farther gone than the rest of the company. He found himself in the garden with Mrs Jevington as a growing cloud obscured the moon. "The creative process is a very extraordinary thing," she was saying, when he made a very unmistakable and grossly physical pass at her. It was so long since the sculptress had regarded sex as anything but a subject for conversation that she was too surprised to pass it off with worldly ease. Not too many people heard her loud expostulation, but enough to create a scandal. It led, at any rate, to a nipping off of Caroline's budding *affaire* with Timothy.

Marie Hélène, though disgusted with Mrs Jevington's lack of *savoir-faire*, saw clearly that Yves would have to go. She set her mind to securing this at the cheapest rate possible, and also, if it could be done, to seeing that Stéphanie remained in her useful new rôle. Where money was concerned she had little pride. What little she had she swallowed and wrote to Elvira. She banked on Elvira's contrition over the scene she had made to dispose her favourably to recompense in general. She made great play with the disappointed expectations of Madame

Houdet, the years of work she had given to Mrs Portway. But to reduce Elvira's sense of guilt from the general to the particular, she dwelt on the constant misery caused to Robin by Yves' presence. It must be admitted that it troubled her conscience to do this, but she felt that the circumstances called for desperate measures. She added that she proposed giving a sum of money to Yves herself, although she did not name the sum.

Larrie had not been exaggerating when he told John that he was in terrible trouble. He had drifted from lodgings to Salvation Army hostels and Rowton Houses after leaving Inge. He was too frightened to seek out John; too work-shy to go to Frank; too miserable and hysterical to resume his old street life in more than a haphazard way. As Vin had told Gerald, he had got into very bad company, if "badness" can be measured in terms of weakness and stupidity. He had met two older Irishmen, but only so much older that they had both reached the age of twenty-five. They were, as Vin had said, burglars, but inefficient, inexperienced burglars. They persuaded Larrie into doing a job on a house in Kensington, and then, having just enough sense to see that they could not dispose of the "stuff" without being traced, they left him with a heavy suit-case to carry. Larrie was quite without any idea of what to do, so he took the case to Frank Rammage's and asked if he could leave it in his old room. "I knew you'd keep the room, as you promised, Frank," he said, "just as you knew I'd return here. If there's still work that you can find me, I'll be glad to do it, for it's work I need." He told Frank that he had to go up West, but that he would be back that night to sleep in his old room. He had just enough self-control to get through this piece of play-acting, but when he turned the corner into Earl's Court Road, hysteria seized him and he began to run. He ran all that evening until he had tracked John to Marie Hélène's.

It was a week later that the police, in the course of their investigations, visited Earl's Court Square and, after a long interview, arrested Frank Rammage on the charge of receiving stolen goods. He appeared in the box at the magistrates' court —pink and plump and bewildered. He seemed particularly distressed at the sordid condition of the two young Irishmen who stood beside him. He was committed for trial, but released on bail. At the Old Bailey, however, the police withdrew the case against him, stating that they could offer no evidence that he had received the goods knowing them to be stolen.

The judge, in dismissing Frank, permitted himself the unusual luxury of a word of admonition. "It would seem," he said, "that you have been involved in this case largely through your own folly. You have taken upon yourself the task of housing criminals and vagrants with some scheme of reformation in your mind. However well-intentioned this may be, I would remind you that there are a number of excellent, organized bodies concerned solely with this task. You would be wise to leave such work to them. You may be more unfortunate next time and find yourself involved in the results of a crime." The two Irishmen received sentences of eighteen months each. Rourke, the third man concerned, was stated by the police to have left the country.

Frank returned to Earl's Court Square in a daze. He resented the judge's remarks and he began at once to "turn out" an upstairs bedroom as the best cure for brooding on his grievance. While he was busy there, Mona, the depressed ex-tart, looked in. She had with her a girl in the tightest of jeans and the largest of slop sweaters. "This is Bobbie," she said, "I want you to fix her up with a room, Frank."

"Are you working, duckie?" Frank asked.

"Yes. She's got a job in a café," Mona said.

"Well. There might be one in a week," said Frank, "but there's nothing now."

"Bobbie's been in trouble," Mona said, and she watched to see Frank's expression change. Surely enough he looked more hopefully at the girl, though his tone was still snappish as he said, "Oh well. We can fix you up with something, I dare say. You can have a li-lo in Mona's room tonight." The girl produced some notes. "Put that away," Frank said. "You'll need all your money the first week of your work. You pay me next week."

As the woman departed, he resumed his scrubbing, but without the same angry violence.

It was lucky that Larrie had a passport all ready for the once proposed summer vacation abroad with John, for now he had to take the holiday without any preparation. They set off for Spain, where they could make the money last longer. Larrie was full of talk as they drove southward. He'd make it all up to John; he'd never forget his friend's kindness; he'd join the Foreign Legion; he'd get a ship at Barcelona; come what might he would never leave John; this was the man's life he'd always wanted, to travel and see the world; sure he'd have no difficulty with foreigners, wasn't he half Spanish himself? and had he never told John the story of his Spanish mother? he'd stand no foreigners taking the mickey out of him; and so on. He insisted that Johnnie should have the holiday that they had once proposed. John pointed out that they could ill afford to hire a car or to waste time dawdling their way through France. Larrie would listen to none of it. Hadn't Johnnie said he wanted to see these caves? Didn't his Johnnie like driving a car? There was no bloody cops that'd stop Larrie Rourke's friend from having what he wanted. John pointed out again and again that there was no danger whatever from police, this was not an extraditable offence, but the less the danger the more Larrie insisted on playing the thrilling game of evading the law. They were made to turn down side roads, to lose their way in complicated routes, and, eventually, in an excess of Larrie's zeal, to sleep in woods and fields.

As the glamour of the journey wore off—and with an unshaved and unwashed Larrie this process was hastened—John became utterly depressed and increasingly irritated. He tried to tell himself that although Larrie was not the charmer he'd been seeing all these months, he was not as worthless as he had sometimes feared. It was, of course, perfectly true: even Larrie's cunning was only an excess of histrionic emotion, he was a stupid, highly-strung, hopeless delinquent. He's a lost boy, John thought to himself, who needs my help. He could not, however, but realize that he was far more completely "lost" himself. He had lived on a heady mixture of ideals and career-ism. He had pepped up the mixture with the extra "kick" of a double life; and now he was left with nothing but the dregs to survive on. He lapsed into moody, self-pitying silence. Larrie talked on and on.

A storm burst over them as they slept in a field outside Limoges and they were soaked to the skin. John's hypo-chondria added a nagging fear of pneumonia to his more real worries. Pictures of foreign hospitals and solitary death came before him, pushing out the comfortable images of Thingy's coddling, the luxury of his flat, the glamour of being a celeb-rity. He was aiding a fugitive criminal; he had shut the door on return to England.

He sneezed and ached and grew really alarmed as they drove under a blistering sun by the bushy woods and meadows of the Lot. In the end, he agreed to Larrie's continuous de-mands to be allowed to drive the car, although the boy was an inexperienced driver and had no licence. Soon they had lost their way among steep red cliffs and scrubby broom and tough grass. Larrie grew irritable with the heat. John shivered with a temperature. Their quarrelling grew more violent.

"It was a terrible day for me," Larrie cried, "when I met you. A terrible day. I was an innocent, decent lad till then."

"You bloody little liar," John shouted.

"I'll not let any man call me a liar. I'll fight the man that says it." The car rocked perilously on the precipitous road.

"Shut up and mind your driving," John said. But Larrie went on calling, "I'll fight. I'll fight you." John refused to make any answer.

Soon Larrie's worked-up rage gave way to tears. "There's no-one, no-one I have in life," he cried. "I wish I were dead." Still John gave no answer. "I'll kill myself," Larrie went on. "I'll kill us both. Indeed, it would be better if the world were rid of our sort."

John reckoned without the determination of hysterics, but Larrie reckoned without his poor command over the car. He swerved to frighten John and, in a moment, the car was over the edge, falling ten or more feet to a ridge below. Larrie was thrown through the windscreen. A vein in his neck was severed and he bled to death among the wild lavender. John lay trapped by his legs beneath the body of the car. It was two hours before he was found. They took him to hospital in Cahors, and to save his life they were forced to amputate his right leg.

CHAPTER THREE

ELVIRA'S immediate reaction to Marie Hélène's letter
was to ignore it. At first she was too preoccupied with
her misery, and then quite suddenly, as the miserable summer
rains changed to a sunny autumn, she was too happy. She fell
in love again with a young painter. As she told her friends, "It's
such wonderful bliss to be in love with someone who's one's
own age and who has some sort of mind—I mean actually in
this case Joe's got a frightfully good one. But this awful obsession I've had for middle-aged men with splendid careers—
forever watching bald spots growing and listening to talk
about stock markets. And it got worse and worse, because
with my last one I almost got a thing about his father, who
must have been quite sixty and a sort of manic-depressive, only
distinguished. And then the heaven of Joe's not being
married!" In fact Joe was five years younger than Elvira and
she began a frantic life of dealing with his socks and getting
him better rooms and seeing that he ate regularly. In the mean-
time, however, she did produce a lot of money for the Houdets—
nearly half, in fact, of what Lilian had left her. She was moved
in part by the wish to free Robin of an incubus as the last thing
she could do for him—Elvira was very romantic. But a far more
potent motive was her feeling that Madame Houdet, at any
rate, deserved reward from both herself and Marie Hélène,
and to produce money freely would be to put Marie Hélène
to shame—Elvira was also a somewhat priggish moralist.
In communicating her offer to Madame Houdet, she said that
she was shortly to marry Joe Adams, an important young
painter of the Lupus Street Group, and asked Stéphanie to
retail the news to the Middletons.

Yves accepted the offer on his mother's behalf very quickly, although he assumed great pique at Elvira's stipulation by which he was only to benefit if he agreed to leave England. He was, in fact, piqued, but not by this. England had proved most uncongenial to his talents, even his Bromley widow proving herself adept at taking what he offered and making inadequate returns. He would not be sorry to leave it. Nevertheless, he was disgusted that neither Elvira's substantial offer nor Marie Hélène's very small contribution was accompanied by any sexual demands upon him.

Madame Houdet was upset that Elvira's offer had been made to her alone. She was horrified that any gains to Yves would mean his departure. She could not bear to be separated from him, yet she hated to leave the little world she had built up in Hampstead. Marie Hélène, who did not wish to lose her services, did everything she could to reach a bargain with her —she would leave her full control of the household economy, she would give her a special room in which to entertain the large circle of decayed Hampstead gentlewomen whom she now patronized. But Stéphanie's love for Yves was too great, and in early September they left together for Mentone. Yves was all smiles and kindness, and Stéphanie persuaded herself that she might have bought as much as a year's peace for herself.

As they crossed the Channel, another loving mother and son passed them en route. Inge had left for Cahors the day that the news of John's accident reached her; and now, thanks to the tireless efforts of Gerald and Robin, the authorities had agreed that there should be no prosecution for John's assistance to Larrie in his escape. The full scandal had not got into the papers, but one way and another his career was at an end. Lovingly now Inge brought him back to Marlow in his wheelchair.

John's difficulties, in fact, had taken up much of Gerald's time during August. Nevertheless, through all the family troubles, and despite the constant nag of the Melpham problem, he retained his new buoyant mood, though not, perhaps, with quite the carefreeness of the night of Marie Hélène's party. He continued to work both on the *History* and on his own book; he started quite suddenly to go to exhibitions of contemporary painting and even bought one or two works by young artists, although when he got them home he decided that he was not sure of his feelings and did not hang them. His interview with the Cressetts left him with a feeling that he would never obtain any evidence even faintly conclusive of his beliefs about Melpham, although he was more certain than ever that they were correct.

One afternoon, however, Derek and Maureen Kershaw came to see him. They wanted news of John.

"Of course, it will be a long business," Gerald said, "learning to walk, but my wife'll take him up to the hospital at Richmond. She'll look after him all right at Marlow."—Derek and Maureen exchanged glances—"He'll be so happy to see you, I'm sure," Gerald said.

Derek said, "Oh, good," but Maureen broke in, "Not at Marlow, he won't, I'm afraid. Johnnie's mother hates Derek's guts."

Derek frowned, but he added, "I'm afraid Johnnie's mother's never been keen on his friends who wanted him to have a life of his own, sir."

Gerald said, "Surely that's not quite fair. After all, John's not a boy any more, hardly even a young man. And then he's had a fine career."

Derek said, "Oh! terrific!" but once more Maureen added, "It could have been first rate." Then she paused and said, "Oh well! he's free of my stepmother now anyway."

Gerald saw an opportunity of deflecting the conversation. "*I'm* in her clutches now," he said.

They both said, "Good God!" simultaneously.

"You think very ill of her," Gerald remarked.

"Very," said Maureen grimly. "What on earth have you got to do with her?"

He told them the story in outline. "Her father died last month," Maureen observed.

"Yes," said Derek. "The old boy had another stroke. The money's hers now."

"Yes," said Maureen. "She only needs Dad's and she'll be set up for life. You know," she said, turning to her husband, "I bet Professor Middleton's right. I know they had a heap of money off that old clergyman. You bet it was blackmail. Look," she said to Gerald, "is this Melpham business important?"

"To historical scholarship, yes."

The Kershaws looked reverent, "I might be able to help," Maureen said. "It's difficult to see Dad on his own, but it can be done. I'll ask him to tea next week if you'll come. She may have said something to him in an unguarded moment. In any case, it'll be good for her to know you're still on the warpath."

Tea at Slough was a curious meal. There was *salami* and *mortadella* and caraway bread. Not that the Kershaws went in for high tea, indeed *ravioli* was in preparation for dinner; it was simply that Maureen could not bear a meal that did not include something from the Continental Delicatessen.

Mr Cressett was only half at ease; he glanced around the room as though at any moment Mrs Cressett's ample form might materialize from behind some of the contemporary furniture. He looked ill and shrunken. "I don't seem to take my meals well," he said. "I bring up most of what I've taken, if you'll pardon the phrase. It's all this agitation I expect. They say it tells when it's over. And then Mr Barker's death, though it had to come some time. And now this move to Cromer. Alice says the sea air'll set me up. But I don't know."

Gerald was surprised at the tact with which Maureen worked round to the subject of the Barkers' indebtedness to Canon Portway, though he guessed that her great affection for her father gave her tact beyond her usual powers. Even so Mr Cressett was alarmed. "I know nothing about it," he said. "It was all before I knew Alice."

But Maureen kept on, and in the end the little man said emphatically, "I've never cared to think about it too much. They got a pile of money from that old man and I've often wondered whether they hadn't got some hold on him."

"You've no idea what hold it could have been?" Gerald asked.

"No," said Mr Cressett, "but the way Alice talks of that old man makes my blood run cold. And Mr Barker, too, when he could still speak. Brutal he was."

Gerald sketched to him his doubts over Melpham.

Mr Cressett clicked his tongue in a shocked way. "It would be a terrible thing if that were true," he said. "There'd be no believing what you read."

It was only later just before he left, that he suddenly said, "I don't know. It may be. I remember once I was reading to them about England—Prehistory from *Pears'*, when Mr Barker laughed, 'They'd look bloody fools, those historians,' he said, 'if I was to tell a thing or two I know.' But Alice shut him up pretty sharp." He looked anxiously at Gerald, "I hope there's no more trouble coming," he said.

It did not seem a very useful meeting and yet it did bear fruit. A few days later Gerald received a visit from Alice, enormous in black. She sat very sedately on the edge of a chair and refused tea. She was wearing a black straw hat, very high in the crown and covered in black ribbon. "You'll be sorry to hear Mr Barker's passed over," she said. Gerald bowed his head slightly but made no comment. He would give her no help.

"I hear you're still concerned about the Melpham excavation," she said. "I've tried to remember everything I could. You'll understand, of course, that in my position that was all above my station. But it does come back to me that Canon Portway was a bit worried in his mind over it. I think he wrote to Professor Stokesay and whatever the gentleman wrote back it eased his mind a little."

"I see," said Gerald, "but he never told you what worried him or what Professor Stokesay said."

"No," Mrs Cressett replied, "and I wouldn't have understood it if he had. But maybe some of Professor Stokesay's folk can tell you what it's all about." She got up to go. "I thought I'd come and tell you what little I could remember," she said, "because me and Mr Cressett are moving to Cromer. We've bought a house to take in lodgers. I'll be very busy from now on. So I won't have time for casual visitors." She smiled comfortably at Gerald and sailed out of the room.

It came to Gerald immediately that if Alice Cressett was speaking the truth then Lionel Stokesay had not only been inept but also dishonest. Both he and Portway had suppressed the proofs of their own stupidity. At one time he had refused any investigation for fear of diminishing Stokesay's scholarly reputation, yet now that his honesty was at stake, Gerald in his new mood thought only he shouldn't have poll-parroted his life away in humbug and hot air. If he could find any proof, he would expose it. Nevertheless, he could not see that he was any nearer his goal; he had seen all Stokesay's historical papers at his death, he had read all Portway's published work, there was no hint to be found there. He had schooled himself for years not to contemplate the possibility of seeing Dollie; it was therefore only some days later that he admitted to himself that she was the only source of information still untapped.

Once he knew that he had to contact her he was filled with delight. She was clearly surprised when he asked to come down to her Cotswold cottage, yet there was no trace on the telephone of the old edgy note in her voice to which he had become accustomed in the years before the war. He did not think, he told her, that his business would take more than a day, but if it did—he and Larwood would put up at the local pub. She said, "Business?" in a surprised voice.

"Nothing to worry about," he replied.

"Well, I wasn't really," she replied. "I never do." He noticed that she no longer said "Toodle-oo" when she rang off.

Although the village shared the excessively picturesque quality of the neighbourhood, Dollie's cottage was a pleasant stone building unornamented with old-world knockers or artily painted doors. The garden was neat, yet it avoided the tea-cosy effect. There were too many copper chrysanthemums for Gerald's liking, but then Dollie's charms had never included good taste. She came out to meet him—one of those frail-looking little elderly women who are in fact tough and wiry. Her face was lined and her hair a washy brown-grey; her legs had become too thin. But she did not look ill and puffy, as she had when he caught sight of her at the airport.

"You look well, Dollie," he said. "Quite different from when I saw you at London airport a few weeks back." He cursed himself as soon as he had said it—no doubt she had been drinking. This was probably her party face got ready for his visit.

"Oh my God! I *had* been sick," she said. "I'd never flown before and I shan't again. It doesn't suit the colour of my eyes. Come to that," she added, "you don't look too bad for your age."

Miraculously, as it seemed to Gerald, they slipped into the old, easy relationship of their happiest days; indeed, even the tension that had *always* been there was somehow relaxed. She apologized before luncheon for the absence of drink. "If you want one, you'll have to go to the pub." Gerald tried to remember if this was one of the usual gambits of secret drinkers. "You're wondering if I keep it in the wardrobe now, aren't you?" she asked, laughing. "People always think that. Luckily it's nothing to do with anybody but myself, so I don't have to convince you. Actually I've stopped drinking altogether."

Gerald said, "I always knew you would." He thought it might help to pass the conversation on to other subjects.

"Did you?" she asked. "I can't think why. I jolly nearly killed myself with the stuff. I got worse than ever after the Pater died—having a bit of money and the war being so frightful. Then I thought I ought to do my bit. I've always been one to wave the Union Jack and when I was in my cups I couldn't put it down. I got a job at the Air Ministry. I wasn't much use for anything, but they were glad to have anyone then. I filed things for a wing-commander and, since I was a lady, they called me a secretary. They weren't glad to have me for long though. I turned up pretty squiffy once or twice and then one day I got completely blotto and they fired me on the spot in front of all the other women. I'd never been treated like that, you know. I'd always been very much the lady. It gave me an 'orrible shock, Gerrie. I really did try after that. I went to doctors and into a home and had injections, but none of it did the faintest good. I was a chronic soak. Then I got put on to the idea of the Alcoholics Anonymous. It sounded a bit pi, I thought. A lot of ex-drunks lending a helping hand and so on. I suppose it *is* a bit. But anyhow it worked. They put me in touch with a marvellous woman. Not my type at all. She'd been a glamour girl, but she knew all the answers. We had some sticky times, but anyhow here I am. It worked, and that's what matters."

"And what do you do with yourself?" asked Gerald.

"Nothing," said Dollie. "At least, not a job. I tried one or two but I was awfully bad and I can't see any point in doing something somebody else can do much better. Anyway I hate regular hours. I'm always busy enough. I garden, and gossip with the neighbours a lot, and then I'm a local J.P., believe it or not. Actually I'm rather good at that. I never believe anyone, but I don't mind their telling me lies, and that seems to be the chief point about it. Oh! and I've written two books about how to play tennis which made me quite a lot of money. The publisher had to do all the grammar. So you see." It was to these books that Clarissa, in her superior authorship, had alluded as a "little hobby".

Dollie moved easily and quickly about like a girl, laying the table and fetching dishes from the kitchen as she talked. She smoked continually. The meal, to Gerald's surprise, was good and the cottage very clean. "Yes," she said, watching his gaze, "you can eat off my floors if you want to. Do you remember how filthy the flat used to get? Poor old Mrs Salad. She must have been the worst char in London,"—Gerald winced slightly —"Oh I didn't mean I wasn't happy then. They were top-hole times. The old girl and I still exchange greetings at Christmas," she said.

Gerald would have continued gossiping all day, but when luncheon was finished, Dollie said, "What on earth's all this about business? Most people mean they want to borrow money. At least that's what I would mean. But you can't, you've always been rolling in the stuff."

Once again Gerald told his story. To be telling it to Dollie seemed a final release, the culmination of the long mental struggle. He was, therefore, a bit disconcerted when she said, "I think you'd better skip the history part, old dear, except where it's essential to what you have to say. I never did understand it very well, though when I was with you I used to think I had a glimmer. But now when I hear you say that you've been worrying all this time about something that happened umpteen years ago, it makes me rather angry. It seems so absolutely piffling."

Feeling like a clergyman searching for a modern parallel in a sermon, he began, "A few moments ago, Dollie, you said that you liked work to be well done. Well, you see . . ."

But she cut him short. "Oh don't worry to explain, Gerrie. I'll take your word for it that it's important. As far as I can see, what you're getting at is this—Gilbert faked the burial as one of his ghastly jokes, mainly to spite the Pater. The Pater knew about it years afterwards but never let on for fear of seeming a fool. And the same goes for old Portway. That Barker man helped Gilbert, and he and his daughter blackmailed old Portway over it. Is that what you're saying?"

Gerald smiled. "Roughly, yes," he said.

"Well," said Dollie, "it all sounds very likely. We both know that Gilbert was a bit off his head at times. But perhaps you didn't know that he played these cruel practical jokes. I

did. I had an awful time with some beastly letters he wrote to
a girl-friend of mine. I suppose nowadays they'd say he was
a—what's the word?—sadist; but I've always thought it was
just because he hadn't grown up on one side. He was like a
filthy-minded schoolboy and a bully. Anyhow, he hated the
Pater, so I can well believe he did it. Poor Pater! He was very
good to me but he *was* the most awful old fraud himself, you
know. Oh, not as an historian, you always said he was the goods
and you'd know. But as a man. He just liked listening to his
own voice and he was the biggest coward I'd ever known. He'd
never have brought himself to speak the truth if it harmed him
or Gilbert, especially after Gilbert was killed. He got softer
and softer. As to old Portway I never liked him, you know. I
wasn't keen on clergymen, and then he was an awful bolshie.
I wouldn't feel quite like that now. Believe it or not, Gerrie, I
go to church on Sundays now. And as to his politics, I dare
say he did a lot of good. Only *he* thought an awful lot of himself too. Lilian had spoilt him. They were a spoilt pair, but, of
course, they had quite a lot to be conceited about. Lilian used
to drive me mad, she was so affected, but then I remember
going to see her in that play, *Candida*. I thought it was awful
tripe, but she made me weep. One thing I can tell you—those
Barkers were n.b.g.: I saw quite a lot of their dishonesty at
Melpham. No, it all sounds awfully likely to me."

Gerald said, "I'm afraid I have to have some proof. You don't
remember anything of what happened on that day, do you?"

Dollie got up and began to make coffee in a percolator. "I
was trying to think," she said. "Lilian told me about the discovery, I remember, and the Pater told me all his theories, but
I didn't listen. Gilbert was particularly nice that day. But
mainly I just remember you."

Gerald was very touched. "That was *my* trouble," he said,
smiling.

But Dollie did not smile back. "Oh dear! The time we
wasted," she said. "One thing I do think is that Gilbert probably left something behind that upset the Pater very badly. It

wasn't just grief he felt when he went through Gilbert's papers, he was horribly shocked. But it may have had nothing to do with Melpham. Gilbert left *me* some drawings—horrible tortures of animals—that upset me for ages. I used to say that was one of the reasons I went on the razzle-dazzle in those war years, but that was probably only an excuse."

"Do you remember," Gerald asked, "if Stokesay ever spoke to you about Melpham?"

"Not about the burial," Dollie said. "He wouldn't talk to me about a thing like that. He kept that sort of thing for people like that Miss Lorimer. No. Portway came to see him once or twice at Highgate and they had a terrific confab, but I've no idea what it was about. I've got the Pater's letters, you know. Two boxes of them. I didn't write to you about them, because, well, when the Pater died, I wasn't keen on seeing you. But I offered them to old Sir Edgar Iffley. He said the Pater had sent all his historical stuff to the Association before he died. So I just held on to them. I *did* have a look at them once for some American who was interested in Gilbert's work, but apart from a few schoolboy letters there was nothing there. He must have destroyed all those letters Gilbert sent from the front. I have a vague idea that I *did* come across something in old Portway's handwriting but I couldn't be sure of that."

She saw him off at the gate; Larwood placed the two boxes of letters in the car. "I envy you the village," Gerald said, "it's charming."

"Is it?" Dollie asked. "It always seems to me a bit got up for tourists, but you have more of an eye for what's beautiful than I have."

Gerald felt ashamed of his remark. "I wish you'd come and see me in London," he said.

"I'd love to," she answered. "I love staying in town now and again, but I don't do it often. Money goes round all right, but only just."

"I could easily put you up at the flat."

"All right," she cried, "I shall hold you to that. Let me know about all this. I feel rather beastly about the Pater."

"So do I," said Gerald.

They neither of them mentioned Gilbert.

When he got back to London that night, Gerald telephoned to Inge to make his regular weekly inquiry after John's progress. She seemed in peculiarly high spirits. "Thank you, Gerald," she answered. "He is so helpless still, but we are very happy. We have now our first fires with the pine cones that give such a lovely scent. We sit at the window and we watch the brown and yellow leaves falling down. Round and round they go, caught in great gusts of wind. Some people are made sad by it. But Johnnie and I are happy. We know that one day will come spring."

"Oh! God," said Gerald somewhat feebly.

"Here is also little Kay," Inge cooed, "with Baby. Kay is a sad little Kay at the moment. She has quarrelled with Donald. He is lazy and he criticizes Kay's family all the time. He has said quite bad things about me. She is so unhappy. But I am telling her to stay here with Baby. Donald is no good to her, Gerald, and she must leave him."

"For heaven's sake, Inge, do take care what you're doing," Gerald shouted down the mouthpiece. "It's probably only a temporary quarrel. Things have been said that they'll be sorry for. But she's got the baby and all her life to think of. It's nothing to do with us after all."

"Oh, it *is*!" Inge cried. "You don't know what cruel things he said about me. And then he made that foolish speech when I had got him such a good job with Robin." There was a pause, then she went on, "It is a pity, I think, that Marie Hélène did not invite me to her party. Many things were said then by you and by Robin that made Donald very bitter. And after all he is an orphan. *I* should have understood better. But now it is too late. Kay must leave him and come to live with me here. I shall be quite happy to have her. I love the baby."

Gerald was seized with horrified panic. "Look," he cried, "I'll come down and discuss it with you both."

"No. Don't come down," Inge said. "That is not at all necessary. We do not need you." Nevertheless Gerald drove down the next morning.

The late September sun shone fitfully and a high gale was whirling the dead leaves down the gravel drive. The air was very cold. Inge swathed in scarves and woollies was wheeling John in his chair. Beside her walked Kay in a sensible woollen costume, her hair blowing across her face. She was pushing Baby in a pram. It might be the Park, Gerald thought.

"Oh, there is Papa come to see us," Inge cried. "We are walking outside, Gerald, so happy in the sun." It was clear that she was going to ignore the cause of his visit.

Gerald decided to go straight to the issue. "What's all this, Kay," he asked, "about your leaving Donald? Do think very carefully about what you're doing."

"I'm quite capable of making up my own mind, thank you," she said.

"Are you?" Gerald asked. "I don't believe you have a mind of your own when your mother's around."

Inge held her blonde head high, her blue eyes ahead of her. She kept them walking up and down the drive in the high wind throughout the interview.

"Oh Lord!" John said. "Can't you go anywhere without making scenes, Father? You ought to see a doctor, you know."

"This has nothing to do with you, John," Gerald said. "I've got things against Donald, Kay, as you well know. It isn't the marriage I'd have chosen for you. But he's fond of you; he's in a difficult position, you've got the baby, you can't just walk out on him because he doesn't get on with your family. It's ridiculous."

"He's taken the family money all the time," Kay said.

"Oh, that!" Gerald cried. "That isn't important in a thing like this. Nor anything he may have said about any of us," and he looked at Inge, but she stared ahead.

"I'm afraid *I* think it's very important that Donald should so completely have failed to understand Mummy." She implied that understanding Inge's faults as the child-like complement of her great virtues was the final test of human worth. She implied also that Gerald, like Donald, had failed to pass it.

"Oh don't be such a childish little fool!" Gerald cried in exasperation. "You don't have to be a priggish head-girl all your life. This is your husband whom you love that you're talking about, not somebody who's let the school side down."

From the mountain air high above their petty human passion, Inge turned the scorn of Brunhild upon him. "How can you say such things to little Kay when she is so unhappy? Poor little Kay with her poor little hand!" Even in her most immortal moments, Inge could not avoid her impulse to speak of Kay's hand.

It was an unfortunate impulse at that moment. Gerald suddenly felt himself shaking with rage. He turned and shouted at her so that Kay and John jumped with the shock. "Shut up, you mad woman," he cried. "How dare you talk about Kay at all? You came near to ruining her life once. Don't you dare touch her again. Do you hear? Don't you dare!"

Inge's eyes rounded with fright. "Don't let him speak of me like that. I can't bear it. I don't want to hear these things."

"There's a great deal you don't want to hear," Gerald cried. "You never have. All your life you've got away with it. But not because anyone loves you, but because they're sorry for you, do you hear! sorry for you. God knows if you've ever been sorry for what you've done."

"Stop talking like that to her," Kay said. "You've done nothing for us. She did everything."

"Yes, everything," Gerald said. "Ask her what she did to your hand."

"I did nothing, nothing," Inge cried. She was weeping now, her huge form shaking.

Gerald felt none of the horror or pity of former days, only anger. "Then tell me how it happened," he said.

Through her tears, Inge began to stutter. "You must not think these dreadful things. You have always thought cruel things of me. It was not my fault, Kay, it *was* not. But you were always touching Baby. And he was so sweet a baby, my Johnnie. And I was tired. I had no servants. I was always working."

"Whose fault was that?" Gerald said.

Inge gave no answer. She went on mumbling now. "I was so alone. I knew nobody. I tried to be friends, but they were difficult, the English people. And so you pulled at Baby and I pushed you and you fell with your hand in the fire. I didn't mean it. Please," she said, "I was only angry for my sweet little baby."

John said, "Oh! my God!"

But Kay put her arm round Inge's waist. "That's all right, darling," she said, "you mustn't worry about it. I guessed something of the kind. You mustn't worry." She turned to Gerald, "*You* gave us no reason to love you, yet you've always been jealous of our loving Mummy. You should be ashamed to treat her like this."

John said, "For God's sake, get out. You're not wanted here."

"You think," Kay cried, "that we don't know her faults. It's because we do that we love her. It's that that gives us a right to speak."

Inge's convulsive sobbing quietened down. She turned a smile upon them. "Don't be unkind to your father," she said. "He is unhappy and bitter. Don't be bitter, Gerald. Things have gone badly for you, my dear. You have failed. But we all have failed in different ways. It is the autumn time in the year and in your life. But you must not be sad. You must open out to the changes. . . ."

Gerald looked at her, then he turned on his heel and walked towards the house, where Larwood waited in the car outside the porch. He looked round at them once. Kay's face was set and bitter. John's eyes were full of hatred. Inge smiled a smile of sweet pathos.

He got into the car. "We'll go straight back," he said to Larwood, and they drove away past the pram and the wheel-chair. He put his head back on the seat and twisted his fingers to prevent himself from crying.

He set himself to the task of going through Professor Stokesay's papers that evening. He dined off an omelette and some Stilton cheese on a tray, and gave himself two strong whiskies and soda. There were two letters from Canon Portway. Mrs Cressett had been telling the truth: both Canon Portway and Professor Stokesay knew of the fraud.

In his last letter Canon Portway had written, "I can only hope that Gilbert was not sane when he played this dreadful joke and I pray for him. It is terrible to feel that all these years we have been so cruelly deceived. Whether, if I had been in your place, I should have destroyed his letter I do not know. You ask me what first gave me the suspicion which I voiced in my letter to you: that I fear I cannot tell you. But let me assure you if it is any comfort that I too have suffered over it. However, now that you have destroyed your son's letter, I must agree with you that we have to regard only the wider issues. Melpham is and will remain a freak, and as such it is not of vital historical importance. To tell the truth would inevitably, human nature being what it is, invite doubt and distrust of so much other work, particularly of the vital local antiquarian work which I have always championed. This doubt would certainly spread out in ever-widening ripples until much genuine work of importance would be in jeopardy from scepticism. Beside this, the erroneous story of Eorpwald's apostasy seems small evil. Nevertheless, I lay great store by your suggestion that whoever of us survives the other should commit the story to paper to be placed at his bank with instructions that it should not be opened for one hundred years. By that time the distorting issues of personality will have disappeared and the wicked joke will be seen in its true perspective without damage to other historical knowledge. For the rest we can only pray that we have acted rightly."

Professor Stokesay, of course, had been the survivor. Gerald made inquiries at his bank, but there were no documents. Perhaps he had left Portway's letters undestroyed as a substitute. It seemed unlikely, but it was more charitable to think so.

With so much of the story pieced together, Gerald felt at liberty to communicate with Sir Edgar. It was agreed that he should present his report to the committee of the Association, to which would be invited for the occasion Cuspatt of the Museum, and Pforzheim. Sir Edgar agreed reluctantly that Gerald should put another matter before the committee on the same occasion. The meeting was fixed for October 9.

At the same time Gerald wrote to Dollie to tell her of his discovery. The presentation of the report to his fellow historians would be an unpleasant task; it would help him so much, he said, if she would come up and stay at the flat that night. She was the only person to whom his personal feelings about the Stokesays would be intelligible: besides it might be that the committee would require a short deposition from her, though he had to add, for truth's sake, that this was not very probable.

Sir Edgar arrived at the Association headquarters in St James's Square in an irritable mood. It served him right, he thought, to be saddled with this unpleasant business when he was chairman. He should have given up the office years ago. The truth was that, without that interest, he would die. It was no superstition, simply a matter of fact. Not that he minded dying, he reflected. He hoped he was as prepared for that as most men; but not to take every precaution to keep alive seemed to him a weak sort of way of going on. It's going to be damned difficult, he thought, to go about this business in a decent manner. The only bit of proof we've got is Portway's letter to Stokesay; it means we can't save their reputations. If only he could really rely on the men who would be at the meeting, but he couldn't. That was another reason why he couldn't resign. Clun was an impossible bounder; Lavenham an R.C.; Cuspatt was all right, but in the last resort these

Museum fellows were as much bureaucrats as they were scholars—tied by a lot of red tape. Pforzheim was a nice Hun, if there was such a thing. The only young fellow they'd got in was Stringwell-Anderson, a funny sort of chap—a vulgar sort of dandy really. As for Rose Lorimer, he dreaded to think what was going to happen there. Middleton, of course, he'd always relied on, but he'd never quite made the grade. Perfectly right, of course, to follow the thing through, but there'd been a sort of over-finicking, high-strung, personal conscience approach about it that didn't do at all. More like a Dissenter than a gentleman. But, of course, he probably came from Quaker stock or something like that. These rich trades-people. Well, they'd have to see. But you couldn't rely on any of them to have the right instinct.

Professor Clun was already waiting in the committee-room when Sir Edgar arrived.

"You're damned early," Sir Edgar said. "Oughtn't to be here before the chairman, you know." He hardly made a joke of it. "Still I suppose I must expect people to be in front of me these days. I can only just hobble with this rheumatism."

"This has been a terrible business for Middleton," Professor Clun said. Sir Edgar grunted, he did not trust Clun's sympathy towards Gerald. He thought to himself, I hope Clun isn't going to start getting sanctimonious. The fellow only has one virtue—his bluntness. He'll be ghastly if he loses that.

"I think," said Professor Clun, "that John Middleton was one of the few valuable figures in public life today. It's a terrible thing when a man like that is crippled. We can only trust that he'll be able to resume his public career. I was astonished at the tone of the ill-natured remarks made in the papers. Pure jealousy, of course."

It was perfectly true, Arthur Clun had been upset by John's accident as he had seldom been in his life before. Sir Edgar, who had heard one or two more-sophisticated rumours, said nothing. He was amazed that Clun should think of anything but Melpham at such a time.

"As you know," Clun went on, "I've not been at all happy at Middleton being chosen as editor of the *History*. Indeed, I've been unwilling to commit myself to contributing. However, the matter now seems settled and I've decided to tell him that I'll write what he's asked for. After all, the *History* must be as good as we can make it. Middleton's had as much to put up with as any man could. I'm not given to strong personal feelings. But to have a son like John Middleton and then see him crippled is a shock that would upset the best of us. I have to admit," he said, and he coughed self-importantly, "that for once a decision has been inspired in me in some degree by a sentimental association. But we have so few men of real individuality in this country that one can't help being affected."

Sir Edgar thought, he's thought better of being left out of the *History* and he's invented all this nonsense about John Middleton to save his face. For once Sir Edgar was wrong.

"You've read the short statement on Melpham which I circulated for the meeting?" he asked.

"Oh, yes," said Professor Clun. "But it doesn't surprise me. I've never believed in the thing. Stokesay was always a charlatan, and, as for Portway, all these local parsons ought to be stopped by their bishops from meddling in things they don't understand."

"I hope there'll be no name-calling at the meeting," Sir Edgar said gravely as the others came in, and, when Clun did not reply, he added, "The essential thing is to keep it away from the newspapers."

"Quite impossible," Clun declared. "The thing's a perfect scoop for the journalists. It's a judgment on Stokesay in my opinion for treating history as a sort of journalism. No hope of keeping it out of the papers, is there, Lavenham?" he asked the priest.

Father Lavenham sighed. "I'm afraid not. We'll have to use every resource to play it down. The whole thing's so sadly un-English."

"Nonsense," said Clun. "There are fools and scoundrels in every country."

"But in England," Professor Pforzheim laughed, "they specialize in Piltdowns." It was clear from the silence that he had overestimated the Englishman's love of a joke against himself.

"Well, Cuspatt, I suppose you're changing your labels," said Professor Clun.

"It's the devil," Mr Cuspatt replied. "The idol is of primary importance, of course, as the sole one found on English soil. *If it was.*"

"We have only Gilbert Stokesay's word to me for that," Gerald said. His voice was at its most drawling. "Not the best evidence I'm afraid, Cuspatt. Like so many truths, this is one that'll be discredited with all the lies. Everyone will call it a fake."

"Hardly, I think," Cuspatt said. "The geiger evidence is conclusive."

"For scholars, perhaps. But not to the popular mind," Gerald replied.

"I really can't see what it's got to do with anyone but scholars," Sir Edgar remarked angrily. "The seventh century is hardly a popular subject."

"It *will* be when the newspapers have finished with it." Gerald felt the urge to transfer some of the misery he had suffered to the others.

"Oh," Jasper remarked grandly, "I think we can trust the more respectable papers to behave well over it. I'll have a word with the people I know on the weeklies."

Nobody at that moment cared to hear of Jasper's smart connections. "The weeklies!" Clun said sharply. He moved over to Gerald. "I trust your son's going along all right," he said.

"Thank you," Gerald answered. "It'll be a slow process."

"It was a terrible tragedy. Terrible," Clun said. "By the way, I've decided to give you the articles for the *History*. You can count on me." Gerald smiled vaguely. He noticed with anxiety that Rose Lorimer alone had not arrived.

Sir Edgar had noticed the same thing. "I fancy Dr Lorimer isn't coming," he said, "so we might begin. Perhaps you'd give us the report in detail, Middleton. I've had Portway's letter bound in that little folder. Will you read it, Clun, and pass it round, please?"

It was only after Gerald had been speaking for five minutes that Rose arrived. She seemed vast and dishevelled, like a huge ill-packed parcel that had been battered and broken open in the post; every crevice seemed to have burst open, every undergarment seemed to have poked its way to the surface. She smiled vaguely around the room and sat quietly in the vacant seat at the table.

When Gerald had finished, they spoke one by one. Sir Edgar thanked him for the clarity of his account. He considered that a short article on the subject should appear in the next number of the proceedings, and he agreed to write it himself. Father Lavenham suggested that among all the regrets, the distaste they must feel, they would inevitably be glad to know that Eorpwald, that saintly man, had been cleared of this absurd slur on his faith. He seemed to imply, too, that an Englishman had been cleared of very un-English behaviour. Clun said that, while they must do everything they could to protect scholarship from ridicule, they must not allow sentiment to lead them into foolish attempts to palliate the cowardly behaviour of Stokesay and Portway. Cuspatt announced that he would have to report to the Trustees of the Museum, but he assured them all that those notable gentleman could be counted upon to act with all the discretion they could require. Pforzheim let everyone feel that Continental scholars would have more regard for the integrity of English historians in scrupulously pursuing the fraud than for any slur that might fall upon individual English scholars. He would simply moderate further his Heligoland report, he said. Stringwell-Anderson felt that the response of younger historians would simply be satisfaction that expert modern archaeological methods made such disasters impossible nowadays. Rose Lorimer said nothing.

There was something, however, which they none of them said. They implied by their reserve that Gerald should have acted on his suspicions earlier; perhaps, in so doing, they revealed their secret wish that he had never acted at all.

At last, when a discreet yet efficient programme had been agreed upon, Gerald rose to his feet again. "There is one other matter which Sir Edgar has given me permission to raise," he said. His drawl almost sounded insolent. "I'm afraid it doesn't concern you, Pforzheim, or Cuspatt. Except perhaps indirectly. Nevertheless, I shall value your views too. So you'll have to forgive me. For the rest, I think all the members of this committee are interested in one way or another. It is in some degree a personal matter and I shall not want you to think I held it in any measure to be of comparable importance to the sad business we've just dealt with. But the two things are connected. The truth is that though I long searched my conscience before I undertook the investigation of the Melpham burial, I think it may be in the minds of many people that I should have acted earlier. I could explain at length the many motives that made me postpone my action, but it will suffice to say that they were personal. It may well be, however, that many will think that a man who failed to act earlier has showed a lack of calibre, seriousness or what you will, that makes him unfitted to edit the *History*. I say unequivocally that I do not feel that,"—Sir Edgar looked up at the extraordinarily buoyant note in Gerald's voice as he said this— "but I should like your opinion on this. I do not have to ask such old colleagues to be quite frank with me. There may be some opposition on the Syndic. If you agree with me I shall fight it. If you do not, then I shall anticipate any such opposition by tendering my resignation now. Sir Edgar's view I have. May I ask the rest of you to give me your views?"

There was silence for a moment, and Gerald, looking at their faces, saw how distasteful the whole Melpham business was to them, and therefore, to some extent, he with it. It was Professor Clun who broke it.

"I hardly think, Middleton," he said, "that you need indulge these personal scruples. They are, if I may say so, rather on a par with those that have delayed your action so long over this Melpham business. I don't pretend to think you're the best man for editor, but for various reasons, which I've explained to Sir Edgar, I've already waived my objections. As I told you earlier I propose now to give you the contributions you asked from me. I was perfectly aware of the points you've just raised when I made that decision. I really think that settled the question."

He looked round at the other historians as though defying them not to follow his lead. It had cost him not a little to change his attitude as a result of his emotions over John Middleton's accident, he was not going to have any nonsensical scruples overset that moral triumph. To Sir Edgar it confirmed his view that in the Divine Order every vice—even Clun's arrogance—had its virtuous purpose.

Gerald bowed his head slightly to Professor Clun. "Thank you," he said.

After Clun's declaration, it was impossible for any of the others—Gerald's friends—not to agree wholeheartedly.

"Sir Edgar, I am glad to say," Gerald announced, "is of your opinion."

Only Rose Lorimer did not speak. "Rose," Gerald said. It was a moment he and Sir Edgar both dreaded. "What do your feel?"

Dr Lorimer rose to her feet. With hat, hair, safety-pins, shawl and everything else askew, she looked more than ever like a mountainous White Queen. She smiled sweetly and mysteriously at them, too, like the White Queen when she told Alice of her ability to read words of one letter. Her little-girl's voice seemed higher than ever as she spoke, almost a squeak.

"I hope no one thinks," she said, "for one minute, that I am taking any notice of all this ridiculous nonsense. I'm not surprised that this story has been concocted. Ever since Professor Pforzheim's wonderful discovery I've been expecting it. I've been far too long familiar with the forces at work. I know their evil strength, their ruthless power far too well. What, I confess, I had not quite expected was the means they would use to pursue their determined aim of suppressing the truth." She turned towards Gerald and, leaning across the table, she addressed him in a loud whisper. "You damned traitor," she said. Then pulling all her falling clothes around as if they were one huge bath-wrap, she sailed out of the room with the same vague smile on her face.

Gerald was about to go after her, but Sir Edgar motioned to him to stay where he was. "There's nothing we can do," he said.

Professor Clun blew his nose noisily. "Well," he said, "there's a good deal come out this afternoon one way and another which should have been revealed some time ago." He was about to say more, but the faces around him were not encouraging. He got up to go, but before he left, he crossed over to Gerald. "When you see the great John Middleton," he said, "be good enough to tell him that Professor and Mrs Clun are eagerly awaiting his return to the public platform."

Gerald made excuses to the others and left as soon as Clun was well out of the way. He was eager to return to Montpelier Square, for by this time Dollie should be back from her shopping.

She was sitting by the fire when he returned. She had put on a short black silk dress with a string of pearls for the evening. He imagined that a younger person with an eye for such things would find her a very "period" figure. She still crossed her legs so that one knee showed; she still wore horn-rimmed spectacles to read the evening paper, but the lenses were thicker.

"How was it?" she asked.

"Hell," he replied, "but all right. It's all over anyway." He paused. "I'll probably be bothered by the newspapers. We shall try to keep it out, but if some chap with bright ideas gets hold of it, he can make a wonderful story of it. They may get on to you too as the only surviving Stokesay."

"Oh Lor!" she cried, "That's not in my line at all. What do I do?"

"Say nothing charmingly, as I'm sure you can," Gerald said.

Dollie looked up at him frowning. "You still say those rude things intended for compliments," she said. "You always had a jolly odd idea of teasing."

She stared into the fire. "It's awfully pretty, the flat," she said. "I suppose all these drawings are all frightfully good. I can't appreciate them. I only like pictures with colours. All the same, you're one of the men who without being cissy can make a house look nice." She's picked up one or two new words since the old days, he thought.

"That's what your neighbour Clarissa Crane said," Gerald observed.

"Oh dear!" Dollie cried, "I'm sorry I said it. It's so awful to think you only got news of me through *her*. She's a dreadful, pushing kind of woman. She always snubs me because I'm only a Philistine, but I'm sure she's a fool. She's always going on about woman's feelings and intuitions as though she was the last word in women. So she is in a sort of way. No man would look at her. She's much too eager." To Gerald's delight she went on reading the paper as though she took the sufficiency of their intimacy for granted.

"I never thought of myself as the last of the Stokesays at all."

"Well, you *are* one only by marriage."

"Yes, and that's such a long time ago. Don't bother about me if you want a drink," she said.

As Gerald was pouring himself out a whisky, the bell rang and Mrs Salad was shown in. Gerald looked at Dollie to see the effect of his surprise. Dollie jumped up from her chair and took the old woman's hands. "Mrs Salad!" she cried. "How very nice." All the same, Gerald couldn't be sure of her reaction.

The old woman was dressed as usual, but though her movements were more shaky, her make-up seemed less profuse and less erratic. "Ah! you look lovely, Miss Dollie," she croaked. "Not changed at all. Or hardly much."

"That sounds more truthful, Mrs Salad. But you look very well too. How is your rheumatism?" Dollie asked.

"Arthritis dear," Mrs Salad corrected. "It's only the dregs that has the rheumatism."

"Well, arthritis then?" Dollie said. Gerald was not quite sure if her tone was sharper.

"Very bad," said Mrs Salad. "Mr Rammage says to put the onions on the 'ands. But I don't do it. It's kind of 'im to make the suggestion, but 'e doesn't reckernise that those 'ands 'ave been kissed by more than peers."

To Gerald's surprise there seemed to be no smile on Dollie's face, she simply said, "Well, I don't really think onions would do much good. I suppose it prevents you sewing much."

"Oh no!" Mrs Salad said, accepting a second glass of brown sherry. "Nobody's doin' the birds and flowers now. It's all the contemporarery. My grandson Vin and Mr Rammage, they showed me. 'Igh colours it is—the reds and the yellers—and the circles and squares. I brought a 'andkerchief I done for you, Miss Dollie." As she handed it over, she repeated with a superior smile, "Ah yes, the birds and the flowers 'ave 'ad their day."

The handkerchief was decorated in scarlet and daffodil yellow, but the forms were significant probably only to Mrs Salad herself.

"Your skin's very white, dear," she said, peering at Dollie's neck. "They're not doin' that now. It's all the buffs and the 'igh yellers." Her eyes took on a distant reminiscent look. "Funny, the changes," she said. "My brother Len married a mulatter. Smooth her skin was but all a light brown. We didn't reckon to like it. My white coffee, 'e called 'er, but 'e couldn't sweeten 'er temper. Ah well!" she sighed, "Other days, other stays, they say. But you'd not remember the whalebone, dear."

Mrs Salad rambled on, and every so often she tried by looks or innuendoes to imply the old relationship between Gerald and Dollie, but somehow Dollie appeared not to notice Gerald while Mrs Salad was there. At last Gerald plucked up courage to say, "Well for me Miss Dollie hasn't changed at all, Mrs Salad."

"Ah!" the old woman said. "You'd need to say that, for you took what there was."

It was the only time that Dollie laughed out loud. "Good heavens, Mrs Salad," she cried, "what an old moralizer you are. You're worse than me."

Shortly afterwards the bell rang. "That'd be my grandson come to fetch me."

Vin was dressed in the perfection of quiet black and oyster-grey silk tie. His hair seemed to have been arranged rather higher than usual. It only required a stuffed bird or a model ship to be the height of fashion at the court of Marie Antoinette.

"This is Vin, Miss Dollie. 'Es a lovely boy. This is Miss Dollie, Vin. You've heard me talk of 'er."

Perhaps Vin was nervous, for he turned to Dollie and said, "I'm sure you look quite marvellous."

Dollie was quite put out. "Your grandmother looks well," she said.

Vin swayed his hips a little as he stood in front of Dollie. "Oh yes, Granny keeps marvellously," he said, then in a confiding whisper, he added, "I try to keep the slap down a bit, you know. I wish I could get rid of that filthy old eye-veil."

Before the Salads departed, Vin said to Gerald rather petulantly, "Well, I must say you didn't take much notice of my advice about that Larrie Rourke. We were all very sorry to hear about Mr John Middleton, of course."

"Thank you," said Gerald. "Yes, I owe you an apology and gratitude for trying to warn me."

Vin was still somewhat reserved. "It was only what duty demanded, I'm sure," he said.

As they were leaving, Gerald felt very warm towards them both. "Let me know how you get on. And keep out of trouble." He turned to Vin. "And that means both of you," he said.

Vin smiled, "I'm sure we try to," he said. "We're more the domestic nowadays really."

When they went into dinner, Dollie said, "Gosh! I've got an appetite. I feel as though I'd been playing Mrs Dale for an hour. You are a terrible snob, Gerrie," she added. During dinner, she asked, "Was that Vin one of those pansy boys?"

Gerald blushed slightly, "I rather fancy so," he replied.

"Funny," she commented, "I've never associated Mrs Salad with *them*. Of course, it's just what she needs really."

As they drank their coffee, she asked, "If I put on my hat and coat, could we go to the cinema? I don't fancy the evening round the fire. I so seldom get to London." And as they were driving up to the West End, she suddenly remarked, "I've grown into a terrific prig. I hope you realize that, Gerrie."

The Salads were having a particularly domestic time that evening, for Vin was giving a party. Mrs Salad had her guest—old Emmie, a hippopotamus-like old woman with only one eye. Many of Vin's guests came in costume with plenty of slap. Mrs Salad and old Emmie sat side by side with huge gins. They thought everything was lovely. When Vin did his dance number with the muslin strips, Mrs Salad said, "I don't know what my gentleman would say."

"That's the Professor," Vin told the company, "you don't know the half of my friends."

Just at midnight, as Vin was doing his Marlene Dietrich turn, Frank bounced in. "That'll be enough of that noise," he said. Somehow or other he was persuaded to stay, however, and at three o'clock he was seated between the two old women, drinking an equally large gin and gossiping happily. Someone had put a crown of silver stars on his bald head. "Well I must say," Vin cried, "you do all right, Frank. It's the fairy god-mother *and* the pumpkin with you."

The same might also have been said for Rose Lorimer as she sat between two old readers some mornings later beneath the great dome of the British Museum reading-room. She was wearing a hat trimmed with water-lilies; her old fur coat, once more in use, seemed bulkier than ever. Ranged on the desk before her were copies of *Crockford's*, the *Catholic Directory* and the *Methodist Handbook*. She had been uncertain about the *Baptist Handbook*, but she had decided by now that the Baptists were probably not in the conspiracy. To all the other clergymen she was busy addressing poison-pen letters. As she was descend-ing the steps of the Museum, she saw Father Lavenham coming in. She crossed over towards him, still with her vague smile.

"Ah! Dr Lorimer!" he cried.

Rose said nothing. She merely swung her two heavy shopping-bags—one, two—against each of his shins. Despite the pain he felt, Lavenham managed to suppress any cry and the incident passed unnoticed. Unfortunately not all the re-cipients of the letters were equally forbearing. Police investi-gations were started, and it was only through the tact of the university authorities that criminal proceedings were avoided. The poor lady was certified, and, by some strange freak of the National Health service, confined in an asylum near Whitby. There for many months she gazed upon the hated ground where, at the famous Synod, the true, the Celtic Church had met its defeat.

It was not long before the newspapers got on to Gerald and, soon after, Dollie in her Cotswold cottage was besieged by visits and telephone calls from journalists. Gerald persuaded her that they could better withstand the attack together and he went to stay at her cottage.

One morning, after they had jointly routed a peculiarly pertinacious woman journalist, Dollie said, "Well, this *is* a lark, Gerrie, and no mistake. I *am* enjoying it."

Gerald smiled back at her across the chintz-covered sitting-room. A few minutes later he said, "Yes. We get on so well. It seems silly not to make something more permanent of it."

Dollie went to the window and looked out on to the little garden where the October sun was shining lustily upon the Michaelmas daisies. "All the same," she said, "I think we'll have a fire."

"Well?" Gerald asked, "I wasn't suggesting anything . . ." His remark tailed away.

"Bed?" Dollie said. "I didn't suppose you were. That *would* be a Fred Karno show at our age."

"I didn't even mean," Gerald explained, "my giving up the flat or you the cottage. Just something a bit permanent."

Dollie had lit the fire; she now knelt before it with a newspaper. "It just wants to draw," she said. "It wouldn't do, Gerrie. I'm sorry, old dear. We'd get on each other's nerves in no time. I'm awfully set since I gave up the drink, you know. And hard. Hard on myself and on others. And a bit pi about things too in a sort of way. Oh! I enjoy life and I'm no nuisance to others, which is about as much as you can ask from an old woman who was brought up as I was. I'd like to come and stay with you when I'm in London. And I'll be glad to see you here as a visitor. But I couldn't *live* with anyone for the world. And nor could you. Only you won't admit it."

Gerald said, "I'm a very lonely person, Dollie."

"No you're not," she cried, "you thrive on being on your own. But you won't leave anything or anybody alone. Look at the way you fuss about your family. You deserve all the raspberries you get from them. And you won't forget the past. Oh! I grant you the Melpham business. That was different. You *had* to act there. But it's over now. You've got to move on."

"I feel," said Gerald, "as though I had moved back when I'm with you. Look at the other evening with Mrs Salad. We might have been back at Fitzroy Square."

Dollie got up and pulled down her skirt, then she said angrily, "That's the only time I've felt disgusted with you since I've seen you again. Oh! I'm not saying anything against Mrs Salad. She's the same pathetic, cunning, dirty old thing that she always was. And quite an old dear too. Naturally we put a halo round her head in those days. We were in love. But to try to build all that up again. Really, Gerald! you've got to grow up." She sat down and began to read the paper. "Here's something rum," she cried a few minutes later. "Look at this."

Gerald read—"Man's body to be exhumed. Echo of recent Civil Service scandal. A Norfolk coroner yesterday ordered the exhumation of the body of Harold Cressett. Mr Cressett died suddenly a fortnight ago at Cromer. Death was certified by a doctor as due to a disorder of the bowel. The expropriation of Mr Cressett's market-garden led to a recent inquiry into Civil Service mismanagement. As a result of the findings of the commission of inquiry a high-up civil servant was severely reprimanded and posted to the Ministry's branch department at Bangor."

"Well," said Gerald, "the mill grinds slowly."

The next morning he received a letter from Inge, forwarded on from Montpelier Square.

"Dear Gerald," she wrote. "Here in Marlow the sun shines, the roses bloom and yet soon we shall burn the wicked traitor Guy Fawkes. I love the English customs. Johnnie already walks a little. One! two! with Thingy's arm. Soon he will be walking. One! two! three! Then we shall have again to fight. To win back his good career. Is England mad now that she wants to lose splendid men because of nasty, dirty little lies? But he will get back his career. With Thingy's arm.

"Why do I write to you? You do not deserve to be forgiven for the wicked things you said. But so is not my way. I want all smiles and happiness. Poor little Kay is not so. She cannot forgive you. She will not hear your name. She must not be judged. It is because she has the poor little hand. Cripples are always so—bitter. But now I will tell you about her. Donald is come here and there will be no divorce. And they are so happy and so pleased with old Thingy who has brought them this happiness that they are together again. Now they will live here and Thingy will have Baby with her. Sometimes Donald has said wicked things like another silly boy I know. But Donald is a good boy and I have forgiven him. But he is also bitter—he is a poor orphan. He is most bitter at things you have said. How you have said that you do not like him for a son-in-law. So please you must not come here, Gerald, for some time, because everything is happy and I do not like to have things which are not pleasant. . . . "

Gerald tossed the letter across to Dollie.

"So John will get back his career with her arm," she commented as she read it. "Does that mean they will appear on T.V. together? There's never been a mother and son act, has there? After all, it wasn't Wee Georgie Wood's *real* mother, or was it?" She looked at Gerald across the Oxford marmalade and the coffee percolator. "Oh, for heaven's sake," she cried, "don't make that hurt face. You've known all this for years. Accept it." She paused. "You do really, of course. You're glad to be free of them but you've got this tommy-rot about loneliness on the brain." She laughed. "Look," she said, "I'll tell you about someone who loves you. There's a girl come down to live here—one of those arty creatures. She's married to a painter. They've taken a perfectly insanitary cottage outside the village with no proper lav and no light, and painted it all colours of the rainbow. Anyhow it seems she's very fond of *you.*"

"What's her name?" Gerald asked.

"Adams," Dollie said. Gerald looked blank.

"Elvira Adams."

"Oh! Elvira!" Gerald cried. "How is she?"

"Blooming, I should have said. She's pretty, but too fat. I met her at tea, and when she heard the name Stokesay, she revealed that she knew you, said how much she admired you, how she wished you'd met in different circumstances, and she wanted to apologize because she's behaved awfully badly to you."

Gerald looked very pleased. "Didn't she tell you she was Lilian Portway's granddaughter? No, I suppose she wouldn't. She never liked Lilian."

"Oh! she's a Portway," Dollie cried. "That accounts for it. They were all dotty."

"Is her marriage working well?" Gerald asked.

"She told me to tell you she was blissfully happy, but she couldn't tell what it really meant because she might be overcompensating. What on earth did she mean, Gerrie?"

"She always fears that excessive emotions may mean the opposite."

"Well, strike me pink," said Dollie. "She asked us to lunch but I refused."

Gerald raised his eyebrows.

"Wait a minute," Dollie said. "*I've been* there. She had two huge gins and I sat getting hungrier and hungrier. After an hour of that, while she talked nonstop, she went to see what there was in the larder. She came back with two tins of stuffed vine leaves but no opener. So we came back here and had eggs. Not again, thank you, Gerrie, not even for one of your girl-friends."

When Gerald was getting into the car to return to London, Dollie said, "Why don't you come here for Christmas? Or will you go to Inge's?"

Gerald was silent for a minute, then he said, "As a matter of fact, I think I shall go abroad."

"That's the stuff to give the troops," Dollie cried.

As he travelled back to London, Gerald realized that Dollie was right. He was fonder of her than anyone, but her "bright" simplicity, her self-confident censoriousness, would make her unbearable to live with. She was, he supposed, his unattainable vision of the noble savage.

Whether it was despite her injunction to keep away from his family or because of it, towards the end of November Gerald rang up Robin. His new-found intimacy with his elder son had been nipped in the bud, but there seemed no reason why he should not see this son he respected, especially as he now regarded the Marlow part of his family as lost to him.

Robin clearly also had a conscience. "Oh, hullo, Father," he answered. "I've been meaning to ring up you for weeks, but I've been so hellishly busy."

"You haven't had a return lunch off me," Gerald said. "When can you make it?"

"Oh! thank you. But you'd much better come to dinner in Hampstead. Marie Hélène'd love to see you."

Gerald agreed reluctantly.

It was the only foggy night of November and Gerald was sorely tempted to cry off, but Larwood got him there somehow. Fog seemed to have seeped into the Regency dining-room. Marie Hélène's complexion and her bottle-green evening dress seemed full of it. The pretentious food tasted of it. There were three other guests—an ex-admiral turned company director and his wife—they talked of their holiday in Majorca—and Elizabeth Sands, the novelist's daughter. She said, "After Mummy's death, I had the usual girl's decision—marriage or career, and as you see I chose career." Gerald could see it all too clearly. The married couple left early because of the fog and took Miss Sands with them. Gerald waited for Larwood to fetch him. He seemed to wait a long time.

He made conversation with Robin about the brandy and with Marie Hélène about Timothy. She told him about the Jevington *débâcle*. "Poor Timothy!" she said. "They take love so seriously at that age. It's quite amusing to see it. However, it was over quickly. He's in love with someone else already. Armand Sarthe liked you very much," she said proudly. "He told me to say that if you want to use any of the

Paris libraries at any time, he will always be glad to recommend you."

"How kind of him," Gerald said.

"The Houdets are in Cannes now. Poor Tante Stéphanie was so sad to leave us. I only hope that Yves doesn't spend all their money. Anyone else but Elvira Portway would have had enough sense to tie it up more carefully," Marie Hélène told him.

Both she and Robin said once or twice, "You don't come to us often enough, Father."

At half past ten Marie Hélène retired to her room. Robin gave his father a whisky and soda. "You're just the man," he said, "to advise me about something. I've got rather interested in this Catholic business. That *affaire* with Elvira made me realize what a sinking sand I've lived on and it's set me thinking about Marie Hélène and how it is she's been such a tower of strength all this time. I don't know that I'm cut out for religion, but I'd like to know a good deal more about it. I can understand a lot of it, but this business of the Pope rather stands in the way. Of course, I could go for instruction, as they call it, and they wouldn't try to influence me, you know: they're far more liberal than people think. But I'd rather find out for myself, to begin with at any rate. What's the best book on the history of the early Church in your opinion, Father?"

Gerald said that this was a very wide question and that he would like to think it over.

"Oh, don't worry," said Robin, "it's not that important."

Gerald realized that he had only been asked out of politeness. Robin, it was clear, would go for instruction anyway.

At last Larwood came to fetch him. "Come and see us again when you feel like it, Father," Robin said, "but I know you're a busy man."

Afterwards in bed Robin said, "My God! that was a sticky evening. I do realize what Mother means about Father, poor old chap." Marie Hélène said, "It was good that we could entertain your father." She preferred to say no more.

A week before Christmas Gerald had to report to the Syndic on the progress of the *History*. There were, as he had expected, some critics, but he had routed them easily. As he came away, Sir Edgar said, "Well done, Middleton, you were in fine form. By the way," he added, "I'd like to see you this week. I've something important to discuss with you."

"Well, I'm afraid that's going to be difficult," Gerald said. "I'm off to London airport now to fly to Mexico."

"Mexico?" Sir Edgar said, amazed.

"Yes," Gerald drawled a little. "I've always wanted to see those Aztec things, and Christmas time seemed to be a good time to go away. The contributions'll be pouring in by the spring and I shan't have much time for travelling. I'm taking *The Confessor* with me, I think I can write quite a bit of it there."

"Ah, well," Sir Edgar said. "You're rich enough to do these things. It's a damned nuisance, though. I may be dead when you get back. I'm very old, you know."

"Nonsense," Gerald answered. "But if it's important why not come down to the airport in the car with me. Larwood'll take you back to Holland Park."

"Very well," Sir Edgar said, and he chuckled. "A few years ago if anyone had asked me to go to an airport and back I'd have thought he was mad. But when you're as old as I am, you might as well do what you're told."

As the car sped through Hammersmith, Gerald noticed the evening newspaper placards. They read, "Cressett Murder Trial. Latest Report."

"I'm going to resign the chairmanship of the Association," Sir Edgar said. "I'm too old for it. But I'll be happier in doing so, if you'll agree to take it on."

There was a moment's silence, then Gerald said, "Thank you. I think I should like to accept."

As they waited for Gerald's flight to be called, a woman in a Persian lamb coat bore down upon them. "Professor Middleton. How very nice!" It was Clarissa Crane.

"You know Sir Edgar Iffley, Miss Crane, don't you?" Gerald asked.

"But of course. How are you, Sir Edgar? Where are you off to, Professor Middleton?"

"Mexico."

Clarissa took care to show no provincial surprise. "Oh, yes," she said, "I didn't know you went in for American archaeology."

"I don't," Gerald answered. "My motives are pure pleasure. I'm giving two lectures at the university there to pay for my keep."

"Lucky man!" Clarissa said, "I'm off to Lisbon on my way to Angola. But I have to *work* for my living. My publishers have commissioned me to write a book about it. They say it's a heavenly country with appalling social conditions."

"Do they?" Gerald commented.

"I had to give up my historical novel, thanks to your awful revelations about Melpham," Clarissa continued. "I think all you historians are frauds really, Sir Edgar. No more fiction for me now, historical or otherwise, just dreary old fact."

"You are lucky," said Sir Edgar, "to be able to distinguish between them."

Gerald's flight number was called. "Good luck for your book, Miss Crane," he said. He turned to Sir Edgar, "I'll send you a postcard of a human sacrifice," he said.

"My dear fellow, I know you won't do anything in such poor taste," Sir Edgar replied. "I'll put your name up to the committee when I send in my letter."

"I'm very honoured," Gerald said gravely and left them. With his black hat, umbrella, smart dark overcoat and despatch case, he looked like almost all the other men travelling on the aeroplane.

"He's *so* good-looking," Clarissa said, "and a charmer. He hasn't *done* much, has he? It's awfully dangerous really for people with brains to have money and good looks. They're practically bound to waste their talents. In any case I suppose one could say that Gerald Middleton had taken life a bit too easily." She cocked her head, bird-like, on one side, as though considering her words. "Don't you think so?" she asked Sir Edgar.

The old man got up from the red American-leather couch. "I can imagine someone who hardly knew him at all saying so. Yes," he said. He raised his bowler hat. "Good day to you," he said. As he walked towards Larwood and the waiting car, he felt ashamed at having lost his temper. I had no right to be rude, he thought, God knows who the woman was, never seen her face or heard her name before. One thing was perfectly clear to him, however: she was a time-waster.

APPENDIX

Extract from Bede's "History of the English Church and People"

Abbot Hadrian, fellow-worker in the word of God with
Archbishop Theodore of blessed memory, sent Eorpwald to
the East Folk and to King Aldbert, their prince. To them
Eorpwald preached the word of God and under their prince
they accepted the mysteries of the Faith. Their king Sabert had
in former times been baptized in Christ and they with him;
but after his death they had apostatized and they offered victims
to devils at their altars. Now Eorpwald was of the East Folk,
but he had early left his people and, when still only a boy, he
had chosen the monastic rather than the secular life. He was of
modest and goodly life and soon acquired great learning. He
was companion to Bishop Wilfrid when the South Saxons
received the word of God. But it was Eorpwald's wish that he
should bring his own people back to the Faith and Sacraments
of Christ, so that he listened joyfully to the command of Abbot
Hadrian when he commanded him to preach the word of God
to the East Folk. And by his teaching, King Aldbert, with all
the nobility and a large number of humble folk, accepted the
Faith and were washed in the cleansing waters of Baptism.
And soon after Eorpwald died and was buried among his own
people in the first year of the reign of King Huthlac, son of
King Aldbert.

Extract from the early thirteenth century
Anonymi Episcopi Vita Eorpwaldi

And after that Saint Eorpwald had brought King Aldbert
and all his people to receive the sacrament of Baptism and had
induced them to forsake their horrible and erroneous beliefs,
he remained among his own people preaching and teaching
and amazing them by the holiness of his life and the modesty
of his behaviour. After a short time he was appointed Bishop
of Sedwich in the East Folk by Abbot Hadrian and he built a
cathedral church there and consecrated it to God and to St
Peter, the keeper of the Heavenly Keys. He diligently governed
the people committed to his care and defended the faithful
from the attacks of ravening wolves. But as history shows, in the
lives of the saints, the efforts of the zealous call forth deeds of
darkness from the hearts of the ungodly. And so it was with
the man of God, for there were those who spoke against him
because he had suppressed sacrilege and put down concubinage
among the laity. And out of their evil hearts they spread
rumours that he had engaged in sorcery and had practised
evil magic. And the holy man was preparing to set out on a
journey to Rome to defend himself before the Holy Father
against these wicked lies when he died. He was buried at
Sedwich in the holy ground of the cathedral. But in after-years
when the Northmen came upon these coasts, devouring all
before them, ravening wolves, the clergy conveyed the body
of the man of God secretly and buried it where no man knows.
Some say it was at Bedbury and some at Melpham, but no man
truly knows the place. And now that we have narrated the
events in the saint's childhood, boyhood, youth, middle age,
old age, let us speak of the wondrous happenings which were
wrought by God's help after his life's work was over, and
which made known to men the sanctity of his life. . . .

Extract from "The Bulletin of the Historical Association," vol. xxii (Summer 1913). Conclusion of "The Significance of Eorpwald's Burial," by the Rev. Reginald Portway, D.D., F.H.A.

It is still somewhat early to assess the significance of the discoveries made last year at Melpham. Thanks to the work of Professor Stokesay, Professor Plummer and Dr Chadwick, our knowledge and understanding of the century of conversion grows yearly more complete; what was once a scene of darkness lit only by the brilliant light of Bede's great beacon lamp is now illumined here and there by the fires of linguistic scholarship and archaeological discovery. Nevertheless, the fires are still only fitful. Each and every discovery can only be examined against historical evidence, and historical evidence means here the story as we receive it from Bede. It is, of course, at once the glory and the bane of our research that the sole chronicler of that obscure age should have been a historian of genius. Bede's ecclesiastical history stands alone, yet by the accident of his greatness it is worth a dozen or more chronicles of later, more documented ages. On the other hand, the very greatness of Bede demands a caution in relation to other evidence that can perhaps impoverish us. One thing stands out from the results of the Melpham excavation: the despised anonymous thirteenth-century *Life of Eorpwald*, written at so late a date and with so evident a propaganda purpose, inherited traditional information of the most extraordinary kind, information apparently unknown to Bede, and that information has been shown to be true. For myself—and I speak as a local historian, deeply committed to the importance of local traditions—the outstanding fact that emerges from the Melpham excavation is its vindication of the value of such traditions. The anonymous biographer of Eorpwald—however late his work, however tendentious his purpose—was a monk of Sedwich, a man of the East Folk. He told us that Eorpwald was charged with sorcery; we now know that those charges had foundation. The lesson is obvious: however obscure, however unique the voice of local tradition, we disregard it at our peril. The intention of the anonymous biographer is obvious: he wished his hero to be numbered among the ranks of the saints. Yet the traditional story of Eorpwald's sorcery was still so widely known in the thirteenth century that his biographer could not omit it from the story of his holy man. Perhaps the story was more widely credited even in the thirteenth century than we can realize; certainly his biographer's plea fell on stony ground. Neither Innocent III nor his successors were prepared to canonize the missionary of the East Folk. However that may be, although Bede must remain our final arbiter for the events of the seventh century, we must recognize that there were other witnesses than Bede whose voices remain to us only in the distorted voices of tradition and folk-lore.

But what of the general historical significance of the burial of Eorpwald? Here, I think, we must speak with the greatest circumspection. One, at least, we now know of the great disciples of Theodore, one of that great band of Missionaries, who completed and made sure of the conversion of our country to Christianity, had feet of clay. So much the existence of the wooden idol in Eorpwald's tomb merely allows us to say. This discovery, however, can say nothing to us that impairs the general picture which we have received from Bede. There is nothing here to lessen the impression of solidity which we have always seen in the work of Theodore, of Hadrian and of Wilfrid, nothing to suggest that the work which was symbolized and sealed at the Synod of Whitby was other than complete. The backsliding, if indeed it can be fully called that, of Eorpwald has nothing in common with the wholesale apostasies that marked the earlier conversions of the Augustinian mission, with the defections of Essex and East Anglia, with King Redwald's setting of idols in the Church of God. Eorpwald's is a singular and peculiar case, and one for which his anonymous chronicler's mention of the charges of sorcery would have prepared us, had we not refused to countenance any evidence that was not comprised by Bede. The circumstances, too, of Eorpwald's life are exceptional. He came from a pagan people, a people who had already once apostatized. It is true that he received his training in a monastery, it is true that he was associated with the great Wilfrid in the conversion of the South Saxons, but he was never of the hard core of Theodore's disciples; we have no evidence that he received any training at Canterbury, let alone at Rome. Hadrian trusted him, it is true, and chose him to convert his own people, but there is nothing to suggest that Eorpwald's faith at that time was not a deep and noble one. He returned to his people and converted them and their king. We now can guess that in that conversion he fell into compromise and from compromise into sacrilege. It is a tragic and singular story of who knows what atavistic impulse working in a man of pagan background. Nevertheless, it is the story of an individual, a theme better suited to literature than history. Without other examples of such apostasy, we cannot even say that the forces of paganism in the late seventh century still had any real hold upon the converts of that age. We can only speak of one man, and that man a member of the most remote of all English kingdoms—the East Folk. The durable, deep conversion that Theodore brought from Rome, the conversion that ended paganism in this country until the coming of the Northmen, the conversion which at the Synod of Whitby decided that the English people should belong to the civilization of Europe, remains untouched by the strange circumstances of Eorpwald's burial. Nothing which is revolutionary for the historian in this discovery—not the unique discovery of an Anglian fertility god in English soil, not the unique discovery of a Christian tomb with pagan relics, and that the tomb of a bishop—has changed our general picture which has been given us by the brilliant sense of history, the steadfast truthfulness of Bede. The lesson of Melpham is a double one—the essential correctness of our historical knowledge only strengthened by exceptions to the rule and the need, for all our great debt to Bede, to be open to the flickering gleam thrown back on those dark times by the uncertain lights of late traditions.

Extract from "The Making of England"
by Professor Lionel Stokesay, C.B.E. (1930)

The qualities that Theodore's men brought with them from
Rome were exactly those which England needed if she was
going to become more than an eccentric fringe of the civilized
world, a last gleam of half light before the darkness of un-
chartered waters. Theodore, Hadrian, Wilfrid and their generation had gifts more valuable than the most precious spices or
Mediterranean works of art to give to the disordered kingdoms
of the Heptarchy. Courage they had in plenty, great zeal and
singleness of purpose, but the Celtic missionaries had these,
perhaps in greater, certainly not in less, degree. But the Roman
missionaries had more: they had organizing ability and political
sense and stern intellectual discipline. In these gifts they were
the heirs of a Rome older than perhaps they realized; and it
was with these gifts rather than with any superiority of argument about questions of tonsure or the date of Easter that they
won the day at Whitby. With a sense of organization and with
superior culture they brought this remote island into the civilized world, as two centuries later Alfred with the same qualities
gave her her first real political unity.

Yet there will always be those for whom Aidan and Cuthbert
will be more dear than Theodore and Wilfrid, and the rule of
Columbanus more attractive than the rule of St Benedict. For
them, the defeated Celts retreating to the Western Islands will
always wear a romantic halo of lost causes, the glamour of the
anchorite and the vagrant missionary, of dreamers to whom
organization and political sense are as vanities beside individual
holiness and the power of the Word. They will recognize, no
doubt, that without the civilizing influence of Rome, England
could never become great, but they will always look askance
at the worldly wisdom, authoritarianism, the collective organization that came with it. These romantic souls, the adherents

of the Celtic cause, the little Englanders among medieval historians, if one may call them so, will find comfort, if tragic comfort, perhaps, in the story of Eorpwald, Bishop of Sedwich.

It is a strange story, indeed, that of Eorpwald. The boy who so hated the dark gods of his people the East Folk that he dared the perils that beset wanderers in those lawless times to seek Christ among strangers. The man who ended his days a bishop, the converter of his own people to the Faith and who had yet returned to the dark gods he had once fled. We do not know the monastery in which he received his learning, but we may guess that he was a lover of intellectual discipline or Abbot Hadrian would not have favoured him, and of zeal and organizing ability or he would have been no companion of Wilfrid, and of culture or he could not have built the cathedral at Sedwich. Yet all his zeal, all his political sense, all his learning did not keep him from a compromise that led to apostasy. In the months after the excavation of his tomb I had leisure and inclination to speculate much on the discovery at which I had assisted and again and again it was the irony and the strangeness that struck me. How did the mind of this man work who was buried with the Cross and with a darker, more sinister deity? How did the tradition of his apostasy regarded as sorcery live on side by side with the tradition of his sanctity to be chronicled obscurely in the thirteenth century? The story has endless overtones, not the least strange of which is the removal of his coffin to Melpham. When the Northmen struck savagely at the land of the East Folk in 867, the priests, zealous for their beloved founder, carried Eorpwald's coffin and buried it secretly at Melpham. How terrified they would have been could they have stood with me on that marshy land on a warm July morning over one thousand years later and seen that their precious burden was a temple to the same unspeakable idol as was worshipped by the terrible barbarians from whom they were fleeing. Yet, when all is said and done, it is not against Eorpwald, the tragic failure of the Roman mission, that we have to set the attractive figures of Cuthbert and Aidan, but against

Wilfrid, that statesmanlike figure of the success of Rome. Cuthbert with Aidan are but sweet side-tracks, as Eorpwald is a dark side-track; the highway runs from Theodore and Hadrian and Wilfrid through Boniface to Dunstan and Lanfranc, the broad track of ecclesiastical history.

Extract from the preface to "The Passing of a Faith," by Dr Rose Lorimer, Ph.D., lecturer in Medieval History (1950)

(This work was refused by the University Presses, but was eventually published by a large commercial publisher of good reputation.)

The contents of this book, then, are controversial. To some readers, unable or unwilling to look beyond the account of England's conversion to Christianity, carefully fostered and imposed upon posterity by the victorious party in the great seventh-century struggle, the story presented here will seem impossible, and, no doubt, ridiculous. The closed mind, it is to be feared, is beyond the reach of argument. To it I cannot hope to speak. There is, however, another and, I trust, wider circle of readers who may pass from interest to conviction as they read the arguments I have assembled here. "Yes," I imagine they may say, "you have convinced us that the cause of beauty, of civilization must have lain with the makers of the Book of Durrow and the Lindisfarne Gospel, with the patrons of Caedmon." They will compare the stiff figures of the evangelists in the Lindisfarne gospels, the contributions of Roman Byzantine civilization, with the inspired free spirit of the abstract patterns in the same manuscript, the contributions of the defeated Celtic cause, and they will perhaps raise their eyebrows at the old reiterated parrot-cry that the triumph of Roman Christianity brought "civilization" to our island. Again, perhaps, they will compare what we know of the characters of Wilfrid, Theodore, Hilda or of the Englishman who took the benefits of the spirit of Roman Christianity to Germany—Boniface—with the little alas! we know of Colman and

Aidan, Columba and Columbanus. "Is there nothing," they may ask, "between the wordly accommodation, the 'Statesmanship' of Lanfranc and the turbulent, intractable pride of Anselm or Thomas of Canterbury? These are Rome's contribution. Is there not also the proud gentleness, the meek determination that make the Celtic saints seem so wondrously near to the Gospel spirit? What has the Roman world of that day to offer that compares with Caedmon's song?" But even those readers to whom conviction may come that the triumph of Rome on those Yorkshire moors in 664 far from England's Salvation was an irreparable tragedy, will still perhaps say, "Yes, you have convinced us that the human spirit lost much with the defeat of the Celts, but history is concerned with facts, with what was rather than with what might have been. Yours is a moving story, but is it worth telling?"

That view of history surely is not far from the one whose influence is presenting us with the terrible menace we face today. The inevitability of history, the grovelling before the face of power have not proved so beneficent to mankind that we need regard as so worthy the scholarship that is concerned with nothing but the victor's story. Truth surely must once again be the historian's goal. But now I think I hear another critic's voice—the facts known to us from that dark age, he says, are too few, too sparse to allow us to create new general pictures of that time, we must be content with small pieces of research, with the minutiae of Dark Age history until good fortune brings us some new fact to work upon. There, let me say, I entirely agree. It was for this reason that I devoted my time for twenty years to the editing of cartularies, the examination of the texts of Anglo-Saxon land grants and literary riddles.

But a far greater riddle than these had been passed by in what I can only call a conspiracy of silence and neglect. I refer to the discoveries made in the excavation of the tomb of Bishop Eorpwald, which are described in detail in this work. The excavation, made by the greatest medieval historian of our time,

Lionel Stokesay, took place in 1912 when I was still at school. Yet as my work progressed I found to my increasing dismay that this extraordinary discovery received only the most casual mention in the works of my colleagues. In Father Lavenham's work on the Mission of Theodore it is not mentioned. Those familiar with the revelations of Roman Catholic "scholarship" made by Dr Coulton, those familiar with Cardinal Gasquet's evasions, will not be surprised at this. The apostasy of the Missionary of the East Folk was an inconvenient discovery for the supporters of the "civilizing" mission of the Roman Church; we need not be surprised therefore that Roman Catholic "scholars" pass it over in silence. We are told so much of the slender hold of Celtic Christian teachers upon the Franks, of the failure of the Irish followers of Columbanus in Germany, we hear less of the backslidings among the Anglo-Saxons a century earlier from King Redwald to Bishop Eorpwald, but then their faith was that of Rome from which backsliding does not exist. Roman Catholic "scholarship", however, has been so much discredited, that we need not concern ourselves too much with its convenient vagaries. More serious, of course, is the timidity with which it has been treated by Protestant and non-Christian teachers. Rome's story even held the day with one of the discoverers of Bishop Eorpwald's tomb—Canon Portway, but then the canon, though an enthusiastic and able antiquarian, was a High Churchman for whom the authoritarianism of Rome was the essence of Christianity, the free and gentle spirit of Lindisfarne only an eccentric weakness. Even Lionel Stokesay, that great historian, the principal excavator at Melpham, speaks in *The Making of England* of Cuthbert and Aidan as "sweet side-tracks" and minimizes the importance of his own great discovery. This is partly the modesty so often to be found in men of genius; nevertheless, it must be said that he conforms to the Roman view more than one could wish. I may say that in his last years Professor Stokesay often spoke to me in a very different vein

"The discoveries at Melpham are either nothing or something far more important than we have dared to think," he told me a few months before his death. His sympathy for the Celtic Church had grown with his changed views and had he lived St Cuthbert might well have been defended by a far worthier pen than mine. It was not to be, however, for, worn out with his valiant struggle for peace in the years that preceded the war, Lionel Stokesay died in 1940. The recent work of Dr Margaret Murray has given a new significance to the dual religion which stares at us from Eorpwald's tomb. I cannot follow Dr Murray in all her conclusions, but sufficient is proved surely to establish a deep-seated survival of the pagan fertility cults, of the old religion, of the royal sacrifice, to suggest that Eorpwald's worship of the old gods and the New God was to be a permanent feature of Christendom for many centuries. We need not look very far for the motives of those who have minimized its importance. . . .

Conclusion of Professor Clun's review of Dr Lorimer's "The Passing of a Faith" (1950)

There are, nevertheless, masterly touches in the book which declare to us—if indeed we need any reminder—that, when the author can forget her central obsession, she remains the most learned and perceptive historian of early Anglo-Saxon history alive in England today. These moments of glorious lucidity occur, as may be anticipated, when neither the Celtic Church nor Anglo-Saxon paganism, those twin monster King Charles's heads of Dr Lorimer's later work, are in question. In *The Christian Debt to the Copts and the Irish* these brilliant passages were many; in *The Passing of a Faith* they have sunk to a scattered few. Nevertheless, even in the present book her analysis of the marriage policies of the reigning houses of the Heptarchy, her summary of the evidences for trade between the Celtic and Saxon areas of these islands, her description of the Anglo-Saxon pilgrimages to Rome before 800, her extraordinary grasp of Merovingian history—all these will remain models to later historians despite their fantastic setting. For fantasy, it must finally be said, her apology for Celtic Christianity, her "case" against Rome, and her ubiquitous pagan survivals are; her book, in the last resort, is more a fit subject for the critic of historical fiction than for the historian proper. It is the great regret indeed of the present reviewer that he cannot leave his task to some critic of fiction, but Dr Lorimer's reputation is a high one, her detailed monographs published over many years command deserved respect, the price of such a high reputation is itself inevitably high. We cannot pass over frivolous or sentimental indulgence in a great scholar as we would in some Ph.D. student or some historical journalist. Dr Lorimer in the course of her apologia for Celtic Christianity impugns the honesty of many historians; the present reviewer is neither a Roman Catholic nor indeed a Christian of any denomination, but the reputation of historical scholarship must be dear to all who profess it. The truth must be written and it is that Dr Lorimer's own scholarship when she touches upon the subjects dear to her sympathies is not without the exaggerations, the omissions and the distortions, which she so freely attributes to other scholars. Some of these I have mentioned in my article; to detail all of them would be tedious. There is one practice, however, against which I should wish to protest and to protest strongly: this is the attribution of views to scholars now dead on the basis of personal conversation. In her preface, Dr Lorimer declares that Stokesay, despite the very cautious attitude he took in his own written book, changed his views about the burial of Eorpwald and took up the view that Dr Lorimer herself adopts—namely, that the apostasy of Eorpwald gives reason for general criticism of the Roman mission of Theodore. The authority for this statement is given as her own conversations with Stokesay in his last years. There may legitimately be more than one view about the value of Stokesay's later work, but this must be firmly said—he was not a man who would fear to put into print a view, however controversial, if he accepted it. To imply, as Dr Lorimer does, that he was prevented from publishing his changed views by pressure of public business is to do ill justice to his lifelong devotion to the service of history.

Extract from "The Times" of January 1955

A pamphlet entitled "The Melpham Burial," published to-day by the Historical Association of Medievalists, gives a concise account of the present view of scholars upon this much disputed Anglo-Saxon antiquity. It now seems clear beyond doubt that the heathen idol found in the coffin of Bishop Eorpwald in 1912 was placed there as a practical joke by Gilbert Stokesay, who assisted his father in the excavations. The full story of this lamentable affair will probably never be known. It is clear, however, that both Lionel Stokesay and Reginald Portway became aware of the fraud during the nineteen-twenties. Devotion to his son's memory appears to have blinded Stokesay to his duty as a scholar; the reason for Portway's acquiescence in this deplorable silence remains obscure. A note of personal sadness marks Professor Middleton's narrative when he deals with the conduct of these two eminent historians. It is a sadness which all who honour Clio must inevitably share. The wretched fraud should not make us forget that the idol itself may well be a unique example of a heathen god unearthed from English soil. Eorpwald, however, whose faith has been so sadly impugned all these years, is now vindicated from all charges of backsliding. By a curious coincidence the exposure of the fraud comes at a time when pagan relics being associated with Christian burial has been once again brought into consideration by the present excavation of Aldwine's grave in Heligoland. Final verdict on this important archaeological discovery must await the definitive report of Professor Pforzheim, the eminent archaeologist in charge of the excavation.